T0057257

"Isaac Marion has a great new voice that hooks you from page one and accomplishes the impossible: it makes you care about young zombie love. *Warm Bodies* is a terrific read."

—Josh Bazell, *New York Times* bestselling author of *Beat the Reaper*

"A jubilant story about two star-crossed lovers, one of them dead and hungry for more than love."

—*Kirkus Reviews*

"Marion is a disarming writer, ruefully humorous, knowingly cinematic in scope. This is a slacker-zombie novel with a heart."

—*The Guardian* (UK)

"*Warm Bodies* is a terrific book—a compelling literary fantasy which is also a strange and affecting pop-culture parable."

—Nick Harkaway, author of *The Gone-Away World*

"R does possess a certain winsome charm, and the upbeat ending will warm many hearts."

—*Publishers Weekly*

"A visually arresting, bleakly Ballardesque world. . . . Wryly playful, cinematic, and ultimately moving."

—*Time Out London*

"A mesmerising evolution of a classic contemporary myth."

—Simon Pegg, *New York Times* bestselling author of *Nerd Do Well*

"Both tender and lacerating, this zombie novel has more to say about being alive than being dead. 'Love' is not a strong enough word for my feelings about this book."

—Maggie Stiefvater, author of the Shiver trilogy and *Books of Faerie*

BY ISAAC MARION

WARM BODIES

THE NEW HUNGER

WARM BODIES

AND

THE NEW HUNGER

A SPECIAL 5TH ANNIVERSARY

EDITION

ISAAC MARION

EMILY BESTLER BOOKS

—

ATRIA

NEW YORK   LONDON   TORONTO   SYDNEY   NEW DELHI

ATRIA PAPERBACK

An Imprint of Simon & Schuster, Inc.
1230 Avenue of the Americas
New York, NY 10020

First Emily Bestler Books/Atria Paperback edition August 2016

EMILY BESTLER BOOKS / ATRIA PAPERBACK and colophon
are trademarks of Simon & Schuster, Inc.

Interior illustrations adapted by Isaac Marion from sources in the public domain.

For information about special discounts for bulk purchases, please contact Simon &
Schuster Special Sales at 1-866-506-1949 or business@simonandschuster.com.

The Simon & Schuster Speakers Bureau can bring authors to your live event. For more
information or to book an event, contact the Simon & Schuster Speakers Bureau
at 1-866-248-3049 or visit our website at www.simonspeakers.com.

Manufactured in the United States of America

10 9 8 7 6 5 4 3 2

ISBN 978-1-5011-5206-1

Author's Note

Warm Bodies began as a seven-page vignette about a day in the "life" of a typical zombie. That little seed bloomed into a novel about a dead man rediscovering humanity. And now, a decade later, it's grown into a four-book saga about people—Living and Dead—fighting the darkness around and inside them as they work to build a better world.

It's safe to say I didn't foresee any of this when I wrote that first story back in 2006. I was a twenty-four-year-old college dropout living in a small farm town, dreaming up stories in the dark of the cobwebbed crawlspaces where I installed heating ducts and sang to the dead rats. Even a few years later, as I germinated a novel while wiping down hospital beds still warm from the people who'd died in them, I never imagined this would become my future.

Now it's been five years since the first book was published and I'm finishing up the last one, and I still can't quite believe it. What began as a goofy little experiment has become the vehicle I've used to navigate my life. This lonely, awkward zombie helped me understand myself and my relationship with the world, and we have transformed each other. I didn't give R his answers from on high as his all-knowing author—we found them together and shared them.

So in some very weird ways, this apocalyptic saga of monsters and magic could be my autobiography. Maybe you'll find a bit of yourself in it too.

—Isaac Marion

WARM BODIES

A NOVEL

For the foster kids I've met

You have known, O Gilgamesh,
What interests me,
To drink from the Well of Immortality.
Which means to make the dead
Rise from their graves
And the prisoners from their cells
The sinners from their sins.
I think love's kiss kills our heart of flesh.
It is the only way to eternal life,
Which should be unbearable if lived
Among the dying flowers
And the shrieking farewells
Of the overstretched arms of our spoiled hopes.

—Herbert Mason,
Gilgamesh: A Verse Narrative

"..."

—*The Epic of Gilgamesh*, Tablet II,
lines 147, 153, 154, 278, 279

wanting

I AM DEAD, but it's not so bad. I've learned to live with it. I'm sorry I can't properly introduce myself, but I don't have a name anymore. Hardly any of us do. We lose them like car keys, forget them like anniversaries. Mine might have started with an "R," but that's all I have now. It's funny because back when I was alive, I was always forgetting *other* people's names. My friend "M" says the irony of being a zombie is that everything is funny, but you can't smile, because your lips have rotted off.

None of us are particularly attractive, but death has been kinder to me than some. I'm still in the early stages of decay. Just the gray skin, the unpleasant smell, the dark circles under my eyes. I could almost pass for a Living man in need of a vacation. Before I became a zombie I must have been a businessman, a banker or broker or some young temp learning the ropes, because I'm wearing fairly nice clothes. Black slacks, gray shirt, red tie. M makes fun of me sometimes. He points at my tie and tries to laugh, a choked, gurgling rumble deep in his gut. His clothes are holey jeans and a plain white T-shirt. The shirt is looking pretty macabre by now. He should have picked a darker color.

We like to joke and speculate about our clothes, since these final fashion choices are the only indication of who we were before we became no one. Some are less obvious than mine: shorts and a sweater, skirt and a blouse. So we make random guesses.

You were a waitress. You were a student. Ring any bells?

It never does.

No one I know has any specific memories. Just a vague, vestigial knowledge of a world long gone. Faint impressions of past lives that linger like phantom limbs. We recognize civilization—buildings, cars, a general overview—but we have no personal role in it. No history. We are just *here*. We do what we do, time passes, and no one asks questions. But like I've said, it's not so bad. We may appear mindless, but we aren't. The rusty cogs of cogency still spin, just geared down and down till the outer motion is barely visible. We grunt and groan, we shrug and nod, and sometimes a few words slip out. It's not that different from before.

But it does make me sad that we've forgotten our names. Out of everything, this seems to me the most tragic. I miss my own and I mourn for everyone else's, because I'd like to love them, but I don't know who they are.

• • •

There are hundreds of us living in an abandoned airport outside some large city. We don't need shelter or warmth, obviously, but we like having the walls and roofs over our heads. Otherwise we'd just be wandering in an open field of dust somewhere, and that would be horrifying. To have nothing at all around us, nothing to touch or look at, no hard lines whatsoever, just us and the gaping maw of the sky. I imagine that's what being full-dead is like. An emptiness vast and absolute.

I think we've been here a long time. I still have all my flesh, but there are elders who are little more than skeletons with clinging bits of muscle, dry as jerky. Somehow it still extends and contracts, and they keep moving. I have never seen any of us "die" of old age. Left alone with plenty of food, maybe we'd "live" forever, I don't know. The future is as blurry to me as the past. I can't seem to make myself care about anything to the right or left of the present, and the present isn't exactly urgent. You might say death has relaxed me.

• • •

I am riding the escalators when M finds me. I ride the escalators several times a day, whenever they move. It's become a ritual. The airport is derelict, but the power still flickers on sometimes, maybe flowing from emergency generators stuttering deep underground. Lights flash and screens blink, machines jolt into motion. I cherish these moments. The feeling of things coming to life. I stand on the steps and ascend like a soul into Heaven, that sugary dream of our childhoods, now a tasteless joke.

After maybe thirty repetitions, I rise to find M waiting for me at the top. He is hundreds of pounds of muscle and fat draped on a six-foot-five frame. Bearded, bald, bruised and rotten, his grisly visage slides into view as I crest the staircase summit. Is he the angel that greets me at the gates? His ragged mouth is oozing black drool.

He points in a vague direction and grunts, "City."

I nod and follow him.

We are going out to find food. A hunting party forms around us as we shuffle toward town. It's not hard to find recruits for these expeditions, even if no one is hungry. Focused thought is a rare occurrence here, and we all follow it when it manifests. Otherwise we'd just be standing around and groaning all day. We do a lot of standing around and groaning. Years pass this way. The flesh withers on our bones and we stand here, waiting for it to go. I often wonder how old I am.

• • •

The city where we do our hunting is conveniently close. We arrive around noon the next day and start looking for flesh. The new hunger is a strange feeling. We don't feel it in our stomachs—some of us don't even have those. We feel it everywhere equally, a sinking, sagging sensation, as if our cells are deflating. Last winter, when so many Living joined the Dead and our prey became scarce, I watched some of my friends become full-dead. The transition was undramatic. They just slowed down, then stopped, and after a while I realized they were corpses. It disquieted me at first, but it's against etiquette to notice when one of us dies. I distracted myself with some groaning.

I think the world has mostly ended, because the cities we wander through are as rotten as we are. Buildings have collapsed. Rusted cars clog the streets. Most glass is shattered, and the wind drifting through the hollow high-rises moans like an animal left to die. I don't know what happened. Disease? War? Social collapse? Or was it just us? The Dead replacing the Living? I guess it's not so important. Once you've arrived at the end of the world, it hardly matters which route you took.

We start to smell the Living as we approach a dilapidated apartment building. The smell is not the musk of sweat and skin, it's the effervescence of life energy, like the ionized tang of lightning and lavender. We don't smell it in our noses. It hits us deeper inside, near our brains, like wasabi. We converge on the building and crash our way inside.

We find them huddled in a small studio unit with the windows boarded up. They are dressed worse than we are, wrapped in filthy tatters and rags, all of them badly in need of a shave. M will be saddled with a short blond beard for the rest of his Fleshy existence, but everyone else in our party is cleanshaven. It's one of the perks of being dead, another thing we don't have to worry about anymore. Beards, hair, toenails . . . no more fighting biology. Our wild bodies have finally been tamed.

Slow and clumsy but with unswerving commitment, we launch ourselves at the Living. Shotgun blasts fill the dusty air with gunpowder and gore. Black blood spatters the walls. The loss of an arm, a leg, a portion of torso, this is disregarded, shrugged off. A minor cosmetic issue. But some of us take shots to our brains, and we drop. Apparently there's still something of value in that withered gray sponge because if we lose it, we are corpses. The zombies to my left and right hit the ground with moist thuds. But there are plenty of us. We are overwhelming. We set upon the Living, and we eat.

Eating is not a pleasant business. I chew off a man's arm, and I hate it. I hate his screams, because I don't like pain, I don't like hurting people, but this is the world now. This is what we do. Of course if I don't eat all of him, if I spare his brain, he'll rise up and follow me back to the airport, and that might make me feel better. I'll introduce him to everyone, and maybe we'll stand around and groan for a while. It's hard to say what "friends" are anymore, but that might be close. If I restrain myself, if I leave enough . . .

But I don't. I can't. As always I go straight for the good part, the part that makes my head light up like a picture tube. I eat the brain, and for about thirty seconds, I have memories. Flashes of parades, perfume, music . . . *life*. Then it fades, and I get up, and we all stumble out of the city, still cold and gray, but feeling a little better. Not "good," exactly, not "happy," certainly not "alive," but . . . a little less dead. This is the best we can do.

I trail behind the group as the city disappears behind us. My steps plod a little heavier than the others'. When I pause at a rain-filled pothole to scrub gore off my face and clothes, M drops back and slaps a hand on my shoulder. He knows my distaste for some of our routines. He knows I'm a little more sensitive than most. Sometimes he teases me, twirls my messy black hair into pigtails and says, "Girl. Such . . . girl." But he knows when to take my gloom seriously. He pats my shoulder and just looks at me. His face isn't capable of much expressive nuance anymore, but I know what he wants to say. I nod, and we keep walking.

I don't know why we have to kill people. I don't know what chewing through a man's neck accomplishes. I steal what he has to replace what I lack. He disappears, and I stay. It's simple but senseless, arbitrary laws from some lunatic legislator in the sky. But following those laws keeps me walking, so I follow them to the letter. I eat until I stop eating, then I eat again.

How did this start? How did we become what we are? Was it some mysterious virus? Gamma rays? An ancient curse? Or something even more absurd? No one talks about it much. We are here, and this is the way it is. We don't complain. We don't ask questions. We go about our business.

There is a chasm between me and the world outside of me. A gap so wide my feelings can't cross it. By the time my screams reach the other side, they have dwindled into groans.

• • •

At the Arrivals gate, we are greeted by a small crowd, watching us with hungry eyes or eyesockets. We drop our cargo on the floor: two mostly intact men, a few meaty legs, and a dismembered torso, all still warm. Call it leftovers. Call it takeout. Our fellow Dead fall on them and feast right there on the floor like animals. The life remaining in those cells will keep them from full-dying, but the Dead who don't hunt will never quite be satisfied. Like men at sea deprived of fresh fruit, they will wither in their deficiencies, weak and perpetually empty, because the new hunger is a lonely monster. It grudgingly accepts the brown meat and lukewarm blood, but what it craves is closeness, that grim sense of connection that courses between their eyes and ours in those final moments, like some dark negative of love.

I wave to M and then break free from the crowd. I have long since acclimated to the Dead's pervasive stench, but the reek rising off them today feels especially fetid. Breathing is optional, but I need some air.

I wander out into the connecting hallways and ride the conveyors. I stand on the belt and watch the scenery scroll by through the window wall. Not much to see. The runways are turning green, overrun with grass and brush. Jets lie motionless on the concrete like beached whales, white and monumental. Moby Dick, conquered at last.

Before, when I was alive, I could never have done this. Standing still, watching the world pass by me, thinking about nearly nothing. I remember effort. I remember targets and deadlines, goals and ambitions. I remember being *purposeful*, always everywhere all the time. Now I'm just standing here on the conveyor, along for the ride. I reach the end, turn around, and go back the other way. The world has been distilled. Being dead is easy.

After a few hours of this, I notice a female on the opposite conveyor. She doesn't lurch or groan like most of us; her head just lolls from side to side. I like that about her, that she doesn't lurch or groan. I catch her eye and stare at her as we approach. For a brief moment we are side by side, only a few feet away. We pass, then travel on to opposite ends of the hall. We turn around and look at each other. We get back on the conveyors. We pass each other again. I grimace and she grimaces back. On our third pass, the airport power dies, and we come to a halt perfectly aligned. I wheeze hello, and she responds with a hunch of her shoulder.

I like her. I reach out and touch her hair. Like me, her decomposition is at an early stage. Her skin is pale and her eyes are sunken, but she has no exposed bones or organs. Her irises are an especially light shade of that strange pewter gray all the Dead share. Her graveclothes are a black skirt and a snug white buttonup. I suspect she used to be a receptionist.

Pinned to her chest is a silver nametag.

She has a name.

I stare hard at the tag; I lean in close, putting my face inches from her breasts, but it doesn't help. The letters spin and reverse in my vision; I can't hold them down. As always, they elude me, just a series of meaningless lines and blots.

Another of M's undead ironies—from nametags to newspapers, the answers to our questions are written all around us, and we don't know how to read.

I point at the tag and look her in the eyes. "Your . . . name?"

She looks at me blankly.

I point at myself and pronounce the remaining fragment of my own name. "Rrr." Then I point at her again.

Her eyes drop to the floor. She shakes her head. She doesn't remember. She doesn't even have syllable one, like M and I do. She is no one. But don't I always expect too much? I reach out and take her hand. We walk off the conveyers with our arms stretched across the divider.

This female and I have fallen in love. Or what's left of it.

I think I remember what love was like before. There were complex emotional and biological factors. We had elaborate tests to pass, connections to forge, ups and downs and tears and whirlwinds. It was an ordeal, an exercise in agony, but it was alive. The new love is simpler. Easier. But small.

My girlfriend doesn't talk much. We walk through the echoing corridors of the airport, occasionally passing someone staring out a window or at a wall. I try to think of things to say but nothing comes, and if something did come I probably couldn't say it. This is my great obstacle, the biggest of all the boulders littering my path. In my mind I am eloquent; I can climb intricate scaffolds of words to reach the highest cathedral ceilings and paint my thoughts. But when I open my mouth, it all collapses. So far my personal record is four rolling syllables before some . . . thing . . . jams. And I may be the most loquacious zombie in this airport.

I don't know why we don't speak. I can't explain the suffocating silence that hangs over our world, cutting us off from each other like prison-visit Plexiglas. Prepositions are painful, articles are arduous, adjectives are wild overachievements. Is this muteness a real physical handicap? One of the many symptoms of being Dead? Or do we just have nothing left to say?

I attempt conversation with my girlfriend, testing out a few awkward phrases and shallow questions, trying to get a reaction out of her, any twitch of wit. But she just looks at me like I'm weird.

We wander for a few hours, directionless, then she grips my hand and starts leading me somewhere. We stumble our way down the halted escalators and out onto the tarmac. I sigh wearily.

She is taking me to church.

The Dead have built a sanctuary on the runway. At some point in the distant past, someone pushed all the stair trucks together into a circle, forming a kind of amphitheater. We gather here, we stand here, we lift our arms and moan. The ancient Boneys wave their skeletal limbs in the center circle, rasping out dry, wordless sermons through toothy grins. I don't understand what this is. I don't think any of us do. But it's the only time we willingly gather under the open sky. That vast cosmic mouth, distant mountains like teeth in the skull of God, yawning wide to devour us. To swallow us down to where we probably belong.

My girlfriend appears to be more devout than I am. She closes her eyes and waves her arms in a way that looks almost heartfelt. I stand next to her and hold my hands in the air stiffly. At some unknown cue, maybe drawn by her fervor, the Boneys stop their preaching and stare at us. One of them comes forward, climbs our stairs, and takes us both by the wrists. It leads us down into the circle and raises our hands in its clawed grip. It lets out a kind of roar, an unearthly sound like a blast of air through a broken hunting horn, shockingly loud, frightening birds out of trees.

The congregation murmurs in response, and it's done. We are married.

We step back onto the stair seats. The service resumes. My new wife closes her eyes and waves her arms.

The day after our wedding, we have children. A small group of Boneys stops us in the hall and presents them to us. A boy and a girl, both around six years old. The boy is curly blond, with gray skin and gray eyes, perhaps once Caucasian. The girl is darker, with black hair and ashy brown skin, deeply shadowed around her steely eyes. She may have been Arab. The Boneys nudge them forward and they give us tentative smiles, hug our legs. I pat them on their heads and ask their names, but they don't have any. I sigh, and my wife and I keep walking, hand in hand with our new children.

I wasn't exactly expecting this. This is a big responsibility. The young Dead don't have the natural feeding instincts the adults do. They have to be tended and trained, and they will never grow up. Stunted by our curse, they will stay small and rot, then become little skeletons, animate but empty, their brains rattling stiff in their skulls, repeating their routines and rituals until one day, I can only assume, the bones themselves will disintegrate, and they'll just be gone.

Look at them. Watch them as my wife and I release their hands and they wander outside to play. They tease each other and grin. They play with things that aren't even toys: staplers and mugs and calculators. They giggle and laugh, though it sounds choked through their dry throats. We've bleached their brains, robbed them of breath, but they still cling to the cliff edge. They resist our curse for as long as they possibly can.

I watch them disappear into the pale daylight at the end of the hall. Deep inside me, in some dark and cobwebbed chamber, I feel something twitch.

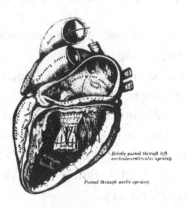

Bristle passed through left auriculo-ventricular opening.

Passed through aortic opening.

I'T'S TIME to feed again.

I don't know how long it's been since our last hunting trip, probably just a few days, but I feel it. I feel the electricity in my limbs fizzling, fading. I see relentless visions of blood in my mind, that brilliant, mesmerizing red, flowing through bright pink tissues in intricate webs and Pollock fractals, pulsing and vibrating with life.

I find M in the food court talking to some girls. He is a little different than me. He does seem to enjoy the company of women, and his better-than-average diction draws them in like dazzled carp, but he keeps a distance. He laughs them off. The Boneys once tried to set him up with a wife, but he simply walked away. Sometimes I wonder if he has a philosophy. Maybe even a worldview. I'd like to sit down with him and pick his brain, just a tiny bite somewhere in the frontal lobe to get a taste of his thoughts. But he's too much of a toughguy to ever be that vulnerable.

"City," I say, putting a hand on my stomach. "Food."

The girls he's talking to look at me and shuffle away. I've noticed I make some people nervous, though I can't guess why.

"Just . . . ate," M says, frowning at me a little. "Two days . . . ago."

I grab my stomach again. "Feel empty. Feel . . . dead."

He nods. "Marr . . . iage."

I glare at him. I shake my head and clutch my stomach harder. "*Need*. Go . . . get others."

He sighs and walks out, bumping into me hard on his way past, but I'm not sure if it was intentional. He is, after all, a zombie.

He manages to find a few others with appetites and we form a small posse. Very small. Unsafely small. But I don't care. I don't recall ever being this hungry.

We set out toward the city. We take the freeway. Like everything else, the roads are returning to nature. We wander down empty lanes and under ivy-curtained overpasses. My residual memories of these roads contrast dramatically with their peaceful present state. I take a deep breath of the sweet, silent air.

We push deeper into the city than usual. The only scents I pick up are rust and dust. The unsheltered Living are getting scarcer, and the ones with shelter are venturing out less frequently. I suspect their stadium fortresses are becoming self-sufficient. I imagine vast gardens planted in the dugouts, bursting with carrots and beans. Cattle in the press box. Rice paddies in the outfield. We can see the largest of these citadels looming on the hazy horizon, its retractable roof wide open to the sun, taunting us.

But finally, we sense prey. The life scent electrifies our nostrils, bright and strong. They are close, and there are a lot of them. Maybe half our own number. We hesitate, stumbling to a halt. M looks at me. He looks at our small group, then back at me. "No," he grunts.

I point toward the crooked, collapsed skyscraper that's emitting the aroma, a cartoon tendril of scent beckoning us *come hither*.

"Eat," I insist.

M shakes his head. "Too . . . many."

"*Eat*."

He looks at our group again. He sniffs the air. The rest of them are undecided. Some of them also sniff warily, but others are more single-minded like me. They groan and drool and snap their teeth.

I'm getting agitated. "Need it!" I shout, glaring at M. "Come . . . on." I turn and start speed-lumbering toward the skyscraper. Focused thought. The rest of the group reflexively follows. M catches up and walks beside me, watching me with an uneasy grimace.

Spurred to an unusual level of intensity by my desperate energy, our group crashes through the revolving doors and rushes down the dark hallways. Some earthquake or explosion has knocked out part of the foundation, and the entire high-rise leans at a dizzying, fun house angle. It's hard to navigate the zigzagging halls, and the inclines make it a challenge to even walk, but the scent is overpowering. After a few flights of stairs I start to hear them as well, clattering around and talking to each other in those steady, melodious streams of words. Living speech has always been a sonic pheromone to me, and I spasm briefly when it hits my ears. I've yet to meet another zombie who shares my appreciation for those silky rhythms. M thinks it's a sick fetish.

As we approach their level of the building, some of us start groaning loudly, and the Living hear us. One of them shouts the alarm and I hear guns cocking, but we don't hesitate. We burst through a final door and rush them. M grunts when he sees how many there are, but he lunges with me at the nearest man and grabs his arms while I rip out his throat. The burning red taste of blood floods my mouth. The sparkle of life sprays out of his cells like citrus mist from an orange peel, and I suck it in.

The darkness of the room is pulsing with gunfire, and by our standards we are grossly outnumbered—there are only three of us to every one of them—but something is tipping things in our favor. Our manic speed is uncharacteristic of the Dead, and our prey are not prepared for it. Is this all coming from me? Creatures without desire don't usually move quickly, but they're following my lead, and I am an angry whirlwind. What has come over me? Am I just having a bad day?

There is one other factor working to our advantage. These Living are not seasoned veterans. They are young. Teenagers, mostly. Boys and girls. One of them has such gruesome acne he's likely to get shot by mistake in this flickering light. Their leader is a slightly older kid with a patchy beard, standing on a cubicle desk in the middle of the room and shouting panicked commands to his men. As they fall to the floor under the weight of our hunger, as dots of blood pointilize the walls, this boy leans protectively over a small figure crouched below him on the desk. A girl, young and blond, bracing her bird-boned shoulder against her shotgun as she fires blindly into the dark.

I lope across the room and grab the boy's boots. I pull his feet out from under him and he falls, cracking his head on the edge of the desk. Without hesitation I pounce on him and bite through his neck. Then I dig my fingers into the crack in his skull, and pry his head open like an eggshell. His brain pulses hot and pink inside. I take a deep, wide, ravenous bite and—

• • •

I am Perry Kelvin, a nine-year-old boy growing up in rural nowhere. The threats are all on some distant coast and we don't worry about them here. Other than the emergency chain-link fence between the river and the mountain ridge, life is almost normal. I'm in school. I'm learning about George Washington. I'm riding my bike down dusty roads in shorts and a tank top, feeling the summer sun broil the back of my neck. My neck. My neck hurts, it—

• • •

I am eating a slice of pizza with my mom and dad. It's my birthday and they are doing what they can to treat me, though their money isn't worth much anymore. I've just turned eleven, and they're finally taking me to see one of the countless zombie movies cropping up lately. I'm so excited I can barely taste my pizza. I take an oversized bite and the thick cheese sticks in my throat. I choke it back up and my parents laugh. Tomato sauce stains my shirt like—

• • •

I am fifteen, gazing out the window at the looming walls of my new home. Clouded gray sunlight drifts down through the stadium's open roof. I'm at school again listening to a lecture about salvage safety and trying not to stare at the beautiful girl sitting next to me. She has short, choppy blond hair and blue eyes that dance with private amusement. My palms are sweating. My mouth is full of laundry lint. When the class ends, I catch her in the hall and say, "Hi."

"Hi," she says.

"I'm new here."

"I know."

"My name's Perry."

She smiles. "I'm Julie."

She smiles. Her eyes glitter. "I'm Julie."

She smiles. I glimpse her braces. Her eyes are classic novels and poetry. "I'm Julie," she says.

She says—

• • •

"Perry," Julie whispers in my ear as I kiss her neck. She twines her fingers into mine and squeezes hard. I kiss her deep and caress the back of her head with my free hand, tangling my fingers in her hair. I look her in the eyes.

"Do you want to?" I breathe.

She smiles. She closes her eyes and says, "Yes."

I crush her against me. I want to be part of her. Not just inside her but all around her. I want our rib cages to crack open and our hearts to migrate and merge. I want our cells to braid together like living thread.

• • •

And now I'm older, wiser, gunning a motorcycle down a forgotten downtown boulevard. Julie is on the seat behind me, her arms clutching my chest, her legs wrapped around mine. Her aviators glint in the sun as she grins, showing her perfectly straight teeth. The grin is not mine to share anymore, and I know this, I have accepted the way things are and the way things are going to be, even if she hasn't and won't. But at least I can protect her. At least I can keep her safe. She is so unbearably beautiful and sometimes I see a future with her in my head, but my head, my head hurts, oh God my head is—

• • •

Stop.

Who are you? Let the memories dissolve. Your eyes are crusted—blink them. Gasp in a ragged breath.

You're you again. You're no one.

Welcome back.

• • •

I feel the carpet under my fingers. I hear the gunshots. I stand up and look around, dizzy and reeling. I have never had a vision so deep, like an entire life spooling through my head. The sting of tears burns in my eyes, but my ducts no longer have fluid. The feeling rages unquenched like pepper spray. It's the first time I've felt pain since I died.

I hear a scream nearby and I turn. It's her. She's here. *Julie* is here, older now, maybe nineteen, her baby fat melted away, revealing sharper lines and finer poise, muscles small but toned on her girlish frame. She is huddled in a corner, unarmed, sobbing and screaming as M creeps toward her. He always finds the women. Their memories are porn to him. I still feel disoriented, unsure where or who I am, but . . .

I shove M aside and snarl, "*No*. Mine."

He grits his teeth like he's about to turn on me, but a gunshot tears into his shoulder and he shuffles across the room to help two other zombies bring down a kid with an Uzi.

I approach the girl. She cowers before me, her tender flesh offering me all the things I'm accustomed to taking, and my instincts start to reassert themselves. The urge to rip and tear surges into my arms and jaw. But then she screams again, and something inside me moves, a feeble moth struggling against a web. In this brief moment of hesitation, still warm with the nectar of a young man's memories, I make a choice.

I let out a gentle groan and inch toward the girl, trying to force kindness into my dull expression. I am not no one. I am a nine-year-old boy, I am a fifteen-year-old boy, I am—

She throws a knife at my head.

The blade sticks straight into the center of my forehead and quivers there. But it has penetrated less than an inch, only grazing my frontal lobe. I pull it out and drop it. I hold out my hands, making soft noises through my lips, but I'm helpless. How do I appear unthreatening when her lover's blood is running down my chin?

I'm just a few feet away from her now. She is fumbling through her jeans for another weapon. Behind me, the Dead are finishing their butchery. Soon they will turn their attention to this dim corner of the room. I take a deep breath.

"*Ju . . . lie*," I say.

It rolls off my tongue like honey. I feel good just saying it.

Her eyes go wide. She freezes.

"Julie," I say again. I put out my hands. I point at the zombies behind me. I shake my head.

She stares at me, making no sign that she understands. But when I reach out to touch her, she doesn't move. And she doesn't stab me.

I reach my free hand into the head wound of a fallen zombie and collect a palmful of black, lifeless blood. Slowly, with gentle movements, I smear it on her face, down her neck, and onto her clothes. She doesn't even flinch. She is probably catatonic.

I take her hand and pull her to her feet. At that moment M and the others finish devouring their prey and turn to inspect the room. Their eyes fall on me. They fall on Julie. I walk toward them, gripping Julie's hand, not quite dragging her. She staggers behind me, staring straight ahead.

M sniffs the air cautiously. But I know he's smelling exactly what I'm smelling: nothing. Just the negative-smell of Dead blood. It's spattered all over the walls, soaked into our clothes, and smeared carefully on a young Living girl, concealing the glow of her life under its dark, overpowering musk.

Without a word, we leave the high-rise and head back to the airport. I walk in a daze, full of strange and kaleidoscopic thoughts. Julie holds limply to my hand, staring at the side of my face with wide eyes, trembling lips.

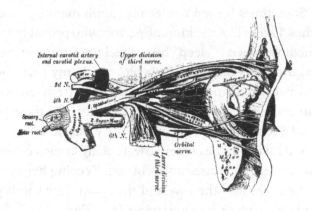

Aᴼᵀᴱᴿ ᴅᴱᴸᴵⱽᴱᴿᴵᴺᴳ our abundant harvest of leftover flesh to the nonhunters—the Boneys, the children, the stay-at-home moms—I take Julie to my house. My fellow Dead give me curious looks as I pass. Because it requires both volition and restraint, the act of intentionally converting the Living is almost never performed. Most conversions happen by accident: a feeding zombie is killed or otherwise distracted before finishing his business, *voro interruptus*. The rest of our converts arise from traditional deaths, private affairs of illness or mishap or classical Living-on-Living violence that take place outside our sphere of interest. So the fact that I have purposely brought this girl home unconsumed is a thing of mystery, a miracle on par with giving birth. M and the others allow me plenty of room in the halls, regarding me with confusion and wonder. If they knew the full truth of what I'm doing, their reactions would be . . . less moderate.

Gripping Julie's hand, I hurry her away from their probing eyes. I lead her to Gate 12, down the boarding tunnel and into my home: a 747 commercial jet. It's not very spacious, the floor plan is impractical, but it's the most isolated place in the airport and I enjoy the privacy. Sometimes it even tickles my numb memory. Looking at my clothes, I seem like the kind of person who probably traveled a lot. Sometimes when I "sleep" here, I feel the faint rising sensation of flight, the blasts of recycled air blowing in my face, the soggy nausea of packaged sandwiches. And then the fresh lemon zing of *poisson* in Paris. The burn of *tajine* in Morocco. Are these places all gone now? Silent streets, cafés full of dusty skeletons?

Julie and I stand in the center aisle, looking at each other. I point to a window seat and raise my eyebrows. Keeping her eyes solidly on me, she backs into the row and sits down. Her hands grip the armrests like the plane is in a flaming death dive.

I sit in the aisle seat and release an involuntary wheeze, looking straight ahead at my stacks of memorabilia. Every time I go into the city, I bring back one thing that catches my eye. A puzzle. A shot glass. A Barbie. A dildo. Flowers. Magazines. Books. I bring them here to my home, strew them around the seats and aisles, and stare at them for hours. The piles reach to the ceiling now. M keeps asking me why I do this. I have no answer.

"Not . . . eat," I groan at Julie, looking her in the eyes. "I . . . won't eat."

She stares at me. Her lips are tight and pale.

I point at her. I open my mouth and point at my crooked, bloodstained teeth. I shake my head. She presses herself against the window. A terrified whimper rises in her throat. This is not working.

"Safe," I tell her, letting out a sigh. "Keep . . . you safe."

I stand up and go to my record player. I dig through my LP collection in the overhead compartments and pull out an album. I take the headphones back to my seat and place the big metal cans on Julie's ears. She is still frozen, wide-eyed.

The record plays. It's Frank Sinatra. I can hear it faintly through the headphones, like a distant eulogy drifting on autumn air.

Last night . . . when we were young . . .

I close my eyes and hunch forward. My head sways vaguely in

time with the music as verses float through the jet cabin, blending together in my ears.

Life was so new . . . so real, so right . . .

"Safe," I mumble. "Keep you . . . safe."

. . . ages ago . . . last night . . .

When my eyes finally open, Julie's face has changed. The terror has faded, and she regards me with disbelief.

"What *are* you?" she whispers.

I turn my face away. I stand and duck out of the plane. Her bewildered gaze follows me down the tunnel.

· · ·

In the airport parking garage, there is a classic Mercedes convertible that I've been playing with for several months. After weeks of staring at it, I figured out how to fill its tank from a barrel of stabilized gasoline I found in the service rooms. Then I remembered how to turn the key and start it, after pushing its owner's dry corpse to the pavement. But I have no idea how to drive. The best I've been able to do is back out of the parking spot and ram into a nearby Hummer. Sometimes I just sit there with the engine purring, my hands resting limply on the wheel, willing a true memory to pop into my head. Not another hazy impression or vague awareness cribbed from the collective subconscious. Something specific, bright, and vivid. Something unmistakably mine. I strain myself, trying to wrench it out of the blackness.

· · ·

I meet M later that evening at his home in the women's bathroom. He is sitting in front of a TV plugged into a long extension cord, gaping at a late-night softcore movie he found in some dead man's luggage. I don't know why he does this. Erotica is meaningless for us now. The blood doesn't pump, the urges don't stir. I've walked in on M with his "girlfriends" before, and they're just standing there naked, staring at each other, sometimes rubbing their bodies together but looking tired and lost. Maybe it's a kind of death throe. A distant echo of that great motivator that once started wars and inspired symphonies, that drove human history out of the caves and into space. M may be holding on, but those days are over now. Sex, once a law as undisputed as gravity, has been disproved. The equation is erased, the blackboard broken.

Sometimes it's a relief. I remember the need, the insatiable hunger that ruled my life and the lives of everyone around me. Sometimes I'm glad to be free of it. There's less trouble now. But our loss of this, the most basic of all human passions, might sum up our loss of everything else. It's made things quieter. Simpler. And it's one of the surest signs that we're dead.

I watch M from the doorway. He sits on the little metal folding chair with his hands between his knees like a schoolboy facing the principal. There are times when I can almost glimpse the person he once was under all that rotting flesh, and it prickles my heart.

"Did . . . bring it?" he asks without looking away from the TV.

I hold up what I've been carrying. A human brain, fresh from today's hunting trip, no longer warm but still pink and buzzing with life.

We sit against the tiles of the bathroom wall with our legs sprawled out in front of us, passing the brain back and forth, taking small, leisurely bites and enjoying brief flashes of human experience.

"Good . . . shit," M wheezes.

The brain contains the life of some young military grunt from the city. His existence isn't particularly interesting to me, just endless repetitions of training, eating, and mowing down zombies, but M seems to like it. His tastes are a little less demanding than mine. I watch his mouth form silent words. I watch his face shuffle through emotions. Anger, fear, joy, lust. It's like watching a dreaming dog kick and whimper, but far more heartbreaking. When he wakes up, this will all disappear. He will be empty again. He will be dead.

After an hour or two, we are down to one small gobbet of pink tissue. M pops it in his mouth and his pupils dilate as he has his visions. The brain is gone, but I'm not satisfied. I reach furtively into my pocket and pull out a fist-sized chunk that I've been saving. This one is different. This one is special. I tear off a bite and chew.

• • •

I am Perry Kelvin, a sixteen-year-old boy, watching my girlfriend write in her journal. The black leather cover is tattered and worn, the inside a maze of scribbles, drawings, little notes and quotes. I am sitting on the couch with a salvaged first edition of *On the Road*, longing to live in any era but this one, and she is curled in my lap, penning furiously. I poke my head over her shoulder, trying to get a glimpse. She pulls the journal away and gives me a coy smile. "No," she says, and returns to her work.

"What are you writing about?"

"Nooot tellinnng," she singsongs.

"Journal or poetry?"

"Both, silly."

"Am I in it?"

She chuckles.

I lace my arms around her shoulders. She burrows into me a little deeper. I bury my face in her hair and kiss the back of her head. The spicy smell of her shampoo—

• • •

M is looking at me. "You . . . have more?" he grunts, and holds out his hand for me to pass it. But I don't pass it. I take another bite and close my eyes.

. . .

"Perry," Julie says.

"Yeah."

We are at our secret spot on the stadium roof. We lie on our backs on a red blanket on the white steel panels, squinting up at the blinding blue sky.

"I miss airplanes," she says.

I nod. "Me too."

"Not flying in them. I never got to do that anyway with Dad the way he is. I just miss *airplanes*. That muffled thunder in the distance, those white lines . . . the way they sliced across the sky and made designs in the blue? My mom used to say it looked like Etch A Sketch. It was so beautiful."

I smile at the thought. She's right. Airplanes were beautiful. So were fireworks. Flowers. Concerts. Kites. All the indulgences we can no longer afford.

"I like how you remember things," I say.

She looks at me. "Well we have to. We have to remember everything. If we don't, by the time we grow up it'll be gone forever."

I close my eyes and let the scorching light blaze red through my lids. I let it saturate my brain. I turn my head and kiss Julie. We make love there on the blanket on the stadium roof, four hundred feet above the ground. The sun stands guard over us like a kind-hearted chaperone, smiling silently.

. . .

"Hey!"

My eyes snap open. M is glaring at me. He makes a grab for the piece of brain in my hand and I yank it away.

"*No*," I growl.

I suppose M is my friend, but I would rather kill him than let him taste this. The thought of his filthy fingers poking and fondling

34

these memories makes me want to rip his chest open and squish his heart in my hands, stomp his brain till he stops existing. This is *mine*.

M looks at me. He sees the warning flare in my eyes, hears the rising air-raid siren. He drops his hand away. He stares at me for a moment, annoyed and confused. "Bo . . . gart," he mutters, and locks himself in a toilet stall.

I leave the bathroom with abnormally purposeful strides. I slip in through the door of the 747 and stand there in the faint oval of light. Julie is lying back in a reclined seat, snoring gently. I knock on the side of the fuselage and she bolts upright, instantly awake. She watches me warily as I approach her. My eyes are burning again. I grab her messenger bag off the floor and dig through it. I find her wallet, and then I find a photo. A portrait of a young man. I hold the photo up to her eyes.

"I'm . . . sorry," I say hoarsely.

She looks at me, stone-faced.

I point at my mouth. I clutch my stomach. I point at her mouth. I touch her stomach. Then I point out the window, at the cloudless black sky of merciless stars. It's the weakest defense for murder ever offered, but it's all I have. I clench my jaw and squint my eyes, trying to ease their dry sting.

Julie's lower lip is tensed. Her eyes are red and wet. "Which one of you did it?" she says in a voice on the verge of breaking. "Was it that big one? That fat fuck that almost got me?"

I stare at her for a moment, not grasping her questions. And then it hits me, and my eyes go wide.

She doesn't know it was me.

The room was dark and I came from behind. She didn't see it. She doesn't know. Her eyes address me like I'm a creature worthy of address, unaware that I recently killed her lover, ate his life and digested his soul, and am right now carrying a prime cut of his brain in the front pocket of my slacks. I can feel it burning there like a coal of guilt, and I reflexively back away from her, unable to comprehend this curdled mercy.

"Why me?" she demands, blinking an angry tear out of her eye. "Why did you save *me*?" She twists her back to me and curls up on the chair, wrapping her arms around her shoulders. "Out of everyone . . . ," she mumbles into the cushion. "Why me."

These are her first questions. Not the ones urgent for her own well-being, not the mystery of how I know her name or the terrifying prospect of what my plans for her might be; she doesn't rush to satisfy those hungers. Her first questions are for others. For her friends, for her lover, wondering why she couldn't take their place.

I am the lowest thing. I am the bottom of the universe.

I drop the photo onto the seat and look at the floor. "I'm . . . sorry," I say again, and leave the plane.

When I emerge from the boarding tunnel there are several Dead grouped near the doorway. They watch me without expressions. We stand there in silence, still as statues. Then I brush past them and wander off into the dark halls.

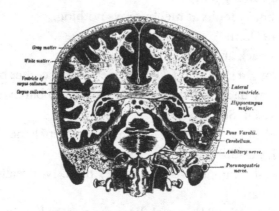

THE CRACKED PAVEMENT rumbles under our truck's tires. It abuses the old Ford's creaky suspension, making a quiet roar like stifled rage. I look at my dad. He looks older than I remember. Weaker. He grips the steering wheel hard. His knuckles are white.

"Dad?" I say.

"What, Perry."

"Where are we going to go?"

"Someplace safe."

I watch him carefully. "Are there still safe places?"

He hesitates, too long. "Someplace safer."

Behind us, in the valley where we used to swim and pick strawberries, eat pizza and go to movies, the valley where I was born and grew up and discovered everything that's now inside me, plumes of smoke rise. The gas station where I bought Coke slushies is on fire. The windows of my grade school are shattered. The kids in the public swimming pool are not swimming.

"Dad?" I say.

"What."

"Is Mom coming back?"

My dad finally looks at me, but says nothing.

"As one of them?"

He looks back at the road. "No."

"But I thought she would. I thought everyone comes back now."

"Perry," my dad says, and the word seems to barely escape his throat. "I fixed it. So she won't."

The hard lines in his face fascinate and repel me. My voice cracks. "Why, Dad?"

"Because she's gone. No one comes back. Not really. Do you understand that?"

The scrub brush and barren hills ahead start to blur in my vision. I try to focus on the windshield itself, the crushed bugs and tiny fractures. Those blur, too.

"Just remember her," my dad says. "As much as you can, for as long as you can. That's how she comes back. *We* make her live. Not some ridiculous curse."

I watch his face, trying to read the truth in his squinted eyes. I've never heard him talk like this.

"Bodies are just meat," he says. "The part of her that matters most . . . we get to keep that."

· · ·

"Julie."

"What?"

"Come here. Look at this."

The wind makes a ripping sound through the shattered plate glass of the hospital we're salvaging. Julie steps to the window's edge with me and looks down.

"What's it doing?"

"I don't know."

On the snowdusted street below, a single zombie walks in a loose circle. It bumps into a car and stumbles, slowly backs up against a wall, turns, shuffles in another direction. It makes no sound and doesn't seem to be looking at anything. Julie and I watch it for a few minutes.

"I don't like this," she says.

"Yeah."

"It's . . . sad."

"Yeah."

"What's wrong with it?"

"Don't know."

It stops in the middle of the street, swaying slightly. Its face displays absolutely nothing. Just skin stretched over a skull.

"I wonder how it feels," she says.

"What?"

"To be like them."

I watch the zombie. It starts swaying a little harder, then it collapses. It lies there on its side, staring at the frozen pavement.

"What's it . . . ?" Julie starts, then stops. She looks at me with wide eyes, then back at the crumpled body. "Did it just *die*?"

We wait in silence. The corpse doesn't move. I feel a wriggling sensation inside me, tiny things creeping down my spine.

"Let's go," Julie says, and turns away. I follow her back into the building. We can't think of anything to say all the way home.

• • •

Stop.

Breathe those useless breaths. Drop this piece of life you're holding to your lips. Where are you? How long have you been here? Stop now. You have to stop.

Squeeze shut your stinging eyes, and take another bite.

IN THE MORNING, my wife finds me slumped against one of the floor-to-ceiling windows overlooking the runways. My eyes are open and full of dust. My head leans to one side. I rarely allow myself to look so corpselike.

Something is wrong with me. There is a sick emptiness in my stomach, a feeling somewhere between starvation and hangover. My wife grabs my arm and pulls me to my feet. She starts walking, dragging me behind her like rolling luggage. I feel a flash of bitter heat pulse through me and I start speaking at her. "Name," I say, glaring into her ear. "Name?"

She shoots me a cold look and keeps walking.

"Job? School?" My tone shifts from query to accusation. "Movie? Song?" It bubbles out of me like oil from a punctured pipeline. "*Book?*" I shout at her. "Food? Family? *Name?*"

My wife turns and spits at me. Actually spits on my shirt, snarling like an animal. But the look in her eyes instantly cools my eruption. She's . . . frightened. Her lips quiver. What am I doing?

I look at the floor. We stand in silence for several minutes. Then she resumes walking, and I follow her, trying to shake off this strange black cloud that's settled over me.

. . .

She leads me to a gutted gift shop and lets out an emphatic groan. Our kids emerge from behind an overturned bookcase full of best-sellers that will never be read. They're each gnawing a human fore-arm, slightly brown at the stumps, not exactly fresh.

"Where did . . . get those?" I ask them. They shrug. I turn to my wife. "Need . . . better."

She frowns and points at me. She grunts angrily, and I avert my eyes, duly chastised. It's true, I haven't been the most involved par-ent. Is it possible to have a midlife crisis if you have no idea how old you are? I could be in my early thirties or late teens. I could be younger than Julie.

My wife grunts at the kids and gestures down the hall. They hang their heads and make a wheezy whining noise, but they follow us. We are taking them to their first day of school.

. . .

Some of us, maybe the same industrious Dead who built the Boneys' stair church, have built a "classroom" in the food court by stacking heavy luggage into high walls. As my family and I ap-proach, we hear groans and screams from inside this arena. There is a line of youngsters in front of the entryway, waiting their turn. My wife and I lead our kids to the back of the line and watch the lesson now in progress.

Five Dead youth are circling a skinny, middle-aged Living man. The man backs up against the luggage, looking frantically left and right, his empty hands balled into fists. Two of the youths dive at him and try to hold his arms down, but he shakes them off. The third one nips a tiny bite in his shoulder and the man screams as if he's been mortally wounded, because in effect, he has. From zombie bites to starvation to good old-fashioned age and disease, there are so many options for dying in this new world. So many ways for the Living to stop. But with just a few debrained exceptions, all roads lead to *us*, the Dead, and our very unglamorous immortality.

The man's pending conversion seems to have numbed him. One of the youths latches her teeth onto his thigh and he doesn't even flinch, he just bends over and starts pummeling her head with both fists until her skull dents and her neck snaps audibly. She stumbles away from him, scowling, her head tilting at a severe angle.

"Wrong!" their teacher roars. "Get . . . throat!"

The children back away and watch the man warily.

"Throat!" the teacher repeats. He and his assistant lumber into the arena and tackle the man, forcing him to the ground. The teacher kills him and stands up, blood streaming down his chin. "Throat," he says again, pointing to the body.

The five children exit shamefaced, and the next five in line are prodded inside. My kids look up at me anxiously. I pat their heads.

We watch as the dead man is hauled off to be eaten and the next one is dragged into the classroom. This one is old and gray haired, but he's big, probably a Security officer at one time in his life. He requires three of our males to haul him in safely. They throw him into a corner and quickly return to guard the entryway.

The five youths inside are nervous, but the teacher shouts at them and they begin to move in. When they get close enough they all five lunge at the same time, two grabbing for each arm and the fifth going for the throat. But the old man is shockingly strong. He twists around and flings two of them hard against the wall of luggage. The impact shakes the wall and a sturdy metal briefcase topples down from the top. The man grabs it by the handle, raises it high, and smashes it down on one of the youths' heads. The youth's skull caves in and his brain squishes out. He doesn't scream or twitch or quiver, he just abruptly collapses into a heap of limbs, flat and flush with the floor as if he's been dead for months already. Death takes hold of him with retroactive finality.

The whole school goes silent. The remaining four children back out of the arena. No one really pays attention as the adults rush inside to deal with the man. We all gaze at the youth's crumpled corpse with sad resignation. We can't tell which of the gathered adults might be his parents, since all our expressions are about the same. Whoever they are, they will forget their loss soon enough. By tomorrow the Boneys will show up with another boy or girl to replace this one. We allow a few uncomfortable seconds of silence for the killed child, then school resumes. A few parents glance at each other, maybe wondering what to think, wondering what this all means, this bent, inverted cycle of life. Or maybe that's just me.

My kids are next in line. They watch the current lesson intently, sometimes standing on tiptoes to see, but they aren't afraid. They are younger than the rest and will probably be matched against someone too frail to put up a fight, but they don't know this, and it's not why they're unafraid. When the entire world is built on death and horror, when existence is a constant state of panic, it's hard to get worked up about any one thing. Specific fears have become irrelevant. We've replaced them with a smothering blanket far worse.

· · ·

I pace outside the 747 boarding tunnel for about an hour before going in. I open the jet's door quietly. Julie is curled up in business class, sleeping. She has wrapped herself in a quilt made of cut-up jeans that I brought back as a souvenir a few weeks ago. The morning sun makes a halo in her yellow hair, sainting her.

"Julie," I whisper.

Her eyes slide open a crack. This time she doesn't jolt upright or edge away from me. She just looks at me with tired, puffy eyes. "What," she mumbles.

"How . . . are . . . ?"

"How do you think I am." She puts her back to me and wraps the blanket around her shoulders.

I watch her for a moment. Her posture is a brick wall. I lower my head and turn to go. But as I step through the doorway she says, "Wait."

I turn around. She is sitting up, the blanket piled on her lap. "I'm hungry," she says.

I look at her blankly. Hungry? Does she want an arm or leg? Hot blood, meat and life? She's Living . . . does she want to eat herself? Then I remember what being hungry used to mean. I remember beefsteaks and pancakes, grains and fruits and vegetables, that quaint little food pyramid. Sometimes I miss savoring taste and texture instead of just swallowing energy, but I try not to dwell on it. The old food does nothing to satisfy us anymore. Even bright red meat from a freshly killed rabbit or deer is beneath our culinary standards; its energy is simply incompatible, like trying to run a computer on diesel. There is no easy way out for us, no humane alternative for the fashionably moral. The new hunger demands sacrifice. It demands human suffering as the price for our pleasures, meager and cheap as they are.

"You know, *food*?" Julie prompts. She mimes the act of taking a bite. "Sandwiches? Pizza? Stuff that doesn't involve *killing* people?"

I nod. "I'll . . . get."

I start to leave but she stops me again.

"Just let me *go*," she says. "What are you *doing*? Why are you keeping me here?"

I think for a moment. I step to her window and point to the runways below. She sees the church service in progress. The congregation of the Dead, swaying and groaning. The skeletons rattling back and forth, voiceless but somehow charismatic, gnashing their splintered teeth. There are dozens of them down there, swarming.

"Keep you . . . safe."

She looks up at me from her chair with an expression I can't read. Her eyes are narrowed and her lips are tight, but it's not exactly rage. "How do you know my name?" she demands.

There it is. It had to come eventually.

"In that building. You said my name, I remember it. How the *fuck* do you know my name?"

I make no attempt to answer. No way to explain what I know and how I know it, not with my kindergarten vocabulary and special ed speech impediments. So I simply retreat, exiting the plane and trudging up the boarding tunnel, feeling more acutely than ever the limitations of what I am.

As I stand in Gate 12 considering where to go from here, I feel a touch on my shoulder. Julie is standing behind me. She stuffs her hands into the pockets of her tight black jeans, looking uncertain. "Just let me get out and walk around a little," she says. "I'm going crazy in that plane."

I don't answer. I look around the hallways.

"Come on," she says. "I walked *in* here and nobody ate me. Let me go with you to get food. You don't know what I like."

This is . . . not entirely true. I know she loves pad thai. I know she drools over sushi. I know she has a weakness for greasy cheeseburgers, despite the stadium's rigorous fitness routines. But that knowledge is not mine to use. That knowledge is stolen.

I nod slowly and point at her. "Dead," I pronounce. I click my teeth and do an exaggerated zombie shuffle.

"Okay," she says.

I lumber around in a circle with slow, shaky steps, letting out an occasional groan.

"Got it."

I take her by the wrist and lead her out into the hallway. I gesture in each direction, indicating the small cliques of zombies wandering in the dim morning shadows. I look her straight in the eyes. "Don't . . . run."

She crosses her heart. "Promise."

Standing so close to her, I find that I can smell her again. She has wiped much of the black blood off her skin, and through the gaps I can detect traces of her life energy. It bubbles out and sparkles like champagne, igniting flashes deep in the back of my sinuses. Still holding her gaze, I rub my palm into a recent gash on my forearm, and although it's nearly dry now, I manage to collect a thin smear of blood. I slowly spread this ink on her cheek and down her neck. She shudders, but doesn't pull away. She is, at the bottom of everything, a very smart girl.

"Okay?" I ask, raising my eyebrows.

She closes her eyes, takes a deep breath, cringes at the smell of my fluids, then nods. "Okay."

I walk and she follows, stumbling along behind me and groaning every three or four steps. She is overdoing it, overacting like high school Shakespeare, but she will pass. We bump through crowds of Dead, large hunting parties shambling past us on both sides, and no one glances at us. To my amazement, Julie's fear seems to be *diminishing* as we walk, despite the obvious peril of her situation. At a few points I catch her fighting a smile after letting out a particularly hammy moan. I feel an unfamiliar but pleasant sensation in my lips, tugging them upward.

This is . . . new.

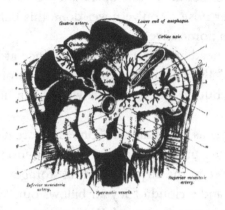

I TAKE JULIE to the food court, and she gives me an odd look when I immediately start moving toward the Thai restaurant. As we get closer she cringes and covers her nose. "Oh God," she moans. The warming bins in front are frothing with dried-up rot, dead maggots, and mold. I'm pretty much impervious to odor by now, but judging by Julie's expression, it's foul. We dig around in the back room for a while, but the airport's intermittent power means the freezers only work part-time, so everything inside is rancid. I head toward the burger joint. Julie gives me that quizzical look again and follows me. In the walk-in freezer we find a few burger patties that are currently cold but have clearly been thawed and refrozen many times. Dead flies speckle the white freezer floor.

Julie sighs. "Well?"

I look off into the distance, thinking. The airport does have a sushi bar . . . but I remember a little about sushi, and if a few hours can spoil a fresh hamachi fillet, I don't want to see what years can do.

"God," Julie says as I stand there deliberating, "you really know how to plan a dinner date." She opens a few boxes of moldy buns, wrinkles up her nose. "You've never done this before, have you? Taken a human home alive?"

I shake my head apologetically, but I wince at her use of the word "human." I've never liked that differentiation. She is Living and I'm Dead, but I'd like to believe we're both human. Call me an idealist.

I raise a finger as if to stall her. "One . . . more place."

We walk to an unmarked side area of the food court. Several doors later, we're in the airport's central storage area. I pry open a freezer door and a cloud of icy air billows out. I hide my relief. This was starting to get awkward. We step inside and stand among shelves stacked high with in-flight meal trays.

"What have we here . . . ," Julie says, and starts digging through the low shelves, inspecting the Salisbury steaks and processed potatoes. Thanks to whatever glorious preservatives they contain, the meals appear to be edible.

Julie scans the labels on the upper shelves she can't reach and suddenly beams, showing rows of white teeth that childhood braces made perfect. "Look, pad thai! I love . . ." She trails off, looking at me uneasily. She points to the shelf. "I'll have that."

I stretch over her head and grab a tray of frozen pad thai. I don't want any of the Dead to see Julie eating this lifeless waste, these empty calories, so I lead her to a table hidden behind some collapsed postcard kiosks. I try to steer her as far away from the school as possible, but we can still hear the wretched screams echoing down the halls. Julie keeps her face utterly placid during even the shrillest wails, doing everything short of whistling a tune to show that she doesn't notice the carnage. Is this for my benefit or hers?

We sit down at the café table and I set the meal tray in front of her. "En . . . joy," I say.

She jabs at the frozen-solid noodles with a plastic fork. She looks at me. "You really don't remember much, do you? How long has it been since you ate real food?"

I shrug.

"How long has it been since you . . . died or whatever?"

I tap a finger against my temple and shake my head.

She looks me over. "Well, it can't have been very long. You look pretty good for a corpse."

I wince again at her language, but I realize she can't possibly know the sensitive cultural connotations of the word "corpse." M uses it sometimes as a rough joke, and I use it myself in some of my darker moments, but coming from an outsider it ignites a defensive indignation she wouldn't understand. I breathe deep and let it go.

"Anyway, I can't eat it like this," she says, pushing her plastic fork into the food until one of the tines snaps. "I'm going to go find a microwave. Hold on."

She gets up and wanders into one of the empty restaurants. She has forgotten her shamble, and her hips sway rhythmically. It's risky, but I find myself not caring.

"Here we go," she says when she comes back, taking a deep whiff of spicy steam. "Mmm. I haven't had Thai in forever. We don't do real food at the stadium anymore, just basic nutrition and Carbtein. Carbtein tablets, Carbtein powder, Carbtein *juice*. Jesus H. Gross." She sits down and takes a bite of freezer-burned tofu. "Oh wow. That's almost *tasty*."

I sit there and watch her eat. I notice she seems to be having trouble getting the clumpy, congealed noodles down her throat. I fetch a lukewarm bottle of beer from the restaurant's cooler and set it on the table.

Julie stops eating and looks at the bottle. She looks at me and smiles. "Why, Mr. Zombie. You read my mind." She twists off the cap and takes a long drink. "I haven't had beer in a while, either. No mind-altering substances allowed in the stadium. Have to stay alert at all times, stay vigilant, blah blah blah." She takes another drink and gives me an appraising look laced with sarcasm. "Maybe you're not such a monster, Mr. Zombie. I mean, anyone who appreciates a good beer is halfway okay in my book."

I look at her and hold a hand to my chest. "My . . . name . . . ," I wheeze, but can't think how to continue.

She sets the beer down and leans forward a little. "You have a name?"

I nod.

Her lip curls in an amused half smile. "What's your name?"

I close my eyes and think hard, trying to pull it out of the void, but I've tried this so many times before. "Rrr," I say, trying to pronounce it.

"Rur? Your name is Rur?"

I shake my head. "Rrrrr . . ."

"Rrr? It starts with 'R'?"

I nod.

"Robert?"

I shake my head.

"Rick? Rodney?"

I shake my head.

"Uh . . . Rambo?"

I let out a sigh and look at the table.

"How about I just call you 'R'? That's a start, right?"

My eyes dart to hers. "R." I feel that upward sensation in my lips again. A slow smile—the first I can remember—creeps across my face.

"Hi, R," she says. "I'm Julie. But you knew that already, didn't you. Guess I'm a fucking celebrity." She nudges the beer toward me. "Have a drink."

I eye the bottle for a second, feeling a strange kind of nausea at the thought of what's inside. Dark amber emptiness. Lifeless piss. But I don't want to ruin this improbably warm moment with my stupid undead hangups. I accept the beer and take a long pull. I can feel it trickling through tiny perforations in my stomach and dampening my shirt. And to my amazement, I can feel a slight buzz spreading through my brain. This isn't possible, of course, since I have no bloodstream for the alcohol to enter, but I feel it anyway. Is it psychosomatic? Maybe a distant memory of the drinking experience left over from my old life? If so, apparently I was a lightweight.

Julie grins at my stupefied expression. "Drink up," she says. "I'm actually more of a wine girl anyway."

I take another pull. I can taste her raspberry lip gloss on the rim. I find myself imagining her dolled up for a concert, her neck-length hair swept and styled, her small body radiant in a red party dress, and me kissing her, the lipstick smearing onto my mouth, spreading bright rouge onto my gray lips . . .

I slide the bottle a safe distance away from me.

Julie chuckles and resumes eating. She pokes at it for a few minutes, ignoring my presence at the table. I'm about to make a doomed attempt at small talk when she looks up at me, all traces of joviality gone from her face, and says, "So, 'R.' Why are you keeping me here?"

The question hits me like a surprise slap to the face. I look at the ceiling. I gesture around at the airport in general, toward the distant groans of my fellow Dead. "Keep you safe."

"Bullshit."

There is silence. She looks at me hard. My eyes retreat.

"Listen," she says. "I get that you saved my life back there in the city. And I guess I'm grateful for that. So, yeah. Thanks for saving my life. Or sparing my life. Whatever. But you walked me *into* this place, I'm sure you could walk me out. So again: why are you keeping me here?"

Her eyes are like hot irons on the side of my face, and I realize I can't escape. I put a hand on my chest, over my heart. My "heart." Does that pitiful organ still represent anything? It lies motionless in my chest, pumping no blood, serving no purpose, and yet my feelings still seem to originate inside its cold walls. My muted sadness, my vague longing, my rare flickers of joy. They pool in the center of my chest and seep out from there, diluted and faint, but real.

I press my hand against my heart. Then I reach slowly toward Julie, and press it against hers. Somehow, I manage to meet her eyes.

She looks down at my hand, then gives me a dry stare. "Are you. Fucking. Kidding me."

I withdraw my hand and drop my eyes to the table, grateful that I'm incapable of blushing. "Need . . . to wait," I mumble. "They . . . think you're . . . new convert. They'll notice."

"How long?"

"Few . . . days. They'll . . . forget."

"Jesus Christ," she sighs, and covers her eyes with her hand, shaking her head.

"You'll . . . be okay," I tell her. "Promise."

She ignores this. She pulls an iPod out of her pocket and stuffs the earbuds into her ears. She returns to her food, listening to music that's just a faint hiss to me.

This date is not going well. Once again the absurdity of my secret thoughts overwhelms me, and I want to crawl out of my skin, escape my ugly, awkward flesh and be a skeleton, naked and anonymous. I'm about to stand up and leave when Julie pulls a bud out of one ear and gives me a squinting, penetrating look. "You're . . . different, aren't you," she says.

I don't respond.

"Because I've never heard a zombie talk, other than 'Brains!' and all that silly groaning. And I've never seen a zombie take any interest in humans beyond eating them. I've *definitely* never had one buy me a drink. Are there . . . others like you?"

Again I feel the urge to blush. "Don't . . . know."

She pushes her noodles around the plate. "A few days," she repeats.

I nod.

"What am I supposed to do here till it's safe to run away? I hope you don't expect me to just sit in your housejet taking blood baths all week."

I think for a moment. A rainbow of images floods my head, probably snippets of old movies I've seen, all sappy and romantic and utterly impossible. I have to get ahold of myself.

"I'll . . . entertain," I say eventually, and offer an unconvincing smile. "Be our . . . guest."

She rolls her eyes and returns to her food. The second earbud is still sitting on the table. Without looking up from her plate she casually offers it to me. I stick it in my ear, and the voice of Paul McCartney drifts into my head, singing all those wistful antonyms, yes/no, high/low, hello/good-bye/hello.

"You know John Lennon hated this song?" Julie says as it plays, speaking in my direction but not really addressing me. "He thought it was meaningless gibberish. Funny coming from the guy who wrote 'I Am the Walrus.'"

"Goo goo . . . g'joob," I say.

She stops, looks at me, tilts her head in pleasant surprise. "Yeah, exactly, right?" She takes a sip of the beer, forgetting the imprint of my lips on the bottle, and my eyes widen in brief panic. But nothing happens. Maybe my infection can't travel through soft moments like these. Maybe it needs the violence of the bite.

"Anyway," she says, "it's a little too chipper for me right now." She skips the song. I hear a brief snippet of Ava Gardner singing "Bill," then she skips a few more times, lands on an unfamiliar pop song, and cranks the volume. I'm distantly aware of the music—one of those dark, dissonant, brutally clanging chants that dominated the airwaves during the last gasps of civilization—but I have tuned out. I watch Julie bob her head from side to side with eyes closed. Even now, here, in the darkest and strangest of places with the most macabre of company, this music moves her and her life pulses hard. I smell it again, a white glowing vapor wafting out from under my black blood. And even for Julie's safety, I can't bring myself to smother it.

What is wrong with me? I stare at my hand, at its pale gray flesh, cool and stiff, and I dream it pink, warm and supple, able to guide and build and caress. I dream my necrotic cells shrugging off their lethargy, inflating and lighting up like Christmas deep in my dark core. Am I inventing all this like the beer buzz? A placebo? An optimistic illusion? Either way, I feel the flatline of my existence disrupting, forming heartbeat hills and valleys.

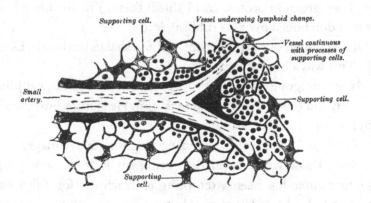

Supporting cell.   Vessel undergoing lymphoid change.

Vessel continuous
with processes of
supporting cells.

Small
artery.

Supporting cell.

Supporting
cell.

"You need to corner sharper. You keep almost running off the road when you turn right."

I crank the skinny leather wheel and drop my foot onto the accelerator. The Mercedes lurches forward, throwing our heads back.

"God you're a leadfoot. Can you go easier on the gas?"

I come to a jerky stop, forget to push in the clutch, and the engine dies. Julie rolls her eyes and forces patience into her voice. "Okay, look." She restarts the engine, scoots over, and snakes her legs across mine, placing her feet on my feet. Under her pressure, I smoothly exchange gas for clutch, and the car glides forward. "Like that," she says, and returns to her seat. I release a satisfied wheeze.

We are cruising the tarmac, taxiing to and fro under the mild afternoon sun. Our hair ruffles in the breeze. Here in this moment, in this candy-red '64 roadster with this beautiful young woman, I can't help inserting myself into other, more classically filmic lives. My mind drifts, and I lose what little focus I've been able to maintain. I veer off the runway and clip the bumper of a stair truck, knocking the Boneys' church circle out of alignment. The jolt throws our heads to the side, and I hear my children's necks snap in the backseat. They groan in protest and I shush them. I'm already embarrassed; I don't need my kids rubbing it in.

Julie examines our dented front end and shakes her head. "Damn it, R. This was a beautiful car."

My son lunges forward in another clumsy attempt to eat Julie's shoulder, and I reach back and smack him. He slumps into the seat with his arms crossed, pouting.

"No biting!" Julie scolds, still inspecting the car's damage.

I don't know why I decided to bring my kids to today's driving lesson. Julie has been attempting to teach me for a few days now, and today I just felt some obscure urge to *father*. To pass on knowledge. I'm aware it's not exactly safe. My kids are too young to recognize Living speech patterns, much less savor them like I do, and I've refreshed Julie's gruesome camouflage several times, but at close range her true nature still seeps into the air. Every now and then my kids smell it, and their slowly developing instincts take hold. I try to discipline them lovingly.

As we circle back toward our home terminal, I notice the congregation emerging from a cargo-loading gate. Like an inverted funeral procession, the Dead march out in a solemn line, taking slow, plodding steps toward the church. A clutch of Boneys leads the pilgrimage, moving forward with far more purpose than any of the fleshclad. They are the few among us who always seem to know exactly where they're going and what they're doing. They don't waver, they don't pause or change course, and their bodies no longer either grow or decay. They are static. One of them looks directly at me, and I recall a Dark Ages etching I've seen somewhere, a rotting corpse sneering at a plump young virgin.

Quod tu es, ego fui, quod ego sum, tu eris.

What you are, I once was.
What I am, you will become.

I break away from the skeleton's hollow stare. As we cruise past their line, some of the Fleshies glance at us with disinterest, and I see my wife among them. She is walking alongside a male, her hand woven into his. My kids spot her in the crowd and stand up on the backseat, waving and grunting loudly. Julie follows their gaze and sees my wife wave back at them. Julie looks at me. "Is that like . . . your wife?"

I don't respond. I look at my wife, expecting some kind of rebuke. But there is almost no recognition in her eyes. She looks at the car. She looks at me. She looks straight ahead and keeps walking, hand in hand with another man.

"Is that your wife?" Julie asks again, more forcefully. I nod. "Who's that . . . *guy* she's with?" I shrug. "Is she cheating on you or something?" I shrug. "This doesn't *bother* you?"

I shrug.

"Stop shrugging, you asshole! I know you can talk; say something."

I think for a minute. Watching my wife fade into the distance, I put a hand on my heart. "Dead." I wave a hand toward my wife. "Dead." My eyes drift toward the sky and lose their focus. "Want it . . . to hurt. But . . . doesn't."

Julie looks at me like she's waiting for more, and I wonder if I've expressed anything at all with my halting, mumbled soliloquy. Are my words ever actually audible, or do they just echo in my head while people stare at me, waiting? I want to change my punctuation. I long for exclamation marks, but I'm drowning in ellipses.

Julie watches me a moment longer, then turns to face the windshield and the oncoming scenery. On our right: the dark openings of empty boarding tunnels, once alive with eager travelers on their way to see the world, expand their horizons, find love and fame and fortune. On our left: the blackened wreckage of a Dreamliner.

"My boyfriend cheated on me once," Julie tells the windshield. "There was this girl his dad was housing while the foster homes were being set up, and they got blackout drunk one night and it just happened. It was basically an accident, and he gave me the most sincere and moving confession of all time, swore to God he loved me so much and would do anything to convince me, blah blah blah, but it didn't matter, I kept thinking about it and running it through my head and just *burning* with it. I cried every night for weeks. Practically wore the binary off all my saddest MP3s." She is shaking her head slowly. Her eyes are far away. "Things are just . . . I feel things *so hard* sometimes. When that happened with Perry, I would have loved to be more . . . like you."

I study her. She runs a finger through her hair and twists it around a little. I notice faint scars on her wrists and forearms, thin lines too symmetrical to be accidents. She blinks and glances at me abruptly, as if I just woke her from a dream. "I don't know why I'm telling you this," she says, annoyed. "Anyway, lesson's over for today. I'm tired."

Without further comment, I drive us home. I brake too late and park the car with the bumper two inches into the grille of a Miata. Julie sighs.

. . .

Later that evening we sit in the 747, cross-legged in the middle of the aisle. A plate of microwaved pad thai sits on the floor in front of Julie, cooling. I watch her in silence as she pokes at it. Even doing and saying nothing, she is entertaining to watch. She tilts her head, her eyes roam, she smiles and shifts her body. Her inner thoughts play across her face like rear-projection movies.

"It's too quiet in here," she says, and stands up. She starts digging through my stacks of records. "What's with all the vinyl? Couldn't figure out how to work an iPod?"

"Better . . . sound."

She laughs. "Oh, a purist, huh?"

I make a spinning motion in the air with my finger. "More real. More . . . alive."

She nods. "Yeah, true. Lot more trouble though." She flips through the stacks and frowns a little. "There's nothing in here newer than like . . . 1999. Is that when you died or something?"

I think about this for a moment, then shrug. It's possible, but the truth is I have no idea when I died. One might try to guess my deathday by my current state of decay, but not all of us rot at the same rate. Some of us stay funeral-parlor fresh for years, and some of us wither to bones in a matter of months, our flesh sloughing away like dry sea foam. I don't know what causes this inequity. Maybe our bodies follow our minds' leads. Some resign themselves easily, others hold on hard.

Another obstacle to estimating my age: I have no idea what year we're in. 1999 could have been a decade ago or yesterday. One might try to deduce a timeline by looking at the crumbling streets, the toppled buildings, the rotting infrastructure, but just like us, every part of the world is decaying at its own pace. There are cities that could be mistaken for Aztec ruins, and there are cities that just emptied last week, TVs still awake all night roaring static, café omelets just starting to mold.

What happened to the world was gradual. I've forgotten what it actually was, but I have faint, fetal memories of what it was like. A smoldering dread that never really caught fire till there wasn't much left to burn. Each sequential step surprised us. Then one day we woke up, and everything was gone.

"There you go again," Julie says. "Drifting off. I'm so curious what you think about when you daze out like that." I shrug, and she lets out an exasperated huff. "And there you go again, shrugging. Stop shrugging, shrugger! Answer my question. Why the stunted musical growth?"

I start to shrug and then stop myself, with some difficulty. How can I possibly explain this to her in words? The slow death of Quixote. The abandoning of quests, the surrendering of desires, the settling in and settling down that is the inevitable fate of the Dead.

"We don't . . . think . . . new things," I begin, straining to kick through my short-sheeted diction. "I . . . find things . . . sometimes. But we don't . . . seek."

"Really," Julie says. "Well that's a fucking tragedy." She continues to dig through my records, but her tone starts to escalate as she speaks. "You don't think about new things? You don't 'seek'? What's that even mean? You don't seek what? Music? Music is *life*! It's physical emotion—you can touch it! It's neon ecto-energy sucked out of spirits and switched into sound waves for your ears to swallow. Are you telling me, what, that it's boring? You don't have time for it?"

There is nothing I can say to this. I find myself praying to the ghastly mouth of the open sky that Julie never changes. That she never wakes up one day to find herself older and wiser.

"Anyway, you've still got some good stuff in here," she says, letting her indignation deflate. "Great stuff, really. Here, let's do this one again. Can't go wrong with Frank." She puts on a record and returns to her pad thai. "The Lady Is a Tramp" fills the plane's cabin, and she gives me a crooked little smile. "My theme song," she says, and stuffs her mouth full of noodles.

Out of morbid curiosity, I pull one off her plate and chew it. There is no taste at all. It's like imaginary food, like chewing air. I turn my head and spit it into my palm. Julie doesn't notice. She seems far away again, and I watch the colors and shapes of her thought-film flickering behind her face. After a few minutes, she swallows a bite and looks up at me.

"R," she says in a tone of casual curiosity. "Who did you kill?"

I stiffen. The music fades out of my awareness.

"In that high-rise. Before you saved me. I saw the blood on your face. Whose was it?"

I just look at her. Why does she have to ask me this. Why can't her memories fade to black like mine. Why can't she just live with me alone in the dark, swimming in the abyss of inked-out history.

"I just need to know who it was." Her expression betrays nothing. Her eyes are locked on mine, unblinking.

"No one," I mumble. "Some . . . kid."

"There's this theory that you guys eat brains because you get to relive the person's life. True?"

I shrug, trying not to squirm. I feel like a toddler caught finger-painting the walls. Or killing dozens of people.

"Who was it?" she presses. "Don't you remember?"

I consider lying. I remember a few faces from that room; I could roll the dice and just pick one, probably some random recruit she didn't even know, and she would let it go and never bring it up again. But I can't do it. I can't lie to her any more than I can spit out the indigestible truth. I'm trapped.

Julie lets her eyes auger into me for a long minute, then she falters. "Was it Berg?" she offers, so quietly she's almost talking to herself. "The kid with the acne? I bet it was Berg. That guy was a dick. He called Nora a mulatto and he was staring at my ass that entire salvage. Which Perry didn't even notice, of course. If it was Berg, I'm almost glad you got him."

I try to catch her gaze to make sense of this reversal, but now she's the one avoiding eye contact. "Anyway," she says, "whoever killed Perry . . . I just want you to know I don't blame them for it."

I tense again. "You . . . don't?"

"No. I mean, I think I get it. You don't have a choice, right? And to be honest . . . I'd never say this to anyone, but . . ." She stirs her food. "It's kind of a relief that it finally happened."

I frown. "What?"

"To be able to finally stop dreading it."

"Perry . . . dying?"

I instantly regret speaking his name. Rolling off my tongue, the syllables taste like his blood.

Julie nods, still looking at her plate. When she speaks again her voice is soft and faint, the voice of memories longing to be forgotten. "Something . . . happened to him. A lot of things, actually. I guess there came a point where he just couldn't absorb any more, so he flipped over into a different person. He was this brilliant, fiery kid, so weird and funny and full of dreams, and then . . . just quit all his plans, joined Security . . . it was scary how fast he changed. He said he was doing everything for me, that it was time for him to grow up and face reality, take responsibility and all that. But everything I loved about him—everything that made him who he *was*—just started rotting. He gave up, basically. Quit his life. Real death was just the next logical step." She pushes her plate aside. "We talked about dying all the time. He just kept bringing it up. In the middle of a wild make-out session he'd stop and be like, 'Julie, what do you think the average life expectancy is these days?' Or, 'Julie, when I die, will you be the one to debrain me?' Height of romance, right?"

She looks out the airplane window at the distant mountains. "I tried to talk him down. Tried *really* hard to keep him here, but over the last couple years it got pretty clear to everyone. He was just . . . gone. I don't know if anything short of Christ and King Arthur returning to redeem the world could have brought him back. *I* sure wasn't enough." She looks at me. "Will he come back to life, though? As one of you?"

I drop my eyes, remembering the juicy pink taste of his brain. I shake my head.

She is quiet for a while. "It's not like I'm not *sad* that he's gone. I am, I . . ." Her voice wobbles a little. She pauses, clears her throat. "I really am. But he wanted it. I knew he wanted it." A tear escapes one eye and she seems startled by it. She brushes it away like a mosquito.

I stand up, take her plate, fold it into the trash bin. When I sit back down her eyes are dry but still red. She sniffs and gives me a weak smile. "I guess I talk a lot of shit about Perry, but it's not like I'm such a shiny happy person either, you know? I'm a wreck too, I'm just . . . still alive. A wreck in progress." She laughs a quick, broken laugh. "It's weird, I never talk about this stuff with anyone, but you're . . . I mean you're so *quiet*, you just sit there and listen. It's like talking to God." Her smile drifts away and she is absent for a moment. When she speaks again her voice is cautious but flat, and her eyes roam the cabin, studying window rivets and warning labels. "I did a lot of drugs when I was younger. Started when I was twelve and tried almost everything. I still drink and smoke pot when I get the chance. I even had sex with a guy for money once, when I was thirteen. Not because I wanted the money—even back then money was pretty worthless. Just because it was awful, and maybe I felt like I deserved it." She looks at her wrist, those thin scars like an entry stamp for some horrible concert. "All the shitty stuff people do to themselves . . . it can all be the same thing, you know? Just a way to drown out your own voice. To kill your memories without having to kill yourself."

There is a long silence. Her eyes roam the floor and mine stay on her face, waiting for her to come home. She takes a deep breath, looks at me, and gives a little shrug. "Shrug," she says in a small voice, and forces a smile.

Slowly, I stand up and go over to my record player. I pull out one of my favorite LPs, an obscure compilation of Sinatra songs from various albums. I don't know why I like this one so much. I once spent three full days motionless in front of it, just watching the vinyl spin. I know the grooves in this record better than the grooves in my palms. People used to say music was the great communicator; I wonder if this is still true in this posthuman, posthumous age. I put the record on and begin to move the needle as it plays, skipping measures, skipping songs, dancing through the spirals to find the words I want to fill the air. The phrases are off key, off tempo, punctuated by loud scratches like the ripping of fascia tissue, but the tone is flawless. Frank's buttery baritone says it better than my croaky vocals ever could had I the diction of a Kennedy. I stand over the record, cutting and pasting the contents of my heart into an airborne collage.

I don't care if you are called—scratch—*when people say you're*—scratch—*wicked witchcraft*—scratch—*don't change a hair for me, not if you*—scratch—*'cause you're sensational*—scratch—*you just the way you are*—scratch—*you're sensational . . . sensational . . . That's all . . .*

I leave the record to play out its normal repertoire and sit back down in front of Julie. She stares at me with damp, red-rimmed eyes. I press my hand against her chest, feeling the gentle thump inside. A tiny voice speaking in code.

Julie sniffs. She wipes a finger across her nose. "What *are* you?" she asks me for the second time.

I smile a little. Then I get up and exit the plane, leaving her question floating there, still unanswerable. In my palm I can feel the echo of her pulse, standing in for the absence of mine.

. . .

That night, lying on the floor of Gate 12, I fall asleep. The new sleep is different, of course. Our bodies aren't "tired," we aren't "resting." But every so often, after days or weeks of unrelenting consciousness, our minds simply can't carry the weight anymore, and we collapse. We allow ourselves to die, to shut down and have no thoughts at all for hours, days, weeks. However long it takes to regather the electrons of our ids, to keep ourselves intact a little longer. There's nothing peaceful or lovely about it; it's ugly and compulsory, an iron lung for the wheezing husks of our souls, but tonight . . . something different happens.

I dream.

Underdeveloped, murky, faded to sepia like centuries-old film, scenes from my former life flicker in the void of sleep. Amorphous figures walk through melting doorways into shadowy rooms. Voices crawl through my head, deep and slurring like drunken giants. I play ambiguous sports, I watch incoherent movies, I talk and laugh with anonymous blurs. Among these foggy snapshots of an unexamined life, I catch glimpses of a pastime, some passionate pursuit long ago sacrificed on the blood-soaked altar of pragmatism. Guitar? Dancing? Dirt bikes? Whatever it was, it fails to penetrate the thick smog choking my memory. Everything remains dark. Blank. Nameless.

I have begun to wonder where I came from. The person I am now, this fumbling, stumbling supplicant . . . was I built on the foundations of my old life, or did I rise from the grave a blank slate? How much of me is inherited, and how much is my own creation? Questions that were once just idle musings have begun to feel strangely urgent. Am I firmly rooted to what came before? Or can I choose to deviate?

I wake up staring at the distant ceiling. The memories, empty as they already were, evaporate completely. It's still night, and I can hear my wife having sex with her new lover behind the door of a nearby staff room. I try to ignore them. I already walked in on them once today. I heard noises, the door was wide open, so I walked in. There they were, naked, awkwardly slamming their bodies together, grunting and groping each other's pale flesh. He was limp. She was dry. They watched each other with puzzled expressions, as if some unknown force had shoved them together into this moist tangle of limbs. Their eyes seemed to ask each other, "Who the hell are you?" as they jiggled and jerked like meat marionettes.

They didn't stop when they noticed me. They just looked at me and kept grinding. I nodded, and walked back to Gate 12, and this was the final weight that broke my mind's kneecaps. I crumpled to the floor and slept.

I don't know why I'm awake already, after just a few feverish hours. I still feel the weight of my accumulated thoughts bearing down on my tender brain, but I don't think I can sleep anymore. A burr and a buzz tickle my mind, keeping me alert. I reach for the only thing that's ever helped in times like these. I reach into my pocket and pull out my last chunk of cerebrum.

As residual life energy fades from the brain, the useless clutter is first to go. The movie quotes, the radio jingles, the celebrity gossip and political slogans, they all melt away, leaving only the most potent and wrenching of the memories. As the brain dies, the life inside clarifies and distills. It ages like a fine wine.

The piece in my hand has shriveled somewhat, taking on a

brownish gray tint. I'll be lucky to get another few minutes of Perry's life out of this, but what blazing, urgent minutes these will be. Closing my eyes, I pop it into my mouth and chew, thinking, *Don't leave me yet, Perry. Just a little longer. Just a little more. Please.*

. . .

I erupt from the dark, crushing tunnel into a flash of light and noise. A new kind of air surrounds me, dry and cold as they wipe the last smears of home off my skin. I feel a sharp pain as they snip something, and suddenly I am less. I am no one but myself, tiny and feeble and utterly alone. I am lifted and swung through great heights across yawning distances and given to Her. She wraps around me, so much bigger and softer than I ever imagined from inside, and I strain my eyes open. I see Her. She is immense, cosmic. She is the world. The world smiles down on me, and when She speaks it's the voice of God, vast and resonant with meaning, but words unknowable, ringing gibberish in my blank white mind.

She says—

. . .

I am in a dark, crooked room, gathering medical supplies and loading them into boxes. A small crew of civilian recruits is with me on this salvage, all of them handpicked by Colonel Rosso except one. One of them picked herself. One of them saw a look in my eyes and worried. One of them wants to save me.

"Did you hear that?" Julie says, glancing around.

"No," I reply instantly, and keep loading.

"I did," Nora says, brushing her frizzy curls out of her eyes. "Pear, maybe we should—"

"We're fine. We scoped it out, we're secure. Just work."

They watch me constantly, tensed like hospital orderlies, ready to intervene. It changes nothing. I won't endanger them but I'll still find a way. When I'm alone, when no one's looking, I'll do it. I'll make it happen. They keep trying and trying but the beauty of their love only drives me deeper. Why can't they understand it's too late?

A noise. I hear it now. A rumble of footsteps up the staircase, a chorus of groans. Are Julie's ears so much more sensitive or have I stopped listening? I pick up my shotgun and turn—

No, I blurt into the middle of the vision. *Not this. This isn't what I want to see.*

To my surprise, everything halts. Perry looks up at me, the voice in the sky. "These are *my* memories, remember? You're the guest here. If you don't want to see it, you can spit it out."

This is a shock. The memory has come unscripted. Am I having a conversation with the very mind I'm digesting? I don't know how much of this is actually Perry and how much is just me, but I'm swept along.

We should be seeing your life! I shout down at him. *Not this! Why would you want your last thought to be a replay of your dirty, meaningless death?*

"You think death isn't meaningful?" he retorts, chambering a round in his shotgun. Julie and the others wait in their positions like background props, fidgeting impatiently. "Wouldn't you want to remember *yours* if you could? How else are you going to reverse-engineer yourself into something new?"

Something new?

"Of course, you dumb corpse." He puts his eye to the sight and makes a slow scan of the room, holding for a moment on Berg. "There are a thousand kinds of life and death across the whole metaphysical spectrum, not to mention the metaphorical. You don't want to stay dead for the rest of your life, do you?"

Well, no . . .

"Then relax, and let me do what I need to do."

I swallow the lump in my throat and say, *Okay . . .*

• • •

—pick up my shotgun and turn, just as the thundering footfalls reach our floor. The door blows open and they burst inside, roaring. We shoot them, we shoot them, we shoot them, but there are too many, and they're *fast*. I crouch over Julie, shielding her as best I can.

No. Oh God. This is not what I wanted.

A tall skinny one is suddenly behind me, grabbing my legs. I fall and hit the table and my vision flashes red. Everything is wrong, but as the red fades to black I still allow an exultant shout, one last selfish orgasm before I go to sleep forever:

Finally. Finally!

And then—

• • •

"Perry." A jab in my ribs. "Perry!"

"What?"

"Don't you go to sleep on me now."

I open my eyes. An hour of sun glaring through my closed lids has faded all the colors of the world to bluish gray, like an old movie poster in a dying local video store. I turn my head to look at her. She smiles wickedly and jabs me again. "Never mind. Go ahead and sleep."

Beyond her face I see the looming white posts of the stadium roof arches, and beyond that, the deep cerulean sky. I slowly alternate my focus between her and the sky, letting her face blur into a peach-and-gold cloud, then refocusing it.

"What?" she says.

"Tell me something hopeful."

"What kind of hopeful?"

I sit up, crossing my arms over my knees. I look out at the surrounding city, the crumbling buildings, the empty streets and lonely sky, clean and blue and deathly quiet without its white-sketching airplanes.

"Tell me this isn't the end of the world."

She lies there for a minute, looking up at the sky. Then she sits up and pulls one of her earbuds out of her tangled blond hair. She gently plugs it into my ear.

The warbled strumming of a broken guitar, the swelling of an orchestra, the oohs and ahhs of a studio choir, and John Lennon's weary, woozy voice, singing limitless undying love. Everyone playing this song is now bones in a grave, but here they are anyway, exciting and inviting me, calling me on and on. The final fadeout breaks something inside me, and tears squeeze out of my eyes. The brilliant truth and the inescapable lie, sitting side by side just like Julie and I. Can I have both? Can I survive in this doomed world and still love Julie, who dreams above it? For this moment at least, tied to her brain by the white wire between our ears, I feel like I can.

Nothing's gonna change my world, Lennon chants, over and over. *Nothing's gonna change my world.*

Julie sings a high harmony and I murmur a low. There on the hot white roof of humanity's last outpost, we look out over our rapidly, hopelessly, irretrievably changing world, and we sing:

Nothing's gonna change my world. Nothing's gonna change my world.

• • •

I am staring at the airport ceiling again. I drop the last chunk of Perry's brain into my mouth and chew, but nothing happens. I spit it out like gristle. The story is over. The life is gone.

I find my eyes burning again, craving tears that my ducts can't supply. I feel as if I've lost someone dear. A brother. A twin. Where is his soul now? Am I Perry Kelvin's afterlife?

I finally drift back to sleep. I'm in the darkness. The molecules of my mind are still scattered, and I float through oily black space, trying to swipe them up like fireflies. Every time I go to sleep, I know I may never wake up. How could anyone expect to? You drop your tiny, helpless mind into a bottomless well, crossing your fingers and hoping that when you pull it out on its flimsy fishing wire it hasn't been gnawed to bones by nameless beasts below. Hoping you pull up anything at all. Maybe this is why I sleep only a few hours a month. I don't want to die again. This has become clearer and clearer to me recently, a desire so sharp and focused I can hardly believe it's mine: I don't want to die. I don't want to disappear. I want to stay.

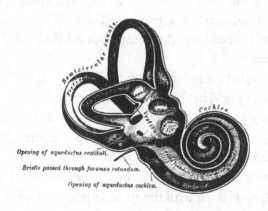

Opening of aqueductus vestibuli.

Bristle passed through foramen rotundum.

Opening of aqueductus cochleæ.

I AWAKE to the sound of screaming.

My eyes snap open and I spit a few bugs out of my mouth. I lurch upright. The sound is far away but it's not from the school. It lacks the plaintive panic of the school's still-breathing cadavers. I recognize the defiant spark in these screams, the relentless hope in the face of undeniable hopelessness. I leap to my feet and run faster than any zombie has ever run.

Following the screams, I find Julie at the Departures gate. She is backed into a corner, surrounded by six drooling Dead. They close in on her, rearing back a little each time she swings her smoke-belching hedge trimmer but advancing steadily. I rush at them from behind and crash into their tight circle, scattering them like bowling pins. The one closest to Julie I punch so hard the bones of my hand shatter into seashell crumbs. His face cracks inward and he drops. The next closest I ram into the wall, then grab his head and smash it into the concrete until his brain pops and he goes down. One of them grabs me from behind and takes a bite out of my rib meat. I reach back, tear off his rotten arm, and swing it at him like Babe Ruth. His head spins a full three-sixty on his neck, then tilts, tears, and falls off. I stand there in front of Julie, brandishing the musclebound limb, and the Dead stop advancing.

"Julie!" I snarl at them while pointing at her. "Julie!"

They stare at me. They sway back and forth.

"Julie!" I say again, not sure how else to put it. I walk up to her and press my hand against her heart. I drop the arm-club and put my other hand on my own heart. "Julie."

The room is silent except for the low grumble of her hedge trimmer. The air is thick with the rotten-apricot smell of stabilized gasoline, and I notice several decapitated corpses I had nothing to do with lying at her feet. *Well done, Julie,* I think with a faint smile. *You are a lady and a scholar.*

"What . . . the *fuck!*" growls a deep voice behind me.

A tall, bulky form is picking itself up off the floor. It's the first one I attacked, the one I punched in the face. It's M. I didn't even recognize him in the heat of the moment. Now, with his cheekbone crushed into his head, he's even harder to identify. He glares at me and rubs his face. "What are . . . doing, you . . ." He trails off, at a loss for even simple words.

"Julie," I say yet again, as if this is an irrefutable argument. And in a way, it is. That one word, a fully fleshed *name*. It's having the effect of a glowing, chattering cell phone raised before a mob of primitives. All the remaining Dead stare at Julie in hushed silence, except M. He is baffled and enraged.

"Living!" he sputters. "Eat!"

I shake my head. "No."

"Eat!"

"No!"

"*Eat,* fucking—"

"*Hey!*"

M and I both turn. Julie has stepped out from behind me. She glares at M and revs the trimmer. "Fuck off," she says. She links an arm into my elbow, and I feel a tingle of warmth spreading out from her touch.

M looks at her, then at me, back to her, then back to me. His permanent grimace is tight. We appear to be in a standoff, but before it can escalate any further the stillness is pierced by a reverberating noise, an eerie, airless horn blast.

We all turn to the escalators. Yellowed skeletons are rising up one by one from the floors below. A small committee of Boneys emerges from the stairs and approaches me and Julie. They stop in front of us and fan out into a line. Julie backs away a little, her bravado flattening under their black, eyeless stares. Her grip on my arm tightens.

One of them steps forward and stops in front of me, inches from my face. No breath wafts from its hollow mouth, but I can feel a faint, low hum emanating from its bones. This hum is not found in me, nor in M, nor in any of the other fleshclad Dead, and I begin to wonder what exactly these dried-up creatures really are. I can no longer believe in any voodoo spell or laboratory virus. This is something deeper, darker. This comes from the cosmos, from the stars, or the unknown blackness behind them. The shadows in God's boarded-up basement.

The ghoul and I are locked in a stare-down, toe to toe, eye to eyesocket. I don't blink, and it can't. What seems like hours pass. Then it does something that slightly undermines the horror of its presence. It raises a stack of Polaroids in its pointy fingers and begins handing them to me, one by one. I'm reminded of a proud old man showing off his grandkids, but the skeleton's grin is far from grandfatherly, and the photos are far from heartwarming. Off-the-hip shots of some kind of battle. Organized ranks of soldiers firing rockets into our hives, rifles popping us off with precision, one two three. Private citizens with their machetes and chain saws hacking through us like blackberry vines, spattering our dark juices on the camera lens. Monumental stacks of freshly rekilled corpses, soaked in gasoline and lit.

Smoke. Blood. Family photos from our vacation in Hell.

But as unsettling as this slide show is, I've seen it before. I've witnessed the Boneys performing it dozens of times, usually for children. They drift around the airport with cameras dangling from their vertebrae, occasionally following us on feeding trips, lingering in the back to document the bloodshed, and I always wonder what it is they're after. Their subject matter follows a precise theme that never varies: Corpses. Battles. Newly converted zombies. And themselves. Their meeting rooms are wallpapered with these photos, floor to ceiling, and sometimes they drag in a young zombie and make him stand there for hours, even days, silently appreciating their work.

Now this skeleton, identical to the rest, hands me these Polaroids slowly and civilly, confident that the images speak for themselves. The message of today's sermon is clear: *inevitability*. The immutable, binary results of our interactions with the Living.

They die / we die.

A noise rises from where the skeleton's throat would be, a crowing sound full of pride and reproach and stiff, rigid righteousness. It says everything it and the rest of the Boneys have to say, their motto and mantra. It says, *I rest my case,* and *That's the way it is,* and *Because I said so.*

Looking straight into its eyesockets, I let the photos fall to the floor. I rub my fingers against each other as if trying to brush off some dirt.

The skeleton does not react. It just stares at me with that horrible, hollow stare, so utterly motionless it seems to have stopped time. The dark hum in its bones dominates everything, a low sine wave prickling with sour overtones. And then, so abruptly it makes me jump, the creature pivots away and rejoins its comrades. It barks out one last horn blast, and the Boneys descend the escalator. The rest of the Dead disperse, sneaking hungry glances at Julie. M is the last to go. He scowls at me, then lumbers away. Julie and I are alone.

I turn to face her. Now that the situation has settled and the blood on the floor is drying, I'm finally able to contemplate what's happening here, and somewhere deep in my chest, my heart wheezes. I gesture toward what I assume is the Departures sign and give Julie a questioning look, unable to hide the hurt behind it.

Julie looks at the floor. "It's been a few days," she mumbles. "You said a few days."

"Wanted to . . . take you home. Say good-bye."

"Why? What's the point? I have to leave. I mean I can't *stay* here. You realize that, right?"

Yes. Of course I realize that.

She's right, and I'm ridiculous.

And yet . . .

But what if . . .

I want to do something impossible. Something astounding and unheard of. I want to scrub the moss off the space shuttle and fly Julie to the moon and colonize it, or float a capsized cruise ship to some distant island where no one will protest us, or just harness the magic that brings me into the brains of the Living and use it to bring Julie into mine, because it's warm in here, it's quiet and lovely, and in here we aren't an absurd juxtaposition, we are perfect.

She finally meets my eyes. She looks like a lost child, confused and sad. "But thanks for, uh . . . saving me. Again."

With great effort, I pull out of my reverie and give her a smile. "Any . . . time."

She hugs me. It's tentative at first, a little scared, and yes, a little repulsed, but then she melts into it. She rests her head against my cold neck and embraces me. Unable to believe what's happening, I put my arms around her and just hold her.

I almost swear I can feel my heart thumping. But it must just be hers, pressed tight against my chest.

• • •

We walk back to the 747. Nothing has been resolved, but she's agreed to postpone her escape. After the messy scene we just caused, it seems prudent to lay low for a bit. I don't know exactly how much the Boneys will object to the irregularity Julie represents, because this is the first time anyone has challenged them. My case has no precedent.

We enter a connecting hallway suspended over a parking lot, and Julie's hair dances in the wind whistling through shattered windows. Decorative indoor shrub beds have been overrun with wild daisies. Julie sees them, smiles, picks a handful. I pluck one from her hands and clumsily stick it in her hair. It still has its leaves, and it protrudes awkwardly from the side of her head. But she leaves it in.

"Do you remember what it was like living with people?" she asks as we walk. "Before you died?"

I wave a hand in the air vaguely.

"Well, it's changed. I was ten when my hometown got overrun and we came here, so I remember what it used to be like. Things are so different now. Everything's gotten smaller and more cramped, noisier and colder." She pauses at the end of the overpass and looks out the empty windows at a pale sunset. "We're all corralled in the stadium with nothing to think about but surviving to the end of the day. No one writes, no one reads, no one really even talks." She spins the daisies in her hands, sniffs one. "We don't have flowers anymore. Just crops."

I look out the opposite windows, at the dark side of the sunset. "Because of *us*."

"No, not because of you. I mean, yeah, because of you, but not *just* you. Do you really not remember what it was like before? All the political and social breakdowns? The global flooding? Wars and riots and constant bombings? The world was pretty far gone before you guys even showed up. You were just the final judgment."

"But we're . . . what's killing you. Now."

She nods. "Sure, zombies are the most obvious threat now. The fact that almost everyone who dies comes back and kills two more people . . . yeah, that's some grim math. But the root problem has to be bigger than that, or maybe smaller, more subtle, and killing a million zombies isn't going to fix it, because there's always going to be more."

Two Dead appear from around a corner and lunge at Julie. I crack their heads together and drop them, wondering if I might have studied martial arts in my old life. I seem to be a lot stronger than my lean frame suggests.

"My dad doesn't care about any of that," Julie continues as we walk down the loading tunnel and enter the plane. "He was an Army general back when the government was still going on, so that's how he thinks. Locate the threat, kill the threat, wait for orders from the big-picture people. But since the big picture is gone and the people who drew it are all dead, what are we supposed to do now? No one knows, so we do nothing. Just salvage supplies, kill zombies, and expand our walls farther out into the city. Basically Dad's idea of saving humanity is building a really big concrete box, putting everybody in it, and standing at the door with guns till we get old and die." She flops across a seat and takes a deep breath, lets it out again. She sounds so tired. "I mean obviously, staying alive is pretty fucking important . . . but there's got to be something beyond that, right?"

My mind drifts through the last few days, and I find myself thinking about my kids. The image of them in that hallway, making a toy out of a stapler, playing together and laughing. *Laughing*. Have I seen other Dead children laugh? I can't remember. But thinking about them, that look in their eyes as they hugged my legs, I feel strange emotions welling up in me. What *is* that look? Where does it come from? In that lovely film projected on their faces, what beautiful score is playing? What language is the dialogue? Can it be translated?

The jet cabin is silent for several minutes. Lying on her back, Julie cranes her head and looks out the window upside down. "You live in an airplane, R," she says. "That's pretty cool. I miss seeing airplanes in the sky. Have I told you about how I miss airplanes?"

I go to the record player. The Sinatra record is still going, skipping on a blank inner groove, so I nudge the needle to "Come Fly with Me."

Julie smiles. "Smooth."

I lie out on the floor and fold my hands over my chest, gazing up at the ceiling, haphazardly mouthing the song's words.

"Have I also told you," Julie says, twisting her head to look at me, "that in a weird way it's actually been kinda nice, being here? I mean aside from almost getting eaten like four times. It's been years since I've had this much time to just breathe and think and look out windows. And you have a pretty decent record collection."

She reaches down and sticks a daisy into my folded hands, then giggles. It takes me a moment to realize I look like the corpse in an old-fashioned funeral. I jolt upright as if struck by lightning, and Julie bursts out laughing. I can't help a little smile.

"And you know the craziest part, R?" she says. "Sometimes I barely believe you're a zombie. Sometimes I think you're just wearing stage makeup, because when you smile . . . it's pretty hard to believe."

I lie down again and fold my hands behind my head. Embarrassed, I keep my face mirthless until Julie falls asleep. Then I slowly let it creep back, smiling at the ceiling as the stars flicker to life outside.

• • •

Early the following afternoon, her soft snoring tapers off. Still lying on the floor, I wait for the sounds of her waking up. The shifting of weight, the tight inhale of breath, the small whimper.

"R," she says groggily.

"Yeah."

"They're right, you know."

"Who?"

"Those skeletons. I saw the pictures they showed you. They're right about what'll probably happen."

I say nothing.

"One of our people got away. When your group attacked us, my friend Nora hid under a desk. She saw you . . . capture me. It might take Security some time to track which hive you took me to, but they'll figure it out soon, and my dad will come here. He'll kill you."

"Already . . . dead," I reply.

"No you're not," she says, and sits up in her chair. "You're obviously not."

I think about what she's saying for a moment. "You want . . . to go back."

"No," she says, and then seems startled. "I mean, yeah, of course, but . . ." She lets out a flustered groan. "It doesn't matter either way, I *have* to. They're going to come here and wipe you out. *All* of you."

I fall silent again.

"I don't want to be responsible for that, okay?" She seems to be pondering something as she talks. Her voice is tight, conflicted. "I've always been taught that zombies are just walking corpses to be disposed of, but . . . look at you. You're more than that, right? So what if there are others like you?"

My face is stiff.

Julie sighs. "R . . . maybe you're sappy enough to find martyrdom romantic, but what about the rest of these people? Your kids? What about them?"

She is nudging my mind down streets it's rarely traveled. For however many months or years I've been here, I've never thought of these other creatures walking around me as people. Human, yes, but not *people*. We eat and sleep and shuffle through the fog, walking a marathon with no finish line, no medals, no cheering. None of the airport's citizens seemed much perturbed when I killed four of us today. We view ourselves the same way we view the Living: as meat. Nameless, faceless, disposable. But Julie's right. I have thoughts. I have some kind of a soul, shriveled and impotent as it may be. So maybe the others do, too. Maybe there's something there worth salvaging.

"Okay," I say. "You have . . . to leave."

She nods silently.

"But I'm . . . going with you."

She laughs. "To the stadium? Tell me that was a lame joke."

I shake my head.

"Well, let's think about that a moment, shall we? You? Are a zombie. As well preserved and kinda charming as you may be, you *are* a zombie, and guess what everyone in the stadium over the age of ten is training seven days a week to do?"

I say nothing.

"Exactly. To kill zombies. So, if I can make this any clearer—you can't come with me. Because they will *kill* you."

I clench my jaw. "So?"

She tilts her head and her sarcasm dissolves. Her voice becomes tentative. "What do you mean 'so'? Do you *want* to be dead? *Really* dead?"

My reflex is to shrug. The shrug has been my default response for so long. But as I lie there on the floor with her worried eyes looking down at me, I remember the feeling that jolted through me the moment I woke up yesterday, that feeling of *No!* and *Yes!* That feeling of *anti-shrug*.

"No," I say to the ceiling. "I don't want to die."

As I say it, I realize I've just broken my syllable record.

Julie nods. "Well, good."

I take a deep breath and stand up. "Need . . . to think," I tell her, avoiding eye contact. "Back . . . soon. Lock . . . door."

I leave the plane, and her eyes follow me out.

● ● ●

People are staring at me. I was always a bit of an outsider here in the airport, but now my mystique has thickened like port wine. When I enter a room, everyone stops moving and watches me. But the looks on their faces aren't entirely cold. There are notes of fascination buried in their reproach.

I find M studying his reflection in a lobby window, sticking his fingers in his mouth and prodding. I think he's trying to put his face back together.

"Hi," I say, standing a safe distance away.

He glares at me for a moment, then looks back at the window. He gives his upper jaw a firm push, and his cheekbone pops back into place with a loud snap. He turns to me and smiles. "How's . . . look?"

I wiggle my hand noncommittally. Half of his face looks relatively normal. The other half is still a bit concave.

He sighs and looks back at the window. "Bad . . . news . . . for the ladies."

I smile. As deeply different as we are, I have to give M some credit. He is the only zombie I've met who's managed to maintain a dangling scrap of humor. Also worthy of note . . . four syllables without pause. He has just matched my former record.

"Sorry," I say to him. "About . . . that."

He doesn't respond.

"Talk to you . . . a minute?"

He hesitates, then shrugs again. He follows me to the nearest set of chairs. We sit down in a dark, defunct Starbucks. Two cups of moldy espresso sit in front of us, abandoned long ago by two friends, two business partners, two people who just met in the terminal and bonded over a shared interest in brains.

"Really . . . sorry," I say. "Irrit . . . able. Lately."

M narrows his brow. "What . . . going on . . . with you?"

"Don't . . . know."

"Brought back . . . Living girl?"

"Yes."

"You . . . crazy?"

"Maybe."

"What's . . . feel like?"

"What?"

"Living . . . sex."

I give him a warning look.

"She's . . . hot. I would—"

"Shut up."

He chuckles. "Fucking . . . with you."

"It's not . . . that. Not . . . like that."

"Then . . . what?"

I hesitate, not sure how to answer. "More."

His face gets eerily serious. "What. Love?"

I think about this, and I find no response beyond a simple shrug. So I shrug, trying not to smile.

M throws back his head and does his best impression of laughter. He thumps me on the shoulder. "My . . . boy! Lover . . . boy!"

"Leaving . . . with her," I tell him.

"Where?"

"Taking . . . her home."

"Stadium?"

I nod. "Keep her . . . safe."

M considers this, watching me with concern clouding his bruised face.

"I . . . know," I sigh.

M folds his arms over his chest. "What . . . going on . . . with you?" he asks me again.

And again, I have no answer but a shrug.

"You . . . okay?"

"Changing."

He nods uncertainly, and I squirm under his probing eyes. I'm not used to having deep conversations with M. Or with any of the Dead, for that matter. I rotate the coffee cup in my fingers, intently studying its fuzzy green contents.

"When . . . figure out . . . ," M finally says, in a tone more earnest than I've ever heard from him, "tell me. Tell . . . *us*."

I wait for him to crack wise, turn it into a joke, but he doesn't. Rare for him or anyone else in this mordant era: he is actually sincere.

"I will," I say. I slap him on the shoulder and stand up. As I walk away, he gives me that same strange look I'm finding on the faces of all the Dead. That mixture of confusion, fear, and faint anticipation.

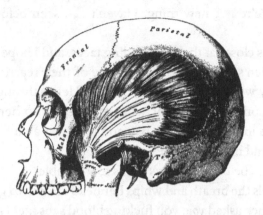

THE SCENE as Julie and I make our way out of the airport resembles either a wedding procession or a buffet line. The Dead are lined up in the halls to watch us pass. Every last one of them is here. They look restless, agitated, and would clearly love to devour Julie, but they don't move or make a sound. Over Julie's heated protests I asked M to escort us out. He follows a few paces behind, huge and vigilant, scanning the crowd like a Secret Service agent.

The unnatural silence of a room full of people who don't breathe is surreal. I swear I can hear Julie's heart pounding. She is trying to look cool and calm, but her darting eyes betray her.

"Are you sure about this?" she whispers.

"Yes."

"There's like . . . hundreds of them."

"Keep you safe."

"Right, right, I'm completely safe, how could I forget." Her voice grows very small. "Seriously, R . . . I mean I've seen you kick a few asses, but you know if they decide to ring the dinner bell right now I'm going to be sushi."

"They . . . won't," I tell her with a surprising degree of confidence. "We're . . . new thing. Haven't . . . seen before. Look at them."

She looks closer at the surrounding faces, and I hope she can see what I've been seeing. The strange array of their reactions to us, to the anomaly we represent. I know they will let us through, but Julie appears unconvinced. A tight wheeze creeps into her breathing. She fumbles in her messenger bag and pulls out an inhaler, takes a hit from it and holds it in, eyes still darting.

"You'll . . . be okay," M says in his low rumble.

She expels the breath and whips her head around to glare at him. "Who the fuck asked *you,* you fucking blood sausage? I should have hedge-trimmed you in half yesterday."

M chuckles and raises his eyebrows at me. "Got . . . a live one . . . 'R.'"

We continue unmolested all the way to the Departures gate. As we step out into the daylight, I feel a nervous buzz in my stomach. At first I think it's just the everpresent terror of the open sky, now looming over us in bruised shades of gray and purple, boiling with high-altitude thunderheads. But it's not the sky. It's the *sound.* That low, warbling tone, like baritone madmen humming nursery rhymes. I don't know if I've just gotten more attuned to it or if it's actually louder, but I hear it even before the Boneys make their appearance.

"Shit, oh shit," Julie whispers to herself.

They march around both corners of the loading zone and form a line in front of us. There are more of them than I've ever seen in one place. I had no idea there even *were* this many, at least not in our airport.

"Problem," M says. "They look . . . pissed."

He's right. There is something different in their demeanor. Their body language seems stiffer, if that's possible. Yesterday they were a jury stepping in to review our case. Today they are judges, announcing the sentence. Or perhaps executioners, executing it.

"Leaving!" I shout at them. "Taking her back! So they won't . . . come here!"

The skeletons don't move or respond. Their bones harmonize in some sour alien key.

"What . . . do you want?" I demand.

The entire front row raises its arms in unison and points at Julie. It strikes me how wrong this is, how fundamentally different these creatures are from the rest of us. The Dead are adrift on a foggy sea of ennui. They don't *do* things in unison.

"Taking her *back!*" I shout louder, faltering in my attempt at reasonable discourse. "If . . . kill her . . . they'll *come here.* Kill . . . *us!*"

There is no hesitation, no time for them to consider anything I've said; their response is predetermined and immediate. In unison, like demon monks chanting Hell's vespers, they emit that noise from their chest cavities, that proud crow of unyielding conviction, and although it's wordless, I understand exactly what it's saying:

> *No need to speak.*
> *No need to listen.*
> *Everything is already known.*
> *She will not leave.*
> *We will kill her.*
> *That is how things are done.*
> *Always has been.*
> *Always will be.*

I look at Julie. She is trembling. I grip her hand and look at M. He nods.

With the pulse-warmth of Julie's hand flooding through my icy fingers, I run.

We bolt left, trying to dodge around the edge of the Boneys' platoon. As they clatter forward to block my path, M surges out in front of me and rams his bulk into the nearest row, knocking them into a pile of hooked limbs and interlocked rib cages. A fierce blast of their invisible horn stabs the air.

"What are you *doing*?" Julie gasps as I drag her behind me. I am actually running *faster* than her.

"Keep you sa—"

"Don't you even *think* about saying 'Keep you safe'!" she shrieks. "This is about as far from safe as I've ever—"

She screams as a skinless hand pinches down on her shoulder and digs in. The creature's jaw opens to sink its filed fangs into her neck, but I grab it by the spine and wrench it off of her. I fling it to the concrete as hard as I can, but there is no impact and no shattering of bones. The thing almost seems to float in defiance of gravity, its rib cage barely touching the ground before it springs upright again, lurching toward my face like some hideous, unkillable insect.

"M!" I croak as it grapples for my throat. "Help!"

M is busy trying to peel skeletons off his arms, legs, and back, but he seems to be standing his ground thanks to his superior size and mass. As I struggle to keep the skeleton's fingers out of my eyes, M lumbers toward me, pulls the thing off me, and flings it into three others about to jump on him from behind.

"Go!" he yells, and shoves me forward, then turns to face our pursuers. I grab Julie's hand and dash toward our target. Finally, she sees it. The Mercedes. "Oh!" she pants. "Okay!"

We jump in the car and I bring the engine to life. "Oh Mercey . . . ," Julie says, stroking the dashboard like it's a beloved pet. "So happy to see you right now." I put the car in gear and release the clutch, gunning us forward. Somehow, it seems easy now.

M has given up trying to fight and is now just running for his life with a mob of skeletons trailing behind him. Hundreds of zombies stand outside the Departures entry area, watching everything in silence. What are they thinking? *Are* they thinking? Is there any chance they're forming a reaction to this event unfolding in front of them? This sudden explosion of anarchy in the state-approved program of their lives?

M cuts across the street, directly across our exit route, and I floor the accelerator. M crosses in front of us, then the Boneys cross in front of us, then four thousand pounds of German engineering smash into their brittle, ossified bodies. They shatter. Bits of anatomy fly everywhere. Two thigh bones, three hands, and half a cranium land inside the car, where they vibrate and twitch on the seats, releasing dry gasps and insectile buzzes. Julie hurls them out of the car and frantically wipes her hands on her sweatshirt, shuddering in revulsion and whimpering, "Oh my God oh my God."

But we are safe. Julie is safe. We roar past the Arrivals gate, onto the freeway, and out into the wider world while the stormclouds churn overhead. I look at Julie. She looks at me. We both smile as the first raindrops begin to fall.

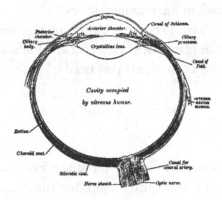

Cornea.
Anterior chamber.
Canal of Schlemn.
Posterior chamber.
Iris.
Ciliary body.
Ciliary process.
Crystalline lens.
Canal of Petit.

Cavity occupied
by vitreous humor.

INTERNAL RECTUS MUSCLE

Retina.

Choroid coat.

Sclerotic coat.

Canal for central artery.

Nerve sheath.

Optic nerve.

TEN MINUTES LATER, the storm has launched into its big opening movement, and we are getting soaked. The convertible was a poor choice for a day like this. Neither of us can figure out how to put the top up, so we drive in silence with heavy sheets of rain beating down on our heads. We don't complain, though. We try to stay positive.

"Do you know where you're going?" Julie asks after about twenty minutes. Her hair is matted flat on her face.

"Yes," I say, looking down the road at the dark gray horizon.

"Are you sure? 'Cause I have no idea."

"Very . . . sure."

I prefer not to explain *why* I know the route between the airport and the city so well. Our hunting route. Yes, she knows what I am and what I do, but do I have to remind her? Can we just have a nice drive and forget certain things for a while? In the sunny fields of my imagination we are not a teenager and a walking corpse driving in a rainstorm. We are Frank and Ava cruising treelined country lanes while a scratchy vinyl orchestra swoons our soundtrack.

"Maybe we should stop and ask directions."

I look at her. I look around at the crumbling districts surrounding us, nearly black in the evening gloom.

"Kidding," she says, her eyes peeking out between plastered wet clumps of hair. She leans back in the seat and folds her arms behind her head. "Let me know when you need a break. You kinda drive like an old lady."

. . .

As the rain pools into standing water at our feet, I notice Julie shivering a little. It's a warm spring night, but she's saturated, and the cab of the old convertible is a cyclone of freeway wind. I take the next exit and we ease down into a silent graveyard of suburban grid homes. Julie looks at me with questioning eyes. I can hear her teeth chattering.

I drive slowly past the houses, looking for a good place to stop for the night. Eventually I pull into a weedy cul-de-sac and park next to a rusted Plymouth Voyager. I take Julie's hand and pull her toward the nearest house. The door is locked, but the dry-rotted wood gives way with a light kick. We step into the relative warmth of some long-dead family's cozy little nest. There are old Coleman lanterns placed throughout the house, and once Julie lights them they provide a flickering campsite glow that feels oddly comforting. She ambles around the kitchen and living room, looking at toys, dishes, stacks of old magazines. She picks up a stuffed koala bear and looks it in the eyes. "Home sweet home," she mumbles.

She reaches into her messenger bag, pulls out a Polaroid camera, points it at me and snaps a shot. The flash is shocking in this dark place. She grins at my startled expression and holds up the camera. "Look familiar? I stole it from the skeletons' meeting room yesterday morning." She hands me the developing photo. "It's important to capture things, you know? Especially now, since the world is on its way out." She puts the viewfinder to her eye and turns in a slow circle, taking in the whole room. "Everything you see, you might be seeing for the last time."

I wave the picture in my hand. A ghostly image begins to take shape. It's me, R, the corpse that thinks it's alive, staring back at me with those wide, pewter-gray eyes. Julie hands the camera to me.

"You should always be taking pictures, if not with a camera then with your mind. Memories you capture on purpose are always more vivid than the ones you pick up by accident." She strikes a pose and grins. "Cheese!"

I take her picture. When it rolls out of the camera she reaches for it, but I pull it away and hide it behind my back. I hand her mine. She rolls her eyes, takes the photo and studies it, tilting her head. "Not bad. I think the rain cleaned you up a little."

She lowers the photo and squints at me for a moment. "Why are your eyes like that?"

I look at her warily. "Like . . . what?"

"That weird gray. It's nothing like how corpse eyes look. Not clouded over or anything. Why are they like that?"

I give this some thought. "Don't know. Happens at . . . conversion."

She's looking at me so hard I start to squirm. "It's creepy," she says. "Looks . . . supernatural, almost. Do they ever change color? Like when you kill people or something?"

I try not to sigh. "I think . . . you're thinking . . . of vampires."

"Oh, right, right." She chuckles and gives a rueful shake of her head. "At least *those* aren't real yet. Too many monsters to keep track of these days."

Before I can take offense, she looks up at me and smiles. "Anyway . . . I like them. Your eyes. They're actually kinda pretty. Creepy . . . but pretty."

It's probably the best compliment I've received in my entire Dead life. Ignoring my idiot stare, Julie wanders off into the house, humming to herself.

· · ·

The storm is raging outside, with occasional thunderclaps. I'm grateful that our house happens to have all its windows intact. Most of the others' were smashed long ago by looters or feeders. I glimpse a few debrained corpses on our neighbors' green lawns, but I'd like to imagine our hosts got out alive. Made it to one of the stadiums, maybe even some walled-off paradise in the mountains, angelic choirs singing behind pearl-studded titanium gates . . .

I sit in the living room listening to the rain fall while Julie putters around the house. After a while she comes back with an armful of dry clothes and dumps them on the love seat. She holds up a pair of jeans about ten sizes too big. "What do you think?" she says, wrapping the waist around her entire body. "Do these make me look fat?" She drops them and digs around in the pile, pulls out a mass of cloth that appears to be a dress. "I can use this for a tent if we get lost in the woods tomorrow. God, these folks must have made a fancy feast for some lucky zombie."

I shake my head, making a gag face.

"What, you don't eat fat people?"

"Fat . . . not alive. Waste product. Need . . . meat."

She laughs. "Oh, so you're an audiophile *and* a food snob! Jesus." She tosses the clothes aside and lets out a deep breath. "Well, all right. I'm exhausted. The bed in there isn't too rotten. I'm going to sleep."

I lie back on the cramped love seat, settling in for a long night alone with my thoughts. But Julie doesn't leave. Standing there in the bedroom doorway, she looks at me for a long minute. I've seen this look before, and I brace myself for whatever's coming.

"R . . . ," she says. "Do you . . . *have* to eat people?"

I sigh inside, so exhausted by these ugly questions, but when did a monster ever deserve its privacy?

"Yes."

"Or you'll die?"

"Yes."

"But you didn't eat me."

I hesitate.

"You *rescued* me. Like three times."

I nod slowly.

"And you haven't eaten anyone since then, right?"

I frown in concentration, thinking back. She's right. Not counting the few bites of leftover brains here and there, I've been gastronomically celibate since the day I met her.

A peculiar little half smile twitches on her face. "You're kind of . . . changing, aren't you?"

As usual, I am speechless.

"Well, good night," she says, and shuts the bedroom door.

I lie there on the couch, gazing up at the water-stained cottage-cheese ceiling.

"What's going on with you?" M asks me over a cup of moldy coffee in the airport Starbucks. "Are you okay?"

"Yeah, I'm okay. Just changing."

"How can you change? If we all start from the same blank slate, what makes you diverge?"

"Maybe we're not blank. Maybe the debris of our old lives still shapes us."

"But we don't remember those lives. We can't read our diaries."

"It doesn't matter. We are where we are, however we got here. What matters is where we go next."

"But can we choose that?"

"I don't know."

"We're Dead. Can we really choose anything?"

"Maybe. If we want to bad enough."

The rain drumming on the roof. The creak of weary timbers. The prickle of the old couch cushions through the holes in my shirt. I'm busy searching my post-death memory for the last time I went this long without food when I notice Julie standing in the doorway again. Her arms are folded on her chest and her hip is pressed against the door frame. Her foot taps an anxious rhythm on the floor.

"What?" I ask.

"Well . . . ," she says. "I was just thinking. The bed's a king-size. So I guess, if you wanted to . . . I wouldn't care if you joined me in there." I raise my eyebrows a little. Her face reddens. "Look, all I'm saying—*all* I'm saying—is I don't mind giving you a side of the bed. These rooms are kinda spooky, you know? I don't want the ghost of Mrs. Sprat crushing me in my sleep. And considering I haven't showered in over a week, you really don't smell much worse than I do; maybe we'll cancel each other out." She shrugs one shoulder, *whatever,* and disappears into the bedroom.

I wait a few minutes. Then, with great uncertainty, I get up and follow her in. She is already in the bed, curled into the fetal position with the blankets pulled tight around her. I slowly ease myself onto the far opposite edge. The blankets are all on her side, but I don't need their warmth. I am perpetually room-temperature.

Despite the pile of luxurious down comforters wrapped around her, Julie is still shivering. "These clothes are . . . ," she mutters, and sits up in bed. "Fuck." She glances over at me. "I'm going to lay my clothes out to dry. Just . . . relax, okay?" With her back to me, she wriggles out of her wet jeans and peels her shirt over her head. The skin of her back is blue-white from the cold. Almost the same hue as mine. In her polka-dot bra and plaid panties, she gets out of bed and drapes her clothes over the dresser, then quickly crawls back under the covers and curls up. "Good night," she says.

I lay my head on my folded arms, staring up at the ceiling. We are both on the very edges of the mattress, about four feet of space between us. I get the feeling that it's not just my ghoulish nature that makes her so wary. Living or Dead, virile or impotent, I still appear to be a man, and maybe she thinks I'll act the same as any other man would, lying so close to a beautiful woman. Maybe she thinks I'll try to take things from her. That I'll slither over and try to consume her. But then why am I even in this bed? Is it a test? For me, or for her? What strange hopes are compelling her to take this risk?

I listen to her breaths slow as she falls asleep. After a few hours, with her fear safely tucked away in dreams, she rolls over, removing most of the gap between us. She's facing me now. Her faint breath tickles my ear. If she were to wake up right now, would she scream? Could I ever make her understand how safe she really is? I won't deny that this proximity ignites more urges in me than the instinct to kill and eat. But although these new urges are there, some of them startling in their intensity, all I really *want* to do is lie next to her. In this moment, the most I'd ever hope for would be for her to lay her head on my chest, let out a warm, contented breath, and sleep.

Now here is an oddity. A question for the zombie philosophers. What does it mean that my past is a fog but my present is brilliant, bursting with sound and color? Since I became Dead I've recorded new memories with the fidelity of an old cassette deck, faint and muffled and ultimately forgettable. But I can recall every hour of the last few days in vivid detail, and the thought of losing a single one horrifies me. Where am I getting this focus? This clarity? I can trace a solid line from the moment I met Julie all the way to now, lying next to her in this sepulchral bedroom, and despite the millions of past moments I've lost or tossed away like highway trash, I know with a lockjawed certainty I'll remember this one for the rest of my life.

• • •

Sometime in the predawn, as I lie there on my back with no real need to rest, a dream flickers on like a film reel behind my eyes. Except it's not a dream, it's a vision, far too crisp and bright for my lifeless brain to have rendered. Usually these secondhand memories are preceded by the taste of blood and neurons, but not tonight. Tonight I close my eyes and it just *happens*, a surprise midnight showing.

We open on a dinner scene. A long metal table laid out with a minimalist spread. Bowl of rice. Bowl of beans. Rectangle of flax bread.

"Thank you, Lord, for this food," says the man at the head of the table, hands folded in front of him but eyes wide open. "Bless it to our bodies. Amen."

Julie nudges the boy sitting next to her. He squeezes her thigh under the table. The boy is Perry Kelvin. I'm in Perry's mind again. His brain is gone, his life evaporated and inhaled . . . yet he's still here. Is this a chemical flashback? A trace of his brain still dissolving somewhere in my body? Or is it actually *him*? Still holding on somewhere, somehow, somewhy?

"So, Perry," Julie's dad says to him—to me. "Julie tells me you're working for Agriculture now."

I swallow my rice. "Yes, sir, General Grigio, I'm a—"

"This isn't the mess hall, Perry, this is dinner. *Mr.* Grigio will be fine."

"Okay. Yes, sir."

There are four chairs at the table. Julie's father sits at the head, and she and I sit next to each other on his right. The chair at the other end of the table is empty. What Julie tells me about her mother is this: "She left when I was twelve." And though I've gently probed, she has never offered me more, not even while we're lying naked in my twin bed, exhausted and happy and as vulnerable as any two people can be.

"I'm a planter right now," I tell her father, "but I think I'm on track for a promotion. I'm shooting for harvest supervisor."

"I see," he says, nodding thoughtfully. "That isn't a *bad* job . . . but I wonder why you don't join your father in Construction. I'm sure he could use more young men working on that all-important corridor."

"He's asked me to, but, ah . . . I don't know, I just don't think Construction is the place for me right now. I really like working with plants."

"Plants," he repeats.

"I just feel like in this day and age there's something meaningful about *growing* things. The soil's so depleted it's hard to get much out of it, but it's pretty satisfying when you finally do see some green coming through that gray crust."

Mr. Grigio stops chewing, blank-faced. Julie looks uneasy. "Remember that little shrub we had in our living room back east?" she says. "The one that looked like a skinny little tree?"

"Yes . . . ," her dad says. "What about it?"

"You loved that thing. Don't act like you don't get gardening."

"That was your mother's plant."

"But you're the one who loved it." She turns to me. "So Dad used to be quite the interior designer, believe it or not; he had our old house decked out like an IKEA showroom, all this modern glass and metal stuff, which my mom couldn't *stand*—she wanted everything earthy and natural, all hemp fiber and sustainable hardwoods . . ."

Mr. Grigio's face looks tight. Julie either doesn't notice or doesn't care.

". . . so to fight back, she buys this lush, bright green shrub, puts it in a huge wicker pot, and sticks it right in the middle of Dad's perfect white and silver living room."

"It wasn't *my* living room, Julie," he interjects. "As I recall we took a vote on every piece of furniture, and you always sided with me."

"I was like eight, Dad, I probably liked pretending I lived in a spaceship. Anyway, Mom buys this plant and they argue about it for a week—Dad says it's 'incongruous,' Mom says either the plant stays or she goes—" She hesitates momentarily. Her father's face gets tighter. "That, um, that went on for a while," she continues, "but then Mom being Mom, she got obsessed with something else and quit watering the plant. So when it started dying, guess who adopted the poor thing?"

"I wasn't going to have a dead shrub as our living room's centerpiece. Someone had to take care of it."

"You watered it every day, Dad. You gave it plant food and pruned it."

"Yes, Julie, that's how you keep a plant alive."

"Why can't you say you loved the stupid plant, Dad?" She regards him with a mixture of amazement and frustration. "I don't get it, what is so wrong with that?"

"Because it's absurd," he snaps, and the mood of the room suddenly shifts. "You can water and prune a plant but you cannot 'love' a plant."

Julie opens her mouth to speak, then shuts it.

"It's a meaningless decoration. It sits there consuming time and resources, and then one day it decides to die, no matter how much you watered it. It's absurd to attach an emotion to something so brief and pointless."

There are a few long seconds of silence. Julie breaks away from her father's stare and pokes at her rice. "Anyway," she mumbles, "my point was, Perry . . . that Dad used to be a gardener. So you should share gardening stories."

"I'm interested in a lot more than gardening," I offer, racing to change the subject.

"Oh?" Mr. Grigio says.

"Yeah, ah . . . motorcycles? I salvaged a BMW R 1200 a while ago and I've been working on bulletproofing it, getting it combat-ready just in case."

"You have mechanical experience, then. That's good. We have a shortage of mechanics in the Armory right now."

Julie rolls her eyes and shovels beans into her mouth.

"I'm also spending a lot of time on my marksmanship. I've been requesting extra assignments from school and I've gotten pretty good with the M40."

"Hey Perry," Julie says, "why don't you tell Dad about your other plans? Like how you've always wanted to—"

I step on her foot. She glares at me.

"Always wanted to what?" her father asks.

"I don't—I'm not really . . ." I take a drink of water. "I'm not really sure yet, sir, to be honest. I'm not sure what I want to do with my life. But I'm almost sixteen; I know I'll have it figured out soon."

What were you going to say? R wonders aloud, interrupting the scene again, and I feel a lurch as we swap places. Perry glances up at him—at *me*—frowning.

"Come on, corpse, not now. This is the first time I met Julie's father and it's not going well. I need to focus."

"It's going fine," Julie tells Perry. "This is my dad these days; I warned you about him."

"You better pay attention," Perry says to me. "You might have to meet him someday, too, and you're going to have a much harder time winning his approval than I did."

Julie runs a hand through Perry's hair. "Aw, babe, don't talk about the present. It makes me feel left out."

He sighs. "Yeah, okay. These were better times anyway. I turned into a real neutron star when I grew up."

I'm sorry I killed you, Perry. It's not that I wanted to, it's just—

"Forget it, corpse, I understand. Seems by that point I wanted out anyway."

"I bet I'll always miss you when I think back to these days," Julie says wistfully. "You were pretty cool before Dad got his claws into you."

"Take care of her, will you?" Perry whispers up to me. "She's been through some hard stuff. Keep her safe."

I will.

Mr. Grigio clears his throat. "I would start planning now if I were you, Perry. With your skill set, you should really consider training for Security. Green shoots coming through the dirt are all well and good but we don't strictly *need* all these fruits and vegetables. You can live on nothing but Carbtein for almost a year before cell fatigue is even measurable. The most important thing is keeping us all alive."

Julie tugs on Perry's arm. "Come on, do we have to sit through this again?"

"Nah," Perry says. "This isn't worth reliving. Let's go somewhere nice."

• • •

We're on a beach. Not a real beach, carved over the millennia by the master craft of the ocean—those are all underwater now. We're on the young shore of a recently flooded city port. Small patches of sand appear between broken slabs of sidewalk. Barnacled streetlamps rise out of the surf, a few of them still flickering on in the evening gloom, casting circles of orange light on the waves.

"Okay guys," Julie says, throwing a stick into the water. "Quiz time. What do you want to do with your life?"

"Oh hi Mr. Grigio," I mutter, sitting next to Julie on a driftwood log that was once a telephone pole.

She ignores me. "Nora, you go first. And I don't mean what do you think you *will* end up doing, I mean what do you *want* to do."

Nora is sitting in the sand in front of the log, playing with some pebbles and pinching a smoldering joint between her middle finger and half a ring finger, missing past the first knuckle. Her eyes are earth brown; her skin is creamy coffee. "Maybe nursing?" she says. "Healing people, saving lives . . . maybe working on a cure? I could get into that."

"Nurse Nora," Julie says with a smile. "Sounds like a kids' TV show."

"Why a nurse?" I ask. "Why not go for doctor?"

Nora scoffs. "Oh, yeah, seven years of college? I doubt civilization's gonna last that long."

"Yes it will," Julie says. "Don't talk like that. But there's nothing wrong with being a nurse. Nurses are sexy!"

Nora smiles and pulls idly at her thick black curls. She looks at me. "Why a doctor, Pear? Is that your target?"

I shake my head emphatically. "I've already seen enough blood and viscera for one lifetime, thanks."

"Then what?"

"I like writing," I say like a confession. "So . . . I guess I want to be a writer."

Julie smiles. Nora tilts her head. "Really? Do people still *do* that?"

"What? Write?"

"I mean is there still like . . . a book industry?"

I shrug. "Well . . . no. Not really. Good point, Nora."

"Sorry, I was just—"

"No, I know, but you're right, it's dumb even for a fantasy. Colonel Rosso says only about thirty percent of the world's cities are still functioning, so unless the zombies are learning how to read . . . not a great time to get into the literary arts. I'll probably just end up in Security."

"Shut the fuck up, Perry," Julie says, punching me in the shoulder. "People still read."

"Do they?" Nora asks.

"Well *I* do. Who cares if there's an industry behind it? If everyone's too busy building things and shooting things to bother feeding their souls, screw them. Just write it on a notepad and give it to me. *I'll* read it."

"A whole book for just one person," Nora says, looking at me. "Could that ever be worth it?"

Julie answers for me. "At least his thoughts would get out of his head, right? At least *someone* would get to see them. I think it'd be beautiful. It'd be like owning a little piece of his brain." She looks at me intently. "Give me a piece of your brain, Perry. I want to taste it."

"Oh my," Nora laughs. "Should I leave you two alone?"

I put my arm around Julie and smile the worldweary smile I've recently perfected. "Oh my little girl," I say, and squeeze her. She frowns.

"What about you, Jules?" Nora says. "What's your pipe dream?"

"I want to be a teacher." She takes a deep breath. "And a painter, and a singer, and a poet. And a pilot."

Nora smiles. I secretly roll my eyes. Nora passes the joint to Julie, who takes a small puff and offers it to me. I shake my head, older than Julie and wiser than Nora. We all gaze out at the glittering water, three kids on the same log watching the same sunset, thinking very different thoughts while white gulls fill the air with mournful calls.

You're going to do those things, R murmurs down to Julie, and he and I swap places again. Julie looks up at me, the corpse in the clouds, floating over the ocean like a restless spirit. She gives me a radiant smile, and I know it's not really her, I know nothing I say here will ever escape the confines of my own skull, but I say it anyway. *You're going to be strong and beautiful and brilliant, and you're going to live forever. You're going to change the world.*

"Thanks, R," she says. "You're so sweet. Do you think you'll be able to let me go when the time comes? Do you think you'll be able to say good-bye?"

I swallow hard. *Will I really have to?*

Julie shrugs, smiling innocently, and whispers, "Shrug."

• • •

In the morning the storm has passed. I am lying on my back in a bed next to Julie. A sharp beam of sunlight cuts through the dust in the air and makes a hot white pool on her huddled form. She is still wrapped tightly in the blankets. I get up and step out onto the front porch. The spring sun bleaches the neighborhood white, and the only sound is rusty backyard swing sets creaking in the breeze. The dream's cold question echoes in my head. I don't want to face it, but I realize that very soon this will be over. I will return her to her daddy's porch by nine, and that will be it. The door will boom shut, and I'll skulk away home. *Will I be able to let her go?* I've never asked a harder question. A month ago there was nothing on Earth I missed, enjoyed, or longed for. I knew I could lose everything and not feel anything, and I rested easy in that knowledge. But I'm growing tired of easy things.

• • •

When I go back inside, Julie is sitting on the edge of the bed. She looks groggy, still half-asleep. Her hair is a natural disaster, post-hurricane palm trees.

"Good morning," I say.

She groans. I try valiantly not to stare at her as she arches her back and stretches, adjusting her bra strap and letting out a little whimper. I can see every muscle and vertebra, and since she's already half-naked I imagine her without skin. I know from grim experience that there is a beauty to her inner layers, too. Marvels of symmetry and craftsmanship sealed away inside her like the jeweled movements of a timepiece, fine works of art never meant to be seen.

"What are we doing for breakfast," she mutters. "I'm starving."

I hesitate. "Can probably . . . get to . . . stadium . . . in hour. Going to . . . need gas . . . though. For Mercey."

She rubs her eyes. She begins to pull her still-damp clothes back on. Once again I try not to stare. Her body wiggles and bounces in ways Dead flesh doesn't.

Her eyes suddenly flash alert. "Shit. You know what? I need to call my dad."

She picks up the corded phone, and I'm surprised to hear a dial tone. I guess her people would have made it a priority to keep the phone lines running. Anything digital or satellite based probably died long ago, but the physical lines, real connections between real objects that need no fragile magic to exist . . . those might endure a little longer.

Julie dials. She waits, tensed. Then relief floods her face. "Dad! It's Julie."

There is a loud burst of exclamations from the other end. Julie pulls the phone away from her ear and gives me a look that says, *Here we go.* "Yeah Dad, I'm okay, I'm okay. Alive and intact. Nora told you what happened, right?" More noise from the other end. "Yeah, I knew you'd be looking, but you were way off. It was that small hive at Oran Airport. They put me in this room with all these dead people, like a food locker or something, but after a few days . . . I guess they just *forgot* about me. I walked right out, found a car and drove off. I'm on my way back now, I just stopped to call you." A pause. She glances at me. "No, um, don't send anyone, okay? I'm in the suburbs down south, I'm almost—" She waits. "I don't know, somewhere close to the freeway, but Dad—" She freezes, and her face changes. "What?" She takes a deep breath. "Dad, why are you talking about Mom right now? No, why are you talking about her, this is *nothing* like that. I'm on my way *back,* I just—Dad! Wait, will you *listen* to me? *Don't send* anyone, I'm coming home, okay? I have a car, I'm on my way, just—Dad!" There is silence from the earpiece. "Dad?" Silence. She bites her lip and looks at the floor. She hangs up.

I raise my eyebrows, full of questions that I'm afraid to ask.

She massages her forehead and lets out a slow breath. "Can you go find the gas by yourself, R? I need . . . to think for a minute." She doesn't look at me as she speaks. Tentatively, I reach out and put a hand on her shoulder. She flinches, then softens, then suddenly turns and embraces me hard, burying her face in my shirt.

"I just need a minute," she says, pulling away and recovering herself.

So I leave her there. I find an empty gas can in the garage and begin working my way around the block, looking for a vehicle with a full tank to drain. As I kneel beside a recently crashed Chevy Tahoe with the siphon tube gurgling in my hand, I hear the sound of an engine starting in the distance. I ignore it. I focus on the taste of gasoline, still harsh and astringent in my mouth. When the can is full I walk back to the cul-de-sac, closing my eyes and letting the sun flood through my eyelids. Then I open them, and just stand there for a while, holding the red plastic can like a belated birthday gift. The Mercedes is gone.

• • •

Inside the house, on the dining room table, I find a note. Something is written on it, letters I can't assemble into words, but next to it are two Polaroids. Both pictures are of Julie, taken by Julie, with the camera extended at arm's length and pointed at herself. In one of them, she is waving. The gesture looks limp, halfhearted. In the other one, she is holding that hand against her chest. Her face is stoic, but her eyes are damp.

Good-bye, R, the picture whispers to me. *It's that time now. It's time to say it. Can you say it?*

I hold the picture in front of me, staring at it. I rub my fingers on it, smearing its fresh emulsion into rainbow blurs. I consider taking it with me, but no. I'm not ready to make Julie a souvenir.

Say it, R. Just say it.

I set the picture back on the table and leave the house. I don't say it.

· · ·

I begin walking back to the airport. I'm not sure what's waiting for me. Full-death? Quite possibly. After the commotion I caused, the Boneys might simply dispose of me like infectious waste. But I'm alone again. My world is small, my options are few. I don't know where else to go.

The journey of forty minutes by car will be a daylong trip on foot. As I walk, the wind seems to reverse direction, and yesterday's thunderheads creep back onto the horizon for an encore. They spiral over me, slowly shrinking the circle of blue sky like an immense camera aperture. I walk fast and stiff, almost marching.

The blue above me darkens to gray, then indigo, then the clouds finally snap it shut. The rain comes. It blasts down in torrents that make last night's shower seem like a gentle produce-aisle mist. To my utter confusion I find myself *cold*. As the water pounds its way through my clothes and into every pore, I actually shiver. And despite the obscene gluttony of sleep I've indulged in lately, I feel the pull again. This is nearly three nights in a row.

I walk off the freeway at the next exit and climb into a triangle of landscaping between the road and the off-ramp. I crash through the brush and duck into the little cluster of trees, a miniforest of ten or twelve cedars arranged in a pleasing pattern for overstressed commuter ghosts.

I curl into a ball at the base of one of these trees, achieving some degree of shelter under its scrawny branches, and close my eyes. As lightning flickers on the horizon like flashbulbs and thunder rumbles in my bones, I drift into darkness.

• • •

I am with Julie on the 747. I realize it's a dream. A *real* dream, not just another rerun of Perry Kelvin's syndicated life. This is coming purely from me. The clarity has improved since the blurry sludge of my brain's first attempt back in the airport, but there's still an awkward, shaky quality to everything, like amateur video to Perry's slick feature films.

Julie and I sit cross-legged, facing each other, floating above the clouds on the plane's bright white wing. The wind ruffles our hair, but no more than a leisurely ride in a convertible.

"So you dream now?" Julie says.

I smile nervously. "I guess I do."

Julie doesn't smile. Her eyes are cold. "Guess you had nothing to dream about till you got some girl problems. You're like a grade school kid trying to keep a diary."

Now we're on the ground, sitting on a sunny green suburban lawn. A morbidly obese couple barbecues human limbs in the background. I try to keep Julie in focus.

"I'm changing," I tell her.

"I don't care," she replies. "I'm home now. I'm back in the real world, where you don't exist. Summer camp is over."

A winged Mercedes rumbles past in the distant sky and vanishes in a muffled sonic boom.

"I'm gone," she says, staring me hard in the eyes. "It was fun, but it's over now. This is how things go."

I shake my head, avoiding her gaze. "I'm not ready."

"What did you think was going to happen?"

"I don't know. I was just hoping for something. A miracle."

"Miracles don't exist. There is cause and effect, dreams and reality, Living and Dead. Your hope is absurd. Your romanticism, embarrassing."

I look at her uneasily.

"It's time for you to grow up. Julie has gone back to her position, and you will go back to your position, and that is the way it is. Always has been. Always will be."

She grins, and her teeth are jagged yellow fangs. She kisses me, gnawing through my lips, biting out my teeth, gnashing up toward my brain and screaming like a dying child. I gag on my hot red blood.

• • •

My eyes flash open and I stand up, pushing dripping branches out of my face. It's still night. The rain is still pummeling the earth. I step out of the trees and climb up onto the overpass. I lean against the railing, looking out at the empty freeway and the dark horizon beyond it. One thought pounds in my head like a migraine of rage: *You're wrong. You fucking monsters are wrong. About everything.*

Out of the corner of my eye, I glimpse a silhouette on the other side of the overpass. The dark form moves toward me with steady, lumbering steps. I hunch my muscles together, preparing for a fight. After wandering alone for too long, the unincorporated Dead will sometimes lose the ability to distinguish their own kind from the Living. And some are so far gone, so deep into this way of life, they just don't care either way. They will eat anyone, anything, anywhere, because they can't fathom any other way to interact. I imagine one of these creatures surprising Julie as she stops the Mercedes to get her bearings, wrapping filthy hands around her face and biting down on her slender neck, and as that image ferments in my head, I prepare to rip this thing in front of me into unrecognizable chunks. The primordial rage that fills me every time I think of someone harming her is frightening. The violence of killing and eating people feels like friendly teasing compared to this consuming bloodlust.

The towering shadow staggers closer. A flash of lightning illuminates its face, and I drop my arms to my sides.

"M?"

I almost fail to recognize him at first. His face has been torn and clawed, and there are countless small pieces bitten out of his body.

"Hey," he grunts. The rain streaks down his face and pools in his wounds. "Let's . . . get out of . . . rain." He walks past my leaky trees and climbs down the slope to the freeway below. I follow him to the dry space under the overpass. We huddle there in the dirt, surrounded by old beer cans and syringes.

"What . . . doing . . . he . . . out . . . out here?" I ask him, fighting for the words. I've been silent less than a day and I'm already rusty.

"Take . . . guess," M says, pointing at his wounds. "Boneys. Drove me out."

"Sorry."

M grunts. "Fuck . . . it." He kicks a sun-faded beer can. "But guess . . . what?" Something like a smile illuminates his mangled face. "Some . . . came with me."

He points down the freeway, and I see about nine other figures moving slowly toward us.

I look at M, confused. "Came . . . with? Why?"

He shrugs. "Things . . . crazy . . . back home. Things . . . shaken." He jabs a finger at me. "You."

"Me?"

"You and . . . her. Something . . . in air. Movement."

The nine zombies stop under the overpass and stand there, looking at us blankly.

"Hi," I say.

They sway and groan a little. One of them nods.

"Where's . . . girl?" M asks me.

"Her name is Julie." This comes off my tongue fluidly, like a swish of warm chamomile.

"Ju . . . lie," M repeats with some effort. "Okay. Where's . . . she?"

"Left. Went home."

M studies my face. He drops a hand onto my shoulder. "You . . . okay?"

I close my eyes and take a slow breath. "No." I look out at the freeway, toward the city, and something blooms in my head. First a feeling, then a thought, then a choice. "I'm going after her."

Six syllables. I have broken my record again.

"To . . . stadium?"

I nod.

"Why?"

"To . . . save her."

"From . . . what?"

"Ev . . . rything."

M just looks at me for a long time. Among the Dead, a piercing look can last several minutes. I wonder if he can possibly have any idea what I'm talking about, when I'm not even sure I do. Just a gut feeling. The soft pink zygote of a plan.

He gazes up at the sky, and a faraway look comes into his eyes. "Had . . . dream . . . last night. *Real* dream. *Memories.*"

I stare at him.

"Remembered . . . when young. Summer. Cream . . . of Wheat. A girl." His eyes refocus on me. "What . . . is it like?"

"What?"

"You've . . . felt. Do you know . . . what it is?"

"What are . . . talking about?"

"My dream," he says, his face full of wonder like a child's at a telescope. "Those things . . . love?"

A tingle runs up my spine. What is happening? To what distant reaches of space is our planet hurtling? M is dreaming, reclaiming memories, asking astonishing questions. I am breaking my syllable records every day. Nine unknown Dead are with us under this overpass, miles from the airport and the hissing commands of the skeletons, standing here awaiting . . . *something*.

A fresh canvas is unfurling in front of me. What do I paint on it? What's the first hue to splash on this blank field of gray?

"I'll . . . go with," M says. "Help you . . . get in. Save her." He turns to the waiting Dead. "Help us?" he asks, not raising his voice above its easy rumble. "Help save . . . girl? Save . . ." He closes his eyes and concentrates. "*Ju . . . lie?*"

The Dead quicken at the sound of the name, fingers twitching and eyes darting. M looks pleased. "Help find . . . something lost?" he asks in a voice more solid than I've ever heard from his tattered throat. "Help . . . exhume?"

The zombies look at M. They look at me. They look at each other. One of them shrugs. Another nods. "Help," one of them groans, and they all wheeze in agreement.

I find a grin spreading across my face. I don't know what I'm doing, how I'm doing it, or what will happen when it's done, but at the very bottom of this rising siege ladder, I at least know I'm going to see Julie again. I know I'm not going to say good-bye. And if these staggering refugees want to help, if they think they see something bigger here than a boy chasing a girl, then they can help, and we'll see what happens when we say *yes* while this rigor mortis world screams *no*.

We start lumbering north on the southbound freeway, and the thunder drifts away toward the mountains like it's scared of us.

Here we are on the road. We must be going somewhere.

taking

I AM YOUNG. I am a teenage boy aflame with health, strong and virile and pounding with energy. But I get older. Every second ages me. My cells spread themselves thinner, stiffening, cooling, darkening. I am fifteen, but each death around me adds a decade. Each atrocity, each tragedy, each small moment of sadness. Soon I will be ancient.

Here I am, Perry Kelvin in the stadium. I hear birds in the walls. The bovine moans of pigeons, the musical chirps of starlings. I look up and breathe deep. The air is so much cleaner lately, even here. I wonder if this is what the world smelled like when it was new, centuries before smokestacks. It frustrates and fascinates me that we'll never know for sure, that despite the best efforts of historians and scientists and poets, there are some things we'll just never know. What the first song sounded like. How it felt to see the first photograph. Who kissed the first kiss, and if it was any good.

"Perry!"

I smile and wave at my little admirer as he and his dozen foster siblings cross the street in a line, hand in hand. "Hey . . . buddy," I call to him. I can never remember his name.

"We're going to the gardens!"

"Cool!"

Julie Grigio grins at me, leading their line like a mother swan. In a city of thousands I run into her almost every day, sometimes near the schools, where it seems probable, sometimes in the outermost corners of the stadium, where the odds are slim. Is she stalking me or am I stalking her? Either way, I feel a pulse of stress hormones shoot through me every time I see her, rushing to my palms to make them sweat and to my face to make it pimply. Last time we met, she took me up on the roof. We listened to music for hours, and when the sun went down, I'm pretty sure we almost kissed.

"Want to come with us, Perry?" she says. "It's a field trip!"

"Oh, fun . . . a field trip to where I just spent eight hours working."

"Hey, there aren't a lot of options in this place."

"So I've noticed."

She waves for me to come over and I immediately comply, while trying my best to look reluctant. "Don't they ever get to go outside?" I wonder, watching the kids march in clumsy lockstep.

"Mrs. Grau would say we *are* outside."

"I mean *outside*. Trees, rivers, etc."

"Not till they're twelve."

"Awful."

"Yeah . . ."

We walk in silence except for the burble of child-speak behind us. The stadium walls loom protectively like the parents these kids will never know. My excitement at seeing Julie darkens under a sudden cloud of melancholy.

"How do you stand it here," I say, barely a question.

Julie frowns at me. "*We* get to go out. Twice a month."

"I know, but . . ."

She waits. "What, Perry?"

"Do you ever wonder if it's even worth it?" I gesture vaguely at the walls. "All this?"

Her expression sharpens.

"I mean, are we really that much better off in here?"

"Perry," she snaps with unexpected vehemence. "Don't you start talking like that, don't you fucking start."

She notices the abrupt silence behind us and cringes. "Sorry," she says to the kids in a confidential whisper. "*Bad words.*"

"Fuck!" my little friend yells, and the whole line explodes with laughter.

Julie rolls her eyes. "Great."

"Tsk tsk."

"You shut your mouth. I meant what I said to you. That's evil talk."

I look at her uncertainly.

"We get to go outside twice a month. More if we're on salvage. And we get to stay alive." She sounds like she's reciting a Bible verse. An old proverb. As if sensing her own lack of conviction, she glances at me, then snaps her eyes forward. Her voice goes quiet. "No more evil talk if you want to come on our field trip."

"Sorry."

"You haven't been here long enough. You grew up in a safe place. You don't understand the dangers."

Dark feelings flood my belly at this, but I manage to hold my tongue. I don't know the pain she's speaking from, but I know it's deep. It makes her hard and yet so terribly soft. It's her thorns and it's her hand reaching out from the thicket.

"Sorry," I say again, and fumble for that hand, nudging it out of her jeans pocket. It's warm. My cold fingers wrap around hers, and my mind conjures an unwelcome image of tentacles. I blink it away. "No more evil talk."

The kids gaze at me eagerly, huge eyes, spotless cheeks. I

wonder what they are and what they mean and what's going to happen to them.

• • •

"Dad."

"Yeah?"

"I think I have a girlfriend."

My dad lowers his clipboard, adjusts his hard hat. A smile creeps into the deep creases of his face. "Really."

"I think so."

"Who?"

"Julie Grigio?"

He nods. "I've met her. She's—hey! Doug!" He leans over the edge of the bulwark and yells at a worker carrying a steel pylon. "That's forty-gauge, Doug, we're using fifty for the arterial sections." He looks back at me. "She's cute. Watch out though; seems like a firecracker."

"I like firecrackers."

My dad smiles. His eyes drift. "Me too, kid."

His walkie-talkie crackles and he pulls it out, starts giving instructions. I look out at the ugly concrete vista under construction. We are standing on the terminating end of a wall, fifteen feet high, currently a few blocks long. Another wall runs parallel to it, making Main Street into an enclosed corridor that cuts through the heart of the city. Workers swarm below, laying concrete pour-forms, erecting framework.

"Dad?"

"Yeah."

"Do you think it's stupid?"

"What?"

"To fall in love."

He pauses, then puts his walkie away. "What do you mean, Pear."

"Like . . . now. The way things are now. I mean everything's so uncertain . . . is it stupid to waste time on stuff like that in a world like this? When everything might fall apart any minute?"

My dad looks at me for a long time. "When I met your mom," he says, "I asked myself that. And all we had going on back then was a few wars and recessions." His walkie starts crackling again. He ignores it. "I got *nineteen years* with your mom. But do you think I would've turned down the idea if I'd known I'd only get one year? Or one month?" He surveys the construction, shaking his head slowly. "There's no benchmark for how life's 'supposed' to happen, Perry. There is no ideal world for you to wait around for. The world is always just what it is *now*, and it's up to you how you respond to it."

I look into the dark window holes of ruined office buildings. I imagine the skeletons of their occupants still sitting at their desks, working toward quotas they will never meet.

"What if you'd only gotten a week with her?"

"Perry . . . ," my dad says, slightly amazed. "The world isn't ending tomorrow, buddy. Okay? We're working on fixing it. Look." He points at the work crews below. "We're building roads. We're going to connect to the other stadiums and hideouts, bring the enclaves together, pool our research and resources, maybe start looking for a cure again." My dad claps me on the shoulder. "You and me, everyone . . . we're going to make it. Don't give up on us yet. Okay?"

I relent with a small release of breath. "Okay."

"Promise?"

"Promise."

My dad smiles. "I'll hold you to that."

. . .

Do you know what happened next, corpse? Perry whispers from the deep shadows of my awareness. *Can you guess?*

"Why are you showing me all this?" I ask the darkness.

Because it's what's left of me, and I want you to feel it. I'm not ready to disappear.

"Neither am I."

I sense a cold smile in his voice.

Good.

• • •

"There you are."

Julie heaves herself up the ladder and stands on the roof of my new home, watching me. I glance at her, then put my face back in my hands.

She makes her way over, cautious steps on the flimsy sheet metal, and sits next to me on the roof edge. Our legs dangle, swinging slowly in the cold autumn air.

"Perry?"

I don't answer. She studies the side of my face. She reaches out and brushes two fingers through my shaggy brown hair. Her eyes pull on me like gravity, but I resist. I stare down at the muddy street.

"I can't believe I'm here," I mumble. "This stupid house. With all these discards."

She doesn't respond immediately. When she does, it's quiet. "They're not discards. They were loved."

"For a while."

"Their parents didn't *leave*. They were taken."

"Is there a difference?"

She looks at me so hard I have no choice but to meet her gaze. "Your mom loved you, Perry. You've never had to doubt that. And so did your dad."

I can't hold the weight. I give in and let it fall on me. I twist my head away from Julie as the tears come.

"Believe that God discarded you if you want to, fate or destiny or whatever, but at least you know *they* loved you."

"What does it even matter," I croak, avoiding her eyes. "Who gives a shit. They're dead. That's the present. That's what matters now."

We don't speak for a few minutes. The cold breeze pricks tiny bumps on our arms. Bright leaves find their way in from the outer forests, spinning down into the stadium's vast mouth and landing on the house's roof.

"You know what, Perry?" Julie says. Her voice is shaky with hurts all her own. "Everything dies eventually. We all know that. People, cities, whole civilizations. Nothing lasts. So if existence was just binary, dead or alive, here or not here, what would be the fucking point in anything?" She looks up at some falling leaves and puts out her hand to catch one, a flaming red maple. "My mom used to say that's why we have memory. And the opposite of memory— hope. So things that are gone can still matter. So we can build off our pasts and make futures." She twirls the leaf in front of her face, back and forth. "Mom said life only makes any sense if we can see time how God does. Past, present, and future all at once."

I allow myself to look at Julie. She sees my tears and tries to wipe one away. "So what's the future?" I ask, not flinching as her fingers brush my eye. "I can see the past and the present, but what's the future?"

"Well . . . ," she says with a broken laugh. "I guess that's the tricky part. The past is made out of facts . . . I guess the future is just hope."

"Or fear."

"No." She shakes her head firmly and sticks the leaf in my hair. "Hope."

• • •

The stadium rises on the horizon as the Dead stumble forward. It looms above most of the surrounding buildings and consumes several city blocks, a gaudy monument to an era of excess, a world of waste and want and misguided dreams that is now profoundly over.

Our cadaverous cadre has been walking for a little over a day, roaming the open roads like Kerouac beats with no gas money. The others are hungry, and there's a brief, mostly wordless debate between M and the rest before they stop at an old boarded-up town house to feed. I wait outside. It's been more days than I can remember since my last meal, but I find myself strangely content. There's a neutral feeling in my veins, balanced precisely between hungry and sated. The screams of the people in the house pierce me more sharply than in all my days of hands-on killing, and I'm not even anywhere near them. I'm standing far out in the street, pushing my palms into my ears and waiting for it to be over.

When they emerge, M avoids my gaze. He wipes the blood off his mouth with the back of his hand and shoots me just one guilty glance before brushing past. The others are not quite there yet, not even to M's level of conscience, but there is something a little different about them, too. They take no leftovers. They dry their bloody hands on their pants and walk in uneasy silence. It's a start.

As we get close enough to the stadium to catch the first whiffs of the Living, I go over the plan in my head. It's not much of a plan, really. It's cartoonishly simple, but here's why it might work: it's never been tried before. There has never been enough will to make a way.

A few blocks from the entry gate, we stop in an abandoned house. I go into the bathroom and study myself in the mirror like the former resident must have done a thousand times. In my head I jog through the maddening repetitions of the morning routine, getting into character. Alarm—shower—clothes—breakfast. Do I look my best? Am I putting my best foot forward? Am I stepping out the door prepared for everything this world has to throw at me?

I run some gel through my hair and straighten my tie. I adjust my shirt to hide a few black wounds. I splash on some cologne.

"Ready," I tell the others.

M sizes me up. "Close . . . enough."

We head for the gates.

• • •

Within a few blocks, the smell of the Living is nearly overpowering. It's as if the stadium is a massive Tesla coil crackling with storms of fragrant pink life-lightning. Everyone in our group stares at it in awe. Some of them drool freely. If they hadn't just eaten, our loosely constructed strategy would collapse in an instant.

Before we get within sight of the gate, we take a side street and stop at an intersection, hiding behind a UPS truck. I step out slightly and look around the corner. Less than two blocks away, four guards stand in front of the stadium's main entrance doors, dangling shotguns over their shoulders and chatting among themselves. Their gruff, military sentences use even fewer syllables than ours.

I look at M. "Thanks. For . . . doing this."

"Sure," M says.

"Don't . . . die."

"Never do. Are . . . ready?"

I nod.

"Look . . . alive . . . out there."

I smile. I brush my hair back one more time, take a deep breath, and run for it.

"Help!" I scream, waving my arms. "Help, they're . . . right behind me!"

With my best possible balance and poise, I run toward the doors. M and the others lumber after me, groaning theatrically.

The guards react on instinct: they raise their guns and open fire on the zombies. An arm flies off. A leg. One of the anonymous nine loses a head and goes down. But not a single weapon points in my direction. Painting Julie's face on the air in front of me, I sprint with Olympian focus. My stride is good, I can feel it; I look normal, *alive,* and so I snap neatly into a category: "human." Two more guards emerge with guns drawn, but they barely even look at me. They squint, they take aim at their targets, and they shout, "Go! Get in there, man!"

Two more zombies hit the ground behind me. As I slip in through the doors, I see M and the remaining Dead veer off and retreat. Their gait suddenly changes. They lose their stumble and run like living things. Not as fast as me, not as graceful, but with purpose. The guards hesitate, the gunfire falters. "What the fuck . . . ?" one of them mutters.

Inside the entrance is a man with a clipboard and a notebook. An immigration officer, ready to take my name and have me fill out a stack of request forms before most likely tossing me out. The Dead have depended on this man for years to provide us with the defenseless stragglers we eat in the ruins outside. He comes toward me, flipping through his notebook, making no eye contact. "Close call, eh, friend? I'm going to need you to—"

"Ted! Look at this shit!"

Ted looks up, looks through the open doors, sees his fellow soldiers standing dumbstruck. He glances at me. "Wait right here."

Ted jogs out and stops next to the guards, staring at the eerily animate zombies dashing off into the distant streets like real people. I imagine the look on the men's faces, their stomachs bubbling with the queasy sensation that the earth under their feet is moving.

Momentarily forgotten, I turn and run. I run through the dark entry corridor toward the light on the other end, wondering if this is a birth canal or the tunnel to Heaven. Am I coming or going? Either way, it's too late to reverse. Hidden in the gloom under a red evening sky, I step into the world of the Living.

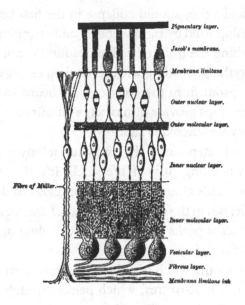

Pigmentary layer.
Jacob's membrane.
Membrana limitans
Outer nuclear layer.
Outer molecular layer.
Inner nuclear layer.
Fibre of Müller.
Inner molecular layer.
Vesicular layer.
Fibrous layer.
Membrana limitans inh

THE SPORTS ARENA Julie calls home is unaccountably large, perhaps one of those dual-event "super-venues" built for an era when the greatest quandary facing the world was where to put all the parties. From the outside there is nothing to see but a mammoth oval of featureless walls, a concrete ark that not even God could make float. But the interior reveals the stadium's soul: chaotic yet grasping for order, like the sprawling slums of Brazil designed by a modern architect.

All the bleachers have been torn out to make room for an expansive grid of miniature skyscrapers, rickety houses built unnaturally tall and skinny to conserve the limited real estate. Their walls are a hodgepodge of salvaged materials—one of the taller towers begins as concrete and grows flimsier as it rises, from steel to plastic to a precarious ninth floor of soggy particleboard. Most of the buildings look like they should collapse in the first breeze, but the whole city is supported by rigid webs of cable running from tower to tower, cinching the grid tight. The stadium's inner walls loom high over everything, bristling with severed pipes, wires, and spikes of rebar that sprout from the concrete like beard stubble. Underpowered streetlamps provide dim orange illumination, leaving this snow globe city smothered in shadows.

The moment I step out of the entry tunnel my sinuses inflame with an overwhelming rush of life-smell. It's all around me, so sweet and potent it's almost painful; I feel like I'm drowning in a perfume bottle. But in the midst of this thick haze, I can sense Julie. Her signature scent peeks out of the noise, calling out like a voice underwater. I follow it.

The streets are the width of sidewalks, narrow strips of asphalt poured over the old Astroturf, which peeks through any unpaved gaps like bright green moss. There are no names on the street signs. Instead of listing off states or presidents or varieties of trees, they display simple white graphics—apple, ball, cat, dog—a child's guide to the alphabet. There is mud everywhere, slicking the asphalt and piling up in corners along with the detritus of daily life: pop cans, cigarette butts, used condoms and bullet shells.

I am trying not to gawk at the city like the rube tourist I am, but something beyond curiosity is gluing my attention to every curb and rooftop. As foreign as it all is to me, I feel a ghostly sense of recognition, even nostalgia, and as I make my way down what must be Eye Street, some of my stolen memories begin to stir.

This is where we started. This is where they sent us when the coasts disappeared. When the bombs fell. When our friends died and rose as strangers, unfamiliar and cold.

It's not Perry's voice—it's everyone's, a murmuring chorus of all the lives I've consumed, gathering in the dark lounge of my subconscious to reminisce.

Flag Avenue, where they planted our nation's colors, back when there were still nations and their colors mattered. Gun Street, where they set up the war camps, planned attacks and defenses against our endless enemies, Living as often as Dead.

I walk with my head down, keeping as close to the walls as I can. When I meet someone coming the other way I keep my eyes straight ahead until the last possible moment, then I allow fleeting contact. We pass briskly with awkward nods.

It didn't take much to bring down the card house of civilization. Just a few gusts and it was done, the balance tipped, the spell broken. Good citizens realized the lines that had shaped their lives were imaginary and easily crossed. They had wants and needs and the power to satisfy them, so they did. The moment the lights went out, everyone stopped pretending.

I begin to worry about my clothes. Everyone I encounter is wearing thick gray denim, a waterproof coat, mud-caked work boots. What world am I still living in where people dress for aesthetics? If no one realizes I'm a zombie, they may still call in a report on the stylish lunatic roaming the streets in a fitted shirt and tie. I quicken my pace, sniffing desperately for Julie's trail.

Island Avenue, where they built the courtyard for the community meetings, where "they" became "we," or so we believed. We cast our votes and raised our leaders, charming men and women with white teeth and silver tongues, and we shoved our many hopes and fears into their hands, believing those hands were strong because they had firm handshakes. They failed us, always. There was no way they could not fail us—they were human, and more importantly, so were we.

I veer off Eye Street and start working my way toward the center of the grid. Julie's scent grows more distinct, but its exact direction remains vague. I keep hoping some clue will emerge from the chanting in my head, but these ancient ghosts have no interest in my insignificant search.

Jewel Street, where we built the schools once we finally accepted that this was reality, that this was the world our children would inherit. We taught them how to shoot, how to pour concrete, how to kill and how to survive, and if they made it that far, if they mastered those skills and had time to spare, then we taught them how to read and write, to reason and relate and understand their world. We tried hard at first, there was much hope and faith, but it was a steep hill to climb in the rain, and many slid to the base.

I notice the maps in these memories are slightly outdated; the street they're calling Jewel has been renamed. The sign is newer, a fresh primary green, and instead of a visual icon it has an actual word printed on it. Intrigued, I turn at this intersection and approach an atypically wide metal building. Julie's scent is still distant, so I know I shouldn't stop, but the pale light coming through the windows seems to prick some new anguish in my inner voices. As I press my nose against the glass, they go quiet.

A large, wide-open room. Row upon row of white metal tables under fluorescent lights. Dozens of children, all younger than ten, divided by row into project groups: a row repairing generators, a row treating gasoline, a row cleaning rifles, sharpening knives, stitching wounds. And at the edge, very near the window I'm staring through: a row dissecting cadavers. Except of course they aren't cadavers. As an eight-year-old girl in blond pigtails peels the flesh away from her subject's mouth, revealing the crooked grin underneath, its eyes flick open and it looks around, struggles briefly against its restraints, then relaxes, looking weary and bored. It glances toward my window and we make brief eye contact, just before the girl cuts out its eyes.

We tried to make a beautiful world here, the voices mumble. *There were those who saw the end of civilization as an opportunity to start over, to undo the errors of history—to relive mankind's awkward adolescence with all the wisdom of our modern age. But everything was happening so fast.*

I hear the noise of a violent scuffle from the other end of the building, shoes scraping against concrete, elbows banging sheet metal. Then a low, wet groan. I traverse the building, searching for a better viewpoint.

Outside our walls were hordes of men and monsters eager to steal what we had, and inside was our own mad stew, so many cultures and languages and incompatible values packed into one tiny box. Our world was too small to share peacefully; consensus never came, harmony was impossible. So we adjusted our goals.

Through another window I see a big open space like a warehouse, dimly lit and scattered with broken cars and chunks of debris as if simulating the outer city landscape. A crowd of older kids surrounds a corral of chain-link fencing and concrete freeway barriers. It resembles the "free speech zones" once used to contain protesters outside political rallies, but instead of being crammed full of sign-waving dissidents, this cage is occupied by just four figures: a teenage boy armored head to toe in police riot gear, and three badly desiccated Dead.

Can the Dark Ages' doctors be blamed for their methods? The blood-letting, the leeches, the holes in skulls? They were feeling their way blind, grasping at mysteries in a world without science, but the plague was upon them; they had to do something. When our turn came, it was no different. Despite all our technology and enlightenment, our laser scalpels and social services, it was no different. We were just as blind and just as desperate.

I can tell by the way they stagger that the Dead in this arena are starving. They must know where they are and what's going to happen to them, but they are far beyond what little self-control they ever had. They lunge for the boy and he aims his shotgun.

The outside world had already sunk under a sea of blood, and now those waves were lapping over our last stronghold—we had to shore up the walls. We realized that the closest we'd ever get to objective truth was the belief of the majority, so we enthroned the majority and ignored all other voices. We appointed generals and contractors, police and engineers; we discarded every inessential ornament. We smelted our ideals under great heat and pressure until the soft parts burned away, and what emerged was a tempered frame rigid enough to endure the cruel world we'd created.

"Wrong!" the instructor shouts at the boy in the cage as the boy fires into the advancing Dead, blowing holes in their chests and blasting off fingers and feet. "Get the head! Forget the rest is even there!" The boy fires two more rounds that miss entirely, thudding into the heavy plywood ceiling. The quickest of the three zombies seizes his arms and wrenches the gun out of his hands, struggles with the pulse-checking safety trigger for a moment, then throws the gun aside and tackles the boy into the fence, biting wildly against the helmet's face guard. The instructor storms into the cage and jabs his pistol into the zombie's head, fires a round and holsters the gun. "Remember," he announces to the whole room, "the recoil on an automatic shotgun will drive the barrel upward, especially on these old Mossbergs, so aim low or you'll be shooting blue sky." He scoops up the weapon and shoves it into the boy's trembling hands. "Continue."

The boy hesitates, then raises the barrel and fires twice. Bits of gore slap against his face guard, spattering it black. He rips the helmet off and stares at the corpses at his feet, breathing hard and struggling not to cry.

"Good," the instructor says. "Beautiful."

We knew it was all wrong. We knew we were diminishing ourselves in ways we couldn't even name, and we wept sometimes at memories of better days, but we no longer saw a choice. We were doing our best to survive. The equations at the roots of our problems were complex, and we were far too tired to solve them.

A snuffling noise at my feet finally tears me away from the scene in the window. I look down to see a German shepherd puppy studying my leg with flaring wet nostrils. It looks up at me. I look down at it. It pants happily for a moment, then starts eating my calf.

"Trina, *no!*"

A little boy rushes up and grabs the dog's collar, pulls her off me and drags her back toward the open doorway of a house. "*Bad* dog."

Trina twists her head around to gaze at me longingly.

"Sorry!" the boy calls from across the street.

I give him an easy wave, *No problem.*

A young girl emerges from the doorway and stands next to him, sticking out her belly and watching me with big dark eyes. Her hair is black; the boy's is curly blond. They are both around six.

"Don't tell our mom?" she asks.

I shake my head, swallowing back a sudden reflux of emotions. The sound of these kids' voices, their perfect, childish diction . . .

"Do you . . . know Julie?" I ask them.

"Julie Cabernet?" the boy says.

"Julie Gri . . . gio."

"We like Julie Cabernet a lot. She reads to us every Wednesday."

"*Stories!*" the girl adds.

I don't recognize this name, but some scrap of memory perks at the sound of it. "Do you know . . . where she lives?"

"Daisy Street," the boy says.

"No, Flower Street! It's a flower!"

"A daisy *is* a flower."

"Oh."

"She lives on a corner. It's Daisy Street and Devil Avenue."

"Cow Avenue!"

"It's not a cow, it's the Devil. Cows and the Devil both have horns."

"Oh."

"Thanks," I tell the kids, and turn to leave.

"Are you a zombie?" the girl asks in a shy squeak.

I freeze. She waits for my answer, twisting left and right on her heels. I relax, smile at the girl, and shrug. "Julie . . . doesn't think so."

An angry voice from a fifth-floor window yells something about curfew and shutting the door and not talking to strangers, so I wave to the kids and hurry off toward Daisy and Devil. The sun is down and the sky is rust. A distant loudspeaker blares out a sequence of numbers, and most of the windows around me go dark. I loosen my tie and start to run.

• • •

The intensity of Julie's scent doubles with each block. As the first few stars appear in the stadium's oval sky, I turn a corner and halt below a solitary edifice of white aluminum siding. Most of the buildings seem to be multifamily apartment complexes, but this one is smaller, narrower, and separated from its tightly packed neighbors by an awkward distance. Four stories tall but barely two rooms wide, it looks like a cross between a town house and a prison watchtower. The windows are all dark except for a third-floor balcony jutting out from the side of the house. The balcony seems incongruously romantic on this austere structure, until I notice the swivel-mounted sniper rifles on each corner.

Lurking behind a stack of crates in the Astroturf backyard, I hear voices inside the house. I close my eyes, luxuriating in their sweet rhythms and tart timbres. I hear Julie. Julie and another girl, discussing something in tones that jitter and syncopate like jazz. I find myself swaying slightly, dancing to their conversational beat.

Eventually the talk trails off, and Julie emerges onto the balcony. It's been only one day since she left, but the sense of reunion that surges in me is decades strong. She rests her elbows on the railing, looking cold in just a loose black T-shirt over bare legs. "Well, here I am again," she says, apparently to no one but the air. "Dad clapped me on the back when I walked in the door. Actually clapped me on the back, like a fucking football coach. All he said was, 'So glad you're okay,' then he ran off to some project meeting or something. I can't believe how much he's . . . I mean, he was never exactly *cuddly,* but . . ." I hear a tiny click and she doesn't speak for a moment. Then another click. "Until I called him he had to have assumed I was dead, right? Yeah, he sent out the search parties, but how often do people really come back from stuff like this? So to him . . . I was dead. And maybe I'm being too harsh but I absolutely can't picture him crying over it. Whoever told him the news, they probably both clapped each other on the back and said

'Soldier on, soldier,' and then went back to work." She stares at the ground as if she's seeing through it, down into the hellish core of the earth. "What's wrong with people?" she says, almost too quiet for me to hear. "Were they born with parts missing or did it all fall out somewhere along the way?"

She is silent for a while, and I'm about to show myself when she suddenly laughs, closing her eyes and shaking her head. "I actually miss that stupid . . . I miss R! I know that's crazy, but is it really *that* crazy? Just because he's . . . whatever he is? I mean, isn't 'zombie' just a silly name we came up with for a state of being we don't understand? What's in a name, right? If we were . . . If there was some kind of . . ." She trails off, then stops and raises a mini cassette recorder to eye level, glaring at it. "Fuck this thing," she mumbles to herself. "Tape journaling . . . not for me." She fast-pitches it off the balcony. It bounces off a supply crate and lands at my feet. I pick it up, tuck it into my shirt pocket, and press my hand against it, feeling its corners dig into my chest. If I ever return to my 747, this memento will go in the stack closest to where I sleep.

Julie hops onto the balcony railing and sits with her back to me, scribbling in her battered old Moleskine.

Journal or poetry?

Both, silly.

Am I in it?

I step out from the shadows. "Julie," I whisper.

She doesn't startle. She turns slowly, and a smile melts across her face like a slow spring thaw. "Oh . . . my God," she half-giggles, then hops off the railing and spins around to face me. "R! You're *here*! Oh my *God*!"

I grin. "Hello."

"What are you *doing* here?" she hisses, trying to keep her voice down.

I shrug, deciding that this gesture, while easy to abuse, does have its place. It may even be vital vocabulary in a world as unspeakable as ours.

"Came to . . . see you."

"But I had to go home, remember? You were supposed to say good-bye."

"Don't know why you . . . say good-bye. I say . . . hello."

Her lip quivers between reactions, but she ends up with a reluctant smile. "God you're a cheeseball. But seriously, R—"

"Jules!" a voice calls from inside the house. "Come here, I wanna show you something."

"One sec, Nora," Julie calls back. She looks down at me. "This is crazy, okay? You're going to get killed. It doesn't matter how changed you are, the people in here won't care, they won't listen, they'll just *shoot* you. Do you understand?"

I nod. "Yes."

I start climbing up the drainpipe.

"Jesus, R! Are you listening to me?"

I get about three feet off the ground before I realize that although I'm now capable of running, speaking, and maybe falling in love, *climbing* is still a ways down the road for me. I lose my grip on the pipe and fall flat on my back. Julie covers her mouth, but some laughter slips through.

"Hey Cabernet!" Nora calls again. "What's going on, are you talking to somebody?"

"Hang *on*, okay? I'm just doing a tape journal."

I stand up and dust myself off. I look up at Julie. Her brows are tight and she bites her lip. "R . . . ," she says miserably. "You can't . . ."

The balcony door swings open and Nora appears, her curls just as thick and wild as they were in my visions, all those years ago. I've never seen her standing, and she's surprisingly tall, at least half a foot above Julie, long brown legs bare under a camouflage skirt. I had assumed she and Julie were classmates, but now I realize Nora is a few years older, maybe in her mid-twenties.

"What are you—" she starts to say, then she notices me, and her eyebrows go up. "Oh my holy Lord. Is that *him*?"

Julie sighs. "Nora, this is R. R . . . Nora."

Nora stares at me like I'm Sasquatch, the Chupacabra, maybe a unicorn. "Um . . . nice to meet you . . . R."

"Likewise," I reply, and Nora slaps a hand over her mouth to stifle a delighted squeak, looks at Julie, then back at me.

"What should we do?" Julie asks Nora, trying to ignore her giddiness. "He just showed up. I'm trying to tell him he's going to get killed."

"Well he needs to get up here, first of all," Nora says, still staring at me.

"Into the house? Are you stupid?"

"Come on, your dad's not back for another two days. Safer for him in the house than on the street."

Julie thinks for a minute. "Okay. Hold on, R, I'll come down."

I go around to the front of the house and stand at the door, waiting nervously in my dress shirt and tie. She opens it, grinning shyly. Prom night at the end of the world.

"Hi, Julie," I say, as if none of the previous conversation happened.

She hesitates, then steps forward and hugs me. "I actually missed you," she says into my shirt.

"I . . . heard that."

She pulls back to look at me, and something wild glints in her eyes. "Hey R," she says. "If I kissed you, would I get . . . you know . . . converted?"

My thoughts skip like a record in an earthquake. As far as I know, only a bite, a violent transfer of blood and essences, has the power to make the Living join the Dead before actually dying. To expedite the inevitable. But then again, I'm fairly sure Julie's question has never, *ever* been asked before.

"Don't . . . think so," I say, "but—"

A spotlight flashes at the end of the street. The sound of two guards barking commands breaks the night quiet.

"Shit, the patrol," Julie whispers, and yanks me inside the house.

"We should get the lights out, it's after curfew. Come on." She runs up the stairs and I follow her, relief and disappointment mixing in my chest like unstable chemicals.

Julie's home feels eerily unoccupied. In the kitchen, the den, the short halls and steep staircases, the walls are white and unadorned. The few pieces of furniture are plastic, and rows of fluorescent lights glare down on stainproof beige carpets. It feels like the vacated office of a bankrupt company, empty echoing rooms and the lingering scent of desperation.

Julie turns lights off as she goes, darkening the house until we reach her bedroom. She switches off the overhead bulb and flicks on a Tiffany lamp by her bed. I step inside and turn in slow circles, greedily absorbing Julie's private world.

If her mind were a room, it would look like this.

Each wall is a different color. One red, one white, one yellow, one black, and a sky-blue ceiling strung with model airplanes. Each wall seems designated for a theme. The red is nearly covered with movie ticket stubs and concert posters, all browned and faded with age. The white is crowded with paintings, starting near the floor with a row of amateur acrylics and leading up to three stunning oil canvases: a sleeping girl about to be devoured by tigers, a nightmarish Christ on a geometric cross, and a surreal landscape draped with melting clocks.

"Recognize those?" Julie says with a grin she can barely contain. "Salvador Dalí. Originals, of course."

Nora comes in from the balcony, sees me with my face inches from the canvases, and laughs. "Nice decor, right? Me and Perry wanted to get Julie the *Mona Lisa* for her birthday because it reminded us of that little smirk she's always—there! Right there!—but, yeah, it's a long way to Paris on foot. We make do with the local exhibitions."

"Nora has a whole wall of Picassos in her room," Julie adds. "We'd be legendary art thieves if anyone still cared."

I crouch down to get a closer look at the bottom row of acrylics.

"Those are Julie's," Nora says. "Aren't they great?"

Julie averts her eyes in disgust. "Nora made me put those up."

I study them intently, searching for Julie's secrets in their clumsy brushstrokes. Two are just bright colors and thick, tortured texture. The third is a crude portrait of a blond woman. I glance over at the black wall, which bears only one ornament: a thumbtacked Polaroid of what must be the same woman. Julie plus twenty hard years.

Julie follows my gaze and she and Nora exchange a glance. "That's my mom," Julie says. "She left when I was twelve." She clears her throat and looks out the window.

I turn to the yellow wall, which is notably unadorned. I point at it and raise my eyebrows.

"That's, um . . . my hope wall," she says. Her voice contains an embarrassed pride that makes her sound younger. Almost innocent. "I'm leaving it open for something in the future."

"Like . . . what?"

"I don't know yet. Depends on what happens in the future. Hopefully something happy."

She shrugs this off and sits on the corner of her bed, tapping her fingers on her thigh and watching me. Nora settles down next to her. There are no chairs, so I sit on the floor. The carpet is a mystery under ancient strata of wrinkled clothes.

"So . . . R," Nora says, leaning toward me. "You're a zombie. What's that feel like?"

"Uh . . ."

"How did it happen? How'd you get converted?"

"Don't . . . remember."

"I'm not seeing any old bites or gunshot wounds or anything. Must've been natural causes. No one was around to debrain you?"

I shrug.

"How old are you?"

I shrug.

"You look twentysomething, but you could be thirtysomething.

You have one of those faces. How come you're not all rotten? I barely even smell you."

"I don't . . . um . . ."

"Do your body functions still work? They don't, right? I mean can you actually still, you know—?"

"Jesus, Nora," Julie cuts in, elbowing her in the hip. "Will you back off? He didn't come here for an interrogation."

I shoot Julie a grateful look.

"I do have one question, though," she says. "How the hell did you get *in* here? Into the stadium?"

I shrug. "Walked . . . in."

"How'd you get past the guards?"

"Played . . . Living."

She stares at me. "They *let* you in? *Ted* let you in?"

"Distrac . . . ted."

She puts a hand to her forehead. "Wow. That's . . ." She pauses, and an incredulous smile breaks through. "You look . . . less gross. Did you comb your hair, R?"

"He's in drag!" Nora laughs. "He's in Living drag!"

"I can't believe that worked on the guards."

"Do you think he could pass?" Nora wonders. "Out on the streets with real people?"

Julie studies me dubiously, like a photographer forced to consider a chubby model. "Well," she allows. "I guess . . . it's *possible*."

I squirm under their scrutiny. Finally Julie takes a deep breath and stands up. "Anyway, you'll have to stay here at least for tonight, till we can figure out what to do with you. I'm going to go heat up some rice. You want some, Nora?"

"Nah, I just had Carbtein nine hours ago." She looks at me cautiously. "Are you, uh . . . hungry, R?"

I shake my head. "I'm . . . fine."

"'Cause I don't know what we're supposed to do about your dietary restrictions. I mean, I know you can't help it, Julie explained all about you, but we don't—"

"Really." I stop her. "I'm . . . fine."

She looks uncertain. I can imagine the footage rolling behind her eyes. A dark room filling with blood. Her friends dying on the floor. Me, crawling toward Julie with red hands outstretched. Julie may have convinced her that I'm a special case, but I shouldn't be surprised to get a few nervous looks. Nora watches me in silence for a few minutes. Then she breaks away and starts rolling a joint.

When Julie comes back with the food, I borrow her spoon and take a small bite of rice, smiling as I chew. As usual it goes down like Styrofoam, but I do manage to swallow it. Julie and Nora look at each other, then at me.

"How's it taste?" Julie asks tentatively.

I grimace.

"Okay, but still, you haven't eaten any people in a long time. And you're still walking. Do you think you could ever wean yourself off . . . live foods?"

I give her a wry smile. "I guess . . . it's *possible*."

Julie grins at this. Half at my unexpected use of sarcasm, half at the implied hope behind it. Her whole face lights up in a way I've never seen before, so I hope I'm right. I hope it's true. I hope I haven't just learned how to lie.

• • •

Around one AM, the girls start to yawn. There are canvas cots in the den, but no one feels like venturing out of Julie's room. This gaudily painted little cube is like a warm bunker in the frozen emptiness of Antarctica. Nora takes the bed. Julie and I take the floor. Nora scribbles homework notes for about an hour, then clicks off the lamp and starts snoring like a small, delicate chain saw. Julie and I lie on our backs under a thick blanket, using piles of her clothes for a mattress on the rock-hard floor. It's a strange feeling, being so utterly surrounded by her. Her life scent is on everything. She's on me and under me and next to me. It's as if the entire room is made out of her.

"R," she whispers, looking up at the ceiling. There are words and doodles smeared up there in glow-in-the-dark paint.

"Yeah."

"I hate this place."

"I know."

"Take me somewhere else."

I pause, looking up at the ceiling. I wish I could read what she's written there. Instead, I pretend the letters are stars. The words, constellations.

"Where do . . . want to go?"

"I don't know. Somewhere far away. Some distant continent where none of this is happening. Where people just live in peace."

I fall silent.

"One of Perry's older friends used to be a pilot . . . we could take your housejet! It'd be like a flying Winnebago, we could go anywhere!" She rolls onto her side and grins at me. "What do you think, R? We could go to the other side of the world."

The excitement in her voice makes me wince. I hope she can't see the grim light in my eyes. I don't know for sure, but there is something in the air lately, a deathly stillness as I walk through the city and its outskirts, that tells me the days of running away from problems are over. There will be no more vacations, no road trips, no tropical getaways. The plague has covered the world.

"You said . . . ," I begin, psyching myself up to express a complex thought. "You said . . . the . . ."

"Come on," she encourages. "Use your words."

"You said . . . the plane's not . . . its own world."

Her grin falters. "What?"

"Can't . . . float above . . . the mess."

She frowns. "I said that?"

"Your dad . . . concrete box . . . walls and guns . . . Running away . . . no better . . . than hiding. Maybe worse."

She thinks for a moment. "I know," she says, and I feel guilty for crashing her brief flight of fancy. "I know this. It's what I've been telling myself for years, that there's still hope, that we can turn things around somehow, blah fucking blah. It's just . . . getting a lot harder to believe lately."

"I know," I say, trying to hide the cracks in my sincerity. "But can't . . . give up."

Her voice darkens. She calls my bluff. "Why are you so hopeful all of a sudden? What are you really thinking?"

I say nothing, but she reads my face like a front-page headline, the kind that announced the atomic bomb and the *Titanic* and all the World Wars in progressively smaller type.

"There's nowhere left, is there," she says.

Almost imperceptibly, I shake my head.

"The whole world," she says. "You think it's all exed? All overrun?"

"Yes."

"How could you know that?"

"I don't. But . . . I feel."

She lets out a long breath, staring at the model planes dangling above us. "So what are we supposed to do?"

"Have to . . . fix it."

"Fix what?"

"Don't know. Ev . . . rything."

She props herself up on one elbow. "What are you talking about?" Her voice is no longer quiet. Nora stirs and stops snoring. "Fix everything?" Julie says, her eyes sparking in the dark. "How exactly are we supposed to do that? If you have some big revelation, please share, 'cause it's not like I don't think about this literally *all* the time. It's not like this hasn't been burning my brain every morning and night since my mom left. How do we fix everything? It's *so* broken. Everyone is *dying*, over and over again, in deeper and darker ways. What are we supposed to do? Do you know what's causing it? This plague?"

I hesitate. "No."

"Then how can you do anything about it? I want to know, R. How are we supposed to 'fix it'?"

I'm staring up at the ceiling. I'm staring at the verbal constellations, glimmering green in distant space. As I lie there, letting my mind rise into those imaginary heavens, two of the stars begin to change. They rotate, and focus, and their shapes clarify. They become . . . *letters*.

T

R

"Ter—" I whisper.

"What?"

"Truh—" I say, trying to pronounce it. It's a sound. It's a syllable. The blurry constellation is becoming a word. "What is . . . that?" I ask, pointing at the ceiling.

"What? The quotes?"

I stand up and indicate the general area of the sentence. "This one."

"It's a line from 'Imagine.' The John Lennon song."

"Which . . . line?"

" 'It's easy if you try.' "

I stand there for a minute, gazing up like an intrepid explorer of the cosmos. Then I lie down and fold my arms behind my head, eyes wide open. I don't have the answers she's asking for, but I can feel their existence. Faint points of light in the distant dark.

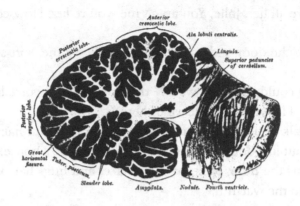

SLOW STEPS. Mud under boots. Look nowhere else. Strange mantras loop through my head. Old bearded mutterings from dark alleys. *Where are you going, Perry? Foolish child. Brainless boy. Where?* Every day the universe grows larger, darker, colder. I stop in front of a black door. A girl lives here in this metal house. Do I love her? Hard to say anymore. But she is all that's left. The final red sun in an ever-expanding emptiness.

I walk into the house and find her sitting on the staircase, arms crossed over her knees. She puts a finger to her lips. "Dad," she whispers to me.

I glance up the staircase toward the general's bedroom. I hear his voice slurring in the dimness.

"This picture, Julie. The water park, remember the water park? Had to haul ten buckets up for just one slide. Twenty minutes of work for ten seconds of fun. Seemed worth it back then, didn't it? I liked watching your face when you flew out of the tube. You looked just like her, even back then."

Julie stands up quietly, moves toward the front door.

"You're all her, Julie. You aren't me, you're *her*. How could she do it?"

I open the door and back out. Julie follows me, soft steps, no sound.

"How could she be so weak?" the man says in a voice like steel melting. "How could she leave us here?"

We walk in silence. The drizzling rain beads in our hair and we shake it out like dogs. We come to Colonel Rosso's house. Rosso's wife opens the door, looks at Julie's face, and hugs her. We walk inside into the warmth.

I find Rosso in the living room, sipping coffee, peering through his glasses at a water-stained old book. While Julie and Mrs. Rosso murmur in the kitchen, I sit down across from the colonel.

"Perry," he says.

"Colonel."

"How are you holding up?"

"I'm alive."

"A good start. How are you settling into the home?"

"I despise it."

Rosso is quiet for a moment. "What's on your mind?"

I search for words. I seem to have forgotten most of them. Finally, quietly, I say, "He lied to me."

"How so?"

"He said we were fixing things, and if we didn't give up everything might turn out okay."

"He believed that. I think I do, too."

"But then he *died*." My voice trembles and I fight to squeeze it tight. "And it was *senseless*. No battle, no noble sacrifice, just a stupid work accident that could have happened to anyone anywhere, any time in history."

"Perry . . ."

"I don't understand it, sir. What's the point of trying to fix a world we're in so briefly? Where's the meaning in all that work if it's just going to disappear? Without any warning? A fucking brick on the head?"

Rosso says nothing. The low voices in the kitchen become audible in our silence, so they drop to whispers, trying to hide from the colonel what I'm sure he already knows. Our little world is far too tired to care about the crimes of its leaders.

"I want to join Security," I announce. My voice is solid now. My face is hard.

Rosso lets out a slow breath and sets his book down. "Why, Perry?"

"Because it's the only thing left worth doing."

"I thought you wanted to write."

"That's pointless."

"Why?"

"We have bigger concerns now. General Grigio says these are the last days. I don't want to waste my last days scratching letters on paper."

"Writing isn't letters on paper. It's communication. It's memory."

"None of that matters anymore. It's too late."

He studies me. He picks up the book again and holds the cover out. "Do you know this story?"

"It's Gilgamesh."

"Yes. *The Epic of Gilgamesh,* one of the earliest known works of literature. Humanity's debut novel, you could say." Rosso flips through the brittle yellow pages. "Love, sex, blood, and tears. A journey to find eternal life. To escape death." He reaches across the table and hands the book to me. "It was written over four thousand years ago on clay tablets by people who tilled the mud and rarely lived past forty. It's survived countless wars, disasters, and plagues, and continues to fascinate to this day, because here I am, in the midst of modern ruin, reading it."

I look at Rosso. I don't look at the book. My fingers dig into the leather cover.

"The world that birthed that story is long gone, all its people are dead, but it continues to touch the present and future because someone cared enough about that world to keep it. To put it in words. To remember it."

I split the book open to the middle. The pages are riddled with ellipses, marking words and lines missing from the tablets, rotted out and lost to history. I stare at these marks and let their black dots fill my vision. "I don't want to remember," I say, and I shut the book. "I want to join Security. I want to do dangerous stuff. I want to forget."

"What are you saying, Perry?"

"I'm not saying anything."

"It sounds like you are."

"No." The shadows in the room pool in the lines of our faces, draining our eyes of hue. "There's nothing left worth saying."

. . .

I am numb. Adrift in the blackness of Perry's thoughts, I reverberate with his grief like a low church bell.

"Are you working, Perry?" I whisper into the emptiness. "Are you reverse-engineering your life?"

Shhhhhh, Perry says. *Don't break the mood. I need this to cut through.*

I float there in his unshed tears, waiting in the salty dark.

. . .

Morning sun streams through the balcony window of Julie's bedroom. The green constellations have faded back into the blue-sky ceiling. The girls are still asleep, but I've been lying here awake for all but a few uneasy hours. Unable to stay motionless any longer, I slip out of the blankets and stretch my creaky joints, letting the sun baste one side of my face, then the other. Nora sleep-mumbles a bit of nursing jargon, "mitosis" or "meiosis," possibly "necrosis," and I notice the dog-eared textbook resting open on her stomach. Curious, I hover over her for a moment, then carefully lift up the book.

I can't read the title. But I immediately recognize the cover. A serenely sleeping face offering its throat of exposed veins to the viewer. The medical reference book *Gray's Anatomy*.

Looking nervously over my shoulder, I whisk the heavy tome out into the hallway and start flipping through its pages. Intricate drawings of human architecture, organs and bones all too familiar to me, although here the filleted bodies are shown clean and perfect, their details unblurred by filth or fluids. I pore over the illustrations as the minutes tick by, wracked by guilt and fascination like a pubescent Catholic with a *Playboy*. I can't read the captions, of course, but a few Latin words pop into my head as I study the images, perhaps distant recalls from my old life, a college lecture or TV documentary I absorbed somewhere. The knowledge feels grotesque in my mind but I grasp it and hold it tight, etching it deep into my memory. Why am I doing this? Why do I want to know the names and functions of all the beautiful structures I've spent my years violating? Because I don't deserve to keep them anonymous. I want the pain of knowing them, and by extension myself: who and what I really am. Maybe with that scalpel, red-hot and sterilized in tears, I can begin to carve out the rot inside me.

Hours pass. When I've seen every page and wrung every syllable from my memory, I gently replace the book on Nora's belly and tiptoe out onto the balcony, hoping the warm sun will grant some relief from the moral nausea churning inside me.

I lean against the railing and take in the cramped vistas of Julie's city. As dark and lifeless as it was last night, now it bustles and roars like Times Square. What is everyone doing? The undead airport has its crowds but no real activity. We don't do things; we wait for things to happen. The collective volition bubbling up from the Living is intoxicating, and I have a sudden urge to be down in those masses, rubbing shoulders and elbowing for space in all that sweat and breath. If my questions have answers, they must certainly be down there, under the pounding soles of those filthy feet.

I hear the girls chatting quietly in the bedroom, finally waking up. I go back inside and crawl under the blankets next to Julie.

"Good morning, R," Nora says, not quite sincerely. I think addressing me like a human is still a novelty for her; she looks like she wants to titter every time she acknowledges my presence. It's aggravating, but I understand. I'm an absurdity that takes some getting used to.

"Morning," Julie croaks, watching me from across the pillow. She looks about as unpretty as I've ever seen her, eyes puffy and hair insane. I wonder how well she sleeps at night and what kind of dreams she has. I wish I could step into them like she steps into mine.

She rolls onto her side and props her head on her elbow. She clears her throat. "So," she says. "Here you are. What now?"

"Want to . . . see your city."

Her eyes search my face. "Why?"

"Want to . . . see how you live. Living people."

Her lips tighten. "Too risky. Someone would notice you."

"Come on, Julie," Nora says. "He walked all the way here, let's give him a tour! We can fix him up, disguise him. He already got past Ted, I'm sure he'll be okay strolling around a little if we're careful. You'll be careful, right, R?"

I nod, still looking at Julie. She allows a long silence. Then she rolls onto her back and closes her eyes, releasing a slow breath that sounds like consent.

"Yay!" Nora says.

"We can *try* it. But R, if you don't look convincing after we fix you up, no tour. And if I see anyone staring at you too hard, tour's over. Deal?"

I nod.

"No nodding. Say it."

"Deal."

She crawls out of the blankets and climbs onto the side of the bed. She looks me up and down. "Okay," she says, her hair sticking out in every direction. "Let's get you presentable."

. . .

I would like my life to be a movie so I could cut to a montage. A quick sequence of shots set to some trite pop song would be much easier to endure than the two grueling hours the girls spend trying to convert me, to change me back into what's widely considered human. They wash my hair. They wear out a fresh toothbrush on my teeth, although for my smile anything above a coffee-addicted Brit is not in the cards. They attempt to dress me in some of Julie's more boyish clothes, but Julie is a pixie and I rip through T-shirts and snap buttons like a bodybuilder. Finally they give up, and I wait naked in the bathroom while they run my old business wear through the wash.

While I wait, I decide to take a shower. This is an experience I had long forgotten, and I savor it like a first sip of wine, a first kiss. The steaming water cascades over my battered body, washing away months or years of dirt and blood, some of it mine, much of it others'. All this filth spirals down the drain and into the underworld where it belongs. My true skin emerges, pale gray, marked by cuts and scrapes and grazing bulletwounds, but clean.

This is the first time I have seen my body.

When my clothes are dry and Julie has sewn up the most noticeable holes, I dress myself, relishing the unfamiliar feeling of cleanness. My shirt no longer sticks to me. My slacks no longer chafe.

"You should at least lose the tie," Nora says. "You're about ten wars behind the fashion curve in that fancy getup."

"No, leave it," Julie pleads, regarding the little strip of cloth with a whimsical smile. "I like that tie. It's the only thing keeping you from being completely gray."

"It sure won't help him blend in, Jules. Remember all the stares we got when we started wearing sneakers instead of work boots?"

"Exactly. People already know you and me don't wear the uniform; as long as R stays with us he could wear spandex shorts and a top hat and no one would mention it."

Nora smiles. "I like *that* idea."

So the tie remains, in all its red silk incongruity. Julie helps me knot it. She brushes my hair and runs some goo through it. Nora thoroughly fumigates me with men's body spray.

"Ugh, Nora," Julie objects. "I hate that stuff. And he doesn't even stink."

"He stinks a little bit."

"Yeah, *now* he does."

"Better he smell like a chemical plant than a corpse, right? It'll keep the dogs away from him."

There is some debate about whether or not to make me wear sunglasses to hide my eyes, but they eventually decide this would be more conspicuous than just letting that ethereal gray show itself.

"It's actually not that noticeable," Julie says. "Just don't have a staring contest with anyone."

"You'll be fine," Nora adds. "No one in this place really looks at each other anyway."

The final step in their remodeling plan is makeup. As I sit in front of the mirror like a Hollywood starlet getting ready for her close-up, they powder me, they rouge me, they colorize my black-and-white skin. When they're done, I stare at the mirror in amazement.

I am alive.

I am a handsome young professional, happy, successful, in the bloom of health, just emerging from a meeting and on my way to the gym. I laugh out loud. I look at myself in the mirror and the joyful absurdity of it just bubbles out.

Laughter. Another first for me.

"Oh my . . . ," Nora says, standing back to look at me, and Julie says, "Huh." She tilts her head. "You look . . ."

"You look *hot!*" Nora blurts. "Can I have him, Julie? Just for one night?"

"Shut your dirty mouth," Julie chuckles, still inspecting me. She touches my forehead, the narrow, bloodless slot where she once threw a knife. "Should probably cover that. Sorry, R." She sticks a Band-Aid over the wound and presses it down with gentle strokes. "There." She steps back again and studies me like a perfectionist painter, pleased but cautious.

"Con . . . vincing?" I ask.

"Hmm," she says.

I offer her my best attempt at a winning smile, stretching my lips wide.

"Oh, God. Definitely don't do that."

"Just be natural," Nora says. "Pretend you're home at the airport surrounded by friends, if you people have those."

I think back to the moment Julie named me, that warm feeling that crept into my face for the first time as we shared a beer and a plate of Thai food.

"There you go, that's better," Nora says.

Julie nods, pressing her knuckles against her smiling lips as if to hold back some outburst of emotion. A giddy cocktail of amusement, pride, and affection. "You clean up nice, R."

"Thank . . . you."

She takes a deep, decisive breath. "Okay then." She pulls a wool beanie over her wild hair and zips up her sweatshirt. "Ready to see what humanity's been up to since you left it?"

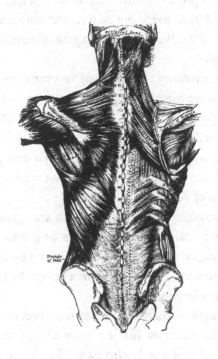

IN MY OLD DAYS of scavenging the city I often gazed up at the stadium walls and imagined a paradise inside. I assumed it was perfect, that everyone was happy and beautiful and wanted for nothing, and in my numb, limited way I felt envy and wanted to eat them all the more. But look at this place. The corrugated sheet metal glaring in the sun. The fly-buzzing pens of moaning, hormone-pumped cattle. The hopelessly stained laundry hanging from support cables between buildings, flapping in the wind like surrender flags.

"Welcome to Citi Stadium," Julie says, spreading her arms wide. "The largest human habitation in what used to be America."

Why did we stay? the voices mutter deep inside me as Julie calls out landmarks and points of interest. *What is a city and why do we keep building them? Take away the culture, the commerce, the business and pleasure; is there anything left? Just a grid of nameless streets filled with nameless people?*

"There are over twenty thousand of us crammed into this fishbowl," Julie says as we push through the dense crowds in the central square. "Pretty soon it'll be so tight we'll all just squish together. The human race will be one big mindless amoeba."

Why didn't we scatter? Head for high ground and plant our roots where the air and water were clean? What is it we needed from each other in this sweaty crush of bodies?

As much as possible I keep my eyes to the ground, trying to blend in and avoid notice. I sneak glances at guard towers, water tanks, new buildings rising under the bright strobe of arc welders, but mostly my view is of my feet. The asphalt. Mud and dog shit softening the sharp angles.

"We're growing less than half what we need to survive," Julie says as we pass the gardens, just a blurry dream of green behind the translucent walls of the hothouses. "So all the real food gets rationed out in tiny servings, and we fill the gaps in our diet with Carbtein." A trio of teenage boys in yellow jumpsuits haul a cart of oranges past us, and I notice one of them has strange sores running down the side of his face, sunken brown patches like the bruises on an apple, as if the cells have simply collapsed. "Not to mention we're burning through a pharmacy worth of medicine every month. Salvage teams can barely keep up. It's only a matter of time before we go to war with the other enclaves over the last bottle of Prozac."

Was it just fear? the voices wonder. We were fearful in the best of times; how could we cope with the worst? So we found the tallest walls and poured ourselves behind them. We kept pouring until we were the biggest and strongest, elected the greatest generals and found the most weapons, thinking all this maximalism would somehow generate happiness. But nothing so obvious could ever work.

"What's amazing to me," Nora says, squeezing past the strained belly of a morbidly pregnant woman, "is that despite all these needs and shortages we have, people keep pumping out kids. Flooding the world with copies of themselves just because that's tradition, that's what's done."

Julie glances at Nora and opens her mouth, then closes it.

"And even though we're about to starve to death under a mountain of poopy diapers, no one's brave enough to even *suggest* that people keep their seed in their nuts for a while."

"Yeah, but . . . ," Julie says, her voice uncharacteristically timid. "I don't know . . . there's something kind of beautiful about it, don't you think? That we keep living and growing even though our world is a corpse? That we keep coming back no matter how many of us die?"

"Why is it beautiful that humanity keeps coming back? So does herpes."

"Oh shut up, Nora, you love people. Being a misanthrope was Perry's thing."

Nora laughs and shrugs.

"It's not about keeping up the population, it's about passing on who we are and what we've learned, so things keep *going*. So we don't just *end*. Sure it's selfish, in a way, but how else do our short lives mean anything?"

"I guess that's true," Nora allows. "It's not like we have any other legacies to leave in this post-everything era."

"Right. It's all fading. I heard the world's last country collapsed in January."

"Oh, really? Which one was it?"

"Can't remember. Sweden, maybe?"

"So the globe is officially blank. That's depressing."

"At least you have some heritage you can hold on to. Your dad was Ethiopian, right?"

"Yeah, but what's that mean to me? He didn't remember his country, I never went there, and now it doesn't exist. All that leaves me with is brown skin, and who pays any attention to color anymore?" She waves a hand toward my face. "In a year or two we're all gonna be gray anyway."

I fall behind as they continue to banter. I watch them talk and gesticulate, listening to their voices without hearing the words.

What is left of us? the ghosts moan, drifting back into the shadows of my subconscious. *No countries, no cultures, no wars but still no peace. What's at our core, then? What's still squirming in our bones when everything else is stripped?*

• • •

By late afternoon, we've come to the road once known as Jewel Street. The school buildings wait for us ahead, squat and self-satisfied, and I feel my stomach knotting. Julie hesitates at the intersection, looking pensively toward their glowing windows. "Those are the training facilities," she says. "But you don't want to see in there. Let's move on."

I gladly follow her away from that dark boulevard, but I stare hard at the fresh green sign as we pass. I'm fairly sure the first letter is a "J."

"What's . . . that street called?" I ask, pointing to the sign.

Julie smiles. "Why, that's Julie Street."

"It used to be a graphic of a diamond or something," Nora says, "but her dad renamed it when they built the schools. Isn't that sweet?"

"It *was* sweet," Julie admits. "That's the type of gesture Dad can manage sometimes."

She takes us around the perimeter of the walls to a wide, dark tunnel directly across from the main gate. I realize these tunnels must be where sports teams once made their triumphal entries onto the field, back when thousands of people could still cheer for things so trivial. And since the tunnel on the other end is the passage into the world of the Living, it seems fitting that this one leads to a graveyard.

Julie flashes an ID badge at the guards and they wave us through the back gate. We step out onto a hilly field surrounded by hundreds of feet of chain-link fencing. Black hawthorn trees curl toward the mottled gray and gold sky, standing guard over classical tombstones, complete with crosses and statues of saints. I suspect these were reappropriated from some forgotten funeral home, as the engraved names and dates have been covered over with crude letters stenciled in white paint. The epitaphs resemble graffiti tags.

"This is where we bury . . . what's left of us," Julie says. She walks a few steps ahead as Nora and I stand in the entry. Out here, with the door shut behind us, the pulsing noise of human affairs is gone, replaced by the stoic silence of the truly dead. Each body resting here is either headless, brainless, or nothing but scraps of half-eaten flesh and bones piled in a box. I can see why they chose to build the cemetery outside the stadium walls: not only does it take up more land than all the indoor farmlands combined, it also can't be very good for morale. This is a reminder far more grim than the old world's sunny yards of peaceful passings and *requiem eternum*. This is a glimpse of our future. Not as individuals, whose deaths we can accept, but as a species, a civilization, a world.

"Are you sure you want to go in here today?" Nora asks Julie softly.

Julie looks out at the hills of patchy brown grass. "I go every day. Today's a day. Today's Tuesday."

"Yeah, but . . . do you want us to wait here?"

She glances back at me and considers for a moment. Then she shakes her head. "No. Come on." She starts walking and I follow her. Nora trails an awkward distance behind me, a look of muted surprise on her face.

There are no paths in this cemetery. Julie walks in a straight line, stepping over headstones and across grave mounds, many still soft and muddy. Her eyes are focused on a tall spire topped by a marble angel. We stop in front of it, Julie and I side by side, Nora still lingering behind. I strain to read the name on the grave, but it doesn't reveal itself. Even the first few letters remain out of reach.

"This is . . . my mom," Julie says. The cool evening wind blows her hair into her eyes, but she doesn't brush it away. "She left when I was twelve."

Nora squirms behind us, then wanders away and pretends to browse the epitaphs.

"She went crazy, I guess," Julie says. "Ran out into the city by herself one night and that was that. They found a few pieces of her but . . . there's nothing in this grave." Her voice is casual. I'm reminded of her trying to imitate the Dead back in the airport, the overacting, the paper-thin mask. "I guess it was too much for her, all of this." She waves a hand vaguely at the graveyard and the stadium behind us. "She was a real free spirit, you know? This wild bohemian goddess full of fire. She met my dad when she was nineteen; he swept her off her feet. Hard to believe it, but he was a musician back then, played keys in a rock band, was actually pretty good. They got married really young, and then . . . I don't know . . . the world went to shit, and Dad changed. Everything changed."

I try to read her eyes but her hair obscures them. I hear a tremor in her voice. "Mom tried. She really did try. She did her part to keep everything together, she did her daily work, and then it was all me. She poured everything into me. Dad was hardly around, so it was always just her and the little brat. I remember having so much fun; she used to take me to this water park back in—" A tiny sob catches her by surprise, choking off the words, and she covers her mouth with her hand. Her eyes plead with me through strands of dirty hair. "She just wasn't built for this fucking place," she says, her voice warbling in falsetto. "What was she supposed to do here? Everything that made her alive was gone. All she had left was this stupid twelve-year-old with ugly teeth who kept waking her up every night wanting to snuggle away a nightmare. No wonder she wanted out."

"Stop," I say firmly, and turn her to face me. "Stop." Tears are running down her face, salty secretions shooting through ducts and tubes, past bright pulsating cells and angry red tissues. I wipe them away and pull her into me. "You're . . . alive," I mumble into her hair. "You're . . . worth living for."

I feel her shudder against my chest, clinging to my shirt as my arms surround her. The air is silent except for the light whistle of the breeze. Nora is looking our way now, twisting a finger through her curls. She catches my eye and gives me a sad smile, as if to apologize for not warning me. But I'm not afraid of the skeletons in Julie's closet. I look forward to meeting the rest of them, looking them hard in the eye, giving them firm, bone-crunching hand-shakes.

As she dampens my shirt with sadness and snot, I realize I'm about to do another thing I've never done before. I suck in air and attempt to sing. "You're . . . sensational . . . ," I croak, struggling for a trace of Frank's melody. "Sensational . . . that's all."

There's a pause, and then something shifts in Julie's demeanor. I realize she's laughing.

"Oh wow," she giggles, and looks up at me, her eyes still glistening above a grin. "That was beautiful, R, really. You and Zombie Sinatra should record *Duets III*."

I cough. "Didn't get . . . warm-up."

She brushes some stray hairs out of my face. She looks at the grave. She reaches into her back pocket and pulls out a wilted airport daisy with four petals remaining. She sets it on the bare dirt in front of the headstone. "Sorry, Mom," she says softly. "Best I could find." She grabs my hand. "Mom, this is R. He's really nice, you'd love him. The flower is from him too."

Even though the grave is empty, I half expect her mother's hand to burst out of the earth and grip my ankle. After all, I'm a cell in the cancer that killed her. But if Julie is any indication, I suspect her mother might forgive me. These people, these beautiful Living women, they don't seem to make the connection between me and the creatures that keep killing everything they love. They allow me to be an exception, and I feel humbled by this gift. I want to pay it back somehow, *earn* their forgiveness. I want to repair the world I've helped destroy.

Nora rejoins us as we leave Mrs. Grigio's grave. She rubs Julie's shoulder and kisses the side of her head. "You okay?"

Julie nods. "As much as ever."

"Want to hear something nice?"

"So badly."

"I saw a patch of wildflowers by my house. They're growing in a ditch."

Julie smiles. She rubs the last few tears out of her eyes and doesn't say anything more.

I peruse the headstones as we walk. They are crooked and haphazardly placed, making the cemetery look ancient despite the dozens of freshly dug graves. I am thinking about death. I'm thinking how brief life is compared to it. I'm wondering how deep this graveyard goes, how many layers of coffins are stacked on top of each other, and what portion of Earth's soil is made from our decay.

Then something interrupts my morbid reflections. I feel a lurch in my stomach, a queer sensation like what I imagine a baby kicking in the womb might feel like. I stop midstep and turn around. A featureless rectangular headstone is watching me from a nearby hill.

"Hold on," I say to the girls, and begin climbing the hill.

"What's he doing?" I hear Nora ask under her breath. "Isn't that . . . ?"

I stand in front of the grave, staring at the name on the stone. A queasy sensation of vertigo rises through my legs, as if a vast pit is opening up in front of me, drawing me toward its edge with some dark, inexorable force. My stomach lurches again, I feel a sharp tug on my brain stem . . . I fall in.

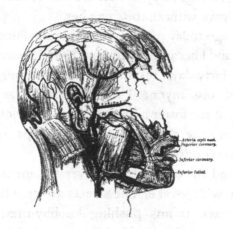

Arteria septi nasi.
Posterior coronary.

Inferior coronary.

Inferior labial.

I AM PERRY KELVIN, and this is my last day alive.

What a strange feeling, waking up to that awareness. All my life I have battled the alarm clock, pummeling the snooze button over and over with mounting self-loathing until the shame is finally strong enough to lever me upright. It was only on the brightest of mornings, those rare days of verve and purpose and clear reasons to live, that I ever sprang awake easily. How strange, then, that I do today.

Julie whimpers as I extract myself from her goose-bumped arms and slip out of bed. She gathers my half of the blankets around her and curls up against the wall. She will sleep for hours more, dreaming endless landscapes and novas of color both gorgeous and frightening. If I stayed she would wake up and describe them to me. All the mad plot twists and surrealist imagery, so vivid to her while so meaningless to me. There was a time when I treasured listening to her, when I found the commotion in her soul bittersweet and lovely, but I can no longer bear it. I lean over to kiss her good-bye, but my lips stiffen and I cringe away from her. I can't. I can't. I'll collapse. I pull back and leave without touching her.

Two years ago today my father was crushed under the wall he was building, and I became an orphan. I have missed him for seven hundred and thirty days, my mother for even longer, but tomorrow I will not miss anyone. I think about this as I descend the winding stairs of my foster home, this wretched house of discards, and emerge into the city. Dad, Mom, Grandpa, my friends . . . tomorrow I won't miss anyone.

It's early and the sun is barely over the mountains, but the city is already wide awake. The streets are crawling with laborers, repair crews, moms pushing knobby-tired strollers and foster moms herding lines of kids like cattle. Somewhere in the distance someone is playing a clarinet; its quavery notes drift through the morning air like birdsong, and I try to shut it out. I don't want to hear music, I don't want the sunrise to be pink. The world is a liar. Its ugliness is overwhelming; the scraps of beauty make it worse.

I make my way to the Island Street administrative building and tell the receptionist I'm here for my seven o'clock with General Grigio. She walks me back to his office and shuts the door behind me. The general doesn't look up from the paperwork on his desk. He raises one finger at me. I stand and wait, letting my eyes roam the contents of his walls. A picture of Julie. A picture of Julie's mother. A faded picture of himself and a younger Colonel Rosso in proper U.S. Army uniforms, smoking cigarettes in front of a flooded New York skyline. Next to this, another shot of the two men smoking cigarettes, this time overlooking a crumbled London. Then bombed-out Paris. Then smoldering Rome.

The general finally sets down his paperwork. He takes off his glasses and looks me over. "Mr. Kelvin," he says.

"Sir."

"Your very first salvage as team manager."

"Yes, sir."

"Do you feel ready?"

My tongue stalls for an instant as images of horses and cellists and red lips on a wineglass flicker through my mind, trying to knock me off course. I burn them like old film. "Yes, sir."

"Good. Here is your exit pass. See Colonel Rosso at the community center for your team assignments."

"Thank you, sir." I take the paperwork and turn to leave. But I pause on the doorway threshold. "Sir?" My voice cracks a little even though I swore I wouldn't let it.

"Yes, Perry?"

"Permission to speak freely, sir?"

"Go ahead."

I moisten my dry lips. "Is there a reason for all this?"

"Pardon me?"

"Is there a reason for us to keep doing all these things? The salvages and . . . everything?"

"I'm afraid I don't understand your question, Perry. The supplies we salvage are keeping us alive."

"Are we trying to stay alive because we think the world will get better someday? Is that what we're working toward?"

His expression is flat. "I suppose."

My voice becomes shaky and very undignified, but I can no longer control it. "What about right now? Is there anything right now that you love enough to keep living for?"

"Perry—"

"Will you tell me what it is, sir? Please?"

His eyes are marbles. A noise like the beginning of a word forms in his throat, then it stops. His mouth tightens. "This conversation is inappropriate." He lays his hands flat on his desk. "You should be on your way now. You have work to do."

I swallow hard. "Yes, sir. Sorry, sir."

"See Colonel Rosso at the community center for your team assignments."

"Yes, sir."

I step through the door and shut it behind me.

In Colonel Rosso's office I conduct myself with utmost professionalism. I request my team assignments and he gives them to me, handing over the manila envelope with warmth and pride in his squinty, failing eyes. He wishes me luck and I thank him; he invites me to dinner and I politely decline. My voice does not crack. I lose no composure.

Marching back through the community center lobby I glance toward the gym and see Nora staring at me through the tall windows. She's wearing snug black shorts and a white tank top, as are all the preteens on the volleyball court behind her. Nora's "team," her sad attempt to distract a few kids from reality for two hours a week. I walk past her without so much as a nod, and as I start to push the front doors open I hear her sneakers slapping the tile floor behind me.

"Perry!"

I stop and let the doors swing shut. I turn around and face her. "Hey."

She stands in front of me with her arms crossed, her eyes stony. "So today's the big day, huh?"

"I guess so."

"What area are you hitting? You got it all planned out?"

"The old Pfizer building on Eighth Ave."

She nods rapidly. "Good, that sounds like a good plan, Perry. And you'll be all done and home by six, right? 'Cause remember we're taking you to the Orchard tonight. We're not letting you spend today moping alone like you did last year."

I watch the kids in the gym, bumping-setting-spiking, laughing and cursing. "I don't know if I'll make it. This salvage might go a little later than usual."

She keeps nodding. "Oh. Oh okay. Because that building is crooked and full of cracks and dead ends and you have to be extra careful, right?"

"Right."

"Yeah." She nods toward the envelope in my hand. "You checked that yet?"

"Not yet."

"Well you should probably check it, Perry." Her foot taps the floor; her body vibrates with restrained anger. "You need to make sure you know everyone's profiles, strengths and weaknesses and all that. Mine, for instance, because I'm on there."

My face goes blank. "What?"

"Sure, I'm going, Rosso put me on yesterday. Do you know my strengths and weaknesses? Is there anything on your agenda you think might be an issue for me? 'Cause I'd hate to jeopardize your very first salvage as team manager."

I rip the top off the envelope and start scanning the names.

"Julie signed up, too, did she mention that?"

My eyes flash up from the page.

"That's right, fucker, will that be a problem for you?" Her voice is strained to breaking. There are tears in her eyes. "Is that a conflict at all?"

I shove open the front doors and burst out into the cold morning air. Birds overhead. Those blank-eyed pigeons, those shrieking gulls, all the flies and beetles that eat their shit—the gift of flight dumped on Earth's most worthless creatures. What if it were mine instead? That perfect, weightless freedom. No fences, no walls, no borders; I would fly everywhere, over oceans and continents, mountains and jungles and endless open plains, and somewhere in the world, somewhere in all that distant untouched beauty, I would find a reason.

• • •

I am floating in Perry's darkness. I am deep in the earth, buried upside down. Somewhere beyond my feet are roots and worms and an inverted graveyard where the coffins are the markers and the headstones are beneath, piercing down into that airy blue emptiness, hiding all the names and pretty epitaphs and leaving me with the rot.

I feel a stirring in the dirt that surrounds me. A hand burrows through and grabs my shoulder.

"Hello, corpse."

• • •

We are in the 747. My piles of souvenirs are sorted and arranged in neat stacks. The aisle is softened with layers of oriental throw rugs. Dean Martin croons on the record player.

"Perry?"

He's in the cockpit, in the pilot's chair with his hands on the controls. He's wearing a pilot's uniform, the white shirt stained with blood. He smiles at me, then gestures at the windows, where streaks of clouds flicker past. "We are now approaching cruising altitude. You're free to move about the cabin."

With slow, cautious movements, I get up and join him in the cockpit. I look at him uneasily. He grins. I rub a finger through the familiar layers of dust on the controls. "This isn't one of your memories, is it?"

"No. This is yours. I wanted you to be comfortable."

"Is it your grave I'm standing on right now?"

He shrugs. "I suppose. I think it's just my empty skull in there, though. You and your friends took most of me home for snacks, remember?"

I open my mouth to apologize again, but he shuts his eyes and waves it away. "Don't, please. We're past all that. Besides, that wasn't really *me* you killed, that was older, wiser Perry. I think this is mostly junior-high Perry you're talking to, young and optimistic and writing a novel called *Ghosts vs. Werewolves*. I'd rather not think about being dead right now."

I eye him uncertainly. "You're a lot more cheerful here than in your memories."

"I have perspective here. It's hard to take your life so seriously when you can see it all at once."

I peer at him. His reality is very convincing, pimples and all. "Are you . . . really you?" I ask.

"What does that mean?"

"All this time I've been talking to you, are you just . . . leftovers from your brain? Or are you really actually you?"

He chuckles. "Does it really actually matter?"

"Are you Perry's soul?"

"Maybe. Kind of. Whatever you want to call it."

"Are you . . . in Heaven?"

He laughs and tugs his blood-soaked shirt. "Yeah, not exactly. Whatever I am, 'R,' I'm in *you*." He laughs again at the look on my face. "Fucked up, isn't it? But Older Wiser went out of this life pretty darkly. Maybe this is our chance to catch up with him and work some things out before . . . you know. Whatever's next."

I look out the window. No glimpse of land or sea, just the silky mountains of Cloud World spread out below us and piled high above. "Where are we headed?"

"Toward whatever's next." He lifts his eyes to the heavens with mock solemnity, then grins. "You're going to help me get there, and I'm going to help you."

I feel my guts twist as the plane surges and drops on erratic air currents. "Why would you help me? I'm the reason you're dead."

"Come on, R, don't you get this yet?" He seems upset by my question. He locks eyes with me and there's a feverish intensity in them. "You and I are victims of the same disease. We're fighting the same war, just different battles in different theaters, and it's way too late for me to hate you for anything, because we're the same damn thing. My soul, your conscience, whatever's left of me woven into whatever's left of you, all tangled up and conjoined." He gives me a hearty clap on the shoulder that almost hurts. "We're in this together, corpse."

A low tremor rumbles through the plane. The control stick

wobbles in front of Perry, but he ignores it. I don't know what to say, so I just say, "Okay."

He nods. "Okay."

Another faint vibration in the floor, like the concussions of distant bombs.

"So," he says. "God has made us study partners. We need to talk about our project." He takes a deep breath and looks at me, tapping his chin. "I've been hearing a lot of inspirational thoughts prancing around in our head lately. But I'm not sure you really understand the storm we're flying into."

A few red lights blink on in the cabin. There is a scraping noise somewhere outside the plane.

"What am I missing?" I ask.

"How about a strategy? We're wandering around this city like a kitten in a dog kennel. You keep talking about changing the world, but you're sitting here licking your paws while all the pit bulls circle in on us. What's the plan, pussycat?"

Outside, the cotton clouds darken to steel wool. The lights flicker, my souvenirs rattle.

"I don't . . . have one yet."

"So when? You know things are moving. You're changing, your fellow Dead are changing, the world is ready for something miraculous. What are we waiting for?"

The plane shudders and begins to dive. I stumble into the copilot chair, feeling my stomach rise into my throat. "I'm not waiting. I'm doing it right now."

"Doing what? What are you doing?"

"I'm trying." I hold Perry's gaze and grip the sides of my seat as the plane shakes and groans. "I'm wanting it. I'm making myself care."

Perry's eyes narrow and his lips tighten, but he doesn't say anything.

"That's step one, isn't it?" I yell over the noise of wind and roaring engines. "That's where it has to start."

The plane lurches and my souvenir stacks collapse, scattering paintings, movies, dishes, dolls and love notes all over the cabin. More lights flare in the cockpit, and a voice crackles on the radio.

R? Helloooo? Are you okay?

Perry's face has gone cold, all playfulness gone. "Bad stuff is coming, R. Some of it's waiting for you right outside this graveyard. You're right, wanting change is step one, but step two is taking it. When the flood comes, I don't want to see you dreaming your way through it. You've got my little girl with you now."

Okay, you're creeping me out. Wake up!

"I know I didn't deserve her," Perry says, his quiet murmur somehow rising above the noise. "She offered me everything and I pissed on it. So now it's your turn, R. Go keep her safe. She's a lot softer than she seems."

God damn it you asshole! Wake up or I'll fucking shoot you!

I nod. Perry nods. Then he turns to face the window and folds his arms across his chest while the controls shake wildly. The storm clouds peel apart and we are diving to earth, hurtling directly toward the stadium, and there they are, the infamous R and J, sitting on a blanket on the rainsoaked roof. R looks up and sees us, his eyes open wide just as we—

. . .

My eyes open wide and I blink reality into focus. I am standing in front of a small grave in an amateur cemetery. Julie's hand is on my shoulder.

"Are you back?" she asks. "What the hell was that about?"

I clear my throat and look around. "Sorry. Daydreaming."

"God you're weird. Come on, I don't want to be here anymore." She strides briskly toward the exit.

Nora and I follow her. Nora keeps pace with me, eyeing me sideways. "Daydreaming?" she asks.

I nod.

"You were talking to yourself a little."

I look at her.

"Some pretty big words, too. I think I heard 'miraculous.'"

I shrug.

The waterfall noise of the city rushes into our ears as the guards open the doors and we step back into the stadium proper. The doors have barely slammed shut behind us when I feel that baby kick in my stomach again. A voice whispers, *Here it comes, R. Are you ready?*

"Oh this is lovely," Julie says under her breath.

There he is, marching around the street corner in front of us: Julie's dad, General Grigio. He strides directly toward us, trailed by three officers of some kind, although none of them wear traditional military attire. Their uniforms are light gray shirts and work pants, no decorations or rank insignias, just pockets and tool loops and laminated ID badges. High-caliber sidearms gleam softly in their belt holsters.

"Be cool, R," Julie whispers. "Don't say anything, just, um . . . pretend you're shy."

"Julie!" the general calls out from an awkward distance.

"Hi, Dad," Julie says.

He and his retinue stop in front of us. He gives Julie's shoulder a quick squeeze. "How are you?"

"Fine. Just went to see Mom."

His jaw muscle twitches, but he doesn't respond. He looks at Nora, gives her a nod, then looks at me. He looks at me very hard. He pulls out a walkie-talkie. "Ted. The individual who slipped past you yesterday. You said it was a young man in a red tie? Tall, thin, poorly complected?"

"Dad," Julie says.

The walkie squawks. The general puts it away and pulls a pair of thumb cuffs from his belt. "You are being detained for unauthorized entry," he recites. "You will be held in—"

"Jesus Christ, Dad." Julie steps forward to push his hands away. "What is wrong with you? He's not an *intruder,* he's visiting from

Goldman Dome. And he almost died on the way here, so cut him some slack on the legalities, will you?"

"Who is he?" the general demands.

Julie edges in front of me as if to block me from responding. "His name is . . . Archie—it was Archie, right?" She glances at me and I nod. "He's Nora's new boyfriend. I just met him today."

Nora grins and squeezes my arm. "Can you believe what a nice dresser he is? I didn't think anyone knew what a tie *was* anymore."

The general hesitates, then puts the cuffs away and forces a thin smile. "Pleased to meet you, Archie. You're aware of course that if you want to stay any longer than three days you'll need to register with our immigration officer."

I nod and try to avoid eye contact, but I can't seem to look away from his face. Although that tense dinner I witnessed in my visions couldn't have been more than a few years ago, he looks a decade older. His skin is thin and papery. His cheekbones protrude. His veins are blue in his forehead.

One of the officers with him clears his throat. "So sorry to hear about Perry, Miss Cabernet. We'll miss him very much." I know this man as well. Colonel Rosso is older than Grigio but has aged more gracefully. He is short and thick, with strong arms and a muscular chest above the inevitable old-man paunch. His hair is wispy and white, blue eyes big and watery behind thick glasses. Julie gives him a smile that seems genuine.

"Thanks, Rosy. So will I."

Their exchange sounds proper but rings false, as if paddling above deep undercurrents. I suspect they have already shared a less professional moment of grief somewhere away from Grigio's officious gaze. "We appreciate your condolences, Colonel Rosso," he says. "However I'll thank you not to replace our surname when addressing my daughter, whatever such 'revisions' she may have embraced."

The older man straightens. "Apologies, sir. I meant nothing by it."

"It's just a nickname," Nora says. "Me and Perry thought she was more of a cab than a . . ."

She trails off under Grigio's stare. He pans slowly over to me. I avoid eye contact until he dismisses me. "We have to be going," he says to no one in particular. "Good to meet you, Archie. Julie, I'll be in meetings all night tonight and then heading over to Goldman in the morning to discuss the merger. I expect to be back at the house in a few days."

Julie nods. Without another word, the general and his men depart. Julie examines the ground, seeming far away. After a moment, Nora breaks the silence. "Well that was scary."

"Let's go to the Orchard," Julie mutters. "I need a drink."

I'm still looking down the street, watching her father shrink into the distance. Just before rounding a corner he glances back at me, and my skin prickles. Will Perry's flood be of water, gentle and cleansing, or will it be a flood of a different kind? I feel movement under my feet. A faint vibration, as if the bones of every man and woman ever buried are rattling deep in the earth. Cracking the bedrock. Stirring the magma.

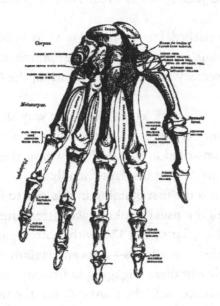

Tᴀᴇ Oʀᴄʜᴀʀᴅ, as it turns out, is not part of the stadium's farming system. It's their one and only pub, or at least the closest thing they have to a pub in this new bastion of prohibition. Reaching its entrance requires an arduous vertical journey through the stadium's Escheresque cityscape. First, we climb four flights of stairs in a ramshackle housing tower while the residents glare at us through cracks in their doors. This is followed by a vertiginous crossing to a neighboring building—boys on the ground try to look up Nora's skirt as we wobble over a wire-mesh catwalk strung between the towers' support cables. Once inside the other building, we plod up three more flights of stairs before finally emerging onto a breezy patio high above the streets. The noise of crowds rumbles through the door at the other end: a wide slab of oak painted with a yellow tree.

I push awkwardly ahead of Julie to open the door for her. Nora grins at her and Julie rolls her eyes. They step inside and I follow them.

The place is packed, but the mood is eerily subdued. No shouting, no high-fiving, no woozy requests for phone numbers. Despite the speakeasy secrecy of its obscure location, the Orchard doesn't serve alcohol.

"I ask you," Julie says as we push our way through the well-behaved crowds, "is there anything sillier than a bunch of ex-marines and construction workers drowning their sorrows at a fucking juice bar? At least it's flask-friendly."

The Orchard is the first building in this city to have some trace of character. All the usual drinking accoutrements are here: dartboards, pool tables, flat-screen TVs with football games. At first I'm amazed to see these broadcasts—does entertainment still exist? Are there still people out there engaging in frivolity despite the times? But then, ten minutes into the third quarter, the images warp like VHS tape and switch to a different game, the teams and scores changing in the middle of a tackle. Five minutes later they switch again, with just a quick stutter to mark the splice. None of the sports fans seem to notice. They watch these abbreviated, eternally looping contests with blank eyes and sip their drinks like players in a historical reenactment.

A few of the patrons notice me staring at them and I look away. But then I look back. Something about this scene is burrowing into my mind. A thought is developing like a ghost on a Polaroid.

"Three grapefruits," Julie tells the bartender, who looks vaguely embarrassed as he prepares the drinks. We settle in on bar stools and the two girls start talking. The music of their voices replaces the jangling classic rock on the jukebox, but then even this fades to a muffled drone. I'm staring at the TVs. I'm staring at the people. I can see the outline of their bones under their muscles. The edges of joints poking up under tight skin. I see their skeletons, and the idea taking shape in my head is something I hadn't expected: a blueprint of the Boneys. A glimpse into their twisted, dried-up minds.

The universe is compressing. All memory and all possibility squeezing down to the smallest of points as the last of their flesh falls away. To exist in that singularity, trapped in one static state for eternity—this is the Boneys' world. They are dead-eyed ID photos, frozen at the precise moment they gave up their humanity. That hopeless instant when they snipped the last thread and dropped into the abyss. Now there's nothing left. No thought, no feeling, no past, no future. Nothing exists but the desperate need to keep things *as they are,* as they *always have been.* They must stay on the rails of their loop or be overwhelmed, set ablaze and consumed by the colors, the sounds, the wide-open sky.

And so the thought hums in my head, whispering through my nerves like voices through phone lines: *What if we could derail them?* We've already disrupted their structure enough to incite a blind rage. What if we could create a change so deep, so new and astonishing, they would simply *break?* Surrender? Crumble into dust and ride out of town on the wind?

"R," Julie says, poking me in the arm. "Where are you? Daydreaming again?"

I smile and shrug. Once again my vocabulary fails me. I'm going to need to find a way to let her into my head soon. Whatever this thing is I'm trying to do, I know it can't be done alone.

The bartender returns with our drinks. Julie grins at me and Nora as we appraise the three tumblers of pale yellow nectar. "Remember how when we were kids, pure grapefruit juice was the toughguy drink? Like the whiskey of kiddie beverages?"

"Right," Nora laughs. "Apple juice, Capri Sun, that stuff was for bitches."

Julie raises her glass. "To our new friend, Archie."

I start to lift my glass off the bar and the girls clang theirs down against it. We drink. I don't exactly taste it, but the juice stings my mouth, finding its way into old cuts in my cheeks, bites I don't remember biting.

Julie orders another round, and when it arrives she hefts her messenger bag onto her shoulder and picks up all three glasses. She leans in close and gives me and Nora a wink. "Be right back." With the drinks in hand, she disappears into the bathroom.

"What's . . . she doing?" I ask Nora.

"Dunno. Stealing our drinks?"

We sit there in awkward silence, third-party friends lacking the connective tissue of Julie's presence. After a few minutes, Nora leans in and lowers her voice. "You know why she said you were my boyfriend, right?"

I shrug one shoulder. "Sure."

"It didn't mean anything, she was just trying to deflect attention away from you. If she said you were *her* boyfriend, or her friend, or anything to do with *her*, Grigio would've grilled the fuck out of you. And obviously if he really *looks* at you . . . the makeup's not perfect."

"I under . . . stand."

"And by the way, just so you know? That was a pretty big deal that she took you to see her mom today."

I raise my eyebrows.

"She doesn't tell people that stuff, ever. She didn't even tell *Perry* the whole story for like three years. I can't say exactly what that means for her, but . . . it's new."

I study the bar top, embarrassed. A strangely fond smile spreads across Nora's face. "You know you remind me a little of Perry?"

I tense. I begin to feel the hot remorse boiling up in my throat again.

"I don't know what it is, I mean you're sure not the blowhard he was, but you have some of that same . . . *sparkle* he had when he was younger."

I should stitch my mouth shut. Honesty is a compulsion that's damned me more than once. But I just can't hold it in anymore. The words build and explode out of me like an uncontainable sneeze. "I killed him. Ate . . . his brain."

Nora purses her lips and nods slowly. "Yeah . . . I thought you might have."

My face goes blank. "What?"

"I didn't see it happen, but I've been putting two and two together. It makes sense."

I look at her, stunned. "Julie . . . knows?"

"I don't think so. But if she did, I'm pretty sure she'd be okay." She touches my hand where it rests on the bar. "You could tell her, R. I think she'd forgive you."

"Why?"

"Same reason I forgive you."

"*Why?*"

"Because it wasn't you. It was the plague."

I wait for more. She watches the TV above the bar, pale green light flickering over her dark face. "Did Julie ever tell you about when Perry cheated on her with that orphan girl?"

I hesitate, then nod.

"Yeah, well . . . that was me."

My eyes dart toward the bathroom, but Nora doesn't seem to be hiding anything. "I'd only been here a week," she says. "Didn't know Julie yet. That's how I met her, actually. I fucked her boyfriend, and she hated me, and then time passed and a lot happened, and somehow we came out the other side as friends. Crazy, right?" She upends her empty glass over her tongue to catch the last drops, then pushes it aside. "What I'm trying to say is, it's a shitty world and shit happens, but we don't have to bathe in shit. Sixteen years old, R—my meth-head parents dumped me in the middle of a Dead-infested slum because they couldn't feed me anymore. I wandered on my own for *years* before I found Citi Stadium, and I don't have enough fingers to count all the times I almost died." She holds up her left hand and wiggles the half-gone finger like a bride-to-be showing off her diamond. "What I'm saying is, when you have weight like that in your life, you have to start looking for the bigger picture or you are gonna *sink.*"

I peer into her eyes, failing to read her meaning like the illiterate I am. "What's . . . the bigger picture . . . of me killing Perry?"

"R, come on," she says, mock-slapping the side of my head. "You're a zombie. You have the plague. Or at least you did when you killed Perry. Maybe you're different now—I sure *hope* you are—but back then you didn't know you had choices. This isn't 'crime,' it's not 'murder,' it's something way deeper and more inevitable." She taps her temple. "Me and Julie get that, okay? There's a Zen saying, 'No praise, no blame, just so.' We don't care about assigning blame for the human condition, we just want to cure it."

Julie emerges from the bathroom and sets the drinks on the bar with a sly grin. "Even grapefruit juice can use a little kick sometimes."

Nora takes a test sip and turns away, covering her mouth. "Holy . . . Lord!" she coughs. "How much did you put in here?"

"Just a few minis of vodka," Julie whispers with girlish innocence. "Courtesy of our friend Archie, and Undead Airlines."

"Way to go *Archie*."

I shake my head. "Can please . . . stop calling me . . ."

"Right, right," Julie says. "No more Archie. But what do we toast to this time? It's your booze, R, you decide."

I hold the glass in front of me. I sniff it, insisting to myself that I can still smell things besides death and potential death, that I'm still human, still whole. A citrus tang pricks my nostrils. Glowing Florida orchards in summer. The toast that enters my head seems unbearably corny, but it comes out anyway. "To . . . life."

Nora stifles a laugh. "Really?"

Julie shrugs. "Corny, but what the hell." She raises her glass and clinks it against mine. "To life, Mr. Zombie."

"*L'chaim!*" Nora bellows, and drains her glass.

Julie drains her glass.

I drain my glass.

The vodka slams into my brain like a round of buckshot. This time it's no placebo. The drink is strong and I *feel* it. I am *feeling it*. How is that possible?

Julie orders another round of grapefruits, then promptly converts them into greyhounds, and she is generous with the pours. I expect the girls to be as lightweight as I am since alcohol is contraband here, but I realize it's probably quite routine to visit the liquor store while out salvaging the city. They quickly outpace me as I sip my second drink, marveling at the sensations that swirl through my body. The noise of the bar fades and I just watch Julie, the focal point in my blurry composition. She is laughing. A free, unreserved kind of laugh that I don't think I've heard before, throwing her head back and letting it just cascade out of her. She and Nora are recounting some shared memory. She turns to me and says something, inviting me into the joke with a word and a flash of white teeth, but I don't respond. I just look at her, resting my chin in my hand, my elbow on the bar, smiling.

Contentment. Is this what it might feel like?

After finishing my drink I feel a pressure in my lower regions, and I realize I have to piss. Since the Dead don't drink, urination is a rare event. I hope I can remember how to do it.

I wobble into the bathroom and lean my forehead against the wall in front of the urinal. I unzip, and I look down, and there it is. That mythical instrument of life and death and first-date backseat fucking. It hangs limp, useless now, silently judging me for all the ways I've misused it over the years. I think of my wife and her new lover, slapping their cold bodies together like poultry in a packing plant. I think of the anonymous blurs in my past life, probably all dead or Dead by now. Then I think of Julie curled next to me in that king-size bed. I think of her body in that comically mismatched underwear, her breath against my eyes as I study every line in her face, wondering what mysteries lie in the glowing nuclei of her cells.

There in the bathroom, surrounded by the stench of piss and shit, I wonder: Is it too late for me? Can I somehow snatch another chance from the skymouth's grinding teeth? I want a new past, new memories, a new first handshake with love. I want to start over, in every possible way.

When I come out of the bathroom the floor is spinning. Voices are muffled. Julie and Nora are deep in conversation, leaning close and laughing. A man in his early thirties approaches the bar and makes some kind of leering comment to Julie. Nora glares at him, says something that looks sarcastic, and Julie shoos him away. The man shrugs and retreats to the pool table, where his friend is waiting. Julie calls out something insulting and the friend laughs, but the man just grins coldly and calls back a retort. Julie looks frozen for a moment, then she and Nora turn their backs to the pool table and Nora starts whispering in Julie's ear.

"What's . . . wrong?" I ask, approaching the bar. I can sense both men at the pool table watching me.

"Nothing," Julie says, but she sounds shaken. "It's fine."

"R, could you give us a quick minute?" Nora says.

I look back and forth between them. They wait. I turn and walk out of the bar, feeling too many things at once. On the patio I slump against the railing, the streets a dizzying seven floors down. Most of the city's lights are out, but the streetlamps flicker and pulse like bioluminescence. Julie's mini cassette player is an insistent weight in my shirt pocket. I pull it out and stare at it. I know I shouldn't but I'm . . . I feel like I just need—

Closing my eyes, swaying gently with one arm on the railing, I rewind the tape for a moment and press play.

"—really that crazy? Just because he's . . . whatever he is? I mean, isn't 'zombie' just a silly name we—"

I press rewind again, and it occurs to me that the gap between the beginning of this entry and the end of the previous one comprises the entire time I've known Julie. Every meaningful moment of my life fits inside a few seconds of tape hiss.

I press stop, then play.

"—thinks no one knows but everyone knows, they're just afraid to do anything. He's getting worse, too. He said he loved me tonight. Actually said those words. Said I was beautiful and I was everything he loved about Mom and if anything ever happened to me he'd lose his mind. And I know *he meant it, I know all of that's really there inside him . . . but the fact that he had to be raging shitfaced drunk to let any of it out . . . it just made the whole thing seem sick. I fucking hated it."*

There is a long pause on the tape. I glance over my shoulder at the bar door, ashamed but desperate. I know these are confidences I should have to earn through months of slow intimacy, but I can't help myself. I just want to listen to her.

"I've thought about making a report," she continues. *"March into the community center and make Rosy go arrest him. I mean, I'm all for drinking, I love it, but with Dad it's . . . different. It's not a celebration for him, it seems like it's painful and scary, like he's numbing himself for some horrible medieval surgery. And yeah . . . I know why, and it's not like I haven't done worse stuff for the same reasons, but it's just . . . it's so . . ."* Her voice wavers and breaks off, and she sniffles hard like a self-rebuke. *"God,"* she whispers away from the microphone. *"Shit."*

Several seconds of tape hiss. I listen closer. Then the door flies open and I whirl around, tossing the player out into the dark. But it's not Julie. It's the two men from the pool table. They stumble out the door, jostling each other and laughing through the sides of their mouths as they light up cigarettes.

"Hey," the one who was talking to Julie calls to me, and he and his friend start ambling in my direction. He's tall, good-looking, his muscular arms sleeved in tattoos: snakes and skeletons and the logos of extinct rock bands. "What's up, man? You Nora's new guy?"

I hesitate, then shrug. They both laugh like I've made a dirty joke.

"Yeah, who ever knows with that chick, right?" He punches his friend in the chest while continuing to saunter toward me. "So you know Julie? You Julie's friend?"

I nod.

"Known her long?"

I shrug, but I feel a coil inside me tensing.

He stops a few feet away from me and leans against the wall, taking a slow drag on his cigarette. "That one used to be pretty wild too, a few years back. I was her firearms teacher."

I need to leave. I need to turn around right now and leave.

"She got all 'pure' after she started dating that Kelvin kid, but man, for a year or so she was ripe fruit." His exhalations form a haze of smoke that stings my dry eyes. "A hundred bucks won't even buy a pack of cigarettes anymore, but it sure went a long way with that bitch."

I lunge forward and crack his head into the wall. It's easy, I just palm his face and thrust forward like a shot putter, punching the wall with the back of his skull. I don't know if I've killed him and I don't care. When his friend tries to grab me I do the exact same to him, two big dents in the Orchard's aluminum siding. Both men slump to the ground. I wobble my way down the stairs and out onto the catwalk. Some kids leaning on the support cables smoking joints stare at me as I shove past them. *Excuse me,* I try to say, but I can't seem to find the syllables. I slide down the four apartment floors and lurch out onto Fairy Street or Tinkerbell Street or whatever the fuck it's called. I just need to get away from all these people for a minute, collect my thoughts. I'm so hungry. God, I'm starving.

After a few minutes of wandering, I'm completely lost and disoriented. A light rain is falling and I'm alone on some dark narrow street. The asphalt glitters black and wet under the crooked streetlamps. Up ahead, two guards converse in a rain-flecked cone of light, grunting to each other with the affected toughness of scared boys straining to be men.

". . . out in Corridor 2 all last week, pouring foundations. We're less than a mile away from Goldman Dome but we've barely got a fuckin' crew anymore. Grigio keeps pulling guys off Construction and dumping 'em into Security."

"What about the Goldman crew? How's their end coming?"

"Goldman is shit. They're barely out their front door. I've been hearing the merger's in bad shape anyway, thanks to Grigio's bad diplomacy. Starting to wonder if he even *wants* the mergers any-more, the way he handled Corridor 1. Wouldn't surprise me if he arranged the collapse himself."

"You know that's bullshit. Don't be spreading that story around."

"Yeah, well, either way, Construction's gone to shit since Kelvin got squished. We're just digging holes and filling 'em in."

"I'd still rather be out building something than playing rent-a-cop in here all night. You get any action out there?"

"Just a couple of Fleshies wandering out of the woods. Pop, pop, game over."

"No Boneys?"

"Haven't seen one of them in at least a year. They stick to their hives nowadays. Fuckin' bullshit."

"What, you *like* running into those things?"

"Hell of a lot more fun than Fleshies. Fuckers can *move*."

"Fun? Are you shitting me? Those things are *wrong;* I don't even like touching 'em with my bullets."

"Is that why your hit rate's one in twenty?"

"Doesn't even seem like they're human remains anymore, you know? They're like aliens or something. Creeps the shit out of me."

"Yeah well that's probably 'cause you're a pussy."

"Fuck you. I'm going to take a leak."

The guard disappears into the dark. His partner stands in the spotlight, pulling his parka tighter as the rain comes down. I'm still walking. I'm not interested in these men; I'm looking for a quiet corner where I can close my eyes and gather myself. But as I approach the light, the guard notices me, and I realize there's a problem. I'm *drunk*. My carefully studied gait has been replaced by an unsteady stagger. I lumber forward, my head lolling from side to side.

I look like . . . exactly what I am.

"Halt!" the guard shouts.

I halt.

He moves toward me a little. "Step into the light, please, sir."

I step into the light, standing on the very edge of the yellow circle. I try to stand as straight as I can, as motionless as I can. Then I realize something else. The rain is dripping off my hair. The rain is running down my face. The rain is washing away my makeup, revealing the pale gray flesh underneath. I stumble back a step, slightly out of the lamplight.

The guard is about five feet away from me. His hand is on his gun. He moves closer and peers at me through slitted eyes. "Have you been drinking alcohol tonight, sir?"

I open my mouth to say, *No, sir, absolutely not, just a few glasses of delicious and heart-healthy grapefruit juice with my good friend Julie Cabernet.* But the words evade me. My tongue is thick and dead in my mouth, and all that comes out is, "Uhhhnnn . . ."

"What the fuck—" The guard's eyes flash wide, he whips out his flashlight and shines it into my gray-streaked face, and I have no choice. I leap out of the shadows and pounce on him, knocking his gun aside and biting down on his throat. His life force rushes into my starved body and brain, soothing the agony of my hideous cravings. I start to tear into him, chewing deltoids and tender abdominals while the blood still pulses through them—but then I stop.

Julie stands in the bedroom doorway, watching me with a tentative smile.

I shut my eyes and grit my teeth.

No.

I drop the body to the ground and back away from it. I can no longer hide behind my ignorance. I know now that I have a choice, and I choose to change no matter what the cost. If I'm a thriving branch on the Tree of Death, I'll drop my leaves. If I have to starve myself to kill its twisted roots, I will.

The fetus in my stomach kicks, and I hear Perry's voice, gentle and reassuring. *You won't starve, R. In my short life I made so many choices just because I thought they were required, but my dad was right: there's no rule book for the world. It's in our heads, our collective human hive-mind. If there are rules, we're the ones making them. We can change them whenever we want to.*

I spit out the meat in my mouth and wipe the blood off my face. Perry kicks me in the gut again and I vomit. I lean over and purge myself of everything. The meat, the blood, the vodka. As soon as I straighten up and wipe my mouth, I'm sober. The fuzz is gone. My head is clear as a glossy new record.

The guard's body begins to twitch back to life. His shoulders slowly rise, dragging the rest of his limp parts with them, as if he's being pinched and pulled upward by unseen fingers. I need to kill him. I know I need to kill him, but I can't do it. After the vow I've just made, the thought of tearing into this man again and tasting his still-warm blood leaves me paralyzed with horror. He shudders and retches, choking and clawing the dirt, straining and dry-heaving, his eyes bulging wide as the gray sludge of new death slithers into them. A wet, wretched groan escapes his mouth, and it's too much for me. I turn and run. Even in my bravest moment, I am a coward.

• • •

The rain is in full force. My feet splash in the streets and spatter mud on my freshly washed clothes. My hair hangs in my face like seaweed. In front of a big aluminum building with a plywood cross on the roof, I kneel in a puddle and splash water on my face. I wash my mouth out with dirty gutter runoff and spit until I can't taste anything. That holy wooden "t" looms overhead, and I wonder if the Lord might ever find cause to approve of me, wherever and whatever he is.

Have you met him yet, Perry? Is he alive and well? Tell me he's not just the mouth of the sky. Tell me there's more looking down on us than that empty blue skull.

Perry doesn't answer. I accept the silence. I get off my knees and I keep running.

Avoiding streetlights, I make my way back to Julie's house. I curl up against the wall, finding some shelter from the balcony over-head, and I wait there while the rain pounds the house's metal roof. After what seems like hours, I hear the girls' voices in the distance, but this time their rhythms stir no joy in me. The dance is a dirge, the music is minor.

They run toward the front door, Nora with her denim jacket pulled over her head, Julie with the hood of her red sweatshirt cinched tight on her face. Nora reaches the door first and rushes inside. Julie stops. I don't know if she sees me in the dark or just smells the fruity stench of my body spray, but something draws her to look around the corner of the house. She sees me huddled in the dark like a lost puppy. She ambles over slowly, her hands stuffed into her sweatshirt pockets. She crouches down and peeks out at me through the narrow opening of her hood. "You okay?" she says.

I nod dishonestly.

She sits next to me on the small patch of dry ground and leans against the house. She takes off her hood and lifts the wool beanie underneath to brush wet hair out of her eyes, then pulls it back down. "You scared me. You just disappeared."

I look at her miserably, but I don't say anything.

"Do you want to tell me what happened?"

I shake my head.

"Did you, um . . . did you knock out Tim and Matt?"

I nod.

A smile of embarrassed pleasure creeps onto her face, as if I've just given her an overlarge bouquet of roses or written her a bad love song. "That was . . . sweet," she says, holding back a giggle. A minute passes. She touches my knee. "We had fun today, didn't we? Despite a few sticky moments?"

I can't smile, but I nod.

"I'm a little buzzed. You?"

I shake my head.

"Too bad. It's fun." Her smile deepens and her eyes become far-away. "You know I had my first drink when I was eight?" There is just a faint slur in her voice. "My dad was a big wine buff and him and Mom used to throw tasting parties whenever Dad was between wars. They'd bring all their friends over and pop a prized vintage and get pretty well toasted. I'd sit there in the middle of the couch taking little sips off the half glass I was allowed and just laugh at all the silly grownups getting sillier. Rosy would get so flushed! One glass and he looked like Santa Claus. He and Dad arm-wrestled on the coffee table once and broke a lamp. It was . . . so great."

She starts doodling in the dirt with one finger. Her smile is wistful, aimed at no one. "Things weren't always so grim, you know? Dad has his moments, and even when the world fell apart we still had some fun. We'd take little family salvage trips and pick up the most crazy wines you can imagine. Thousand-dollar bottles of '97 Dom Romanée-Conti just rolling around on the floors of abandoned cellars." She chuckles to herself. "Dad would have absolutely lost his shit over those back in the day. By the time we moved here he was kinda . . . muted. But God, we drank some outrageous stuff."

I'm watching her talk. Watching her jaw move and collecting her words one by one as they spill from her lips. I don't deserve them. Her warm memories. I'd like to paint them over the bare plaster walls of my soul, but everything I paint seems to peel.

"And then Mom ran off." She pulls her finger out of the dirt, inspecting her work. She has drawn a house. A quaint little cottage with a smoke cloud in the chimney, a benevolent sun smiling down on the roof. "Dad thought she must have been drunk, hence the booze ban, but I saw her, and she wasn't. She was very sober."

She is still smiling, as if this is all just easy nostalgia, but the smile is cold now, lifeless.

"She came into my room that night and just looked at me for a while. I pretended I was asleep. Then right as I was about to pop up and yell 'boo' . . . she walked out. I didn't get to say anything."

She reaches a hand down to wipe away her drawing, but I touch her wrist. I look at her and shake my head. She regards me silently for a moment. Then she scoots around to face me and grins, inches from my face.

"R," she says, "if I kiss you, will I die?"

Her eyes are steady. She's *barely* drunk.

"You said I won't, right? I won't get infected? Because I really feel like kissing you." She fidgets. "And even if you do pass something to me, maybe it wouldn't be all bad. I mean, you're different now, right? You're *not* a zombie. You're . . . something new." Her face is very close. Her smile turns serious. "Well, R?"

I look into her eyes, splashing in their icy waters like a ship-wrecked sailor grasping for the raft. But there is no raft.

"Julie," I say. "I need . . . to show you something."

She cocks her head with gentle curiosity. "What?"

I stand up. I take her hand and start walking.

The night is still except for the primeval hiss of the rain. It drenches the dirt and slicks the asphalt, liquefying the shadows into shiny black ink. I stick to the narrow backstreets and unlit alleys. Julie follows slightly behind me, staring at the side of my face.

"Where are we going?" she asks.

I pause at an intersection to retrace the maps of my stolen mem-ories, calling up images of places I've never been, people I've never met. "Almost . . . there."

A few more careful glances around corners, furtive dashes across intersections, and there it is. A five-story house looms ahead of us, tall, skinny, and gray like the rest of this skeletal city, its windows flickering yellow like wary eyes.

"What the hell, R?" Julie whispers, staring up at it. "This is . . ."

I pull her to the front door and we stand there in the shelter of the eaves, the roof rattling like military drums in the rain. "Can I . . . borrow your hat?" I ask without looking at her.

She doesn't move for a moment, then she pulls it off and hands it to me. Overlong and floppy, dark blue wool with a red stripe . . .

Mrs. Rosso knitted this for Julie's seventeenth birthday. Perry thought she looked like an elf in it and would start speaking to her in Tolkien

*tongues whenever she put it on. She called him the biggest nerd she'd ever
met, and he agreed, while playfully kissing her throat and—*

I pull the beanie low over my face and knock a slow waltz on
the door, eyes glued to the ground like a shy child. The door opens
a crack. A middle-aged woman in sweatpants looks out at us. Her
face is puffy and heavily lined, dark bags under bloodshot eyes.
"Miss Grigio?" she says.

Julie glances at me. "Hi, Mrs. Grau. Um . . ."

"What are you doing out? Is Nora with you? It's after curfew."

"I know, we . . . got a little lost on our way back from the Orchard. Nora's staying at my house tonight but um . . . can we come
in for a minute? I need to talk to the guys."

I keep my head down as Mrs. Grau gives me a cursory appraisal.
She opens the door for us with an annoyed sigh. "You can't stay
here, you know. This is a foster home, not a flophouse, and your
friend here is too old for new residency."

"I know, sorry, we'll . . ." She glances at me again. "We'll just be
a minute."

I can't endure formalities right now. I brush past the woman and
into the house. A toddler peeks around a bedroom door and Mrs.
Grau glares at him. "What did I tell you?" she snaps, loud enough
to wake the rest of the kids. "Back in bed right now." The boy disappears into the shadows. I lead Julie up the staircase.

The second story is identical to the first, except there are rows of
preadolescents sleeping on the floor on small mats. So many now.
New foster homes pop up like processing plants as mothers and
fathers disappear, chewed up and swallowed down by the plague.
We step over a few tiny bodies on our way to the stairs, and a little
girl grasps feebly at Julie's ankle.

"I had a bad dream," she whispers.

"I'm sorry, honey," Julie whispers back. "You're safe now, okay?"

The girl closes her eyes again. We climb the stairs. The third
floor is still awake. Young teens and patch-beard semiadults sitting
around on folding chairs, hunched over desks writing in booklets

and flipping through manuals. Some kids snore on stacked bunks inside narrow bedrooms. All the doors are open except one.

A few older boys look up from their work, surprised. "Wow, hey Julie. How's it going? You holding up okay?"

"Hey guys. I'm . . ." She trails off, and her ellipsis eventually forms a period. She looks at the closed door. She looks at me. Gripping her hand, I move forward and open the door, then shut it behind us.

The room is dark except for the faint yellow glow of streetlamps through the window. There is nothing in here but a plywood dresser and a stripped bed, with a few pictures of Julie taped to the ceiling above it. The air is stale and much colder than the rest of the house.

"R . . . ," Julie says in a quivery, dangerous voice. "Why the *fuck* are we here?"

I finally turn to face her. In the yellow dimness, we look like actors in a silent sepia tragedy. "Julie," I say. "That theory . . . about why we . . . eat the brain . . ."

She starts to shake her head.

"True."

I look into her reddening eyes a moment longer, then kneel down and open the bottom drawer of the dresser. Inside, under piles of old stamps, a microscope, an army of pewter figurines, there is a stack of paper bound together with red yarn. I lift it out and hand it to Julie. In so many strange and twisted ways, I feel like the manuscript is mine. Like I've just handed her my own bloody heart on a platter. I am fully prepared for her to claw it to shreds.

She takes the manuscript. She unties the yarn. She stares at the cover page for a full minute, breathing shakily. Then she wipes her eyes and clears her throat.

"'*Red Teeth*,'" she reads. "'By Perry Kelvin.'" She glances down the page. "'For Julie Cabernet, the only light left.'" She lowers the manuscript and looks away for a moment, trying to hide a spasm in her throat, then steels herself and turns the page to the first chapter. As she reads, a faint smile peeks through the tear tracks. "Wow," she says, wiping a finger across her nose and sniffling. "It's actually . . . kinda good. He used to write such dry and detached bullshit. This is . . . cheesy . . . but in a sweet way. More like how he really was." She glances at the cover page again. "He started it less than a year ago. I had no idea he was still writing." She flips to the last page. "It's not finished. Cuts off in the middle of a sentence. 'Outmanned and outgunned, certain of death, he kept fighting, because—'"

She rubs her thumbs into the paper, feeling its texture. She puts it near her face and inhales. Then she closes her eyes, closes the manuscript, and reties the yarn. She looks up at me. I am nearly a foot taller than her and probably sixty pounds heavier, but I feel small and featherweight. Like she could knock me down and crush me with a single whispered word.

But she doesn't speak. She sets the manuscript back in the drawer and gently slides it shut. She straightens up, dries her face with her sleeve, and embraces me, resting her ear against my chest.

"Thump-thump," she murmurs. "Thump-thump. Thump-thump."

My hands hang limp at my sides. "I'm sorry," I say.

With her eyes closed, her voice muffled by my shirt, she says, "I forgive you."

I raise a hand and touch her straw-gold hair. "Thank you."

These three phrases, so simple, so primal, have never sounded so complete. So true to their basic meanings. I feel her cheek move against my chest, her zygomaticus major pulling her lips into a faint smile.

Without another word, we shut the door on Perry Kelvin's room and leave his home. We descend the stairs past beleaguered teens, past tossing and turning kids, past deeply dreaming babies, and out into the street. I feel a nudge low in my chest, closer to my heart than my belly, and a soft voice in my head.

Thank you, Perry says.

• • •

I would like to end it here. How nice if I could edit my own life. If I could halt in the middle of a sentence and put it all to rest in a drawer somewhere, consummate my amnesia and forget all the things that have happened, are happening, and are about to happen. Shut my eyes and go to sleep happy.

But no, "R." No sleep of the innocent. Not for you. Did you forget? You have blood on your hands. On your lips. On your teeth. Smile for the cameras.

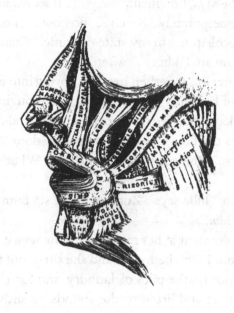

"Julie," I say, bracing to confess my final sin. "I need . . . to tell you . . ."

BANG.

The stadium's field halogens flare like suns and midnight becomes daylight. I can see every pore in Julie's face.

"What the hell?" she gasps, whipping her head around. A piercing alarm further shatters the night's stillness, and then we see it: the Jumbotron is aglow. Hanging from the upper reaches of the open roof like a tablet descending from Heaven, the screen plays a blocky animation of a quarterback running from what appears to be a zombie, arms outstretched and clutching. The screen blinks between this and a word that I think might be:

BREACH

"R . . . ," Julie says, horrified, "did you *eat* someone?"

I look at her desperately. "No ch . . . no choi . . . no *choice*," I stutter, my diction collapsing in my state of panic. "Guard . . . stopped me. Didn't . . . mean. Didn't . . . *want*."

She presses her lips together, her eyes boring into me, then gives a single shake of her head as if banishing one thought, committing to another. "Okay. Then we need to get inside. God damn it, R."

We run into the house and she slams the door. Nora is at the top of the stairs. "Where have you guys been? What's going *on* out there?"

"It's a breach," Julie says. "Zombie in the stadium."

"You mean *him*?"

The disappointment in her reply makes me wince. "Yes and no."

We hurry into Julie's bedroom and she turns out the lights. We all sit on the floor on the piles of laundry, and for a while nobody speaks. We just sit and listen to the sounds. Guards running and shouting. Gunfire. Our own heavy breathing.

"Don't worry," Julie whispers to Nora, but I know it's for me. "It won't spread much. Those shots were probably Security taking him out already."

"Are we in the clear, then?" Nora asks. "Will R be okay?"

Julie looks at me. Her face is grim. "Even if they think the breach started from a natural death, that guard obviously didn't eat himself. Security will know there's at least one zombie unaccounted for."

Nora follows Julie's eyes to mine, and I can almost imagine my face flushing. "It was you?" she asks, straining for neutrality.

"Didn't . . . mean. Was . . . going . . . kill me."

She says nothing. Her face is blank.

I meet her stare, willing her to feel my crushing remorse. "It was my last," I say, straining to force language back into my idiot tongue. "No matter what. Swear to the skymouth."

A few agonizing moments pass. Then Nora slowly nods, and addresses Julie. "So we need to get him out of here."

"They shut everything down for breaches. All the doors will be locked and guarded. They might even shut the roof if they get scared enough."

"So what the hell are we supposed to do?"

Julie shrugs, and the gesture looks so bleak on her, so wrong. "I don't know," she says. "Once again, I don't know."

. . .

Julie and Nora fall asleep. They fight it for hours, trying to come up with a plan to save me, but eventually they succumb. I lie on a pile of pants and stare up at the starry green ceiling. *Not so easy, Mr. Lennon. Even if you try.*

It seems trivial now, a thin silver lining on a vast black storm-cloud, but I think I'm learning to read. As I look up at the phosphorescent galaxy, letters come together and form words. Stringing them into full sentences is still beyond me, but I savor the sensation of those little symbols clicking together and bursting like soap bubbles of sound. If I ever see my wife again . . . I'll at least be able to read her nametag.

The hours ooze by. It's after midnight but bright as noon outside. The halogens ram their white light against the house, squeezing in through cracks in the window shades. My ears tune to the sounds around me. The girls' breathing. Their small shifting movements. And then, sometime around two in the morning, a phone rings.

Julie comes awake, gets up on one elbow. In some distant room of the house, the phone rings again. She throws off her blankets and stands up. Strange to see her from this angle, towering over me instead of cowering under. I'm the one who needs protecting now. One mistake, one brief lapse of my newfound judgment—that's all it took to unravel everything. What a massive responsibility, being a moral creature.

The phone keeps ringing. Julie walks out of the bedroom and I follow her through the dark, echoing house. We step into what appears to be an office. There is a large desk covered in papers and blueprints, and on the walls various kinds of telephones are screwed to the drywall, different brands and styles from all different eras.

"They rerouted the phone system," Julie explains. "It's more like an intercom now. We have direct lines to all the important areas."

Each phone has a nametag sticker stuck below it, with the location Sharpied onto the blank. *Hi, my name is:*

GARDENS
KITCHENS
WAREHOUSE
GARAGE
ARMORY
CORRIDOR 2
GOLDMAN DOME
LEHMAN ARENA
AIG FIELD

And so on.

The phone that's ringing, a pea-green rotary-dialer covered in dust, is labeled:

OUTSIDE

Julie looks at the phone. She looks at me. "This is weird. That line is from the phones in the abandoned outer districts. Since we got walkie-talkies nobody uses it anymore."

The phone clangs its bells, loud and insistent. I can't believe Nora is still asleep.

Slowly, Julie picks up the receiver and puts it to her ear. "Hello?" She waits. "What? I can't under—" Her brow furrows in concentration. Then her eyes widen. "*Oh.*" They narrow. "*You.* Yeah this is Julie, what do *you*—" She waits. "Fine. Yeah, he's right here."

She holds the phone out to me. "It's for you."

I stare at it. "What?"

"It's your friend. That fat fuck from the airport."

I grab the phone. I put the earpiece to my mouth. Julie shakes her head and flips it around for me. Into the receiver I breathe a stunned "*M?*"

His deep rumble crackles in my ear. "Hey . . . loverboy."

"What's . . . Where are you?"

"Out in . . . city. Didn't know . . . what would get with . . . phone, but had . . . to try. You're . . . okay?"

"Okay but . . . trapped. Stadium . . . locked down."

"Shit."

"What's . . . going on? Out there?"

There is silence for a moment. "R," he says. "Dead . . . still coming. More. From airport. Other places. Lots . . . of us now."

I'm silent. The phone wanders away from my ear. Julie looks at me expectantly.

"Hello?" M says.

"Sorry. I'm here."

"Well we're . . . *here*. What now? What should . . . do?"

I rest the phone on my shoulder and look at the wall, at nothing. I look at the papers and plans on General Grigio's desk. His strategies are all gibberish to me. I have no doubt it's all important—food allocation, construction plans, weapon distribution, combat tactics. He's trying to keep everyone alive, and that's good. That's foundational. But like Julie said, there must be something even deeper than that. The earth *under* that foundation. Without that firm ground, it's all going to collapse, over and over, no matter how many bricks he lays. This is what I'm interested in. The earth under the bricks.

"What's going on?" Julie asks. "What's he saying?"

As I look into her anxious face, I feel the twitch in my guts, the young, eager voice in my head.

It's happening, corpse. Whatever you and Julie triggered, it's moving. A good disease, a virus that causes life! Do you see this, you dumb fucking monster? It's inside you! You have to get out of these walls and spread it!

I angle the phone toward Julie so she can listen. She leans in close.

"M," I say.

"Yeah."

"Tell Julie."

"What?"

"Tell Julie . . . what's happening."

There's a pause. "Changing," he says. "Lots of us . . . changing. Like R."

Julie looks at me and I can almost sense her neck hairs standing on end. "It's not just you?" she says, moving away from the phone. "This . . . reviving thing?" Her voice is small and tentative, like a little girl poking her head out of a bomb shelter after years of life in the dark. It almost quivers with tight-leashed hope. "Are you saying the plague is healing?"

I nod. "We're . . . fixing things."

"But *how?*"

"Don't know. But we have to . . . do more of it. Out there . . . where M is. 'Outside.'"

Her excitement cools, hardens. "So we have to leave."

I nod.

"Both of us?"

"Both," M says, his voice crackling in the earpiece like an eaves-dropping mother. "Julie . . . part of it."

She eyes me dubiously. "You want *me.* Skinny little human girl. Out there in the wild, running with a pack of zombies?"

I nod.

"Do you grasp how insane that is?"

I nod.

She is silent for a moment, looking at the floor. "Do you really think you can keep me safe?" she asks me. "Out there, with them?"

My incurable honesty makes me hesitate, and Julie frowns.

"Yes," M answers for me, exasperated. "He can. And I'll . . . help."

I nod quickly. "M will help. The others . . . will help. Besides," I add with a faint smile, "you can . . . keep yourself safe."

She shrugs nonchalantly. "I know. I just wanted to see what you'd say."

"So you'll . . . ?"

"I'll go with you."

"You're . . . sure?"

Her eyes are distant and hard. "I had to bury my mom's empty dress. I've been waiting for this a long time."

I nod. I take a deep breath.

"The only problem with your plan," she continues, "is that you seem to be forgetting you *ate* someone last night, and this place is going to stay clamped shut until they find and kill you."

"Should we . . . attack?" M says. "Get you . . . out?"

I put the phone back to my ear, gripping the receiver hard. "No," I tell him.

"Have . . . army. Where's . . . battle?"

"Don't know. Not here. These are . . . people."

"Well?"

I look at Julie. She looks at the ground and rubs her forehead. "Just wait," I tell M.

"Wait?"

"A little longer. We'll . . . figure it out."

"Before . . . they kill you?"

"Hopefully."

A long, dubious silence. Then: "Hurry up."

• • •

Julie and I stay up all night. In our rain-wet clothes we sit on the floor in the cold living room and don't say a word. Eventually my eyes sag shut, and in this strange calm, in what may be my last few hours on Earth, my mind creates a dream for me. Crisp and clear, alive with color, unfolding like a time-lapse rose in the sparkling darkness.

In this dream, *my* dream, I am floating down a river on my house-jet's severed tail fin. I am lying on my back under the blue midnight, watching the stars drift by above me. The river is uncharted because the maps have burned and the satellites have crashed, and I have no idea where it leads. The air is still. The night is warm. I've brought only two provisions: a box of pad thai and Perry's book. Thick. Ancient. Bound in leather. I open it to the middle. An unfinished sentence in some language I've never seen, and beyond it, nothing. An epic tome of empty pages, blank white and waiting. I shut the book and lay my head down on the cool steel. The pad thai tickles my nose, sweet and spicy and strong. I feel the river widening, gaining force.

I hear the waterfall.

. . .

"R."

My eyes open and I sit up. Julie is cross-legged next to me, watching me with grim amusement.

"Having some nice dreams?"

"Not . . . sure," I mumble, rubbing my eyes.

"Did you happen to dream up any solutions to our little problem?"

I shake my head.

"Yeah, me either." She glances at the wall clock and bunches her lips ruefully. "I'm supposed to be at the community center in a few hours to do story time. David and Marie are going to cry when I don't show up."

David and Marie. I repeat the names in my head, savoring their contours. I would let that dog eat my whole leg for the chance to see those kids again. To hear a few more clumsy syllables tumble from their mouths before I die. "What are . . . you reading them?"

She looks out the window at the city, its every crack and flaw brought into sharp relief by the blinding white light. "I've been trying to get them into the Redwall books. I figured all those songs and feasts and courageous warrior mice would be a nice escape from the nightmare they're growing up in. Marie keeps asking for books about zombies and I keep telling her I can't read nonfiction for *story* time, but . . ." She notices the look on my face and trails off. "Are you okay?"

I nod.

"Are you thinking about your kids at the airport?"

I hesitate, then nod.

She reaches out and touches my knee, looking into my stinging eyes. "R? I know things look bleak right now, but listen. You can't quit. As long as you're still breathe—sorry, as long as you're still *moving*, it's not over. Okay?"

I nod.

"Okay? Fucking say it, R."

"Okay."

She smiles.

"TWO. EIGHT. TWENTY-FOUR."

We jolt away from each other as a speaker in the ceiling blares out a series of numbers followed by a shrill alert tone.

"This is Colonel Rosso with a community-wide notice," the speaker says. *"The Security breach has been contained. The infected officer has been neutralized, with no further casualties reported."*

I release a deep breath.

"However . . ."

"Shit," Julie whispers.

". . . the original source of the breach remains at large within our walls. Security patrols will now begin a door-to-door search of every building in the stadium. Since we don't know where this thing might be hiding, everyone should come out of their houses and congregate in a public area. Do not confine yourself in any small spaces." Rosso pauses to cough. *"Sorry about this, folks. We'll get it taken care of, just . . . sit tight."*

There's a click, and the PA goes quiet.

Julie jumps to her feet and storms into the bedroom. She pulls open the blinds, letting the floodlights burst through the window. "Rise and shine, Miss Greene, we're out of time. Do you remember any old exits in the wall tunnels? Wasn't there a fire escape somewhere by the skybox? R, can you climb a ladder?"

"Wait, what?" Nora croaks, trying to shield her eyes. "What's happening?"

"According to R's friend, maybe the end of this shitty undead world, if we don't get killed first."

Nora finally comes awake. "Sorry, *what*?"

"I'll tell you later. They just announced a sweep. We have maybe ten minutes. We need to find . . ." Her voice fades and I watch her mouth move. The shapes her lips make for each word, the flick of tongue against glistening teeth. She is holding on to hope but my grip is slipping. She twists at her hair as she talks, her golden tresses stiff and matted and in need of a wash.

The spicy smell of her shampoo, flowers and herbs and cinnamon dancing with her natural oils. She would never say what brand she used. She liked to keep her scent a mystery.

"R!"

Julie and Nora are staring at me, waiting. I open my mouth to speak, but I have no words. And then the front door of the house bangs open so hard it resonates through the metal walls all the way to where we're standing. Heavy, booted footfalls pound the stairs.

"Oh Jesus," Julie says in a panicked breath. She herds us out of the room and into the hallway bathroom. "Get his makeup back on," she hisses to Nora, and slams the door shut.

As Nora fumbles her compact out of her purse and tries to re-rouge my rain-stained face, I hear two voices out in the hall.

"Dad, what's going on? Did they find the zombie?"

"Not yet, but they will. Have you seen anything?"

"No, I've been here."

"Are you alone?"

"Yeah, I've been here since last night."

"Why is the bathroom light on?"

Footsteps pound toward us.

"Wait, Dad! Wait a second!" She lowers her voice. "Nora and Archie are in there."

"Why did you just tell me you're here alone? This is not a time for games, Julie, this is not a time for hide-and-seek."

"They're . . . you know . . . *in there.*"

There is the briefest of hesitations. "Nora and Archie," he shouts at the door, his voice compressed and extremely loud. "As you just heard on the intercom there is a breach in progress. I cannot begin to imagine a worse time for lovemaking. Come out immediately."

Nora straddles me against the sink and buries my face in her cleavage just as Grigio yanks the door open.

"*Dad!*" Julie squeals, flashing Nora a quick look as she jumps off of me.

"Come out immediately," Grigio says.

We step out of the bathroom. Nora straightens her clothes and pats down her hair, doing a pretty good job of looking embarrassed. I just look at Grigio, unapologetic, limbering up my diction for its first and probably last big test. He looks back at me with that taut, angular face, peering into my eyes. There are less than two feet between us.

"Hello, Archie," he says.

"Hello, sir."

"You and Miss Greene are in love?"

"Yes, sir."

"That is wonderful. Have you discussed marriage."

"Not yet."

"Why delay. Why deliberate. These are the last days. Where do you live, Archie?"

"Goldman . . . Field."

"Goldman Dome?"

"Yes, sir. Sorry."

"What work do you do at Goldman Dome."

"Gardens."

"Does that work allow you and Nora to feed your children?"

"We don't have children, sir."

"Children replace us when we die. When you have children you will need to feed them. I'm told things are bad at Goldman Dome. I'm told you are running out of everything. It's a dark world we live in, isn't it, Archie."

"Sometimes."

"We do the best we can with what God gives us, don't we. If God gives us stones when we ask for bread, we will sharpen our teeth and eat stones."

"Or make . . . our own bread."

Grigio smiles. "Are you wearing makeup, Archie?"

Grigio stabs me.

I didn't even notice the knife coming out of its sheath. The five-inch blade sinks into my shoulder and pokes out the other side. I don't feel it and I don't flinch. The wound doesn't bleed.

"Julie!" Grigio roars, stepping back from me and drawing his pistol, his eyes wild in their deep sockets. "Did you bring the Dead into my city? Into my home? Did you let the Dead touch you?"

"Dad, listen to me," Julie says, holding her hands out toward him. "R is different. He's *changing*."

"The Dead don't change, Julie! They are not people, they are things!"

"How do we *know* that? Just because they don't talk to us and tell us about their lives? We don't understand their thoughts so we assume they don't have any?"

"We've done tests! The Dead have never shown any signs of self-awareness or emotional response!"

"Neither have *you*, Dad! Jesus Christ—R saved my life! He

protected me and brought me home! He's *human*! And there are more like him!"

"No," Grigio says, abruptly calm. His hands stop wavering and the gun steadies, inches from my face.

"Dad, please listen to me? Please?" She takes a step closer. She is trying to stay cool but I can tell she is terrified, and I hate myself for being the cause. "When I was at the airport, something happened. We sparked something, and whatever it is, it's spreading. The Dead are coming back to life, they're leaving their hives and trying to change what they are, and we have to find a way to help. Imagine if we could *cure* the plague, Dad! Imagine if we could clean up this mess and start over!"

Grigio shakes his head. I can see his jaw muscles tightening under his waxy skin. "Julie, you are young. You don't understand. We can stay alive and we can kill the things that want to kill us, but there is no grand solution. We searched for years and never found one, and now our time is up. The world is over. It can't be cured, it can't be salvaged, it can't be saved."

"Yes it *can*!" Julie screams at him, losing all composure. "Who decided life has to be a nightmare? Who wrote that fucking rule? We can fix it, we've just never *tried* before! We've always been too busy and selfish and scared!"

Grigio grits his teeth. "You are a dreamer. You are a child. You are your mother."

"Dad, *listen*!"

"No."

He cocks the gun and presses it against my forehead, directly onto Julie's Band-Aid. Here it comes. Here is M's everpresent irony. My inevitable death, ignoring me all those years when I wished for it daily, arriving only after I've decided I want to live forever. I close my eyes and brace myself.

A spatter of blood warms my face—but it's not mine. My eyes flash open just in time to see Julie's knife glancing off Grigio's hand. The gun flies out of his grip and fires when it hits the floor, then again and again as the recoil knocks it against the walls of the narrow hall like a ricocheting Super Ball. Everyone drops for cover, and the gun finally spins to rest touching Nora's toes. In the deafened silence she stares down at it, wide-eyed, then looks at the general. Cradling his gashed hand, he lunges. Nora snatches the gun off the floor and aims it at his face. He freezes. He flexes his jaw and inches forward as if about to pounce anyway. But then Nora pops out the spent ammo clip, whips a fresh one out of her purse, shoves it into the gun and chambers a round, all one liquid motion without ever taking her eyes off his. Grigio steps back.

"Go," she says, her eyes flicking to Julie. "Try to get out somehow. Just try."

Julie grabs my hand. We back out of the room while her dad stands there vibrating with rage.

"Good-bye, Dad," Julie says softly. We turn and run down the stairs.

"*Julie!*" Grigio howls, and the sound reminds me so much of another sound, a hollow blast from a broken hunting horn, that I shiver in my damp shirt.

• • •

We are running. Julie stays in front, leading us through the cramped streets. Behind us, angry shouts ring out from the direction of Julie's house. Then the squawk of walkie-talkies. We are running, and we are being chased. Julie's leadership is less than decisive. We zigzag and backtrack. We are rodents scrambling in a cage. We run as the looming rooftops spin around us.

Then we hit the wall. A sheer concrete barrier laced with scaffolding, ladders, and walkways to nowhere. All the bleachers are gone, but one staircase remains; a dark hallway beckons to us from the top. We run toward it. Everything on either side of the staircase has been stripped away, leaving it floating in space like Jacob's ladder.

A shout flies up from the ground below just as we reach the opening. "Miss Grigio!"

We turn and look down. Colonel Rosso is at the bottom of the steps, surrounded by a retinue of Security officers. He is the only one without his gun drawn.

"Please don't run!" he calls to Julie.

Julie pulls me into the hallway and we sprint into the dark.

This inner space is clearly under construction, but most of it remains exactly as it was abandoned. Hot dog stands, souvenir kiosks, and overpriced pretzel booths sit cold and lifeless in the shadows. The shouts of the Security team echo behind us. I wait for the dead-end that will halt us, that will force me to turn and face the inevitable.

"R!" Julie pants as we run. "We're going to get out, okay? We're *going* to!" Her voice is cracking, halfway between exhaustion and tears. I can't bring myself to respond.

The hallway ends. In the faint light creeping through holes in the concrete, I see a sign on the door:

EMERGENCY EXIT

Julie runs faster, dragging me behind her. We slam into the door and it flies open—

"Oh shhh—" she gasps, and whips around, grabbing on to the door frame as one foot dangles out over an eight-story drop.

Cold wind whistles around the doorway, where torn stumps of a fire escape protrude from the wall. Birds flutter past. Below, the city spreads out like a vast cemetery, high-rises like headstones.

"Miss Grigio!"

Rosso and his officers roll to a stop about twenty feet behind us. Rosso is breathing hard, clearly too old for hot pursuit.

I look out the door at the ground below. I look at Julie. I look down again, then back at Julie.

"Julie," I say.

"What?"

"Are you *sure* you want . . . to come with me?"

She looks at me, straining to force breath through her rapidly constricting bronchial tubes. There are questions in her eyes, maybe doubts, surely fears, but she nods. "Yes."

"Please stop running," Rosso groans, leaning against his knees. "This is not the way."

"I have to go," she says.

"Miss Cabernet. *Julie.* You can't leave your father here. You're all he has left."

She bites her lower lip, but her eyes are steely. "Dad's dead, Rosy. He just hasn't started rotting yet."

She grabs my hand, the one I shattered on M's face, and squeezes so hard I think she might break it even further. She looks up at me. "Well, R?"

I pull her to me. I wrap my arms around her and hold tight enough to fuse our genes. We are face-to-face and I almost kiss her, but instead I take two steps backward, and we fall through the doorway.

We plummet like a shot bird. My arms and legs encircle her, almost completely enveloping her tiny body. We crash through a roof overhang, a support bar tears into my thigh, my head bounces off a beam, we tangle in a cell phone banner and rip it in half, and then, finally, we hit the ground. A chorus of cracks and crunches shoots through me as my back greets the earth and Julie's weight flattens my chest. She rolls off me, choking and gasping for breath, and I lie there staring up at the sky. Here we are.

Julie raises herself on hands and knees and fumbles her inhaler out of her bag, takes a shot and holds it, supporting herself against the ground with one arm. When she can breathe again she crouches over me with terror in her eyes. Her face eclipses the hazy sun. "R!" she whispers. "Hey!"

As slow and shaky as the day I first rose from the dead, I lift myself upright and hobble to my feet. Various bones grind and crackle throughout my body. I smile, and in my breathy, tuneless tenor, I sing, "You make . . . me feel so young . . ."

She bursts out laughing and hugs me. I feel the pressure snap a few joints back into place.

She looks up at the open doorway. Rosso is framed in it, looking down at us. Julie waves to him, and he disappears back into the stadium with a swiftness that suggests pursuit. I try not to begrudge the man his paradigm—perhaps in his world, orders are orders.

So Julie and I run into the city. With each step I feel my body stabilizing, bones realigning, tissues stiffening around cracks to keep me from falling apart. I've never felt anything like this before. Is this some form of *healing*?

We dash through the empty streets, past countless rusty cars and drifts of dead leaves. We violate one-way streets. We blow stop signs. Ahead of us: the edge of town, the high grassy hill where the city opens up and the freeway leads elsewhere. Behind us: the relentless roar of assault vehicles gunning out of the stadium gate. *This cannot stand!* declare the steel-jawed mouths of the rulemakers. *Find those little embers and stomp them out!* With these howls at our backs, we crest the hill.

We are face-to-face with an army.

They stand in the grassy field next to the freeway ramps. Hundreds of them. They mill around in the grass, staring at the sky or at nothing, their gray, sunken faces oddly serene. But when the front line sees us they freeze, then pivot in our direction. Their focus spreads in a wave until the entire mob is standing at attention. Julie gives me an amused glance as if to say, *Really?* Then a disturbance ripples through the ranks and a burly, bald, six-foot-five zombie pushes his way into the open.

"M," I say.

"R." He gives Julie a quick nod. "Julie."

"Hiiii . . . ," she says, leaning into me warily.

Our pursuers' tires screech and we hear a rev of engines. They are very close. M steps up to the peak of the hill and the mob follows him. Julie huddles close to me as they sweep in around us, absorbing us into their odorous army, their rank ranks. It could be my imagination or a trick of the light, but M's skin looks less ashen than usual. His partial lips seem more expressive. And for the first time since I've known him, his neatly trimmed beard is not stained with blood.

The trucks barrel toward us, but as the swarm of the Dead rises into view on the hilltop, the vehicles slow down, then grumble to a stop. There are only four of them. Two Hummer H2s, a Chevy Tahoe, and an Escalade, all spray-painted military olive drab. The hulking machines look small and pitiful from where we stand. The Tahoe's door opens, and Colonel Rosso slowly emerges. Clutching his rifle, he scans row upon row of swaying bodies, weighing odds and strategies. His eyes are wide behind his thick glasses. He swallows, then lowers his gun.

"I'm sorry, Rosy," Julie calls down to him, and points at the stadium. "I can't do it anymore, okay? It's a fucking lie. We think we're surviving in there but we're *not*."

Rosso is looking hard at the zombies arrayed around him, peering into their faces. He's old enough that he's probably been around since the beginning of all this. He knows what the Dead are supposed to look like, and he can tell when something's different, no matter how subtle, subliminal, subcutaneous.

"You can't save the world by yourself!" he yells. "Come back and we can discuss this!"

"I'm not by myself," Julie says, and gestures at the forest of zombies swaying around her. "I'm with these guys."

Rosso's lips twist in a tortured grimace, then he jumps in his vehicle, slams the door, and revs back toward the stadium with the other three right behind. A brief respite, a quick suck of breath, because I know they aren't quitting, they *can't* quit, they're just gathering their strength, their weapons, their brute-force determination.

And well they should, because look at us. We are several hundred monsters and a hundred-pound girl, standing on the edge of their city with fire in our eyes. Deep under our feet Earth holds its molten breath, while the bones of countless generations watch us and wait.

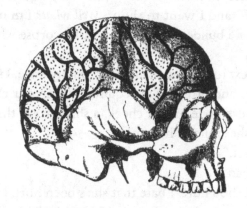

We ARE MASSED on the freeway on-ramp. Behind us, the city. In front of us, angular hills of alders and landscaped medians leading back toward the airport. Julie stands close by my side, looking a lot less confident than the brash revolutionary she just portrayed for Rosso. I put a hand on her shoulder and address the crowd.

"Julie!"

The crowd shivers, and I hear one or two sets of teeth snap. I raise my voice. "*Julie!* We keep her safe."

A few of them look tempted, but for the most part what I see in their eyes isn't hunger. It's the same fascination I saw back in the airport, intensified. More focused. They're not just looking at her, they're studying her. *Absorbing* her. Strange spasms ripple through their bodies every few seconds.

I catch M giving her a slightly different kind of stare, and I snap my fingers in his face.

"Come on," he says as if I'm being unreasonable.

I sit down on the concrete barrier, struggling to think. The noise of Rosso's trucks is still fading into the distance. Everyone is looking at me. Impatient stares from every direction. It's a look that says, *Well?* and I want to shout, *Well what?* I'm not a general or a colonel or a builder of cities. I'm just a corpse who wants not to be.

Julie sits next to me and puts a hand on my knee. I finally notice all the scrapes and bruises she acquired during our chuteless skydive. There's even one on her cheek, a shallow cut that makes her wince when she smiles. I hate it.

"You're hurt," I say.

"Not too bad."

I hate that she's hurt. I hate that she's been hurt, by me and by others, throughout the entire arc of her life. I barely remember pain, but when I see it in her I feel it in myself, in disproportionate measure. It creeps into my eyes, stinging, burning.

"Why did . . . you come?" I ask her.

"To help, remember? And to keep you safe."

"But why?"

She gives me a soft smile, and the cut on her cheek brightens with fresh blood. "Because I like you, Mr. Zombie." She wipes the blood away, looks at it, then smears it down my neck. "There. Now we're even."

Watching her sitting next to me, this blue-eyed angel surrounded by the drooling Dead, this fragile girl smiling with bloody lips into a highly uncertain future, I feel something surge in me. My vision blurs, and a wet trail streaks down my face. The burning in my eyes cools.

Julie touches my cheek and looks at her finger. She stares at me with such fascination I can't return her gaze. Instead I stand up and blurt, "We're going back to the airport."

The Dead look at me. They look at M.

"Why?" M says.

"Because it's where . . . we live. Where . . . we start."

"Start . . . what? War? Fight Boneys?"

"Not war. Not . . . that kind."

"Then what?"

As I stand there trying to answer, trying to distill the whirlwind of images in my head—music in the airport's dark halls, my kids coming out of their hiding places and dusting off their pinkening skin, a movement, a change—as I stand there dreaming, the hushed city air shivers with a scream. A frantic, gurgling howl like a cow thrashing around half-butchered.

Someone is coming toward us from farther down the freeway. He's running, but his lumbering gait betrays his biological status. M rushes out to meet the newcomer. I watch them converse, the newcomer waving his hands and gesturing in a way that creates a sinking feeling in my stomach. He is, without question, a bringer of bad news.

He merges into our crowd and M walks slowly back to me, shaking his head.

"What?" I ask.

"Can't . . . go home."

"Why not?"

"Boneys . . . going crazy. Coming in . . . from everywhere. Killing all who . . . differ."

I look at the newcomer. What I at first took for severe decomposition is actually severe injury, countless bites and claw marks. Farther down the road, there are more like him. Some are on the freeway, some stumble through the mud and grass in the medians, a widely dispersed crowd of hundreds.

"Ones like us . . . trying to escape," M continues. "And Boneys . . . chasing them."

Just as he says this, as if cued by the sound of their name, Death's publicists make their entrance. One, then two, then five and six spindly white shapes burst out of the distant trees and overtake two of the fleeing zombies. I watch the skeletons drag them down and hammer their heads against the pavement. I watch them stomp out their brains like so much rotten fruit. And I watch them multiply, rolling out of the trees and down the freeway slopes as far back as I can see, gathering on the road in a vast, clattering swarm.

"Oh fuck this . . . ," Julie whispers.

"New plan?" M inquires with forced calm.

I stand there in a trance of indecision. I am back in Julie's bedroom, lying next to her on a pile of her laundry, and she's saying, *There's nowhere left, is there?* And I am grimly shaking my head, telling her that the entire world is now covered in death. In the back of my awareness I can hear the rumble of SUVs, a lot more than four, barreling down Main Street to snuff me out and drag Julie back to their concrete tomb, embalm her like a princess and lay her down for eternity in some fluorescent-lit ossuary.

So here we are. Trapped in the gap between the cradle and the grave, no longer able to fit in either.

"New plan!" M says, jolting me out of my reverie. "Go into . . . city."

"Why the hell would we go in there?" Julie says.

"Lead Boneys in. Let Living . . . clean up."

"Wrong," she snaps at him. "Security doesn't discriminate between Boneys and Fleshies. They'll wipe you all out equally."

"We'll . . . hide," M says. He points down the freeway slope to a wide valley of rambler homes and grassy roundabouts gone to seed. It's the northern extremity of the suburbs where Julie and I nested for a night, once upon a time in a mildewed fairy tale.

"What, just hide out and hope Security and the skeletons deal with each other?"

M nods.

Julie pauses for two seconds. "That's a terrible plan, but okay, let's go." She turns to run, but M puts his hand on her shoulder. She claws it off and whirls on him. "What are you doing? Don't fucking touch me!"

"You . . . go with R," M says.

"What?" I ask him, perking to attention, and he fixes his dry gray eyes on me as he strains for language.

"We draw them . . . this way. You take her . . . that way."

"Excuse me?" Julie squeaks. "He's not 'taking me' anywhere, why the fuck would we split up?"

M points to a bruised and bleeding gash on her arm, then the cut on her cheek. "Because you're . . . fragile," he says in a surprisingly tender voice. "And . . . important."

Julie looks at M. She says nothing. She and I have somehow found ourselves outside the rim of the crowd, and everyone is watching us. The Boneys are close enough now for us to hear them. The scraping of their brittle feet and the low, warbling hum of whatever dark energy powers them. The shadowblack marrow seething in their bones.

I nod to M and he nods back. I take Julie's hand. She resists briefly, keeping her eyes on the crowd, then she turns and looks at me, and we run. M and the others disappear from view as we scramble down the embankment and dash into the crumbled downtown streets. The old ghosts in my head rise from their sleep and run alongside us, eagerly cheering us on.

Something unknown to us, something we've never seen. Memory can't overtake the present; history has its limits. Are we all just Dark Age doctors, swearing by our leeches? We crave a greater science. We want to be proven wrong.

• • •

Within minutes we hear the battle. Machine-gun fire that echoes down the narrow canyons of the streets. Muffled explosions that thump in our chests like distant bass music. The occasional shriek of a Boney, so shrill and piercing it conducts across the distance like electricity through water.

"Should we hide out in one of those?" Julie asks, pointing out a few brick and steel towers. "Just wait it out?"

I nod but I hesitate in the street. I don't know why I hesitate. What else is there now but hiding?

Julie runs to the nearest building. She tries the door. "Locked." She crosses the street to an apartment complex. "Locked." She approaches an old brownstone and rattles the door. "This might—" A window shatters above her; a skeleton scuttles down the wall like a spider and drops onto her back. I sprint across the street and grab the creature by the spine to wrench it off of her, but its pointy fingers are digging into her flesh like barbs. With both hands I grip its skull and strain against it as it tries to bury its teeth in her neck. Despite its withered neck tendons, the thing is unbelievably strong. Its jaws snap, inching toward her.

"Against . . . wall!" I grunt at Julie. She stumbles backward and slams the skeleton against the brick. Its strength falters just long enough for me to twist its head away from her and bash it against the window ledge. The skull cracks. The eyeless face squeezed between my palms seems to look right at me. And although its expression is a permanent grin, I can hear its outraged screams in my head:

STOP. STOP. WE ARE THE SUM OF EVERYTHING.

I bash it against the brick again. The skull cracks wider and the creature's grip on Julie weakens.

YOU WILL BECOME US. WE WILL WIN. ALWAYS HAVE, ALWAYS W—

I wrench the thing to the pavement and ram my shoe through its face. The bones clatter to rest. The hum goes quiet.

I'm about to grab Julie and force my way through the brownstone's rickety door when something happens that I don't understand. The skull under my foot twitches, and as the crushed brain disintegrates, the jaw falls open and releases a wretched, mournful call like an injured bird. It sounds nothing like the bone hum or the horn roar or the skeleton's screaming voice, and I wonder with horror if this is the human being it once was, the last gasp of its freeze-dried soul dissolving into the void. The hairs on my neck stand up. Julie shivers. And as if in response to this plaintive wail, a sound begins to rise in the distant streets. A scrabbling clatter from all directions, a circle of noise tightening in on where we stand. I catch a flicker of motion in the corner of my eye and I look up. The windows of all the buildings are filled with hollow faces. Their naked teeth grin through the glass, leering down like a nightmare jury.

"What is happening?" Julie pleads, exhaustion washing over her face.

I don't want to answer. I'm worried that she is near the brink, and the answer I have is not hopeful. But looking up at the self-satisfied skulls behind those windows, I see no other conclusion. "I think they want . . . *us*," I say. "You and me. They know . . . who we are."

"Who *are* we?"

"Ones who . . . started it."

"Are you shitting me?" she explodes, her eyes darting down the streets as the marching clatter gets louder. "Are you telling me these things hold *grudges*? They're going to *hunt us down* because we accidentally started a little scuffle in their stupid haunted-house airport?"

Julie, Julie, Perry whispers inside my head. I can hear him smiling. *Look at me, babe. Look at R's face and read it there. It's not a grudge. These creatures are far too pragmatic to care about revenge. They're onto you. It's not because you started this scuffle, it's because they know you're going to finish it.*

Julie's look of panic freezes in sudden comprehension. "Oh my God," she whispers.

I nod.

"They're *afraid* of us?"

"Yes."

She considers this a moment, then nods rapidly and looks at the ground, chewing her lip, eyes flicking back and forth. "Okay," she says. "Okay, okay, yes, I've got it. Come on."

She grabs my hand and runs. Directly toward the sound of the oncoming mob.

"What are . . . you doing?" I pant as I run behind her.

"This is Main Street," she says. "This is where Dad's troop met me when I drove home. Right around that corner should be . . ."

It's there. The old red Mercedes, parked halfway into the street, just sitting there waiting for us like a faithful chauffeur. And three blocks ahead: the Boneys' front line, pouring into the street and racing toward us with single-minded purpose. We jump into the car, Julie starts it, and we make a screeching U-turn, weaving in and out of the abandoned vehicles that litter the street—the city's final traffic jam. The Boneys rush in behind us, loping forward with the relentless commitment of the Reaper himself, but we're losing them.

"Where are . . . we going?" I ask as the potholed pavement rattles my jaw.

"Back to the stadium."

I look at her with wide eyes. "What?"

"If the skeletons are after us, specifically *us*, then they'll chase us there, right? They'll give up on the rest of your people and come after us. We can lead them right to the gates."

"And . . . then what?"

"We hide inside while Security takes care of them. There's no way they're going to breach the stadium walls, unless they can fly or something." She glances at me. "They can't fly, can they?"

I look ahead through the windshield, gripping the dash as Julie careens through the ruined streets at extremely unsafe speeds. "Back to . . . the stadium," I repeat.

"I know what you're thinking. It sounds like suicide for you, going back, but I think we can get away with it."

"How? Your dad—"

"My dad wants to kill you, I know. He's just . . . he can't see things anymore. But I think Rosy can. I've known him since I was a kid; he's practically my grandpa, and he's not blind, no matter what he looks like in those glasses. I'm pretty sure he gets what's going on."

Having lost the Boneys in the tangled side streets, we circle back around to Main, slipping through an unfinished section of Corridor 1. Inside the concrete walls, the street is swept clean of cars and debris, pointing toward the stadium straight as a runway. Julie drops into low gear and accelerates until the antique engine rattles. The stadium roof rises on the horizon, rearing up like some monolithic beast. *Climb into my mouth*, it teases. *Come on, kids, don't mind the teeth.*

With certain death rattling behind us, we fly through the heart of the city toward death slightly less certain. Soon we hear an all-too-familiar sound. The rev of big engines and the popcorn of gunfire, but close now, no longer muffled by distance. As the corridor walls dissolve into collapsed concrete and bent rebar frames, the view opens up, and Julie and I stare in horror.

Citi Stadium is already under siege. As if anticipating our plan, separate streams of Boneys are rushing toward the walls from other parts of the city, leaping over cars and scrambling on all fours like skeletal cats. Bullets and bombs blow out storefronts and topple traffic lights as Security does its job, but the skeletons are replenishing from every direction, needing no help from the group advancing behind us. My mind flashes back to the last time I was in this car. Frank and Ava joyriding through their Golden Age romance, a warm bubble of blossoms and birdsong and smiling eyes in Technicolor blue. Was this fiery hellscape there all along, swirling just outside our bubble? These swarms of demons clawing to get in?

This is wrong. It's all wrong. I stare at the growing horde as if I've never seen a walking corpse before. Where are they all coming from? With everything I thought I knew about our decomposition process, there is no accounting for these numbers. It usually takes *years* for us to fully shed our flesh. Even if they're answering some call to arms and pouring in from nearby cities . . . there just shouldn't be this many.

Is this the new face of the plague? Stronger, crueler, gaining traction and speed? Is the hole in the hourglass widening?

Julie looks at me with fresh fear in her eyes. "Do you think . . . ?"

"Don't," I tell her. "Just keep going. Too late . . . to change plans."

She keeps going. She swerves around grenade craters, bounces over curbs, drives on the sidewalk and crashes into pedestrian Boneys like a reeling drunk. Elegant Mercey is starting to look like a crumpled roadside tragedy.

"There!" she shouts suddenly. "That's him!" She revs toward the gate, blaring on the horn. As we get closer I recognize Colonel Rosso standing at the main doors, calling out orders from behind a blockade of armored Suburbans. Julie skids to a stop in front of the trucks and jumps out of the car. "Rosy!" she yelps as she runs toward the doors with me just behind. "Let us in let us in!"

The soldiers raise their rifles, looking at me and then at Rosso. I prepare myself for the bullet that will enter my brain and put an end to all this. But Rosso waves a hand at them. They lower their weapons. We run to the doors and the soldiers close their circle around us, taking aim at our pursuers.

"Miss Cabernet," Rosso says, perplexed. "You saved the world already?"

"Not quite," she pants. "Ran into some snags."

"I see that," he says, surveying the army of dirty yellow bones flooding in through the remains of the corridor.

"You guys can handle them, right?"

"I think so." He watches as his men take down the first wave, then fumble to reload before the next one crashes. "I hope so." He starts to pull open the massive door, then stops and looks at me. "Is what your father said true?" he asks Julie in a very calm voice. "Is this boy what I think he is?"

"Let us in, Rosy. He's my friend."

"Did he kill the guard?"

Julie takes his veiny hand and squeezes it. "Rosy. Please. Please trust me right now."

With his other hand on the door, Rosso stares at me, his squinty eyes unreadable. I stare back. Silently, he opens the door a crack and steps aside. Julie pecks him on the cheek and slips in through the gap. I hesitate at the threshold. The colonel and I regard each other for a moment. Then I give him a nod, he returns it slowly, and I follow Julie inside.

• • •

Once again we are skulking through the rat-maze streets of the stadium, fugitives no matter where we go. Julie speed-walks, scanning street signs, making decisive turns. Her breath sounds tight but she doesn't stop for her inhaler. Bloody and dirty, clothes torn and lungs wheezing, she and I have never been a better match.

"Where are . . . you going?" I ask.

She points at the Jumbotron. A picture of Nora's face is blinking on the screen with a sequence of words:

NORA GREENE

ARMED ASSAULT

ARREST ON SIGHT

"We're going to need her," Julie says. "Whatever happens next, I want to make sure she's with us, not locked in the locker rooms."

I look up at Nora's huge, pixelated face. Her cheerful grin seems incongruous on a wanted poster. "Is that why . . . we came back?" I ask the back of Julie's head. "For her?"

"Fifty-fifty."

A faint smile creeps onto my face. "You have . . . plans," I say in my best attempt at an insinuating tone. "Not just . . . keeping safe."

"I really thought I was finished with this place," she says without slowing down, and leaves it at that.

We stick to the stadium's edges, following the wall around the perimeter. Anchored to the concrete above us, the thick steel support cables twang like sci-fi lasers as the buildings sway and creak in the breeze. The muddy streets are empty. Security forces are probably all outside dealing with the Boneys, while the civilians huddle in their flimsy homes waiting for it to be over. The early evening sky is hazy orange, with high-altitude clouds rippling past the sun. It would be almost peaceful if not for the armies outside, sending their argument through the walls like inconsiderate neighbors.

"I have an idea where she might be," Julie says as she leads us through a dark doorway. "We used to hang out in the walls a lot when we were younger. We'd sit in the VIP rooms and pretend we were celebrities or something. The world was mostly over by then, so it was fun imagining we still mattered."

We ascend several long flights of stairs into an upper level. Most of the doors appear sealed off, but Julie doesn't bother with any of them. She finds a narrow gap in the wall that's been covered over with plastic sheeting, and we squeeze in through a girl-sized tear.

We are in what appears to be the stadium's luxury skybox. Expensive leather chairs lie on their sides around cracked glass tables. Silver snack trays offer clumps of dry mold. On the bar, tumblers wait next to purses like patient boyfriends, unaware that their dates are never coming back from the bathroom.

Nora is sitting in front of the huge viewing window that angles out over the stadium's distant floor. She takes a sip from the bottle of wine in her hand and gives us a big smile. "Look," she says, pointing at the Jumbotron flashing her face. "I'm on TV."

Julie runs over to her and hugs her, spilling a little wine in the process. "You're okay?"

"Sure. Why'd you come back?"

"Have you picked up what's going on outside?"

A distant grenade-blast punctuates the question.

"Lots of skeletons?"

"Yeah. They chased me and R here. They're hunting us."

Nora waves at me. "Hi, R."

"Hi."

"Want some wine? It's an '86 Mouton Rothschild. I'd describe it as yummy, with notes of fucking delicious."

"No thanks."

She shrugs and looks back at Julie. "Hunting you? Why?"

"We think they know what we're trying to do."

A pause. "What are you trying to do?"

"I'm not sure. Fix the world?"

Nora's face looks exactly like Julie's last night on the phone with M, listening to the news she never thought she'd hear. "Really?" she says, the wine bottle dangling between her fingers.

"Yeah."

"How?"

"We don't know yet. We're just going to try. We'll figure it out while trying."

At that moment the Jumbotron goes blank, and the stadium's huge, ceiling-mounted speakers crackle to life. A familiar voice booms across the sky like an insane god.

"Julie. I know you're here. This tantrum you are throwing will end now. I will not let you become your mother. Soft flesh is eaten by hard teeth. She died because she refused to harden."

Down on the ground below, I can see the few remaining guards staring up at the speakers, looking at each other uneasily. They can hear it in his voice. Something is wrong with their commander in chief.

"Our world is under attack and this may be the last of our last days, but you are my priority. Julie. I can see you."

As his words reverberate through the speakers I feel the chill of eyes on my back, and I turn around. On the far opposite side of the stadium, I can just make out the shape of a man standing behind the glass of the dark announcer's booth, gripping a microphone. Julie stares bleakly across the distance.

"When every real thing decays there is nothing left but principle and I will hold to it. I'm going to reset things back to right. Wait, Julie. I'll be there soon."

The speakers click off.

Nora hands the wine bottle to Julie. *"L'chaim,"* she says quietly.

Julie takes a drink. She hands it to me. I take a drink. The wine's bright red spirits dance around in my stomach, oblivious to the somber stillness in the room.

"What now?" Nora says.

"I don't know," Julie snaps before Nora finishes asking. "I don't know." She grabs the bottle from me and takes another long pull.

I stand in front of the viewing window and gaze out over the streets and rooftops below, that microcosmic parody of urban contentment. I'm so weary of this place. These tight rooms and claustrophobic hallways. I need some air.

"Let's go to the roof," I say.

The girls both look at me. "Why?" Julie says.

"Because it's . . . the only place left. And because I like it there."

"You've never been there," Julie says.

I look her in the eyes. "Yes I have."

There is a long silence.

"Let's go up," Nora says, glancing uncertainly from Julie to me. "It's probably the last place they'll look, so it'll at least . . . I don't know . . . buy us some time."

Without breaking eye contact with me, Julie nods. We travel through the dark corridors, which grow less and less crowd-friendly, more and more industrial as we go. Our path ends at a ladder. White light streams down from above.

"Can you climb this?" Nora asks me.

I grasp the ladder and tentatively pull myself up. My hands tremble on the cold steel, but the skill is there. I advance another rung, then look down at the girls. "Yes," I say.

They come up behind me and I ascend, *climbing a ladder*, rung after rung like I've done it a hundred times. The feeling is exhilarating, even better than the escalators, my own numb hands drawing me up toward daylight.

We emerge from a hatch doorway, and we're on the roof. The smooth panels shine white under the setting sun. Structural beams arch overhead like sculpture. And there's the blanket, damp and maybe a little mildewy from weeks of rain, but laid out exactly as I remember it, bright red against the white roof.

"Oh Lord . . . ," Nora whispers, looking out at the surrounding city. The ground below is alive with skeletons, now outnumbering Security by vast margins. Have we miscalculated? Have we erred? In my head I can hear Grigio exulting as they scale the walls and flood through the gates to kill every last person. *You dreamers. You ridiculous children. You dancing grinning fuckups. Here is your bright future. Your earnest, saccharine hope. How does it taste dripping from the neck of everyone you love?*

Perry! I call out into my head. *Are you there? What do we do?*

My voice echoes like a prayer in a dark cathedral. Perry is silent.

I watch the skeletons kill and devour another soldier, then I turn away. I block out the screams, the explosions, the compressed pops of sniper fire from the tier just below us. I block out the skeletons' hum, even though it's now an immense chorus, howling in stereo from every direction. I block all this out and sit on the red blanket. While Nora paces the roof watching the battle, Julie walks slowly to the blanket and sits next to me. She tucks her knees against her chest, and we both look out at the horizon. We can see the mountains. They're blue like the ocean. They're lovely.

"This plague . . . ," Julie says in a very soft voice. "This curse . . . I have an idea where it came from."

The clouds are thin and pink overhead, stretched out into delicately textured swirls. A bracing cold wind whips across the roof and makes us squint.

"I don't think it's from any spell or virus or nuclear rays. I think it's from a deeper place. I think we brought it here."

Our shoulders are pressed together. She is cool to the touch. As if her warmth is retreating, curling deep inside her to escape the extinguishing wind.

"I think we crushed ourselves down over the centuries. Buried ourselves under greed and hate and whatever other sins we could find until our souls finally hit the rock bottom of the universe.

And then they scraped a hole through it, into some . . . dark place."

I hear pigeons cooing somewhere in the eaves. Starlings zip and dive against the distant sky, pretty much unaffected by the end of our silly civilization.

"We released it. We poked through the seabed and the oil erupted, painted us black, pulled our inner sickness out for everyone to see. Now here we are in this dry corpse of a world, rotting on our feet till there's nothing left but bones and the buzz of flies."

The roof shudders under us. With a low, grinding rumble, the entire expanse of steel begins to move, sliding shut to shield the people inside from what is quickly becoming a full-scale invasion. As it booms closed, footsteps clang toward us from the ladder. Nora pulls Grigio's pistol out of her purse and rushes to the hatch.

"What do we do, R?" Julie finally looks at me. Her voice is shaky, her eyes are raw, but she doesn't surrender to tears. "Are we stupid to think we can do anything? You made me start hoping again, but here we are, and I think we're about to die. So what do we do?"

I look into Julie's face. Not just at it, but into it. Every pore, every freckle, every faint gossamer hair. And then the layers beneath them. The flesh and bones, the blood and brain, all the way down to the unknowable energy that swirls in her core, the life force, the soul, the fiery will that makes her more than meat, coursing through every cell and binding them together in millions to form *her*. Who is she, this girl? What is she? She is everything. Her body contains the history of life, remembered in chemicals. Her mind contains the history of the universe, remembered in pain, in joy and sadness, hate and hope and bad habits, every thought of God, past-present-future, remembered, felt, and hoped for all at once.

"What do we do?" she pleads, confounding me with her eyes, the vast oceans in her irises. "What do we have left?"

I have no answer for her. But I look into her face, her pale cheeks, her red lips bright with life and tender as an infant's, and I understand that I love her. And if she is everything, maybe that's answer enough.

I pull Julie into me and kiss her.

I press her lips against mine. I pull her body against mine. She wraps her arms around my neck and squeezes me hard. We kiss with our eyes open, staring into each other's pupils and the depths inside them. Our tongues taste each other, our saliva flows, and Julie bites my lip. I feel the death in me stirring, the anti-life surging toward her glowing cells to darken them. But as it reaches the threshold, I *halt* it. I hold it back and hammer it down, and I feel Julie doing the same. We hold this thrashing monster between us in a relentless grip, we bear down on it together with determination and rage, and something happens. It changes. It warps and squirms and twists inside-out. It becomes something altogether different. Something new.

A surge of ecstatic agony rushes through me, and we fall back from each other with a gasp. My eyes are aching with some deep, twisting pain. I look at Julie's and see that her irises are shimmering. The fibers twitch, and their hue begins to change. Vivid sky blue fades to pewter gray—but then hesitates, flickers, and flashes back as gold. A brilliant shade of solar yellow that I have never seen before on any human being. As this happens, my sinuses ignite with a new smell, something similar to the life energy of the Living but also vastly different. It's coming from Julie, it's her scent, but it's also *mine*. It rushes out from us like an explosion of pheromones, so potent I can almost see it.

"What . . . ," Julie whispers, staring at me with her mouth slightly open, "just happened?"

For the first time since we sat down on this blanket, I look around and see my surroundings. Something has changed on the ground below. The armies of skeletons have stopped advancing. They stand completely motionless. And it's hard to tell from this distance, but they all seem to be looking directly at *us*.

"Julie!"

The voice shatters the unearthly stillness. There is Grigio, standing in front of the ladder hatch while Rosso clambers up behind him, breathing hard and keeping his eyes on the general. Nora sits slumped against the hatch with her hands cuffed to the ladder, her bare legs sprawled against the cold steel roof. Her gun lies at Grigio's feet, just out of reach.

Grigio's jaw muscles look tight enough to burst. When Julie turns and he sees her changed eyes, his entire body clenches. I can hear his teeth grinding.

"Colonel Rosso," he says in the driest voice I have ever heard. "Shoot them."

His face is ashen, the skin dry and flaky.

"Dad," Julie says.

"Shoot them."

Rosso glances from Julie to her father. "Sir, she's not infected."

"Shoot them."

"She's not infected, sir. I'm not even so sure the *boy* is infected. Look at their eyes, they're—"

"They're *infected!*" Grigio barks. I can see the shape of his teeth under his pursed lips. "This is how the infection travels! This is how it works! There is no—" He chokes off his words as if deciding he's said enough.

"Sir . . . ," Rosso says.

Grigio draws his pistol and points it at his daughter.

"John!" Rosso grabs Grigio's arm and wrenches it down, grappling for the gun. With trained precision Grigio twists Rosso's wrist and snaps it, then jabs him hard in the ribs. The old man falls to his knees.

"Dad, stop!" Julie screams, and he replies by cocking the gun and taking aim once again. His face is empty now, expressing absolutely nothing. Just skin stretched over a skull.

Rosso stabs a knife into his ankle.

Grigio doesn't cry out or visibly react. But his leg gives under him, and he topples backward. He slides down the roof's steep slope, rolling and twisting, fingers grasping for purchase on the smooth steel. His gun spins past him and drops over the edge, and he nearly follows it—but he stops. His hands cling to the rim of the roof as the rest of him dangles over the drop. All I can see are his white-knuckled fingers and his face, tight with exertion but still eerily impassive.

Julie runs to help him, but the slope is too steep and she starts to slip. She crouches there and stares at her father, helpless.

Then a curious thing happens. As Grigio's skinny hands clutch the roof edge, another set of fingers rises up and clamps down over his. But these fingers have no flesh. Just dry bone, yellowed and browned by dust and age and ancient blood from ancient murders. They grip the roof, digging into the steel, and hoist up a grinning, humming skeleton.

It is not fast. It doesn't leap or sprint. It moves leisurely, lacking the relentless, bloodthirsty drive that pursued us through the city. And despite the desperation of that pursuit, it seems in no hurry now to get to me or Julie. It doesn't even seem to notice us. It bends over to hook its claws into Grigio's shirt and drags him up onto the ledge. Grigio struggles to stand, and the skeleton hauls him to his feet.

Grigio and the skeleton regard each other, their faces inches apart.

"Rosy!" Julie screams. "Fucking shoot it!"

Rosso is struggling for breath, clutching his wrist and ribs, unable to move. He gives Julie a look that pleads forgiveness, not just for this failure but for all the failures leading to it. All the years of knowing and not acting.

The skeleton takes hold of Grigio's arm gently, tenderly, as if leading him into a dance. Then it pulls him close, gazes into his eyes, and bites a chunk out of his shoulder.

Julie shrieks, but everyone else is dumbstruck. Grigio doesn't fight. His eyes are wide and feverish, but his face is a blank mask as the creature chews into him, taking slow, almost sensual bites. Pieces of flesh fall through its hollow jaw and hit the roof.

I am transfixed. I stare at Grigio and the skeleton in rapt horror, trying to grasp what I'm witnessing. They are perched there on the edge of the roof, silhouetted against a smoldering sky of pink clouds and sickly orange haze, and in that otherworldly light, their figures are indistinguishable. Bones devouring bones.

Julie sprints to the hatch. She picks up Nora's gun and points it at the skeleton. It finally looks at her, finally acknowledges our presence, and rears back its head to release a roar, a piercing blast like the trumpets at the end of time, rusted and broken and forever out of tune.

Julie fires. The first few shots miss completely, then a bullet snaps off a rib, a clavicle, a hip bone.

"Julie."

She pauses, the gun trembling in her hands. Her father stares at her vacantly as the blood drains from his body. "I'm sorry," he says in a quiet murmur.

"Dad, push it off you! *Fight it!*"

Grigio closes his eyes and says:

"No."

The skeleton grins at Julie, and eats her father's throat.

Julie screams with all the anguish and rage in her battered young heart and fires one more time. The creature's skull vanishes in a burst of dust and bone shards. With its fingers still embedded in Grigio's shoulders, it reels backward and tips off the edge of the roof.

Grigio goes with it.

They fall together, entangled, and Grigio's body shudders in the air, convulsing. Converting. His remaining flesh peels away in the wind, dry scraps floating up like ashes, leaving the pale bones underneath, and there is a message in those bones that I'm finally able to read. A warning etched into each femur, each humerus, each grasping metacarpal:

This is the plague. This is the curse. So potent now, so deeply rooted and ravenous for souls, no longer content to wait for death. Now reaching out and simply taking what it wants.

But a decision has been made today. We will not be robbed. We will cling tight to what we have, no matter how hard the curse pulls. We will fight it.

On the ground below, the Boneys watch Grigio's remains plummet to earth and shatter. They stare at the fragments in the dirt, those little white shards, broken and inconsequential. Then all at once, with movements devoid of purpose or intent . . . they wander off. Some walk in circles, some bump into each other, but little by little they disperse and disappear into the buildings and trees. I feel a tiny thrill creeping through me. What signal have they received? Between the fall of those bones and the strange new energy pulsing out from this rooftop like radio waves, is there a notice blaring loud in their empty skulls? An announcement that their time is over?

Julie lets the gun fall from her fingers. She inches her way to the edge of the roof and crouches there, gazing down at the pile of bones below. Her eyes are red, but there are still no tears. The only sound on the roof is the wind, whipping at the tattered remnants of state and country flags. Rosso watches Julie for a moment, then unlocks Nora's cuffs and helps her to her feet. Nora rubs her wrists and they share a look that makes words unnecessary.

Julie makes her way over to us with dazed, dragging steps. Rosso touches her shoulder. "I'm so sorry, Julie."

She sniffs, staring down at her feet. "I'm okay." Her voice is like her eyes, raw and wrung out. Now that I have the ability, I want to do her crying for her. Julie has become an orphan, but she is much more than the tragic waif that word implies. Her grief will catch up to her eventually and demand its due, but for the moment she is here with us, alive and standing.

Rosso brushes his left hand against her hair, tucking a lock behind her ear. She squeezes his callused palm against her cheek and offers a faint smile.

Rosso turns his attention to me. I can see his eyes flicking left and right, studying my irises. "Archie, was it?"

"Just R."

He puts his hand out to me, and after a moment's confusion, I put out mine. Rosso shakes my broken hand, enduring his broken wrist with a fierce grimace. "I don't know exactly why," he says, "but I'm thrilled to know you, R."

He walks back to the hatch.

"Will we be having a community meeting tomorrow?" Nora asks.

"I'm going to announce it as soon as I get down this ladder. We have some urgent developments to address." He looks out at the retreating skeletal army. "And I'd certainly love to hear your take on just what the hell happened today."

"We might have some theories," Nora says.

Rosso descends the ladder, gripping carefully with his left hand. Nora looks at Julie. Julie nods. Nora smiles at her, then at me, then disappears into the hatch.

We are alone on the rooftop. Julie squints up at me, studying me as if she's never seen me before. Then her eyes widen, and she takes in a sharp breath. "Oh my God," she says. "R, you're . . ." She reaches up and peels the Band-Aid off my forehead. She touches the place where she stabbed me on the day we first met, ages ago, last month.

Her finger comes away red.

"You're *bleeding!*"

As she says this I begin to notice things. Sharp points of pain all over my body. I *hurt.* I pat myself down and find my clothes sticky with blood. Not the dead black oil that once clogged my veins. Bright, vivid, living-red *blood.*

Julie presses her hand into my chest so hard it's almost kung fu. Against the pressure of her palm, I feel it. A movement deep inside me. A *pulse.*

"R!" Julie nearly shrieks. "I think . . . you're *alive!*"

She pounces on me, wrapping herself around me and squeezing so hard I feel my semihealed bones creaking. She kisses me again, tasting the salty blood from my lower lip. Her warmth radiates into my body, and I feel a rush of sensations as my own warmth finally pushes back.

Julie goes still. She releases me and pulls back a little, glancing downward. A wondering smile creeps across her face.

I look down at myself, but I don't need to. I can feel it. My hot blood is pounding through my body, flooding capillaries and lighting up cells like Fourth of July fireworks. I can feel the elation of every atom in my flesh, brimming with gratitude for the second chance they never expected to get. The chance to start over, to live right, to love right, to burn up in a fiery cloud and never again be buried in the mud. I kiss Julie to hide the fact that I'm blushing. My face is bright red and hot enough to melt steel.

Okay, corpse, a voice in my head says, and I feel a twitch in my belly, more like a gentle nudge than a kick. *I'm going now. I'm sorry I couldn't be here for your battle; I was fighting my own. But we won, right? I can feel it. There's a shiver in our legs, a tremor like the Earth speeding up, spinning off into uncharted orbits. Scary, isn't it? But what wonderful thing didn't start out scary? I don't know what the next page is for you, but whatever it is for me I swear I'm not going to fuck it up. I'm not going to yawn off in the middle of a sentence and hide it in a drawer. Not this time. Peel off these dusty wool blankets of apathy and antipathy and cynical desiccation. I want life in all its stupid sticky rawness.*

Okay.

Okay, R.

Here it comes.

living

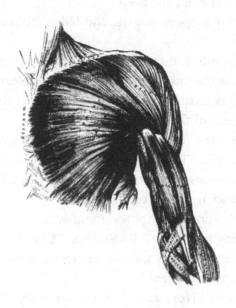

Nora Greene is in the square by the stadium's main gate, standing with General Rosso in front of a huge crowd. She is a little nervous. She wishes she had smoked before coming out today, but it seemed inappropriate somehow. She wanted a clear head for this occasion.

"Okay, folks," Rosso begins, straining his reedy voice to reach the back of the assembly spilling out into the far streets. "We've prepared you for this as best we could, but I know it may still be a little . . . uncomfortable."

Not everyone in the stadium is here, but everyone who wants to be is. The rest are hiding behind locked doors with guns drawn, but Nora hopes they'll come out eventually to see what's going on.

"Let me just assure you once again that you are not in any danger," Rosso continues. "The situation has changed."

Rosso looks at Nora and nods.

The guards pull open the gate, and Nora shouts, "Come on in, guys!"

One by one, still clumsy but walking more or less straight, they wander into the stadium. The Half-Dead. The Nearly-Living. The crowd murmurs anxiously and contracts as the zombies form a loose line in front of the gate.

"These are just a few of them," Nora says, moving forward to address the people. "There are more out there every day. They're trying to cure themselves. They're trying to cure the plague, and we need to do whatever we can to help."

"Like *what*?" someone shouts dubiously.

"We're going to study it," Rosso says. "Get close to it, knead it and wring it until answers start to emerge. I know it's vague, but we have to start somewhere."

"Talk to them," Nora says. "I know it's scary at first, but look them in the eyes. Tell them your name and ask them theirs."

"Don't worry," Rosso says. "Each one will have a guard assigned to them at all times, but try to believe that they won't hurt you. We have to entertain the idea that this will work."

Nora steps back to let the crowd come forward. Cautiously, they do. They approach the zombies, while wary guards keep rifles trained. For their part, the zombies are handling this awkward experience with admirable patience. They just stand there and wait, some of them attempting affable grins while trying to ignore the laser dots jittering on their foreheads. Nora moves to join the people, crossing her fingers behind her back and hoping for the best.

"Hi there."

She turns toward the voice. One of the zombies is watching her. He steps forward from the line and gives her a smile. His lips are thin and slightly mangled under a short blond beard, but they, along with countless other wounds on his body, appear to be healing.

"Um . . . hello . . . ," Nora says, glancing up and down his considerable height. He must be well over six feet. He's a little heavyset, but his muscular arms strain his tattered shirt. His perfectly bald head gleams like a pale gray pearl.

"I'm Nora," she says, tugging at her curls.

"My name is Mm . . . arcus," he says, his voice a velvety rumble. "And you're . . . the most beautiful woman . . . I've ever seen."

Nora giggles and twirls her hair faster. "Oh *my*." She reaches out a hand. "Nice to meet you . . . Marcus."

• • •

The boy is in the airport. The hallways are dark, but he's not scared. He runs through the shadowed food court, past all the unlit signs and moldy leftovers, half-finished beers and cold pad thai. He hears the rattle of a solitary skeleton in an adjacent corridor and quickly changes course, darting around the corner without pausing. The Boneys are slow now. The moment the boy's dad and stepmom first came back here, something happened to them all. Now they wander aimlessly like bees in winter. They bump into walls and stand motionless, obsolete things waiting to be replaced.

The boy is carrying a box. It's empty now, but his arms are tired. He runs into the connecting overpass and stops to get his bearings.

"Alex!"

The boy's sister appears behind him. She's carrying a box, too. She has bits of tape stuck all over her fingers.

"All done, Joan?"

"All done!"

"Okay. Let's go get more."

They run down the corridor. As they hit the conveyer, the power comes back on and the belt lurches under their feet. The boy and the girl are running barefoot at the speed of light, flying down the corridor like loping deer while the morning sun drifts up behind them. At the end of the corridor they nearly collide with another group of kids, all holding boxes.

"All done," says a boy whose charcoal skin is turning warm brown.

"Okay," Alex says, and they run together. Some of the kids still wear tatters. Some of them are still gray. But most of them are alive. The kids lacked the instinctual programming of the adults. They had to be taught how to do everything. How to kill easily, how to wander aimlessly, how to sway and groan and properly rot away. But now the classes have stopped. No one is teaching them, and like perennial bulbs dried up and waiting in the winter earth, they are bursting back to life all on their own.

The fluorescent lights flicker and buzz, and the sound of a record needle scratches onto the speakers overhead. Some enterprising soul has hijacked the airport PA system. Sweet, swooning strings swell into the gloom, and Francis Albert Sinatra's voice echoes lonely in the empty halls.

Something wonderful happens in summer . . . when the sky is a heavenly blue . . .

The dusty speakers pop and sizzle, short out and distort. The record skips. But it's the first time in years this place's inert air has been stirred by music.

As the kids run to the Arrivals gate to get fresh boxes, fresh rolls of tape, they pass a pale figure shambling down the hall. The zombie glances at the Living children as they run past, but doesn't pursue them. Her appetite has been waning lately. She doesn't feel the hunger like she used to. She watches the kids disappear around the corner, then continues on her way. She doesn't know where she's going exactly, but there's a white glow at the end of this hallway, and it looks nice. She stumbles toward it.

Something wonderful happens in summer . . . when the moon makes you feel all aglow . . . You fall in love, you fall in love . . . you want the whole world to know . . .

She emerges into the waiting area of Gate 12, flooded with bright morning sunlight. Something in here is different than before. On the floor-to-ceiling windows overlooking the runways, someone has taped small photos to the glass. Side by side and stacked about five squares high, they form a strip that runs all the way to the end of the room.

Something wonderful happens in summer . . . and it happens to only a few. But when it does . . . yes when it does . . .

The zombie approaches the photos warily. She stands in front of them, staring with mouth slightly agape.

A girl climbing an apple tree. A kid spraying his brother with a hose. A woman playing a cello. An elderly couple gently touching. A boy with a cat. A boy crying. A newborn deep in sleep. And one older photo, creased and faded: a family at a water park. A man, a woman, and a little blond girl, smiling and squinting in the sun.

The zombie stares at this mysterious and sprawling collage. The sunlight glints off the nametag on her chest, so bright it hurts her eyes. For hours she stands there, motionless. Then she takes in a slow breath. Her first in months. Dangling limply at her sides, her fingers twitch to the music.

• • •

"R."

I open my eyes. I am lying on my back, arms folded behind my head, looking up at a flawless summer sky. "Yes?"

Julie stirs on the red blanket, scooting a little closer to me. "Do you think we'll ever see jets up there again?"

I think for a moment. I watch the little molecules swim in my eye fluids. "Yes."

"Really?"

"Maybe not us. But I think the kids will."

"How far do you think we can take this?"

"Take what?"

"Rebuilding everything. Even if we can completely end the plague . . . do you think we'll ever get things back to the way they were?"

A lone starling swoops across the distant sky, and I imagine a white jet trail sketching out behind it, like a florid signature on a love note. "I hope not."

We are silent for a while. We are lying in the grass. Behind us, the battered old Mercedes waits patiently, whispering to us in sizzles and pings as its engine cools. Mercey, Julie named it. Who is this woman lying next to me, so overflowing with life she can grant it to a car?

"R," she says.

"Yeah."

"Do you remember your name yet?"

On this hillside on the edge of a crumbled freeway, the bugs and birds in the grass perform a tiny simulation of traffic noise. I listen to their nostalgic symphony, and I shake my head. "No."

"You could give yourself one, you know. Just pick one. Whatever you want."

I consider this. I thumb through the index of names in my brain. Complex etymologies, languages, ancient meanings passed down through generations of cultural traditions. But I'm a new thing. A fresh canvas. I can choose what history I build my future on, and I choose a new one.

"My name is R," I say with a little shrug.

She twists her head to look at me. I can feel her sun-yellow eyes on the side of my face, as if they're trying to tunnel into my ear and explore my brain. "You don't want to get your old life back?"

"No." I sit up, folding my arms over my knees and looking down into the valley. "I want this one."

Julie smiles. She sits up with me and faces what I'm facing.

The airport spreads out below us like a thrown gauntlet. There was no global transformation after the skeletons surrendered. Some of us are on our way back to life, some are still Dead. Some are still lingering here at the airport, or in other cities, countries, continents, wandering and waiting. But to fix a problem that spans the globe, an airport seems like a good place to start.

We have big plans. Oh yes. We're fumbling in the dark, but at least we're in motion. Everyone is working now; Julie and I are just pausing for a moment to enjoy the view, because it's a beautiful day. The sky is blue. The grass is green. The sun is warm on our skin. We smile, because this is how we save the world. We will not let Earth become a tomb, a mass grave spinning through space. We will exhume ourselves. We will fight the curse and break it. We will cry and bleed and lust and love, and we will cure death. We will *be* the cure. Because we *want it*.

THE NEW HUNGER

HUNGER

A WARM BODIES NOVELLA

A Note on Prequels

The story you're about to read takes place roughly seven years before the one you just finished. So why didn't it come first? Most stories are told in forward chronological order; it's how we perceive time, so it's fair to wonder why a prequel goes "backwards." Some readers feel this is a mistake and take it upon themselves to rearrange it into the "correct" sequence. I want to assure you there's a reason for the jumble.

The New Hunger is not a beginning. We jump into the early lives of characters we already know, and that knowledge colors everything we see. It provides context, a reason to care, and added undercurrents of meaning. Prequels are unique because they tell a story in two overlaid layers of time: the one playing out on the page in front of you, and the one playing along with it in your memory of the future. There's a special kind of poignancy in that, like nostalgia in reverse.

That's what I wanted to capture by telling this story this way. We may perceive time in a straight line, but we experience our lives on a much messier path, a crazy zigzag between past and present, memory and hope. And the beauty of that mess is what these stories are all about.

—Isaac Marion

For Jenae and Kevon.
Wherever you are, I hope you found good people.

The past speaks to us in a thousand voices, warning and comforting, animating and calling to action.

—Felix Adler

beginning

beginning

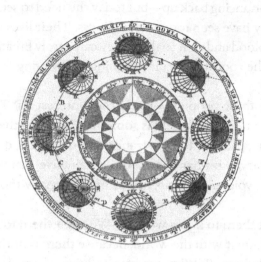

T HIS IS NOT the beginning.

The beginning is darkness and fire, microbes and worms—the very first of us, killing by the billions on their way up the ladder. There is little to learn from the beginning. We prefer the middle, where things are getting interesting.

Who are we? We are everyone. We are every thought and action. Time is just a filing system for the vastness of our Library, but we linger in the present with the unfinished books, watching them write themselves. The world is changing. The globe is bulging and straining, erupting and blazing with miracles, and we don't know what shape it will take when it cools. Even with all of history inside us, we don't know, and this is a little scary.

So we narrow our focus. We zoom in on a country, then a city, then the white rooftop of a stadium, where three young people are sitting on a blanket.

The sky is dark. They are the only ones awake for miles around. It's hard to catch a sunrise in the middle of summer—the sun barely sets before bouncing back up—but today the need to see beauty was urgent. They have seen too much ugliness. Their lives are smeared with it like blood and shit, so thick they can barely breathe, so today they're on the roof in the cold morning air, waiting for the sun to wash them.

Who are these people? Why do they interest us? They are not special—no one is—but there is something in them that draws our gaze. A short, pale girl full of strange dreams. A tall, dark girl with a promise carved on her heart. And a half-alive man whose head buzzes with voices, who talks to us and listens without knowing we exist.

We want them to know we exist. We want them to read our Library and share it with the world, because there is nothing sweeter than being known. But first we have to know them. We are books that read our readers, not a story but a conversation, and we open it with a question:

Who are you?

We circle around them, peering in the windows of their souls.

What's in there? Where did it come from? Show us and we'll show you.

Up and down the Library, from its bright ceiling to its black basement, pages begin to flutter.

THE NEW
HUNGER

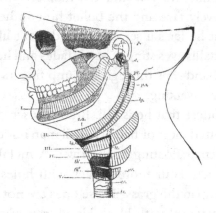

A DEAD MAN LIES near a river, and the forest watches him. Gold clouds drift across a warming pink sky. Crows dart through dark pines that hover over him like morbid onlookers. In the deep, wild grass, small living things creep around the dead man's face, eager to eat it and return it to the soil. Their faint clicks mingle with the rush of the wind and the screams of the birds and the roar of the river that will wash away his bones. Nature is hungry. It is ready to take back what the man stole from it by living.

But the dead man opens his eyes.

He stares at the sky. He feels an impulse: *move.* So he sits up. His eyes are open but he can't see anything. Just a blur that he doesn't know is a blur, because he has never seen clarity.

This is the world, he reasons. *The world is blurry.*

Hours pass. Then his eyes remember how to focus, and the world sharpens. He thinks that he liked the world better before he could see it.

Lying next to him is a woman. She is beautiful, her hair pale and silky and matted with blood, her blue eyes mirroring the sky, tears drying rapidly under the hot sun. The man tilts his head, studying the woman's lovely face and the bullet hole in her forehead. For a brief moment he feels a sensation he doesn't like. His features bend downward; his eyes sting. Then it fades and he stands up. The revolver in his hand slips through his limp fingers and falls to the ground. He starts walking.

The man notices that he is tall. Branches scrape his scalp and tangle in his matted mess of hair. The tall man notices other things, too. A leather chair floating in the river. A metal suitcase hanging from a branch. Four more bodies with holes in their heads, sprawled out limp in the grass. These ones are not beautiful. They are pale and spattered with black blood, regarding the sky with strange, metallic gray eyes. He feels another unpleasant sensation, and he kicks one of the bodies in the head. He kicks it again and again, until his shoe sinks into the putrid mess of its brain, and then he forgets why he's doing this and keeps walking.

The tall man does not know who he is. He does not know what he is or where he is, how he came here or why. His head is so empty it hurts; the vacuum of space is twisting it apart, so he forces a thought into it just to ease the pain:

Find someone.

He walks away from the blond woman. He walks away from the bodies. He walks away from the column of smoke rising out of the trees behind him.

Find another person.

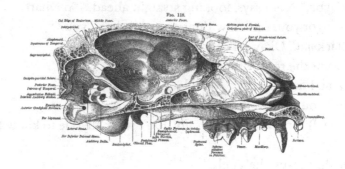

Fig. 118.

A GIRL AND HER BROTHER are walking in the city. Her brother breaks the silence.

"I know who you like."

"What?"

"I know who you like."

"No you don't."

"Yeah I do."

"I don't like anybody."

"Do too. And I know who it is."

Nora glances back at Addis, who is such a painfully slow walker she wants to put him on a leash and drag him.

"Okay, who do I like?"

"I'm not telling."

She laughs. "That's not how blackmail works, dumb-ass."

"What's blackmail?"

"It's when you know a secret about somebody and you threaten to tell people unless they do what you want. But it doesn't work if you don't say what you know."

"Oh. Okay, you like Evan."

Nora fights a surprised smile. The little shit's got eyes.

"You *do*!" Addis crows. "You like Evan!"

"Maybe," Nora says, looking straight ahead. "So what?"

"So I got you. And now I'm gonna blacknail you."

"Black*mail*. Okay, let's hear your demands."

"I want the rest of the Teddy Grahams."

"Deal. I don't like the chocolate ones."

"And you have to carry the water an extra day."

"Fine. But only because I *really* don't want anyone to know I like Evan."

"Yeah, because he's ugly."

"No, because he has a girlfriend."

"But he *is* ugly."

"I like ugly. Beauty is a trick."

Addis snorts. "No one likes ugly."

"I like you, don't I?" She reaches back and grabs a handful of his woolly hair, shakes his head around. He laughs and wrestles free. "Okay, so are we good here?" she says. "Do we have a deal?"

"One more."

"All right, but only one, so you better make it good."

Addis studies the pavement scrolling by under his feet. "I want us to look for Mom and Dad."

Nora walks in silence for a few sidewalk squares. "No deal."

"But I'm blackmailing you!"

"No deal."

"Then I'm gonna tell everyone you like Evan."

Nora stops walking. She cups her hands to her mouth and sucks in a deep breath. "Hey everyone! *I like Evan Kenerly!*"

Her voice echoes through long canyons of crumbled high-rises, gutted storefronts, melted glass and scorched concrete. It rolls down mossy streets and bounces off piles of rusted cars, frightening crows out of a copse of alders that sprouts through the roof of an Urban Outfitters.

Her brother scowls at her, betrayed, but Nora is tired of this. "We were just playing a game, Addy. Evan's probably dead by now."

She starts walking again. Addis hangs back a moment, then follows, still scowling. "You're mean," he says.

"Yeah, maybe. But I'm nicer than Mom and Dad."

They walk in silence for five minutes before Addis looks up from his gloomy study of the sidewalk. "So what *are* we looking for?"

Nora shrugs. "Good people. There are good people out there."

"Are you sure?"

"There's got to be one or two."

"Do I still get the cookies?"

She stops and raises her eyes skyward, letting out a slow sigh. She slips off her backpack and pulls out the bag of Teddy Grahams, hands it to her brother. He shoves the last two into his mouth and Nora studies him as he chews furiously. He's getting thinner. A seven-year-old's face should be round, not sharp. It shouldn't have the angular planes of a fashion model. She can see the exhaustion in his dark eyes, creeping in around the sadness.

"Let's crash," she says. "I'm tired."

Addis beams, revealing white teeth smeared black with cookie gunk.

They set up camp in a law firm lobby, wrapped in the single wool blanket they share between them, the marble floor softened with chair cushions. The last red rays of the sunset leak through the revolving door and crawl across the floor, then abruptly vanish, severed by the rooftops.

"Can we make a fire?" Addis whimpers, although the night is warm.

"In the morning."

"But it's scary in here."

Nora can't argue with that. The building's steel skeleton creaks and groans as the day's warmth dissipates, and she can hear the ghostly rustle of paperwork in a nearby office, brought to life by a breeze whistling through a broken window. But it's a law firm. A place utterly useless to the new world, and thus invisible to scavengers. One threat out of a hundred checked off her list—she will sleep one percent better.

She pulls the flashlight out of her pack and squeezes its handle a few times until the bulb begins to glow, then gives it to Addis. He hugs it to his chest like a talisman.

"Good night, Adderall," she says.

"Good night, Norwhale."

Even with the powerful protection of a two-watt bulb against the creeping jungle of night, he still sounds scared. And she can still hear his stomach, growling louder than any monsters that may lurk in the dark.

Nora reaches across their makeshift bed and squeezes her brother's hand, marveling at its softness. Wondering how mankind survived as long as it did with hands this soft.

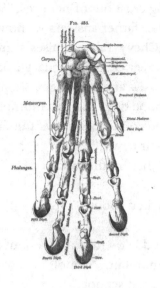

FIG. 483.

FOR THE FIRST TIME in weeks, Julie Grigio is having a dream that's not a nightmare. She is sitting on a blanket on a high white rooftop, gazing into a sky full of airplanes. There are hundreds of them, gleaming against the sky like a swarm of butterflies, writing letters on the blue with their contrails. She is watching these planes next to someone who loves her, and she knows with warm certainty that everything will be okay. That there is nothing in the world worth fearing.

Then she wakes up. She opens her eyes and blinks the world into focus. The tiny cage of the SUV's cabin surrounds her, spacious for a vehicle, suffocating for a home.

"Mom?" she blurts before she's fully conscious, a reflex born from years of bad nights and cold-sweat awakenings.

Her mother twists around in the front seat and gives her a gentle smile. "Morning, honey. Sleep okay?"

Julie nods, rubbing crust out of her eyes. "Where are we?"

"Getting close," her father answers without taking his eyes off the road. The silver Chevy Tahoe cruises at freeway speeds down a narrow suburban street called Boundary Road. It used to terrify her, watching mailboxes and stop signs streak past her window, imagining neighborhood dogs and cats thumping under their tires, but she's getting used to it. She knows the faster they drive, the sooner they'll find their new home.

"Are you excited?" her mother asks.

Julie nods.

"What are you excited about?"

"Everything."

"Like what? What do you miss most about real cities?"

Julie thinks for a moment. "School?"

"We'll find you a great school."

"My friends."

Her mother hesitates, struggling to maintain her smile. "You'll make new friends. What else?"

"Will they have libraries?"

"Sure. Maybe no librarians, but the books should still be there."

"What about restaurants?"

"God, I hope so. I'd kill for a cheeseburger."

Julie's father clears his throat. "Audrey . . ."

"What else?" her mother continues, ignoring him. "Art galleries? I bet we could find somewhere to show your paintings—"

"Audrey."

She doesn't look away from Julie but she stops talking. "What."

"The Almanac said 'functioning government,' not 'thriving civilization.' "

"I know that."

"So you shouldn't be getting her hopes up."

Audrey Grigio smiles stiffly at her husband. "I don't think any of us are in danger of a hope overdose, John."

Julie's father keeps his eyes on the road and doesn't reply. Her mother turns back to her and tries to resume the daydream. "What else, Julie? Boys? I hear the boys are cute in Vancouver."

Julie wants to keep playing but the moment has died. "Maybe," she says, and looks out the window. Her mother opens her mouth to say more, then closes it and turns around to face the road.

Behind the perfect movie set of beige houses and green lawns, the border wall looms like a studio soundstage, making suspension of disbelief impossible. Big red maple leaves painted every hundred feet serve as stern reminders of who built this barrier, and who's keeping out whom. Julie loves her mother. She has high hopes for this new life in Canada. But she has seen more nightmares come true than dreams.

"There it is," her father announces. The truck hops a curb and descends into the border park lawn, tearing muddy grooves in the weedy grass. They drive past the booths where glorified mall cops once pretended to interrogate nervous college kids. *How long will you be staying? Are you carrying any alcohol? Where were you on September 11th?*

All that quaint border-crossing pageantry is over now. There is only one question still of interest to the gatekeepers of nations:

Are you infected?

The Tahoe rolls to a stop in front of the gate and Julie's father gets out. He approaches the black glass scanning window with his hands upraised. "Colonel John Grigio, US Army," he shouts. "Requesting immigration."

The wall is an impressive feat of construction for something built in such desperate times: thirty feet of reinforced concrete running from half a mile off the coast of Washington to somewhere deep in the Quebecois wilderness, and the whole length of it garnished with razor wire. The "gate" is just two tall slabs of galvanized steel, fitted flush to the concrete to make any prying or tampering impossible. Not that the automated guns mounted above it would allow the attempt.

The scanning window emits a few beeps. The guns twitch on their arm mounts. Then silence.

Julie's father glances around expectantly. "Colonel John Grigio, US Army," he repeats, "requesting immigration."

Silence.

"Hello!" He lowers his hands to his sides. "I have a wife and kid with me. We came from New York by way of the north and middle territories and have plenty of intel to share. Colonel John Grigio, requesting immigration!"

A red light blinks on behind the black glass, then fades. The twin surveillance cameras wobble briefly but remain pointed at random spots in the grass, as if fascinated by some caterpillars.

"How old was that Almanac?" Julie whispers to her mother, gripping the seat to pull herself forward.

"Two months," her mother says, and the tightness in her voice pushes Julie's heart underwater.

"We have skills!" her father yells, his voice filling with an emotion that startles her. "My wife is a veterinarian. My daughter is combat trained. I was an O-6 colonel and commanded federal forces in twelve secession conflicts!"

He stands in front of the gate, waiting with apparent patience, but Julie can see his shoulders rising and falling dangerously. She realizes she is seeing a rare sight: a glimpse into her father's secret bunker. His hopes were as high as his wife's.

"Requesting immigration!" he roars savagely, and hammers the butt of his pistol into the scanning window. It bounces pitifully off the bulletproof glass, but this action finally elicits a reaction. The red light blinks on again. The surveillance cameras wobble. A garbled electronic voice fills the air—*ARNING—SAULT RESPONSE—ETHAL FORCE*—and the guns begin spraying bullets.

Julie screams as geysers of dust erupt inches from her father's feet. He leaps backward and runs—not toward the truck but into the grass of the park. But the guns don't follow him. They spin on their arms, strafing the road, bending downward and bouncing bullets off the steel door itself, then they abruptly go limp, barrels bouncing against the concrete.

Julie's mother hops out of the car and runs to her husband's side. They both stare at the wall in shock.

FILE, it declares in its buzzing authoritarian baritone. *RESPONSE FILE CORRU—RETINA SCAN—AILED. REQUESTING RESPONSE FROM FEDERAL AUTHORIT—PASSWORD. PASSWOR—EQUIRED. WORK VISA. DUTY-FREE. APPLE MAGGOT.*

The guns rise.

Julie's parents jump into the Tahoe and her father slams it in reverse, lurching backward just as the guns spray another wild arc across the road. When they're out of range he pulls a sharp slide in the muddy grass, flipping the Tahoe around, and they all pause to catch their breath as Canada loses its mind. The guns have stopped spinning and are both pointed down at the same spot, diligently pounding bullets into the dirt.

"What the *fuck*?" Julie's mother says between gasps.

Julie digs through the duffel bag on the seat next to her and pulls out her father's sniper scope. She runs it along the top of the wall, past coil after coil of razor wire, scraps of clothing and the occasional bit of dried flesh. Then she sees an explanation, and her heart finishes drowning.

"Dad," she mumbles, handing him the scope. She points. He looks. He sees it. A uniformed arm dangling over the edge of the wall. Two helmets caught in the razor wire, one containing a head. And three city-sized plumes of smoke rising from somewhere beyond the wall.

Her father hands the scope back to her and drives calmly toward the freeway, steering clear of the gun turrets that bristle from the Peace Arch. His face is flat, all traces of that unnerving lapse into passion now gone. For better or worse, he is himself again.

After five minutes of silence, her mother speaks, her voice as flat as her husband's face. "Where are we going."

"South."

Five more minutes.

"To where."

"Rosso's heard chatter about an enclave in South Cascadia. When we get in radio range we'll check in with him."

"What happened?" Julie asks in a small voice. Her only answer is the roar of the tires on the cracked pavement of I-5 South. There are dozens of answers for her to choose from, everything from anarchic uprising to foreign invasion to the newer, more exotic forms of annihilation that have recently graced the world, but the relevant portion of every answer is the same: Canada is gone. The land is still there, and maybe some of its people, but Canada the safe haven, the last vestige of North American civilization, the new place to call home—that Canada is as lost as Atlantis, sunk beneath the same tide of blood and hunger that drowned the home she fled.

Suddenly exhausted, she closes her eyes and slips into nightmares again. Graveyards rising out of the ocean. Her friends' corpses in the light of their burning school. Skeletons ripping open men's chests and crawling inside. She endures it patiently, waiting for the horror film to end and the theater to go dark, those precious few hours of blackout that are her only respite.

Julie Bastet Grigio has reasons to sleep darkly. Her life has seen little light. She is twelve years old but has a woman's weathered poise. Her abyss-blue eyes have a piercing focus that some adults find unsettling. Her mother ties her hair in a ponytail but Julie pulls it out, letting it fall into a loose mess of yellow and gold. She has fired a gun into a human head. She has watched a pile of bodies set alight. She has starved and thirsted, stolen food and given it away, and glimpsed the meaning of life by watching it end over and over. But she has just turned twelve. She likes horses. She has never kissed a boy.

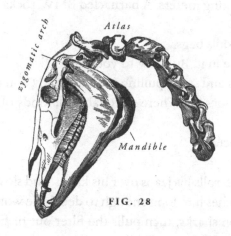

Atlas

zygomatic arch

Mandible

FIG. 28

WHAT CITY IS THIS? When did it die? And which of the endless selection of disasters killed it? If print news hadn't vanished years ago, Nora could find a paper blowing in the street and read the bold headlines declaring the end. Now she's left to wonder. Was it something quick and clean? Earthquakes, showers of space debris, freak tornados and rising tides? Or was it one of the threats that linger? Radiation. Viruses. People.

She knows that knowing wouldn't change anything. Death will introduce itself in its own time, and when she has shaken its hand and heard its offer, she will try her best to bargain with it.

"Can I go swimming?" Addis pleads.

"We don't know what's in there. It could be dangerous."

"It's the ocean!"

"Yeah, but not really."

They are standing on a new coastline. The ocean has grown tired of living on the beach and has moved to the city. Gentle waves lap against telephone poles. Pink and green anemones compete for real estate on parking meters. A barnacled BMW rocks lazily in the shifting tides.

"Pleeease?" Addis begs.

"You can wade in it. But only to your knees."

Addis whoops and starts pulling off his muddy, shredded Nikes.

"Keep your shoes on. There's probably all kinds of nasty stuff in there."

"But it's the ocean!"

"Shoes on."

He surrenders, rolls his jeans over his knees, and sloshes into the waves. Nora watches him long enough to decide he won't drown or be eaten by urban sharks, then pulls the filter out of her pack and kneels at the water's edge to fill her jug. She remembers a photo of her grandmother doing the same in some filthy Ethiopian river, and how it always made her glad she was born in America. She smiles darkly.

It took only eight feet to drown every port in the world. New York is a bayou. New Orleans is a reef. Whatever city this is, it's lucky to be sitting on a hill—the ocean has claimed only a few blocks. While her brother splashes and squeals, Nora scans the waterline for any trace of actual beach, some little patch of sand on the last remaining high ground. She remembers the feeling of sweaty toes digging into cool mud. She remembers sprinting on the thin after-waves that slid over each other like sheets of glass. When she ran with the waves it looked like she wasn't moving. When she ran against them it looked like she was flying. She refuses to believe her brother will never know these things. Somewhere, they will find sand.

When she looks back at him he's in up to his neck, swimming.

"Addis Horace Greene!" she hisses. "Out, right now!"

"Brr!" he squeals as he dog-paddles past the post office, through soggy clusters of letters floating like lily pads. "It's cold!"

• • •

Nora is grateful that it's summer. The heat is unpleasant but it won't kill them. They can sleep in doorways or alleyways or in the middle of the street with nothing more than their tattered blanket to keep off the dew. She wonders how long her parents debated their decision. If they might have waited a few months for the weather to warm. She would like to believe in this tiny kindness, but she finds it hard.

"Do we have *anything* left to eat?" Addis asks, shivering in his wet jeans. "Even some crumbs?"

Nora digs through her backpack reflexively, but no miracle has taken place. No fishes or loaves have appeared. It contains the same flashlight, blanket, filter, and bottle it always has, nothing more. Not counting the Teddy Grahams, Addis's last meal was two days ago. Nora can't remember when hers was.

She turns in a circle, examining the surrounding city. All the grocery stores are long since gutted. She found their last few morsels in the kitchen of a homeless shelter—five cookies and half a can of peanuts—but that was an unlikely windfall. Actual restaurants are the lowest of low-hanging fruit and were probably stripped bare on this city's first day of anarchy. But something on the horizon catches her eye. She bunches her lips into a determined scowl.

"Come on," she says, grabbing her brother's hand.

They wriggle through a tangle of rebar from a bombed-out McDonald's, climb over a rusty mountain of stacked cars, and there it is, rising in the distant haze: a white Eiffel Tower with a UFO on top.

"What's that?" Addis asks.

"It's the Space Needle. I guess we're in Seattle."

"What's the Space Needle?"

"It's like . . . I don't know. A tourist thing."

"What's that round thing on the top? A space ship?"

"I think it's a restaurant."

"Does it go into space?"

"I wish."

"But it's the *Space* Needle."

"Sorry, Addy."

He frowns at the ground.

"But spaceships aren't full of food. A restaurant might be."

He raises his eyes, hopeful again. "Can we get up there?"

"I don't know. Let's go see if the power's still on."

•　•　•

It's eerier to be alone in a city that's lit up and functioning than in one that's a tomb. If everything were silent, one could almost pretend to be in nature. A forest. A meadow. Crickets and birdsong. But the corpse of civilization is as restless as the creatures that now roam the graveyards. It flickers and blinks. It buzzes to life.

When the first signs of the end came—a riot here, a secession there, a few too many wars to shrug off with "boys will be boys"—people started to prepare. Every major business installed generators, and when the oil derricks started pumping mud and the strategic reserves burned on a doomsday cult's altar, solar power suddenly didn't seem so whimsical. Even the brashest believers in America's invincibility shut their mouths and gazed at the horizon with a wide-eyed *oh shit* stare. Solar panels appeared everywhere, glittering blue on high-rise roofs and suburban lawns, nailed haphazardly onto billboards, blocking out the faces of grinning models like censorship bars.

By then it was too late for such baby steps, of course. But at least this last desperate effort will provide a few extra years of light for the next generation, before it too flickers out.

Nora gives her brother's hand a squeeze as they make their way toward the Space Needle. The sun is setting and the monument's lights are coming on one by one. The tip of the needle blinks steadily, a beacon for planes that will never leave the ground.

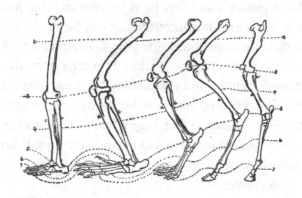

IN A REMOTE PATCH of forest that has never known human footprints, nature is witnessing a strange sight. A dead thing is moving. Crows circle it uncertainly. Rats sniff the air wafting from it, trying to settle the disagreement between their eyes and noses. But the tall man is unaware of his effect on the surrounding wildlife. He is busy learning how to walk.

This is a complex procedure, and the man is proud of his progress. His gait is far from graceful, but he has put appreciable distance between himself and the grisly scene of his birth. The black smoke is a far-off smudge, and he can no longer smell any trace of the blond woman's rotting body.

Right leg up, forward, down. Left leg up, body forward, right leg back, left leg down.

Repeat.

He knows he should be doing something with his arms as well but hasn't yet deduced what it could be. Waving? Flapping? He raises them straight ahead just to get them out of his way while he concentrates on the ancient art of ambulation. One step at a time.

A few other things have come back to him. Words for common

objects—grass, trees, sky—and a general overview of reality. He knows what a planet is and that he is on one and that its name is Earth. He is not sure what a country is, but he thinks this one is called America. He knows the strip of cloth around his neck is a tie, and that it's the same color as the blood oozing from the bite on his leg, although that is rapidly darkening. The vacuum in his head is not as painful as it was, but there is another emptiness building in him. A hollow sensation that begins in his belly and creeps up into his mouth, pulling him forward like a horse's bit. *Where are we going?* he asks the emptiness. *Are you taking us to people?*

There is no answer.

As far as the tall man can tell, Earth is a world of grass and trees and water. He feels like it should be more beautiful than it is. The river is a sickly greenish brown. The sky is blue but not pretty. Too pale, almost gray. He remembers a sky that looked different— *sitting on the roof under noonday sun, listening to his father yell*—and rivers that were clean—*sinking to the bottom and holding his breath, wishing he never had to come up*—but the hollowness yanks him out of his reverie. He keeps walking.

The trees reach closer to the river until there is no more room to skirt around them, so he stops and regards the dark area where there are a lot of them together—*forest.* A smell of mildew and earthy rot emanates from it, stirring inexplicable terror in him— *Hole. Worms. Darkness. Sleep. Vast mouth and endless throat, down, down, down*—but he has no choice. He enters the forest.

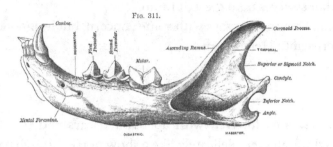

Fig. 311.

JULIE WATCHES THE BACKS of her parents' heads, looming like stone idols in the front seats. No one has spoken in two hours. She watches the trees and empty fields become buildings, gas stations, college campuses. *Welcome to Bellingham,* an overpass mural declares, or used to declare before some cheery vandal sprayed the *B* into an *H* and crossed out *ingham.*

A spark of recognition goes off in her head and she lurches toward the front seats. "Hey! This is where Nikki lives!"

Her father glances at her in the mirror. "Who?"

"My pen pal? The deliveryman's niece?"

"The one who sent you a bottle of whiskey when you were ten?"

"Yes, Dad, that one. We have to stop!"

"Bellingham is exed. Nothing there to stop for."

"But I got a letter from her right before we left Omaha."

"That was almost a year ago."

"She could still be here."

"Not likely."

"Dad, we have to check!" She tries to catch her father's eyes. "She's my friend."

He doesn't answer. She waits, preparing herself to digest yet another wish denied. Then to her surprise, and without comment, her father swerves onto the exit ramp.

"John?" her mother says with some concern, but he ignores her. They drive into Hellingham.

. . .

The streets are cluttered with abandoned cars and the Tahoe weaves through them delicately like a show horse through barrels. Julie presses her face to the glass, scanning the windows of houses for any sign of movement. Most are boarded over. The ones that aren't boarded are broken. She sees movement in one, a sluggish shape lurching in the darkness of the living room, but she says nothing.

"Where does Nikki live?" her father asks in a genial, optimistic tone that draws a cold look from his wife.

"Downtown," Julie says quietly. "Holly Street."

They turn right on Holly, the thoroughfare Nikki always talked about in her letters. She made it sound like it was Mardi Gras every weekend, she and her college buddies gathering in riotous numbers, stumbling into the street and blocking traffic, laughing and singing, trying to forget the world that was crumbling around them. Julie had always wanted to see this street. To watch her friend drink and flirt and to learn firsthand how people keep living.

But Holly Street is paved with corpses. And other, less rotted corpses stagger through the mess like scavenging dogs, picking for scraps on the bones of their friends.

"What's the address?" her father queries loudly as the Tahoe runs over a body, his voice not quite masking the crunch.

Julie can't speak.

"Address?" he asks again as he swerves to hit a creature chewing on a girl's foot. Its brief grunt of surprise, the thumps and cracks as the SUV grinds over it . . .

"Twelve-twelve," she whispers.

Her mother is silent in the front seat, keeping her eyes carefully hidden from the mirror.

"Is this it?"

The Tahoe rolls to a stop, its tires crackling on gravel and glass. Julie rolls down her window and regards the old house. Front porch lined with moldy couches. Beer bottles and cigarette butts, muddy boot marks on the crooked walls . . . it was probably a ruin before the collapse, but it's a different kind now. Not the kind created by an excess of life. Not the result of seven young people crammed into a small house, desperate to enjoy themselves before the world they inherited burns up. The windows are empty holes lined with glass teeth. The front door is wide open and creaking in the breeze, and everything inside is dark.

"Nikki?" Julie manages to croak, despite the obvious. "Hello?"

Her father shakes his head and puts the truck in gear. Julie makes no objection as they pull away from the house. She says nothing as they head back to I-5.

"Was that really necessary, John?" her mother mutters.

"She needs to understand."

"Understand what? That all her friends are dead? That the world's a pile of shit? Christ."

His reply is the rev of the engine as he resumes their southward course.

Audrey Grigio twists her head around the seat to look at her daughter. "I'm sorry, honey."

Julie doesn't meet her gaze. She stares out the window as her friend's city recedes, giving way to pines and cedars, deep valleys and high mountains silhouetted against the browning sun. She wonders how many of her letters are moldering in the drop-off boxes. She wonders how long she's been writing to a ghost. She wonders what her friend's voice sounded like, and if she died in panic or acceptance, and if her twenty-one years had any effect on the relentless spinning of the world.

Fig. 337.

"WHAT ABOUT THESE?" Addis asks, holding up a pair of pruning shears.

"Too small."

He grabs a power drill. "This?"

"Nothing electric."

He picks up a nail-pull bar and holds it out. Nora considers it. "Nah. You need to be able to pierce a skull without much windup. Something with more focused weight."

The fluorescent lights buzz overhead as she and her brother browse the aisles of a hardware store in search of weapons. Their parents took the guns. Nora would like to believe it was for safety, that they didn't trust her not to shoot herself or Addis by mistake, but no. They've seen her shoot a militia sniper out of a seventh-story window, calmly aiming the family Glock in the dim morning light while they were still trying to untangle their blankets. She can find few excuses for her parents, and she wonders what she will tell Addis when he's old enough to demand real answers.

"How about *this*?"

He hefts a big, oak-handled axe. He presses his lips into a tough-guy scowl and takes a test swing, making a *whoosh* sound with his mouth. The axe slips out of his hands and crashes into a display of detergent bottles, spewing milky blue Tide all over the floor.

"It's the right idea," Nora giggles, "but maybe something a little more manageable."

She pulls two hatchets off the rack and hands one to Addis. He swings it, making the *whoosh* followed by a grisly *splat,* then grins at Nora. There is a savageness in this grin, a bloodlust that in any other era would have been patiently lectured out of him as he grew up. It scares Nora a little, but she says nothing. This is not any other era. This is now.

"These'll have to do," she says. "Now let's go find some food."

* * *

The Space Needle's lobby has been completely ransacked over the months or years, however long it's been since this particular city surrendered to the march of regress. All the T-shirts and hats are gone. All the mugs, sunglasses, and "Space Noodles" pasta. None of the looters took an interest in the snow globes, fridge magnets, or souvenir spoons. Even the paperweights—which could potentially be used as bludgeons—are still here.

The lights in the lobby are broken out, but when Nora pushes the elevator button she hears machinery grinding into motion. Addis looks up at her, wriggling with excitement. Nora pulls her hatchet out of her backpack and waits.

The doors open with a polite *ding.* There is nothing inside that wants to kill them.

"Let me push it!" Addis shouts, and begins scanning the rows of buttons.

"Not the top one, that's probably the view deck. There. That's the restaurant."

Addis pushes the button. The elevator soars upward, making Nora's knotted stomach groan in protest.

"Whoa . . . ," Addis gasps, pressing his face against the window as the city recedes below, spreading out to a hazy horizon of blue islands and waves. The disc at the top of the Space Needle rushes down and envelops them in darkness, then the doors open on the restaurant. Nora steps out and gives Addis a formal bow.

"Welcome to Sky City, sir. Do you have a reservation?"

He looks concerned. "What? What's a—"

She laughs and shoves him in the face. "Never mind. Come on."

She walks into the dining area and glances around, searching for the kitchen. Addis pauses at the edge of the disc's outer rim, which rotates slowly.

"It's *moving!*" he says.

"Yeah, I've heard about that. Cool, huh?"

"Are you *sure* it's not a spaceship?"

"Let's go look around. Maybe we'll find the cockpit."

Compared to most of the city below, the restaurant is in good shape. One table is missing its cloth and silverware and there's a wad of bloody bandages on one of the benches, but the place is otherwise unspoiled. No broken windows, no graffiti, no corpses. But they aren't here for the atmosphere.

They stand in front of the door of the walk-in freezer, paralyzed with suspense like game show contestants watching the wheel. Bankrupt or jackpot? Starve or keep going?

Nora pulls the door open. The freezer is full of food. Tubs of sliced vegetables, stacks of baguettes, bins stuffed with chicken breasts and steaks, a dozen sausage ropes hanging from the ceiling. And all of it is rotten. A room-temperature cornucopia of mold.

Addis's lips bunch and his brows squeeze down tight. He walks stiffly back into the kitchen and stands in a corner with his face to the wall, fists clenched at his sides.

Nora takes a deep breath and holds it, steps into the freezer and stares at the festering heaps of locally sourced organic ingredients. She thinks about those game show contestants, how they always took losing so well. They were college kids and single moms, hungry dropouts and desperate debt-cripples, and when the wheel informed them they'd just lost a life-changing sum of money and would go home with nothing, they laughed and sighed and clapped for their own demise. *Aw, darn!*

This is a different kind of show. The prize is not cash or a set of golf clubs; it's another day of life for Nora and her brother, and she is not about to lose politely.

She dives into the compost heap, knocking aside tubs of slimy asparagus, dumping bins of green chicken breasts, digging down through the mess as furry green sausages slap against her face. She gags from the smell and nearly vomits when her hand sinks into a turkey frothing with maggots. But at the bottom of it all, in a corner under some rat-gnawed bags of flour, she finds a box. She opens the box, and it's full of cans.

"Addis!" she shouts.

It's not a large box. Just three cans and a plastic tub: peeled potatoes, green beans, tofu, and some slightly rancid margarine. Not a life-changing win . . . but enough to pay off their hunger debts with a little left to spare.

She stands up with the box and finds Addis in the doorway, wide-eyed. "Guess what, Addy." She grins, savoring the novelty of what she's about to say. "We're going to have dinner tonight."

• • • •

Pommes frites, fried in margarine. Green beans, sautéed in margarine. Margarine-infused tofu, with margarine sauce. It's the tastiest meal Nora has eaten since this impromptu family vacation began.

"You're a disaster," she says, watching Addis shovel handfuls of dripping potatoes into his mouth. He has wasted no time staining the white linen tablecloth and spilling all his water on the floor. "You're lucky you know the chef."

They have the best table in the house and the view is spectacular: all of Seattle spreads out for them through the floor-to-ceiling windows, fading east into the blue of the Cascades. Nora imagines bow-tied servers checking in on them, asking if they've saved room for dessert. She has always wondered what crème brûlée tastes like.

"These fries are way better than the ones at that gas station," Addis says through a mouthful.

"Glad you think so. Healthier, too."

"Really?"

"Slightly."

"That's good."

Nora smiles. A few months ago, the word "healthy" would have made him spit out his food. It's a bittersweet thing to see him finally valuing nutrition.

"Do you think they have music?" he wonders.

"I don't know if that's a good idea."

"Why?"

"If someone comes up the elevator, we might not hear them."

"So? They'll hear us and then they can have dinner with us."

"Addis . . ."

"What?"

Nora glances around. Addis watches her.

"Fine. Let me go check."

She makes a quick circuit of the restaurant, looking for the stereo controls but looking even harder for any signs that they're not alone. Those bandages. The blood is brown; they're at least a day or two old. She finds no other traces, so when she finds the stereo, plugged into some cleanup crewman's battered iPod, she spins through its playlists with a certain thrill, hoping to find something they can both enjoy.

"Billie Holiday?" she yells at Addis.

"Boring!"

"The Beatles?"

"They suck!"

"You little shit," she laughs. "I'm putting it on shuffle."

She presses play without looking and walks back to the table.

Some soft piano begins, then a high, whispery voice layered with fragile harmonies.

"What's this?" Addis says, wrinkling his nose.

"Sounds like Sigur Rós."

"Why do you always listen to *old* music!" Addis groans.

"This isn't that old."

"It's like a million years old."

Nora sighs and flicks one of Addis's spilled green beans onto his shirt. A glint comes into his eye. He picks up a fry.

"No," Nora snaps, pointing her fork at him. "We are absolutely not food-fighting with this meal. Put it down."

Addis hesitates, sizing up her resolve.

"Sir," she says in cop-voice, "I need you to put the fry down immediately."

He pops it in his mouth. Nora nods and eats some tofu. They smile at each other as they chew.

The restaurant moves so slowly it's barely perceptible, but Nora notices they've made half a revolution since they arrived. The Cascade Mountains have been replaced by Puget Sound, pink and red, set ablaze by the setting sun. In the evening dimness, with the buildings all just silhouettes, the city looks perfectly normal. Many of the downtown high-rises are dark, but a few still have power, their tiny windows blinking on and off like Christmas lights. She watches her brother shoving fries into his mouth and somehow getting them in his hair, and she wonders where she's taking him. When they spend a whole day walking, where are they walking to? She has been avoiding this thought, but here it is again, insistent: she has no idea. She has no destination, or even a direction. She is making them walk because motion is the only plan she has. Because stillness is death.

Addis is looking out the window now, following her gaze. Her focus shifts to their reflections in the glass, ghostly faces surrounded by constellations of ceiling lights, and she is struck again by how different they are. He is tiny even for his age; Nora is already taller than her mother. His skin is dark like their father's; hers is a shade more Irish. Her hair is a briar of loose coils; his is a tightly woven nest that floats over his head collecting leaves, cobwebs, French fries. It's in desperate need of grease, so dry she could probably snap a chunk off in her fingers. His skin, too, so ashy he almost looks dead. It hits her suddenly how fragile he is. How constantly vulnerable. She doubted her ability to be a mother even before the end of the world. How is she going to do it now?

"Nora?"

He is looking at her uneasily. She wonders what her face has been doing for the last few minutes. She blinks away the beginnings of a tear.

"I need to go to the bathroom," she says, and stands up. The music has shifted to something modern, one of those new pop songs Addis and his friends used to listen to back in DC. It murmurs and clangs, slow and dark, the singer's androgynous voice doubled note for note by a mournful viola. It gives her goose bumps, and she makes a note to skip it on her way back. She never thought she'd be out of touch with youth culture by age sixteen. The darkness came so abruptly her tastes never had a chance to adjust, and now it all just scares her. She retreats into the past, to the records Auntie Shirley used to play while they built Legos in the living room. Some Ella or Billie or Frank would be nice right now, despite Addis's protests. There are worse feelings than boredom.

She pushes into the women's restroom and leans against the sink, fighting for composure. She looks in the mirror at her tired red eyes. She sees a large mound in the corner of the room, heaving slowly under a tablecloth.

• • •

"Addis, get your stuff."

"What?"

"We're leaving."

"But I'm not done eat—"

"Addis!"

He looks up at her, startled.

"Get your stuff."

Addis grabs his NPR tote bag and stuffs his hatchet into it next to a few bags of leftover food. Nora takes his hand and marches toward the elevator.

"What's going on?"

"There's something in the bathroom."

"Something?"

"Something or someone."

"Someone bad?"

"I don't know. It doesn't matter."

"But what if it's someone good?"

"Doesn't matter."

She drags her brother into the elevator and presses the lobby button. The elevator drops, pushing stomach bile into her throat.

"But I thought that's why we're walking around! I thought we're trying to find people who can help us."

"This person can't help us."

"How do you know?"

"Because they're lying on the floor under a bloody tablecloth."

"Are they hurt?"

"At least."

"Then shouldn't we help *them?*"

Nora pauses. She looks at her brother. It's a strange feeling, being judged by a child. He's seven years old; where the hell did he get a moral compass? Certainly not from his parents. Not even from her. She supposes there must be people in the world who stick to their principles, who always do the right thing, but they are few and far between, especially now. Where does a child get an idea as unnatural as goodness?

The elevator reaches the bottom. Addis watches Nora hopefully. She sighs and presses the restaurant's floor. They ascend.

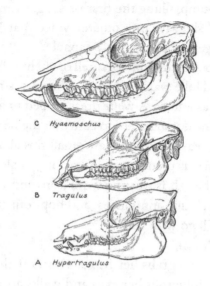

C   *Hyaemoschus*

B   *Tragulus*

A   *Hypertragulus*

THE SILVER TAHOE is low on gas. Julie can hear her father muttering about it every few minutes, scanning the surrounding landscape for likely filling stations. Eventually, on some obscure cue, he takes an exit into what appears to be a primeval forest. There are no signs advertising food or gas or civilization of any kind, but after a few miles a tiny truck stop appears, halfway hidden in the trees. Most of the city stations are drained dry. To find gas or anything else of value anymore, they have to look where no one else would. They have to turn logic backward and trust intuition, a skill Julie was surprised to find in Colonel John Grigio's stern repertoire.

"Does Dad have super smell?" she asks her mother as they watch him hook the hand pump into the station's diesel reservoir.

"What?"

"How'd he know there was gas out here?"

"I don't know. He's just smart that way." She watches her husband work the pump, filling the first of six gas cans. "You have to appreciate that," she says in a quieter voice that Julie can barely hear. "If nothing else, he's certainly capable."

The sickly sweet, rotten apricot smell of chemically preserved fuel floods the air, and Julie watches her mother press a fold of her dress against her nose as a filter. A *white* dress, pulled in at the waist by a bright red sash. She doesn't seem to care that the hem is brown with dirt and engine grease, that there are small rips all over it revealing bare skin. The dress is pretty, so she wears it. Julie loves her for that, even though she herself is wearing work jeans and a gray T-shirt.

"I have to pee," Julie announces, and hops out of the car.

"Not alone. I'll go with you."

"I'm twelve, Mom."

"You're veal." She grabs her Ruger 9mm off the dash and gets out of the truck. Julie rolls her eyes and walks around the back of the station with her mother in tow. She drops her jeans, her mother hikes her dress, and they crouch in the bushes.

"Remember those wine parties you and Dad used to throw?" Julie says.

"Sure."

"I wish we could have one now. I'm old enough to have a whole glass, right?"

"I'd say so. Don't know about your dad, though."

"I'll talk him into it."

Her mother smiles. "Maybe we can do something when we find the enclave. A housewarming party."

Julie watches her urine pool around her work boots. She browses the decades of graffiti scratched and sprayed onto the station's wall.

Big Dick Tim was here

Tim sux big dick

God still loves us!

God loves himself

~~NEVER~~ GIVE UP

"I want to get wasted," Julie mutters.

Her mother laughs.

Julie wipes with a leaf and buttons her jeans. A dead thorn branch catches on her mother's dress and pulls away with her when she stands. Her husband is waiting around the corner and he watches her tug at the branch until it finally rips free, tearing another hole in the bodice.

"You need some real clothes," he says. "We're not out for a picnic."

"Fuck off, John," she says cheerfully, and brushes past him.

"By the time we get to the enclave you're going to be wearing a bikini."

"The better to seduce their leader."

They drive back to the freeway in brittle silence, and Julie thinks about wine parties. She thinks about their old house. She thinks about the day she found out her father used to have a band, and how her mother played his album for her and she laughed even though it was good, because how else could she react to the revelation that her father was human?

She peers into the passing trees, searching for wildlife. Birds, deer, something stupid and innocent that she can pretend to be for a while. Surely creatures that simple know how to be happy.

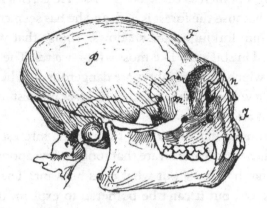

T HE TALL MAN is in pain.

The feeling that began in his stomach has now spread through his entire body and somehow beyond it. It radiates out from him like a cloud of ghosts, countless hands clutching at the air, reaching out for . . . something. He wishes he knew what it wanted, but it's a mindless brute. It lashes him onward with unintelligible grunts of need.

In some distant compartment of his mind, he is aware that the forest is beautiful. Despite the darkness and the musty tomb smell, there is a silence and softness that he finds comforting. He runs his hands along mossy tree trunks as he passes, enjoying their texture. *Like wool,* he thinks. *Like blankets. Her skin was—*

Something shifts. He can still feel the moss but it has been reduced to information: *Soft. Cool. Damp.* He no longer understands why he is wasting energy touching a tree, so he drops his hands and walks faster.

He is in a forest. He is surrounded by trees. He is wearing a tie the color his blood used to be, and slacks the color his blood is now. He is tall and thin but strong for his build—he surprises himself by snapping a branch as thick as his wrist. He carries it for a while like a club, because the forest is dark and he has seen creatures that aren't like him lurking in the shadows. Things that walk on four legs, covered in soft stuff like moss—fur—*wolves*. The forest is full of wolves, which he remembers are dangerous, and he feels afraid. But after a few hours the fear fades; he loses interest in the branch and tosses it aside.

It is becoming harder for him to maintain interest in anything but the hollowness. He is aware that tools and weapons might help him get what he wants, but what does he want? The hollowness seems to know, but it can't be bothered to explain. It pulses and pounds with one vague agenda, reflexively vetoing all other initiatives, even ones that might help it achieve its goals—such as carrying a weapon. The tall man will get no help from these impulses. He must decipher himself by himself.

He thinks about the wolves. He understands that they are not like him and that they want to hurt him. Maybe he wants to hurt them too. Maybe that's what he wants. Maybe creatures that are not like each other are supposed to hurt each other to find out which one is stronger, so that the stronger one can take the things it wants. A competition. A game. *War! Sex! Football!*

His eyes widen with these sudden bursts of insight. He is happy that he is remembering things. Perhaps soon he will have enough information to do whatever the brute in his belly is demanding.

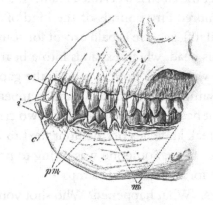

"Hello?"

The thing under the tablecloth continues to heave. The blood-stain in the middle of the cloth is bright red. Spreading.

"Hey. Are you alive?"

Nora stands in the bathroom doorway with her hatchet at the ready. Addis stands behind her, trembling despite all his noble ideals.

Nora takes a step inside.

"Listen. If you're still alive, you need to give me some kind of sign or we're gonna leave."

The cloth shifts slightly. A hand slides out from under it, palm down on the floor.

"Okay, that shows me you're still moving, but I need to know you're capital-L *Living*. So if you're not Dead, tap twice."

There is a long hesitation. The hand taps twice.

Addis grabs her shirt hem. She rubs his head.

"Okay," she says under her breath, and approaches the heaving mound. Holding her hatchet high, ready to strike, she pulls the tablecloth away.

Addis hides his eyes behind his hands and starts whimpering.

The man under the cloth is a certified giant. At least six foot five, probably two hundred fifty pounds of the kind of hard bulk that looks like fat until it flexes. He is bald except for some light stubble on the sides of his head, which expands into a beard surrounding big, soft lips. But what Nora notices most is the gaping hole in his stomach, slowly saturating his white T-shirt. It appears to be a gunshot wound, but it has been sliced open with two crude, crisscrossing incisions. A steak knife lies on the floor next to him, as well as two bloody dinner forks. Someone was trying to perform surgery using dinnerware for a scalpel and clamps.

"Hey," she says. "What happened? Who shot you?"

The man's pale blue eyes fixate on her, dilating unsteadily. He opens his mouth, but all that comes out is a croak. He makes a vague waving motion and closes his eyes as if to say, *Doesn't matter.*

Nora lowers her voice. "Are they still here?"

He faintly shakes his head, eyes still closed.

"Who tried to take the bullet out? Is someone else with you?"

His eyes open. His hand moves like he's trying to point somewhere, but he can't summon the strength. He moves his lips on his next exhalation, and Nora hears the outline of a word, perhaps a name, but it's too faint. A ghost. He closes his eyes again. Tears glint in the corners.

Nora feels her stomach clenching. She stares at the hole in his belly, its ragged edges and dark center, a well of blood leading down into his inner depths. A wave of nausea sweeps through her; drops of perspiration pop out on her forehead.

"Listen," she says, "I'm not . . . I don't know how to . . ." She gingerly touches the edge of the wound. The sliced flaps of skin spread apart and she shudders. "I don't know what to do."

The man's head moves slightly. Nora would like to think it's a nod. That he understands. His eyes roll into his head, then return to hers.

Nora glances back at Addis. He is standing in the doorway, wringing his hands in front of his crotch and biting his lip.

He wasn't wrong. They did the right thing. But they shouldn't have.

She touches the man's fiery forehead. "I'm sorry."

He holds her gaze for a moment longer, then closes his eyes. A long, slow breath comes out of him and doesn't come back.

Nora stands up. "Addis, wait outside for a sec. I need to do something."

"Is he dead?"

"Yeah. Wait outside."

"Why?"

"Because I need to do something."

Addis looks at the hatchet clenched in her hand. His lips tremble and he backs out of the room.

Nora stands over the man, staring at his shiny bald head. She has never done this before. Her mind moves ahead to the sensations that will vibrate up her arms through the hatchet when it cracks the skull and sinks into the rubbery tissues inside. She raises the hatchet. She shuts her eyes. The toilet stall behind her creaks open and something groans and Nora screams and runs. She doesn't turn around to see what's there, she just runs. She grabs her brother's hand and drags him down the hall at a full sprint. Standing in the elevator pounding the "door close" button, she sees movement reflected in the restaurant's windows and hears a ragged howl, low and guttural but distinctly female. Then the doors slide shut, and they descend.

• • •

Addis is crying. Nora can't believe he still cries so easily after all the things they've been through. He cried when his mother dragged them out of bed and hid them in the bathroom while their father killed a looter with a crowbar. He cried when their apartment and the rest of Little Ethiopia went up in flames, his snot smearing against the window of the family Geo. He cried all the way from DC to Louisiana and then again when he saw New Orleans, yelling at his mother that the Bible said God would never again destroy the earth with a flood. He cried when his father said God is a liar.

Crying. Expelling grief from the body in the form of salt water. What's its purpose? How did it evolve, and why are humans the only creatures that do it? Nora wonders how many years it takes to dry up that messy urge.

"It's okay, Addy," she says as the elevator settles on the ground floor. "We're okay."

His sniffles don't completely subside until the Space Needle is hidden behind buildings far in the distance.

"What *was* that?" he finally asks as they trek north on Highway 99, the first words out of his mouth in thirty minutes.

"Guess," she says.

He doesn't.

They cross the Aurora Bridge just as the sun disappears behind the western mountains. Nora stops, although she knows she shouldn't. They are standing on a narrow sidewalk hundreds of feet above what was once a busy waterway, now a graveyard for sunken and sinking boats, million-dollar yachts floating on their sides, palaces for king crabs.

"Where are we going?" Addis asks.

"I'm not sure."

He pauses to think about this. "How far are we gonna have to walk?"

"I don't know. Probably a million miles."

He sags against the railing. "Can we find somewhere to sleep? I'm really tired."

Nora watches the last red glow of the sunset glitter on the water. Just before the sky goes completely dark, she catches movement out of the corner of her eye and glances back the way they came. On the edge of the hill, just before the bridge leaps out over the chasm, she sees a silhouette. A big silhouette of a big man, standing in the street and swaying slightly.

"Yeah," she mumbles. "Let's go."

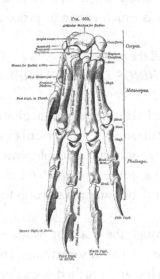

Fig. 460.

HE CLOUD OF HANDS has grown so large and strong it has begun to feel like an extra sense. Some warped hybrid of sight and smell and intuition. The tall man feels it reaching through the forest, its wispy fingers brushing through ferns and poking under rocks, seeking whatever it seeks. He struggles to ignore its constant moaning, which has begun to form words but is still too simple to be understood.

Get. Take. Fill.

He tries to distract himself by remembering more things. *What is your name?* Nothing. *How old are you?* Nothing. He hesitates before his next question. *Who was the woman by the river?* Something surges up from his core, a surprise heave of emotional vomit, but he gags it back down. *Her name was—the weight in your hand, the trigger—*

GUNS CAN KILL YOU! YOUR BRAIN IS IMPORTANT! DO NOT GET SHOT IN THE HEAD!

He is deeply relieved when this second voice interrupts. Its simple information is much easier to process than that terrifying eruption of feeling.

What you did—all the people you—

FIND OTHER THINGS LIKE YOU! THEY CAN HELP YOU GET THINGS YOU WANT!

And so a strange bartering session begins in his mind. He gives up the grief he felt upon seeing the woman and remembers what guns do and that he should avoid people who have them. He hands over his guilt and the desire to atone and receives the knowledge that he will be safer if he can find a group to join. It seems a very fair bargain.

A jolt ripples through the cloud of hands and his eyes snap open wide. His new sense has found something. The hands have reached very far, perhaps miles, and touched something that arouses them. They stretch off into the darkness of the woods, sending pulses of excitement back to him like Morse code.

Come. Follow. Take.

He obeys.

His muscles, which begin to cool and stiffen anytime he stands still, become supple again with whatever unknown energy drives them, and he walks at a brisk pace. The forest grows darker as he nears its heart. He glimpses strange things from the corner of his eyes: crystalline frogs and birds that glow, doors in the dirt and cyclones of bones, but he doesn't stop to wonder at these things. He has traded wonder for hunger. He follows the brute.

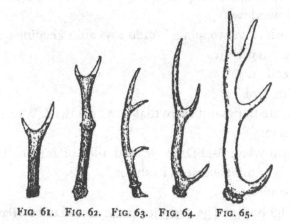

FIG. 61. FIG. 62. FIG. 63. FIG. 64. FIG. 65.

The sun sets faster than it used to. Nora is almost sure of this. It plummets like a glob of wax in a lava lamp, so rapidly she swears she can trace its motion, and she wonders if the earth has sped up. If perhaps somehow, all the bombs pummeling its crust have increased its spin. A ridiculous thought, but she still raises her walking pace. It's unfair to Addis's little legs, but he doesn't complain. He maintains a half run to keep up.

"Why don't we find a car?" he pants.

"Dad never showed me how to hotwire."

"What if somebody left their keys?"

"Those ones are probably all gone by now. But keep an eye out."

Addis abruptly stops and turns around. "What was that?"

Nora didn't actually hear it, so she feels okay saying, "Nothing. Probably boats knocking against each other. Come on."

They pass several motels on their way up the hill, but a bed isn't much use if you can't sleep, and she knows she won't tonight without a gun under her pillow. She pushes forward, scanning the storefront windows.

"Why aren't we stopping?" Addis says after keeping quiet for an impressive ten minutes.

"We need guns."

"But I'm *tired*."

"There are things out there that don't get tired. We need guns." Addis sighs.

"Tell you what, A-D-D. If we find a lot of bullets, I'll let you shoot the next thing we need to shoot."

Addis smiles.

The neighborhood gets seedier as they move north. Pawn shops, smoke shops, dark alleys littered with condoms and syringes. This is encouraging. The "bad neighborhoods" of yesterday are the survival buffets of today, full of guns and drugs and all the other equipment necessary for living the low life. No neighborhood built for prosperity has any place in the new era—no one needs parks or cafés or fitness centers, much less schools or libraries. What's useful now is the infrastructure of the underworld, with its triple-bolted doors and barred windows, its hidden passages and plentiful supplies of vice. The slums and ghettos had the right idea all along. They were just ahead of their time.

"There!" Addis says, pointing at a storefront.

Nora stops and stares at it. A lovingly painted plywood sign, declaring in thousand-point font:

GUNS

She chuckles to herself. She almost walked past it.

• • •

Naturally, a cache this obvious has been thoroughly looted, but they search anyway. The display cases are empty, the ammo boxes are gone. There are more than a few puddles of dried blood on the floor, but no bodies. Whoever made this mess was careless. Everyone living in these times knows the most important rule of conservation: if you have to kill someone, make sure they stay dead. It may be a losing battle, the math may be against the Living, but diligence in this one area will at least slow down the spread of the plague. Responsible murder is the new recycling.

"This is the worst gun store ever," Addis says, scanning row after empty row.

"Pretend you're a looter. What places would you check last?"

"What are looters like?"

"I don't know, hungry? Scared?"

"Okay. That's easy."

"So you run into this place, you're hungry and scared, maybe you shoot some people . . . what do you do next?"

"Well . . ." A little smile blooms on his face as he gets into character. Nora realizes this is inappropriate make-believe to play with a seven-year-old, and for a moment she feels bad. But only a moment.

Addis runs around the store aiming an invisible pistol, making *blam* sounds near all the blood pools and taking little grabs at the empty shelves. Then he turns to deliver his findings.

"I'd grab all the ones off the shelves first. Then the stuff in the cases. All the stuff that's right in front, 'cause I'd be scared to go into any back rooms or corners."

"Well I already checked the back room . . ."

"What if I was the owner of the shop?" His eyes widen with inspiration. "I bet I'd be even more scared then!"

"Okay, what if you were the owner?"

"I'd put guns in secret spots all over the store. So I could grab one no matter where I was."

Nora checks the cash register. Its drawer is open, empty. She checks the shelves under it. Empty.

"But if there was lots of shooting all the time," Addis continues like a scientist explaining his breakthrough theorem, "I'd probably be hiding on the *floor* a lot."

Nora shrugs and lies down on the floor behind the cash register, playing along. "Oh shit," she laughs. She grabs the Colt .45 taped to the cabinet molding and jumps up, aiming it at an imaginary target.

"Blam," she says.

Addis grins with huge, Christmas-morning eyes.

Nora checks the magazine. Full.

"I love you, Addis Greene," she says. "Let's go find somewhere to sleep."

• • •

When choosing their lodging, they ignore all the feeble enticements on the billboards. Fragmented advertisements with letters either missing or added by vandals.

CLEAN & QUI T
FREE INTERNmEnT
MONTHLY RA p ES

They base their choice solely on the thickness of the window bars.

Not wanting to damage their room's lock, Nora kicks in the office door instead, finds the key for the room farthest from the street, and enters the civilized way. Once inside, she locks the doorknob, latches the chain, hooks the hook, turns the deadbolt, the mortise, and the night latch.

This is a good motel.

A scan of the room brings a grim smile to her face. Peeling beige wallpaper. Dark orange carpet with wall-to-wall stains. Teal bedspread with a pink floral pattern. She tries the light switch but isn't surprised when nothing happens. Businesses in areas like this probably only bought gas generators, leaving the solar and hydrogen to the downtown folk. As a general rule, she doesn't expect to find electricity anywhere she can't find art galleries.

The moment she feels satisfied with the room's security, a wave of exhaustion washes over her. She plops down on the bed next to Addis and stares out the window into the darkness. After a while she feels Addis looking at her. She senses another round of questions building in him.

"What, Addy," she mumbles.

He doesn't answer. She notices a slight tremble in his chin.

"What's wrong?" she asks more gently.

"Mom and Dad . . . ," he says. "Where did they go?"

Her lips press into a thin line. "I don't know."

"Why aren't we looking for them?"

She hesitates, but she's too tired to protect him anymore. She lets it out in a breath. "Because they're not looking for us."

Addis's eyes focus on something far away. Nora braces herself, hoping he's still young enough to accept this and move on the way he does with a skinned knee or a bee sting. A good, hard cry, then back to playing, though the pain is still there.

"They're mean," he mumbles, glowering at the sheets.

Nora takes a deep breath. "Yeah, they are. But Addy?" She puts a hand on his shoulder. "It doesn't matter."

"Why not?"

"Because Mom and Dad are just people. Same as Auntie Shirley, Evan, anyone. Just because they *made* us doesn't mean they *are* us. They're mean and stupid and we're smart and cool, and we don't have to let what they do decide how we feel."

He looks at the floor, doesn't answer.

Nora raises an eyebrow at him. "At least . . . *I'm* smart and cool. Aren't you smart and cool?"

He lets out a heavy sigh. "Yeah."

"I thought so."

"I'm super smart and super cool."

"I knew it." She raises a palm. He slaps it weakly. "You ready for bed?"

Instead of answering, he crawls under the covers and curls into a ball with his back to her. Five minutes later, he's snoring. She sits there for a while, watching his breaths rise and fall under that hideous teal blanket. How much longer will simple logic and guidance-counselor pep talks be able to numb his wounds? Or hers, for that matter?

She slips under the blankets and stares at the mildewed ceiling. Despite her urgent exhaustion, her eyes won't close. Then sometime around midnight, she glances out the window and sees a man watching her through the bars.

For Addis's sake she stifles her scream. Biting her lip, her whole body shaking, she gets up and swipes the curtains shut. She stands there a moment, just breathing. She checks all the locks and turns in a slow circle, making sure there are no other doors or possible access points to the room. There aren't. And the door, in addition to its six different locks, has steel hinges as thick as her thumb. The owner of this motel must have been an avid reader of the signs of the times. The room is a vault.

Clutching the Colt, she pulls the curtains back for one last peek. The man is still there. His eyes, now pewter gray instead of sky blue, slowly track over to meet hers. Other than the desaturation of his irises and skin, he hasn't changed physically. He hasn't begun to rot. But it's astonishing how different he looks. He's not quite empty, his eyes still show a dim light of awareness, but whoever he was before, he is no longer. His face fits him like a cheap Halloween mask.

Nora knows she should shoot him right now, tell Addis the bang was just another of his nightmares and soothe him back to sleep, but she decides to leave it till morning. The man *could* throw rocks through the window, maybe shove a piece of wood through the bars if he's unusually motivated, but there really isn't much he can do to hurt them through those narrow gaps. And she has to admit, violence seems to be the last thing on his mind, if he has one anymore. He's just standing there, hands limp at his sides, looking at her. If she had to take a guess at reading his expression, she would say he looks . . . lost.

She shuts the curtain and climbs back in bed. She doesn't put the gun under her pillow as planned. She keeps it tight in her hand, safety off, polished steel cold against her thigh.

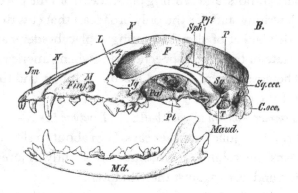

JULIE WATCHES THE SUN change from a fierce point of light to a sad orange blob that sags against the horizon like rotting fruit. She shivers when it disappears, imagining evil eyes snapping open in the trees surrounding the Tahoe, hungry mouths hissing *at last.* She knows this is stupid; her fear of the dark makes her feel like a child instead of a strong and capable twelve-year-old. There are monsters in the dark, of course, plenty of them. But there are just as many in the light.

Everything is going to be fine, the rich baritone on the truck's radio assures her. *The dark is always darkest before the brightness. Embrace your inner—Avoid major highways during militia activity. Stay in your homes until assistance arrives—Seahawks lead the Broncos forty-three to eight with three minutes on the clock . . .*

"For the love of God, John," her mother says. "Turn that shit off."

"You'd rather sit here in dead silence all night?"

"Yes! Absolutely yes."

The radio mumbles a constant stream of cultural non sequiturs. Fragments of sports broadcasts from games that ended years ago, ads for long-forgotten blockbusters, inspirational quotes from popular self-help authors, and calming platitudes from the government's own hack writing staff. It's the only broadcast that cuts through the nationwide blanket of signal jamming, a placeholder station once used for state-of-the-union speeches back when America was still a union. The government skipped town in a hurry, and they forgot to turn off the radio.

This summer, hold on to your balls. . . . Dwayne Lee is—

"Please, John," Julie's mother says. "I'm about to slit my wrists."

He turns the volume down, but only slightly. Audrey sighs in exhaustion and leans against the window.

"We could talk," Julie offers.

"I think it's bedtime," her father announces, and pulls off into a deserted rest stop alongside I-5. He shuts off the engine and Audrey visibly relaxes when the radio's schizophrenic chatter goes silent.

Julie's legs are numb, so she gets out of the truck and paces around, stamping her feet to revive the nerves. Her father opens the rear doors and grabs his shotgun off the ceiling-mounted rack. The rack holds three weapons: a big Army-issue riot gun for him, an automatic twelve-gauge for his wife, and a twenty-gauge Mossberg Mini for his daughter, which he procured after noticing the bruises her big Remington was inflicting on her shoulder. He gave it to her after they had to leave Omaha, and she got to use it the very next day, when Denver didn't work out either.

"What are you doing?" she asks him.

"Perimeter check." He starts toward the rest stop bathrooms.

"Hey Dad?"

He stops, turns.

"Is Seattle exed?"

"It's still a question mark in the Almanac, but probably. DBC takes their sweet time assessing the bigger cities."

"Do you think we'll find any people there?"

"No."

Julie releases a low sigh that gets lost in the wind. Her father finishes checking the buildings and heads out into the evergreen blackness. Her mind suddenly recalls one of last night's dreams and begins to flood with images—a deep, murky hole lined with teeth, a voice from the bottom beckoning her father—so she retreats to the Tahoe and sits in the driver's seat next to her mother. Her stomach growls like the voice in the hole. She reaches around the seat for the bag of Carbtein, tears open one of the little foil packages, and pops a dusty white cube in her mouth.

"Hungry?" she asks her mother, offering her a cube as she attempts to chew the one in her mouth. Her mother stares at it like she's never seen one before. Like she hasn't been eating these nutrient-packed billiards chalks and little else for months. She scratches at the sunken brown spots on her neck and shakes her head. Julie forces herself to swallow the lump of gritty, astringent mortar, then slumps into her seat, relieved to have it over with. She begins to wonder what they'll do when that bag is empty, but she stops herself. The bag is half full. That's what matters tonight.

Her mother switches the radio on and quickly flips away from Fed FM, which is currently playing a selection from its ten-song playlist of lab-tested pop hits. She leaves it on one of the many frequencies of static and leans her seat back, lying with her arms folded, gazing at the ceiling.

"At least static doesn't have commercials," Julie says.

Her mother's lips curve just slightly. "I would love to hear a commercial. I'd listen to commercials all day if it meant there were people out there making and selling things."

"Even those suicide pill commercials?"

"Especially those."

Julie doesn't understand this comment but it creates a cold feeling in her chest. She looks away from her mother.

"Has your life gone on long after the thrill of living is gone?" her mother quotes with a bitter smirk. "Are the dreams in which you're dying the best you've ever had?"

Julie starts flipping through stations, looking for something to change the subject.

"Knock, knock, knock on Heaven's door, with Enditol. Because only the good die young."

Each station plays a different genre of static. There's the bass hum station, the harsh crackle station, and Julie's favorite, the classical white noise station. Someone out there could be broadcasting a world-changing message, a solution, a cure, and unless Julie's family drove within a dozen miles of the source, it would be chewed up and swallowed by the jammers. She is not expecting to find anything worth hearing, just some static jarring enough to distract her mother from her dark thoughts. But then she lands on 90.3, and her mother's smirk vanishes.

"Mom!" Julie squeals under her breath.

For the first time in 1,394 miles, there is music on the radio.

It's an oldie. Something from the late nineties, long before pop music began to resemble horror movie scores. Julie's mother is transfixed as it streams through a gap in the clouds of static.

Starting and then stopping . . . taking off and landing . . . the emptiest of feelings . . .

She watches the radio as if the singer is inside it. Her eyes begin to glisten.

Floors collapsing, falling . . . bouncing back and one day . . . I am gonna grow wings . . . a chemical reaction . . .

The song ends. A young woman's voice replaces it, soft and shaky between spasms of static.

This is KEXP, 90.3 Seattle, bringing you the perfect soundtrack for huddling with your loved ones waiting to die.

To Julie's surprise, her mother laughs. She wipes at her eyes and grins at her daughter.

If you've been listening for a while I apologize for the repetitiveness. We usually try to keep things diverse here, but our door's being battered down as I record this and I didn't have much time to put a playlist together. . . .

Her grin starts to stiffen.

But anyway, if you're hearing this it means they didn't break the equipment, so enjoy the loop for as long as the power lasts. Consider it the last mixtape from us to you before our big breakup. I'm sorry, Seattle. America. World. We knew it couldn't last.

Julie's mother hits the radio's off button and sinks back into her chair. Her smile is gone with no trace.

"Mom?" Julie says softly.

Her mother doesn't respond or react. Her damp eyes regard the ceiling, as blank as a corpse's. Julie feels horrible things crawling in her belly. She gets out of the truck.

Her father is still securing the area, marching around with his gun in position, all procedure and tactics. Her mother has told her stories of when they were both young and wild. How they met on an airplane while in line for the bathroom, how he stole her away from her friends at the airport and showed her around Brooklyn, how they holed up in his tiny apartment for days and played music and drank wine and talked philosophy and causes and things they wanted to fight for. She knows he changed when the world changed. Adapted to survive. And there is a small part of her—a tender, bleeding organ that's been battered and bruised for too many years—that's starting to envy him.

She wanders out toward the trees that surround the rest stop like an infinite void. She sticks her earbuds in and clicks play on an iPod she found on a dead girl somewhere in Pennsylvania. There is a song on this dented, cracked device that she reserves for moments like these, when she needs a reminder that there's still a world out there. That her family is not alone on a spinning ball of rock.

The song is called "For Hannah." She has never heard of the band and the song isn't especially good. What makes it her favorite is the date listed on the file. It's the most recent date she's seen on a song by at least three years. Everything else in her collection was released back when there were still remnants of a music industry, money to be made and goods to spend it on. She has come to believe that this song—a sappy little ballad strummed clumsily on an out-of-tune guitar—is the last song ever recorded in the sunset of civilization.

Can you hear me? it begins. *Look up.* . . .

She stands at the edge of the forest, listening to the indefensible beauty of the singer's tuneless tenor, and whispers the melody into the shadows.

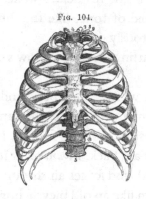

Fig. 104.

THE TALL MAN watches the girl. He stands absolutely still, staring at her through a gap in the bushes, and although she is so close he can see the freckles on her ears, she does not notice him.

What is she?

She is different from him. Smaller, softer, yes—he knows what a female is—but also something else. A fundamental contrast that has nothing to do with her physical shape. Something ephemeral that he can't explain.

The brute knows what it is. The brute is ecstatic about it. Its cloud of hands swarms around the girl, caressing her face, hissing into the man's mind:

This. This. This.

The man doesn't understand. He feels his hollowness lurching toward her, an angry prisoner flinging itself against the walls of his belly, but he doesn't move. *What?* he asks. *What do you want?*

THIS.

His foot lifts off the ground. Left leg up, forward—

"Look up. . . . Look up. . . ."

He halts. A sound is coming out of the girl's mouth. He has

heard similar sounds inside his head—*words*—but they are always short and blunt, devoid of tone, like the thud of heavy boots on asphalt. This is wondrously different.

"The clouds are parting . . . the window's open . . . time to grow a pair of wings . . ."

These are not just words. They bend and stretch and toy with pitch in a way that somehow elevates their meaning.

TAKE! the brute insists, growing furious. *FILL!*

Not yet, the man snaps back. *I want to try it . . .*

He opens his mouth and forces air through it. A harsh, phlegmy note honks out of him like an old bicycle horn. He wants to blush, but his blood is too congealed.

The girl's mouth clamps shut. She pulls out her earbuds and scans the trees with wide eyes.

"Dad . . . ?" she says, backing away.

The tall man starts to move toward her, but another person appears by her side, this one holding a gun.

"What's wrong?" this much bigger person says in a much different voice, harsher and less tonal, closer to the boot stomp of the tall man's thoughts.

"Nothing," the girl says. "I thought I heard something."

The sound of her special words—*singing*—rings in the tall man's head, gently teasing the tone-deaf idiot that lives there. *Come on,* they seem to say. *Try a little harder.* The idiot in his head backs away from the girl's voice as he backs away from her father's gun.

He is glad he has information in his head instead of feelings. He is proud of himself for knowing what to do. The brute screams in protest as he creeps back into the forest, but he shoves it down. When he is a safe distance away, back in the smothering darkness of the woods, it finally surrenders. The cloud of hands goes limp, dejected, then slowly gathers itself and floats off in a new direction.

Soon, it growls at him, and although the man still isn't sure what he's agreeing to, he nods.

Soon.

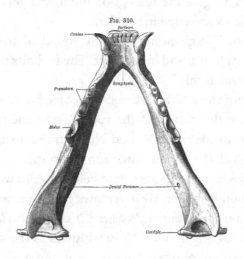

Nora is in Washington, DC, at the community center, doing practice volleys with her teammates.

Bump. Set. Spike.

She has managed to reduce everything to this. When a cult burns down her school, when a soldier corners her in a dark room, when she finds her parents on the floor with a pipe and powder, laughing and screaming like things born in Hell, she comes here. She puts on shorts. She hits the shiny white ball again and again and as long as she's here, the ball is all she has to think about. Keeping it aloft.

The community center is the one place that hasn't changed much in the upheaval. Its ping-pong table, its stained furniture, its snack machines and painfully earnest free condom dispensers—everything is still familiar, even the tired faces behind the help counter. Not because the place is somehow safe from the decline, but because it was already at the bottom before things fell. Nothing here will change until the bottom drops out. Until the president appears on TV to give the final good night and good luck, to cut everyone loose to scavenge in the dark.

"Girls!" a staff lady shouts over the sound of their squeaking sneakers. They all stop and look at her. The ball hits the floor. "You should come watch this."

They file into the lobby. All the staff people are crowded around the small TV in the corner of the room. Someone raises the volume until the speakers rattle, and Nora strains to make out the words through all the digital distortion and static.

Logic is no longer enough, says a man being interviewed in what appears to be a bomb shelter. *We have moved past the point where science alone can offer answers to our predicament. It's grown too large for that.*

"What's he talking about?" Nora whispers to the staff lady. The lady doesn't respond or move her eyes from the screen.

My question for you, Doctor, the host says, *is whether you felt this way yesterday, or if this is simply a reaction to today's news.*

Today's news? The doctor chuckles bitterly. *This isn't today's news. This is us finally acknowledging what's been happening all over the world for years.*

And when did you learn about it?

Last summer. A few days after my wife died in a car crash, when I woke up and looked out my bedroom window and saw her standing in the front yard, gnawing on a human head.

"What's he talking about?" Nora asks more loudly. Still no one looks at her. Signal interference spatters the screen with red pixels. She hears low laughter in the girls' restroom.

What is our reaction to that? How can we understand it? In the space of a few decades we've suffered nearly every catastrophe we ever imagined and now, with civilization already on the brink, we're given this. Our friends and families, all the casualties of all our conflicts, getting up again to keep the tragedy flowing. To consummate it.

The signal sputters and cuts off, detaching the two men's heads, scrambling their faces in a flurry of pixels and ear-piercing noise. Someone clicks the TV off and there is silence.

"What's he *talking* about?" Nora shouts, but no one answers her. Her friends stand with their backs to her, staring at the blank screen, unblinking. A warbling hum begins to fill the room.

She glances out the window and sees her baby brother playing alone in the mud of the playground. A gaunt black wolf stands behind him, drooling, grinning. Her teachers and teammates stare at the blank TV, ignoring her screams as the wolf's jaws stretch open.

• • •

"*Nora!*"

Her eyes snap open just in time to see Addis shutting the window curtain and dashing back to the bed, his eyes wide with panic.

"It's okay, Addy," she murmurs groggily.

"There's . . . there's a—"

"I know. He was there last night. He can't get in."

She climbs out of bed and approaches the window, fingering the Colt's trigger. She opens the curtain. The big man doesn't seem to have moved all night.

"Go away!" she shouts, her face mere inches from his. No reaction. She waves her hands in aggressive shooing motions. "Get the fuck out! Leave us alone!"

Nothing.

She raises the pistol and points it at his forehead.

Addis jams his hands against his ears. But before Nora can give her brother his next lesson on the brutality of modern life, the man pulls back. His expression remains blank, but he backs away from the window and steps aside like a gentleman holding a door for a lady. It unnerves Nora more than she would have expected.

"Get your stuff," she says to her brother, still aiming the gun.

"Aren't you gonna shoot him?"

"Not yet."

"Why?"

"Because he backed up."

"But isn't he a zombie?"

Nora hesitates before answering. "I don't know what he is. No one does."

She slips her backpack on and undoes the door locks, keeping her eyes and pistol trained on the man through the window. Addis huddles close behind her, gripping his hatchet.

"We're coming out!" she yells, having no idea if the man still understands language. "You stay away from us or I'm shooting you!"

She opens the door a crack. He doesn't move. She opens it the rest of the way and steps out, keeping him firmly sighted. "All clear, Addis?"

Addis runs to each corner of the motel and peeks around, securing the perimeter like a seasoned police officer. His father taught him at least one thing well.

"All clear."

Nora walks backward toward him, not taking her eyes off the big man's dull silver gaze.

"Nora?" Addis says quietly.

"What."

"You should shoot him."

She glances back at her brother to make sure the voice really came from him.

"Auntie said we're not supposed to let them stay alive. If you don't kill him he's gonna kill someone else."

"I know what Auntie said." She keeps her sights on the center of the man's forehead. "And Dad said don't waste bullets on other people's problems."

"But Dad is mean."

Her teeth are grinding. The gun is getting slippery in her hands. The big man watches her calmly, standing a safe twenty feet away, arms hanging at his sides.

She doesn't want to shoot him.

She doesn't know what possible good it could do to spare his life, but she knows she wants to. Is it as simple as empathy? That uniquely human reluctance to kill? It can't be. She's killed two people since her fourteenth birthday. Yes, she did it in self-defense to protect her family, but does that really matter? Is the difference between killing with satisfaction and killing with horror nothing more than context?

"I can look away," Addis offers.

"What?"

"If you don't want to shoot him 'cause of me, I can look away when you do it."

"Addis, just shut up, okay?"

He shuts up. There is a long silence.

"Hey!" Nora shouts at the man. "You're infected, right? You're not just mute or sleepwalking or something? You're capital-D Dead?"

No response. As if she needs one. As if his skin, his eyes, and the gaping wound in his stomach weren't enough. She knows exactly what he is, but . . .

"Hey," she almost pleads, knowing she is talking to no one, nothing. "Can you understand me?"

He nods.

Nora gasps. Her gun lowers.

She hears the creak of a door behind her and whirls around. A naked woman is standing three feet from her face, skin gray and mottled and split open in places, head tilted to the side, a beard of brown blood running down her mouth and neck. Her jaw creaks open and she moans, a hollow sound of pain and hunger, and she lunges.

Nora is a good shot. She has excellent spatial awareness and eye-hand coordination, making her naturally talented with guns. But she is not a killer. She is not a war vet, she is not trained by the Army or National Guard or even local militias. The art of murder is not embedded in her muscle memory and she is not immune to shock. So when this drooling wreck of rotting flesh surges toward her, she doesn't calmly fire a round into its frontal lobe and walk away. She screams like a teenage girl and empties all seven rounds into its chest.

She doesn't have time to pull out her hatchet. The bullets slow the corpse about as much as paintballs. Its fingertips swipe for her face. She stumbles backward and trips, falls on her butt, kicks hard at the corpse's ankle and feels it snap like brittle plastic. The corpse topples onto its side and Nora scrambles to her feet, sprints to her brother and stands protectively in front of him while the corpse staggers upright. It takes two steps toward her with its loose, floppy foot dragging against the pavement, then stops, looks down at the broken foot, steps on it with the other, and heaves. Its foot tears off like a stubborn shoe. The corpse advances, stumping forward on its bare tibia like a peg leg.

Nora has seen all she can handle. Without premeditation or planning, she grabs Addis's wrist and runs back toward downtown Seattle, not because there is shelter or food or ammo there, but because it's downhill. She manages one final glance toward the motel. The Dead woman is giving slow pursuit, but the man hasn't moved. He stands where Nora left him, just watching her go.

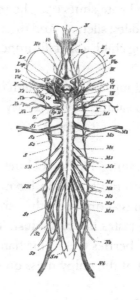

THE TALL MAN has been cheated. Some of the information he bartered for is false. He knows that he is in a North American forest and that there should be things like wolves and bears and deer in it but instead there are strange things that shouldn't be here or anywhere. Floating eyes and trees that breathe and snakes with silky blue fur. He does not know where to send his complaints. He does not know how he'll ever get a grasp on this world if it keeps changing.

He has been walking in the dark for six hours. His mind is losing what little rigidity it had, melting into mercury and oozing through the cracks. The brute in his belly is in a panic, screaming at him over and over, and he is growing weary of its ranting.

TAKE GET STEAL HAVE FILL

Shut up! he finally snaps. *I can't do it until you tell me what it is! So shut up!*

To his surprise, the brute shuts up. The man walks onward, his mind ringing in the sudden silence. And then, in a sour grumble, as if pried out of a pouting child, a specific imperative finally emerges:

Eat.

The man stops walking and slaps a palm over his face. That was it? *Eat?* He remembers eating. Eating is easy.

Why did you dance around it so long?

The brute is silent.

The man begins foraging. He finds a huckleberry bush and pops a handful of the plump red globes in his mouth. He bites down, expecting juicy sweetness—and feels the sensation of biting into a dead moth. The juice tastes like attic dust. The texture is dry and flaky, despite how the berries feel in his hands. He spits them out and stares with horror at the pulpy mess on his shirt.

The brute smirks.

He searches until he finds some wild mushrooms and shoves one in his mouth. Although he can feel its fleshy softness in his fingers, his mouth tells him he's crunching into a ball of dead wasps. He spits it out with a moan.

The brute laughs.

The cloud of hands mobilizes again, darting deeper into the forest, and a rich new scent pulses back to him through the cloud. *Blood. Flesh.* He follows it into a small clearing and discovers the source: a young deer hobbling through the underbrush, blood pouring from its claw-raked haunches.

This? he asks the brute, and the response is a mumbled, slightly sarcastic *maybe.*

The deer's dark, round eyes regard him with desperation. Part of him recoils from the impulses surging into his hands and teeth, but that part is no longer in charge. He seizes the deer and bites into its neck.

Blood pours down his throat. He rips out big chunks of meat and his mouth plays no tricks on him. The meat tastes like meat. The blood tastes like blood, salty and metallic. But when it hits his stomach, there is no spreading warmth of satiety. He drops the deer and stands up, waiting for it, but when his stomach finally responds, it's not the answer he expected. A dark rush of wrenching, twisting hunger knifes into him, as if he's suddenly minutes from starvation.

Eyes bulging, he leans over and vomits.

Wrong! the brute giggles into his ears. *Wrong wrong wrong.*

He vomits until it feels like his stomach will twist inside out, then stands over the deer gasping and shuddering. *What do you want? Tell me!*

Eat, the brute purrs, retreating back into the shadows, as if the answers to all questions are contained in this single word.

The cloud of hands drifts toward an opening in the trees, beckoning him with long, curling fingers, and he follows. He squints as he emerges from the dank woods into crisp air and blinding light. He is on a hill overlooking a valley, and there is something amazing in this valley. Towering rectangles of concrete and glass. A tangled web of streets winding through *houses* and *businesses* and *banks* and *bars.*

City.

All these words return to him at once, conjuring a wild spray of images. *People swarming in shopping malls, flashing plastic cards, putting paint on their faces and rings on their fingers. People sleeping in alleys, sticking bottles in their mouths and needles in their arms. People naked in beds, kissing. People naked in showers, crying. An old man in a tall building, grinning and sipping a drink as his soldiers fill the streets.*

THERE, the brute shouts, interrupting his daydream, and the images fade. *GO. TAKE. EAT.*

The cloud of hands surges down into the city like a squid on the hunt. With his head bowed, the man goes where he's led.

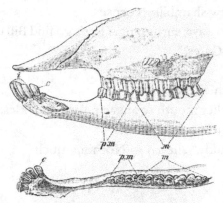

FIG. 235.—TEETH OF SHEEP (*Ovis aries*).

"ARE WE GOING BACK to the Space Needle?" Addis asks when the motel has vanished from sight and they have recovered some composure.

"No."

"Why are we going over this bridge again?"

"I don't know."

"You don't know?"

"Surprise. Big sister doesn't know everything."

Silence.

"Maybe we should go up there." He points east, toward a distant hill topped by three radio towers.

"Why?"

"I don't know."

"If you want to go places for no reason, just keep following me. You get to be our new leader when you come up with a plan."

"Maybe there's people up there. Look at all the houses."

Nora considers the plateau of colonial homes, balconies and roof decks, stunning water views. That must be where all Seattle's money used to go. Surely those estates have good enough security to keep out a few shambling corpses.

"Okay," Nora says, shrugging. "Let's go find Bill Gates's house."

"Who's Bill Gates?"

"A rich guy."

"What's 'rich' mean?"

Nora opens her mouth to answer, then chuckles, pondering the vocabulary of future generations.

"Nothing, Addy," she says. "Nothing much."

• • •

When they reach the bottom of the highway hill, she looks back to see how far they've come and notices two figures in the distance, cresting the peak. They are so far away they'd be invisible except that they're the only things in her field of vision that are moving. She can't make out any details of their faces or features, but one of them is much taller than the other and the short one is limping severely.

So they travel together on their little murder spree. Boney and Clyde. How cute.

"Those things are following us," Nora tells Addis as they exit the highway and start heading east, toward the trio of radio towers that tops the hill like a tiara. "We need to find more bullets."

"I'm really hungry," Addis says.

"Did you finish your leftovers?"

"Yeah."

"Check mine."

He unzips her backpack and digs around in it while Nora waits. He pulls out one small Ziploc of fried tofu.

Nora frowns at it. "Is that all I saved?"

"Yeah."

"God. What a fatty."

Addis opens it and squeezes a clump of tofu into his mouth.

He offers the bag to her and she starts to take it, then looks at her brother's face. His cheekbones.

"You have it," she says. "I'm not hungry."

Her stomach chooses that moment to growl ferociously.

"Are too," Addis says.

"Okay I'm lying. But you're a growing boy and I'm a crusty old teenager. You eat it."

"Do you think there's food in those houses?"

"Probably. Hopefully."

He relents. He squeezes out another precious helping of tofu and cold margarine and they keep walking.

They pass a small Airstream trailer turned on its side, napkins and plastic forks spewed out into the street. A menu Sharpied onto its steel panels advertises grass-fed burgers on locally baked brioche, but the stench emanating from it advertises maggots.

"Food," Addis points out.

"All yours."

Addis sighs and shoves his face into the Ziploc, licking out the last of the tofu.

"We'll look for food as soon as we get safe," Nora says. "Bullets before burgers."

He gives her an accusatory glare that's somewhat undermined by the globs of margarine in his eyebrows. "Are you gonna kill them next time?"

"I'm at least gonna kill the lady one."

"Why not the man?"

"I don't know. I'll probably kill him too. But he's a little different."

"Because he didn't try to eat us?"

"Maybe."

"Why didn't he?"

Nora doesn't answer right away. She is in good shape, but the hill is steep and stealing her breath. "Remember when we stayed with Auntie Shirley on our way out here?"

He watches the pavement under his feet. "Yes."

"Remember how when she got bitten, she just stood in the kitchen all day, washing the dishes over and over?"

"Yes."

"And she didn't try to eat Mom until two days later?"

"Yes."

"Sometimes when people turn into . . . 'zombies' or whatever . . . it takes a while for them to figure out what they're supposed to do. Maybe their personalities don't disappear right away, so at first they're just confused, and they don't know who they are or what's happening to them."

Addis is quiet for a while, digesting this. "So why is that one following us?"

"I don't know. Maybe 'cause his girlfriend wants to eat us. Or maybe just 'cause I was the last person he saw before he died."

Addis smiles. "Maybe he likes you."

"Maybe the girl likes you."

His smile vanishes.

• • •

By the time they reach the hill's main thoroughfare, Broadway Avenue, the sun is on its way down. Nora realizes they must have slept a lot later than she intended. She can't remember if they ever actually slept the night before. The days of scheduled meals and bedtimes feel like ancient myths. She struggles to remember the color of her mother's eyes.

They have entered a neighborhood that looks like it was once vibrant. Colorful storefronts with artful graffiti. Concert posters smothering every pole. Stylishly dressed corpses littering the streets, their scooped-out skulls brimming with rainwater.

Nora opens her mouth to tell Addis not to look at them, then realizes how absurd that is. She lets him quietly absorb the massacre, hoping he will somehow process all his horrible experiences without too much damage. That he will find a way to bathe in poison without letting it inside.

"Look!" he says, pointing toward the park on the other side of the street. "A swimming pool!"

The park is huge, and may once have been beautiful. Rolling hills of grass, now overgrown with weeds. Tall, elegant lampposts, now rusted. Its towering central fountain still produces a trickling stream where it must have once cascaded. The stream flows into a shallow pool less than a foot deep and fully accessible, none of the usual municipal railings and warnings, as if the city actually wanted people to play in it. Perhaps that headless couple holding hands in the bus stop used to sit on the benches here and watch their toddlers splash. Perhaps the college kids now feeding flies in the street used to get drunk and lie on their backs in this pool late at night, staring up at the stars, dreaming big dreams for themselves and each other. Nora is going to cry again. This fucking city. This fucking world. When will she harden to it?

She watches Addis peel off his shoes and socks, sweaty and filthy, spotted red from bleeding blisters. She watches him cool his feet in the algae-slimed water. She wants to join him—she is drenched in sweat and the summer air seems to ripple around her in little pulses—but she needs to stay ready. They are not safe.

"Oh! Fuck!" she gasps as Addis palms a huge spray of water down the front of her tank top. Addis almost falls over laughing.

"You *ass*hole!" she snaps, but she can't hide the smile on her face and Addis keeps laughing. She whips off her shoes and runs into the pool. Addis squeals and flees. Nora kicks water at his back as he hops out of the pool and sprints off into the shaggy grass.

"Hey!" Nora shouts. "Come back!"

"Can't catch me!" he giggles, and keeps running. Nora can see in the blurring speed of his feet that he's beyond her discipline. The feeling of running barefoot in a field of grass, tendons flexed tight, feet bouncing off the ground like springs. Like running on a beach.

She lets him run. He won't get far; he's going in circles. She tries not to think about the precious calories he's burning right now, maybe half a meal's worth. If they can't spare the energy for a brief sprint in a park, they might as well go join the corpses on Broadway.

She hears a low growl behind her. Not a groan, not a moan, not a shout or a war cry; none of the sounds she's used to hearing when something wants to kill her. Just a wet, rattling growl, like seashore rocks tumbling in the undertow. She turns around. A wolf is staring at her from under a nearby picnic table. Its eyes are ice blue. Like her mother's, she suddenly recalls.

It creeps slowly from under the table, eyes fixed on hers. A big Canadian timber wolf, thin and desperate, fur caked in mud, too weary to bother cleaning itself anymore. Another phantasm pulled from the dying world's fever dreams. Next will be dragons. Vampires. Demons. Ghosts. By the time the last human being—and there *will* be a last one, if only for a moment—realizes she is alone, the world will be nothing but the sum of her nightmares. Why should reality hold together with no minds left to force it?

Nora reaches for her hatchet and the wolf snarls as if it knows what a hatchet is. She glances right and sees Addis watching from a distant knoll, frozen with terror. She glances left and sees two more wolves slinking out from the trees near the edge of the park, leafy shadows stretching toward her as the sun sinks to the rooftops. Is this really how she's going to die? In a world with so many options for exit, wandering a ruined city with no food or medicine, surrounded by murderers and the hungry Dead, she's going to be killed by *wolves*?

And yet it fits. It's appropriate. If the Library of Congress can be destroyed by arson, the Louvre by mold and neglect, if all the cultural accomplishments of ten thousand years on this planet can be erased by a few decades of carelessness, why shouldn't this young American be devoured by wild animals in the middle of a city park?

Her bare feet dip into the warm water of the wading pool. Her back bumps against the fountain and she feels the thin trickle of regurgitated rainwater flowing down her spine. The wolves circle in, grinning.

The big man steps around the fountain and stands between her and the wolves. He groans loudly at them and it almost sounds like a word, but too hoarse to understand.

The nearest wolf leaps at him. It's no doubt aiming for his throat, but his throat is nearly six feet high so it gets a mouthful of his T-shirt instead. He grabs the animal and strangles it, or maybe breaks its neck—it takes only a few seconds for the wolf to go limp. The other two bite into his legs. He reaches down, seizes them by the scruff of the neck, and hammers their heads into the concrete until their yelps go quiet. Everything goes quiet. The big man, his bald head gleaming gray in the evening light, looks at the dead predators at his feet. He looks at Nora.

Nora runs.

"Did you *see* that?" Addis squeals when she comes to a stop next to him on the hill.

"Uh, no. I was watching the sunset."

"It was just like in *Beauty and the Beast!*"

The man picks up one of the wolves, sniffs it, tears off a leg and rips out a bite of the hot muscle, chews for a moment, then casually vomits into the fountain.

"Yeah . . ." Nora mumbles. "Kind of."

The man drops the wolf and looks up at Nora. There is plenty of distance between them and plenty of directions for her to run, so she stays put for now, waiting to see what he does. But he doesn't do anything. He just stands there, looking at her.

"Why'd you do that?" she shouts.

He doesn't react. She glances around, making sure his girlfriend can't spring any more horror-movie shock-entrances on her, maybe popping out of a garbage can this time since there are no doors nearby.

"Stop following us, okay? Leave us alone!"

A sound gurgles in his throat and passes through his lips. It's faint and he's far away, but this time she's sure it was a word.

"Did you hear him?" she asks Addis. "Did he just say something?"

Addis is squinting at the man, a queer expression on his face. "I think he said 'please.' "

"What the fuck . . . ," Nora mutters.

Out from behind the fountain, the man's girlfriend staggers into view, still visibly female but hard to call a woman anymore. Its shoulders are now bare bone with nearly transparent scraps of skin dangling off. Its internal organs have shrunk away from the bullet wounds in its chest; Nora can see the lovely sunset shining through the holes. Since she last encountered this creature just a few hours ago, its decay has advanced about a month.

"Leave us *alone!*" she screams, and drags Addis away from the park, her fingers white-knuckled on his wrist.

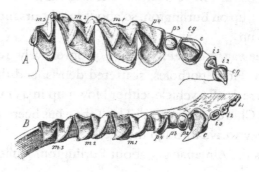

"Q!"

"Where?"

"Right there. 'Food next exit . . . Quiznos.'"

"Oh come on!"

"Stick that in your sandwich hole."

"I hate you, Mom."

Julie and her mother are playing the Alphabet Game. It is significantly harder without any passing license plates to read. They haven't seen another car on the road since Idaho, and that one rammed them into the median and disgorged two men who thought they'd found a nice little family to rob. That game of Alphabet ended with Julie and her mother wiping blood off the Tahoe's beige leather upholstery. She hopes this one will end with her being the first to spot the Seattle Zoo.

As always, she awoke to the hum of the tires and the seat belt cutting into her neck. Her father gets up at an hour that's only technically morning and usually has them on the road well before sunrise. She has always wanted to witness his mysterious morning routine but has never managed to wake up for it. She imagines him perusing old editions of the *New York Times* and sipping a cup of instant coffee while cleaning the family shotguns.

"How close are we to Seattle?" she asks him.

"Coming up on Burlington, so about two hours more unless the road clears up."

The freeway has been getting progressively rougher since Bellingham. Huge potholes, scattered debris, and the occasional scorched wreck of a vehicle, either blown up in a crash or burned by the Fire Church's "Ardents." The Tahoe has been steadily losing speed as they weave through the mess.

"What's the Almanac say about Burlington?" Julie asks. "Exed, right?"

"Last month's said there were still a few communes and markets functioning. Small towns last longer than cities sometimes."

"Why?"

"Not enough resources to attract militias and not enough Living to attract the Dead. If they're small enough, they get left alone."

"Why don't we live in a small town then?"

He looks over at his wife and smiles slightly. "Audrey?"

"Your dad thinks we should," she says. "What do you think, Julie? Should we move to a place that's too boring for zombies?"

"There are worse things than boredom," her husband counters.

"I'm not convinced of that."

He stares at her for a moment. He cocks his head. "What do you want, Audrey?" Anger simmers beneath his perplexity. "What is it you'd like us to do?"

Audrey leans back in her seat like she's settling in for a speech.

"You want to go back to Brooklyn? You want to work for the Axiom Group, help them claim the country? You want to clean their toilets and rub their feet while I go out and shoot little boys for a strong new America?"

"No, John," Audrey sighs.

"Then maybe you want to join one of the militias? The Brooklyn Bulldogs are probably wiped out by now. Bronx United's going to get shot in the back while they're fighting the Queens Kings.

The Wall Street Traitors have a chance, but it's a pretty close match across the board . . ."

"John."

"I'm thinking it'll keep going till they've all killed each other or the floods force them off the island, but if you're tired of driving, we can—"

"John!"

He slams on the brakes; Julie's face smacks into the front seat as the Tahoe screeches to a stop. Stunned, she feels her nose to see if it's bleeding, then reluctantly follows her parents' gaze.

They have just crested a hill, and directly in front of them is a police spike strip. In front of the strip is a wall of wrecked cars that extends across all eight lanes of the freeway. And beyond the wall, stretching across a wide, green valley of overgrown farm fields, is what appears to be a war zone. What was once a shopping district has been reduced to a plain of pockmarked asphalt. The gutted, scorched interiors of big-box retailers are visible through gaping holes in their walls. The only vehicles in the parking lots are tanks, some with their turrets blown off, some lying on their sides, treads hanging like entrails; some marked *Army*, some spray-painted with the logos of various militias. And behind all this, as a perfectly hellish backdrop: the concrete skeletons of buildings engulfed in white flames of Fire Church phosphorous, left to burn for days as a warning. A monument. Or whatever their muddled message may be.

"Why?" Julie asks in a very small voice, unable to be more specific. There is, of course, no answer.

Her father grabs his shotgun and steps out of the truck, slipping into the hyper-alert posture of a soldier on perimeter check. Julie can't see anything moving down in the valley. It could have been deserted weeks ago and set ablaze recently by passing Ardents for a little morning devotional. She's hoping it's as empty as it looks.

"John," her mother calls to her father's back. "Let's just go around. We can take the back roads till I-5 clears up."

He doesn't answer. Julie can see in the set of his jaw and the animal blankness in his eyes that he didn't even hear her. He's in procedure mode. He will scout the area and ascertain possible threats before making any further decisions.

"John!"

He climbs into the bed of the pickup and pulls out his scope, begins scanning the smoldering valley below. Julie's mother sighs and grabs her gun. "Stay here," she tells Julie, locking the doors as she climbs out.

Julie watches her mother approach her father, her irritation visible in the stiffness of her stride. She watches them argue, their voices not quite audible through the window. Then she sees movement in her periphery and her window shatters. A man's arm reaches through and pulls the door open. She manages to grab her shotgun out of the ceiling rack just as two hands clamp around her ankles and yank her out of the truck. Her head hits the dirt hard and her vision swims. She sees a man's face hovering over her—not a man. A boy. Just a few years older than her. Fourteen or fifteen. His beautiful brown eyes are wild with desperation. His black hair is matted and filthy. The knife in his hand is crusted with dried blood.

Julie shoots him in the chest.

The world moves very slowly as she drags herself upright, clinging to the side of the truck. She is distantly aware of her parents shooting the boy's parents, who were emerging from a van with guns drawn and firing—she even notices the blood oozing from a graze on her father's thigh. But mostly, she notices the boy dying on the ground in front of her.

"Jesus Christ," she hears her mother muttering. Her parents are standing next to her now. She doesn't look at them. She looks at the boy, listens to his last breath leaking out of him, a slow hiss like a popped tire.

The three of them stand in silence for a moment. Then Julie's father bends down and picks up her gun—she doesn't remember dropping it. He places it in her hands.

"Are you serious?" Her mother's eyes are ice picks boring into her father's. "Are you fucking serious, John?"

"It's her third kill and we can't keep hiding this part from her. She needs to face it."

The boy's eyes begin to vibrate. Their color drains.

"She's *twelve years old!* She doesn't need to face this yet!"

"This is the world, Audrey. She knows that as well as we do."

Julie's mother shakes her head in disbelief. A wet, sloppy breath attempts to inflate the boy's punctured chest. Fixing her husband with a murderous glare, she steps toward the boy and starts to raise her pistol—then yelps as the boy's face vanishes in a spray of blood.

The valley reverberates with thunder. Audrey Grigio stares openmouthed at her daughter, and at the ghost of smoke creeping out of her daughter's shotgun.

Julie hops into the truck and snaps the gun into the rack. She fastens her seat belt and stares ahead with hollow eyes, waiting to leave.

Silently, her parents climb into the front seats. Her father drives into the grassy median to get around the blockade, working his way through the edge of the war zone to reach the residential side streets, which will be slower than the freeway but marginally safer.

"Hey Mom," Julie says.

"Yes honey."

Her mother's voice is faint and shaky. Julie hopes her own sounds stronger. She points at the markings on a destroyed tank, the American flag's red and blue scorched gray but the word "Army" still visible. "Found an 'R.'"

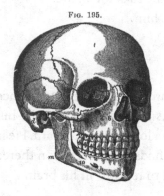

Fig. 195.

Despite everything he's traded away, the tall man still feels a faint sense of awe as he wanders through the city. These towering structures, this elaborate urban circulatory system . . . whatever sort of creature he is, he can tell by the shape of the doors and stairs and benches that this was all designed for bodies like his, and this pleases him. He must have some value if something this magnificent was built for him. The wolves have fast legs and sharp teeth but they don't have *cities*. He is excited to learn more about what he is—what he's called and what he's here for. Surely it's something wonderful.

The cloud of hands has not wavered since he arrived here, so he doesn't worry about getting lost. Each smoky tendril stretches off in the same direction, sending faint pulses of sensation back to him. A strange sort of smell that bypasses his nose and saturates his whole body. Floral sweetness spiked with sharp, electrical bitterness, like a lavender bush struck by lightning. But he finds it hard to enjoy this perfume when his body is collapsing from the inside out. Whatever energy drives his muscles is almost gone, and he can feel his cells beginning to shrivel up like raisins. The gentle hill he's climbing may prove an insurmountable summit.

How much farther? he asks the brute.

The brute ignores him.

Are we almost there?

Nothing.

How about now?

EAT, the brute snaps, then resumes its silence.

The tall man sulks as he staggers up the hill. Finally, the cruel incline levels out into a long, flat boulevard. He instinctively glances at the street sign but finds no information there. The symbols on it blur and spin and fail to register in his brain.

I can't read.

This thought surprises him, as he is not even sure what reading is. But what surprises him even more is the feeling that comes with it.

Loss.

What did he lose? What did he have? For reasons he can't explain, his enthusiasm for learning his nature dims.

His foot strikes something and he stumbles. He falls to the pavement and lands with his face inches from a round thing that looks like a face but has empty holes where eyes and a nose should be. He pulls himself upright and regards the long, spindly object attached to it—a body. The object is a body, brown and dry and withered. There are more like it all over the street. The cloud of hands pokes at them, mumbling something that's probably *eat,* then loses interest and floats off into the city without comment. But the man is intrigued. The bodies resemble him in shape, but like the ones by the river there is a fundamental difference that goes beyond the condition of their flesh. It's the same chasm that separated him from the girl in the woods, but yawning in the opposite direction.

An insight begins to bubble in his head.

Dead.

The bodies are *dead* and the girl is . . . *alive.*

He tilts his head and frowns. *Then what am I?*

A pulse ripples through the cloud of hands. It has found something.

Eat? the man prompts.

No answer. The brute is silent, pensive, as if studying a puzzle. What could possibly hold the attention of that drooling monomaniac? The man increases his pace, stepping over heap after rotted heap.

. . .

The sun is nearly set, bathing the bodies in a warm orange glow that makes them look slightly less inert. He can almost imagine them standing up and dusting themselves off, groaning and chasing after him, but he knows that's absurd. He knows what *dead* means now. It means gone forever. Lost. Irretrievable.

He sees a familiar shape ahead and feels a rush of happiness when he realizes what it is. A *person*. Not a body, not an object in the street waiting to become dirt—an actual person, like him. A man, to be specific, even taller than him and also big, a bearded, bald giant in a white T-shirt. He is just standing alone in the street, his eyes on the pavement, swaying slightly.

The tall man approaches the big man with quick, clumsy strides, tripping over corpses, bumping into cars, making no attempt at stealth, but the big man doesn't look up. His face is almost entirely blank, with just a faint trace of . . . an emotion . . . something bad maybe, but never mind; the tall man is too excited to focus on decoding emotional cues right now. He stops in front of the man and stands there, both of them swaying, but the big man still doesn't look up.

A trembling spasm begins to form in the back of the tall man's throat. He is going to speak.

He is going to say "hi."

"Hhh . . ." he says, managing only this throaty hiss.

The big man doesn't react.

"Hhh . . . hhh . . . *hi.*" He feels profoundly satisfied. He has just greeted another person.

The big man's eyes slide up to meet his, and the tall man begins to notice things. The big man's eyes are silvery gray. The same gray that stared up at him as he kicked the corpse by the river over and over, filled with some desperate rage that seems utterly foreign to him now. The big man's skin is also gray, the same gray as the tall man's. And there is a gaping wound in his barrel-like belly, visible through the bloody hole in his shirt.

An insight:

The big man is dead.

And yet . . .

The brute studies this man intently. The cloud of hands pokes and prods at him like a doctor. Whatever the scent is that they've been following, that electric lavender perfume, it's completely absent from this man. But there is *something* there. A sort of anti-scent, a negative. He is not alive like the girl in the woods, but not dead like the bodies in the street. He is . . .

He's like you.

The tall man looks at his hands, his arms, the black blood oozing from his calf.

This is what you are.

A moan emanates from the big man's throat, and the tall man suddenly recognizes the emotion on his face. It's the feeling of understanding a terrible truth. Of learning something that changes everything.

A piercing screech sounds from the doorway of a nearby building, and another creature emerges onto the steps above them. A female corpse, nearly as rotten as the ones in the street, her hair hanging in mangy clumps, her naked body shriveled and sagging, full of holes and tears and exposed bones.

This is what you will be.

The woman is holding something. It is an arm. A scrawny thing, black tattoos of dice and dragons and dollar bills barely visible on its brown skin, blood still trickling from its red stump. With another triumphant screech, the woman throws the arm down the stairs. It bounces and twists and lands in front of the big man, who stares at it a moment, then snatches it up and bites into its bicep.

This is what you do.

The tall man is hungry. He is so hungry. The sight of the arm has sent the brute into a frenzy, and the hollowness is so strong it's tearing him apart. The woman disappears back into the building and the tall man follows her.

The building is a coffee shop. A quaint, cozy little place lined with books, ancient bagels moldering in the pastry case, a few laptops left unattended and still not stolen. The tall man sees all this by the light of a tiny campfire in the middle of the room. A few smashed table legs stacked on a pile of crumpled book pages, burning hot and bright.

Next to the fire are two bodies. A man and a woman, one brown, one pink, one missing an arm, the other missing everything.

The tall man's mind has ceased to function. All his senses have been absorbed by the hunger. All he can see is the cloud of hands flailing in his face. All he can smell or taste or even feel is the scent. The perfume.

Life.

And all he can hear is the brute screaming at him to take it.

THIS, it bellows over and over as its myriad fingers jab at the bodies. *THIS THIS THIS.*

While the rotten woman gnaws on the brown man's thigh, the tall man kneels beside his head. Glazed eyes stare up at him, a mouth frozen open in surprise, as if gasping, *What happened? How did I get here? How could I have known that my choices mattered?*

The tall man sees his hands reaching out and picking up the man's remaining arm. He feels the brute prying his mouth open and shoving his head down. He feels himself chewing. And yes, he feels relief, a warm river of energy washing over his dried-up cells and reconstituting them, pooling in his chest and inflating him like a sad, sagging party balloon. But he feels no pleasure. He wishes he could feel nothing at all. He wishes he could trade everything for information, the dullest, numbest information feelings can buy, but the trading floor is closed. He bangs on the door as he satiates himself with this person's dwindling life, but the only answer is the thin, cold voice of his own thoughts.

This is what you are and why you're here. You are not a person. You are not even a wolf. You are nothing, and no city was ever built for you.

He looks up from his meal and sees the big man watching him through the book-fire's flames. He understands that they will travel together now. They will look for other creatures like themselves and gather more and more so that they can eat more and more. And he understands that no matter how many they gather, even if they become a mob of thousands, each and every one of them will be alone.

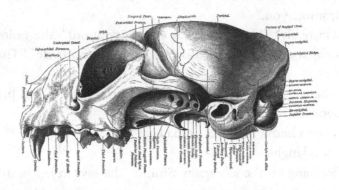

THE CARNAGE THICKENS as Nora and her brother work their way up Pine Street. The bodies are so dense she has to walk with eyes to the ground to avoid tripping over them, or worse: stepping in them. Her earlier impulse to shield Addis from the sight of death feels even more absurd now. He picks his way through the corpses with practical care, as if they're nothing more than fallen branches to be avoided. Is he indifferent to the dead? Does he make no connection between these husks and the living people he loves? Or is he simply too hungry to care?

Nora can feel her own hunger slowly consuming her loftier concerns, grinding layer after layer off the hierarchy of needs. The grand pyramid of a fully realized life eroded long ago into a practical trapezoid, and may soon collapse to the baseline of an animal.

"A police station!" Addis yelps, pointing to a blue and white building a few blocks up the hill. "Maybe there's guns!"

Nora rouses herself from her bleak forecasting and puts on a smile for her brother. "Maybe. Should we start our own police department?"

He grins.

"Want to be sheriff? I'll be your deputy."

"No, you have to start out as a regular officer and then maybe I'll promote you."

"Oh really? Do I have a lot of competition?" She points at a uniformed corpse slumped over a police motorcycle. "That guy, maybe?"

"That's . . . Sergeant Smith. He's our best guy, he'll probably beat you."

"I don't know, he looks kinda lazy."

Addis laughs.

"Sleeping on the job again, Smith?" she says in her best tough-chief growl and begins frisking the dead cop. "That's it! I want your badge on my desk, *pronto!*" She's not surprised that his gun is gone—if he still had it, why would he be dead?—but she does find a few things of interest in his pockets. Some kind of keycard and a baggie of pot. She confiscates both and they approach the station entrance.

The door is locked, which is an auspicious sign. Most easily accessed areas are stripped of anything useful. The harder a place is to reach, the more likely reaching it will be worthwhile. Nora and Addis work together to lift an empty *Seattle Times* kiosk and ram it through the tempered-glass windows.

Once inside the lobby, her hopes sink a little. The reception desk is bare and there are no posters or placards on the walls, as if the station closed down officially instead of being abandoned intact like most businesses these days. They roam through empty hall-ways and locker rooms, past ceramic-tiled holding cells smeared with graffiti in various mediums. The anarchy "A" drawn in blood. The Fire Church's burning Earth drawn in ash. A gigantic frown face drawn in what looks like vomit. This one strikes Nora as the most eloquent. It should replace the American flag and fly proudly over city hall, the first raw honesty to touch that place in years.

"Why didn't Dad take us here?" Addis asks as they dig through a pile of blue uniforms.

"Probably didn't know where it was."

"But he was a policeman. He should have known about it."

"He should have a lot of things."

"What if him and Mom came here? What if they took all the bullets and stuff already?"

"Addy, there are plenty of people for us to worry about without bringing Mom and Dad into it."

"No there aren't."

"Well . . . maybe not here. But other places."

"Why is everywhere always empty? Where do people go?"

"Some of them find shelter. Like skyscrapers or stadiums."

"And the other ones die, right? Like all those people out in the road?"

She pauses. "Right."

"Okay."

He finds a riot helmet and crams it down over his springy hair. "Halt!" he orders in cop-voice, and Nora smiles through a rush of bittersweet sadness that takes her a moment to understand. Nostalgia for the present. Her brother is still here, but she has already begun missing him.

"I like this place," he says. "Maybe we should stay here tonight."

Nora looks around the station, considering it. "We broke the window. Anything could come in here and get us."

"We could lock ourselves in the jail!" He starts giggling halfway through this idea.

"We need a simple building we can lock from the inside and get out of easily if we have to. This place has too many places to get trapped in. Once we're done in here, we'll go find a house."

"Aww," he says with genuine disappointment, and Nora wonders if being in the police station feels like being with his father. She wonders if he remembers the time Ababa Germame—aka Bob Greene—showed his kids around the DC precinct when Nora was twelve and Addis was three. The man was so proud. He had worked so hard, overcome such odds. None of his friends from the neighborhood could believe he had made it through the academy, even in its drastically simplified mid-apocalyptic form. Neither could his wife, who mocked and resented every forward step he took. And maybe all that doubt finally convinced him, because it was less than a year before he decided his shift would be easier with some amphetamines in his veins and shot a teenager for flipping him off, ending his brief foray into the world of unbroken people.

Nora glances over her shoulder. One dark thought leads to another and she feels shadows creeping across her back. "Wait here a second," she tells her brother. "I'm gonna go check outside."

"Why?"

"To see if those things are still following us."

"But they're slow. We can just walk away from them."

"Not if they trap us in a cramped building like this. And there might be more of them around here."

"Really?" Addis's eyes widen as if he's never considered this, which worries Nora.

"Of course, Addy, duh. What do you think ate the brains out of all those people in the street?"

"If there's more, where are they?"

"Could be anywhere. I don't think there's a hive in Seattle, so they'll just be wandering around. That's why we have to be super careful."

"Okay."

"Be right back."

She jogs out into the lobby and crawls through the shattered window. The street is still motionless, just a desolate garden of sun-wrinkled corpses. Could it be that Boney and Clyde finally gave up? Went off in search of easier heists?

She hurries back to the station locker room, but her brother is not there. "Addis!" she shouts down the hall. She runs back into the lobby, then through the briefing room. "*Addis!*"

She finds him on the basement level, in a corner of the station they haven't yet explored.

"Look at this," he says, staring through the bars of a holding cell.

"I told you to wait," she hisses at him, but something in the way he's looking into the cell distracts her from her discipline.

"What is that?" he says, and Nora moves in behind him to see.

"Holy shit . . . ," she whispers. In the corner of the cell sits a pile of small cubes, glittering like diamonds in their foil wrappers. "I think that's . . ."

She scans the wall around the cell door, finds the lock mechanism, and slips the cop's keycard into it. The steel door unlocks with a loud *clack* and Nora heaves it open.

"What is it, what is it?" Addis demands, hopping on his toes.

Nora picks up one of the cubes and studies the wrapper. "Carbtein," she reads incredulously. "Oh my God Addy this is *Carbtein!*"

"What's Carbtein!"

"It's . . . *food*. Like . . . *super* food, for soldiers and cops and stuff. Oh my God I can't believe this."

"What's super food?"

"Here, just shut up and eat one." She tears open the wrapper and hands the white cube to Addis. He regards it skeptically.

"This is food?"

"It's like . . . concentrated food. They break stuff down to the basic nutrients and it just . . . goes right into your cells."

Addis turns the cube in his hand, grimacing. He licks it cautiously. "It's salty." He nibbles a tiny bite off the corner. "But kinda sour, too." He swallows hard, then closes his eyes and shudders. "Gross."

Nora unwraps a cube and bites it in half. It has the texture of moist chalk, like a candy Valentine heart, but its flavor is a disorienting mix of dissonant notes: sweet, sour, salty, bitter, and a few that her mind can't quite label. She concurs with her brother's review.

"This is what we're gonna eat?" Addis moans.

Nora is still chewing her first bite. The stuff resists her saliva; it won't dissolve. She keeps chewing it into smaller and smaller particles until she finally convinces her throat to swallow. She gags, but when it hits her stomach she feels something remarkable. A wave of warmth spreads out from her core like she's just taken a shot of whiskey. It will stay in her belly for hours, slowly releasing nutrients like an IV drip feed, and despite the awful taste lingering in her mouth, she smiles. Up until this moment, her plans for their future have been very small. Walk a little farther. Live a few more days. She has not allowed her mind to wander past tomorrow because tomorrow was a wall and beyond it a smothering black void she dared not approach. But a horizon has appeared.

"Eat as much as you can," she tells her brother. "If you can get that whole cube down, you won't get hungry for two or three days."

He moans again and takes a halfhearted bite.

Nora begins cramming the little foil packages into her backpack. Addis watches in dismay.

"Hey," she says. "This is the best thing that's ever happened to us."

"Is not," he mumbles.

"There's probably two hundred cubes here! We can live off this for a *year*!"

He groans.

"Oh so you'd rather starve?"

"Maybe."

She stops packing and fixes him with a hard stare. She knows he's just a seven-year-old whining about food just like any seven-year-old in any era, but she is suddenly filled with rage. "You listen to me," she says. "We are not at Auntie's house, okay? It is not your fucking birthday. We are *dying*. Do you understand that?"

Addis is quiet.

"You get a few bites to eat and you forget what starving feels like. Well I don't. It's my job to take care of you now and I'm doing the best I can, but I'm scared shitless and all I ever dream about is failing. So don't you fucking tell me you'd rather starve."

He looks at the ground. "Sorry."

"I'll let you know next time I find pizza and ice cream but for now let's just try to stay alive, okay?"

He sighs and takes another bite of his cube.

"Okay," Nora says. "Let's go find somewhere to sleep."

When they emerge from the police station the sun is all the way down, leaving only a residual orange glow as it journeys west. Down where Pine intersects Broadway, a few street lamps flicker on. Nora sees the big man and his woman trudging steadily up the hill. And now someone else. Another man trailing an awkward distance behind them, like a surly teen who doesn't want to be seen with his parents. So they're gaining converts. Trying to start a hive. Even the Dead want a family.

Well you can't have mine, she mutters under her breath, and pulls Addis the other way.

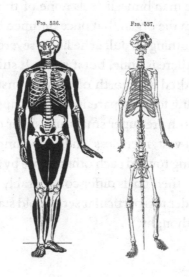

FIG. 536.   FIG. 537.

Tʜɪʀᴛʏ-ꜰᴏᴜʀ ᴍɪʟᴇꜱ ɴᴏʀᴛʜ of the police station, a young girl who recently killed a young boy is watching beige houses flicker through the headlights of her family's SUV. Her father's eyes are tight on the road, her mother's on everything around the road, pistol at the ready should anything incongruous emerge from this idyllic suburban scene. They are traveling later than they usually do, later than is safe, and the girl is glad. She hates sleeping. Not just because of the nightmares, but because everything is urgent. Because life is short. Because she feels a thousand fractures running through her, and she knows they run through the world. She is racing to find the glue.

Thirty-four miles south of this girl, a man who recently learned he is a monster is following two other monsters up a steep hill in an empty city, because he can smell life in the distance and his purpose now is to take it. A brutish thing inside him is giggling and slavering and clutching its many hands in anticipation, overjoyed to finally be obeyed, but the man himself feels none of this. Only a coldness deep in his chest, in the organ that once pumped blood and feelings and now pumps nothing. A dull ache like a severed stump numbed in ice—what was there is gone, but it hurts. It still hurts.

And three hundred feet north of these monsters are a girl and boy who are looking for new parents. Or perhaps becoming them. Both are strong, both are super smart and super cool, and both are tiny and alone in a vast, merciless, endlessly hungry world.

All six are moving toward each other, some by accident, some by intent, and though their goals differ considerably, on this particular summer night, under this particular set of cold stars, all of them are sharing the same thought:

Find people.

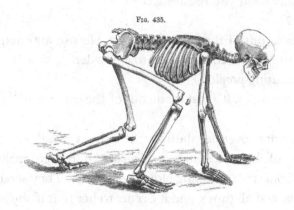

Fig. 435.

"CAN I GET my flashlight?" Addis asks as they enter a tree-lined residential area. Nora recognizes a few of the towering mansions they saw from the highway.

"The stars are plenty bright. I don't want people seeing us."

"But I thought we're *looking* for people!"

"Not at night. Bad people come out at night."

"We're out at night."

"Okay, bad people and stupid people. But we're not looking for either of those."

He swallows hard and takes a deep breath. "I *just* swallowed the bite I took back at the police station."

"I know it's gross, Addy, but look on the bright side. You'll never have to poop."

His face freezes, then he snickers. "*What?*"

"There's zero waste in this stuff. Your body absorbs all of it. So no poop."

He laughs explosively, and Nora laughs at his laughter. "Poop," he repeats with supreme satisfaction, as if savoring a perfectly crafted joke.

361

"Basically what you're eating is *life*."

"What?"

"It's made out of the same stuff our cells use for energy. So it's basically human life condensed into a powder."

"We're eating *people*?"

"It's not people. It's just made out of the same stuff."

"Oh."

Nora glances over her shoulder. The street is dark except for the faint sheen of the crescent moon. She has to strain to make out the distant silhouettes stumbling along behind her. They seem to keep a steady pace at all times, and it occurs to her that if she and Addis were to sprint at full speed for as long as they could, they might be able to lose their stalkers. Except that despite being slow, the Dead have two big advantages: they can smell the Living from half a mile away, and they never have to stop. Nora realizes that sooner or later, she will have to deal with them.

"What about there?" Addis says, stopping to look at a relatively modest two-story estate. The place is an odd study in contrasts. It's an elegant, old-fashioned building, rustic red brick with white window frames and knob-topped railings on its second-floor balcony, but it has the security measures of an inner-city bank branch. Thick, wrought-iron bars on all the windows, cameras on every door, and a tall iron fence around the whole yard. The fence isn't much help due to the front gate lying flat on the ground, but still . . .

"Let's take a look," Nora says.

She pulls out her flashlight and her hatchet. Addis does the same. They begin with a quick circuit of the yard, checking the window bars, checking the doors. All intact, all locked. A convertible covered in dried blood and claw marks is the only thing out of the ordinary. In fact, the yard is oddly well kept, the shrubberies still in neat rows, the lawn weedy but not wild.

"All clear," Addis says in cop-voice.

"These window bars are pretty wide. Think you could fit?"

He tests his head against the bars. Pushing his ears flat, he could probably squeeze through. "Want me to break in?" he asks, smiling deviously. He might make a better robber than cop.

"Let's check the rest of the doors first."

They come back around to the front. Nora is surprised to find the front door—a huge, solid oak slab with reinforced hinges—unlocked. Slightly ajar. They step inside. Nora locks it behind them and clicks on her flashlight. The interior is no less luxurious than she expected. The usual exotic hardwoods and leather, paintings by real artists hanging casually in the hall.

"God," Nora whispers, aiming her flashlight at a messy, intricate collage. "That's a Rauschenberg."

"It's way too big," Addis says in a tone that means *Don't even think about it*. He remembers when the family stopped at a museum to search for weapons on dead security guards and Nora stuffed the Geo full of Picassos. He remembers when some thugs stole the car and they had to continue on foot, and she made him put all her clothes in his bag so she'd have room for some rolled-up Dali canvases. He doesn't have to worry anymore. She's much more practical these days.

They begin to explore the house. The white circles of their flashlights roam the walls like infant ghosts. Nora flicks a light switch and is surprised to see a chandelier blaze to life. She quickly switches it off.

"Why'd you turn it off?" Addis says.

"You know why."

Addis sighs. They step quietly down the hall and into the dining room. "What's that smell?" he asks, wrinkling his nose.

Nora sniffs. "Burnt plastic?" She starts to move toward the kitchen to investigate and Addis yelps, so sudden and sharp Nora almost drops her flashlight. She dashes to his side, hatchet raised. His light is creeping slowly over the faces of three corpses. Old corpses. Skeletons. No flesh but a few leathery ligaments clinging to the joints. Even their clothes have disintegrated. They recline peacefully in the living room, an adult in the easy chair and two smaller ones on the couch, their lipless mouths locked in that insane snarl that lurks behind every smile.

Addis pulls his light away and the grim tableau disappears into the shadows. He is breathing a lot harder than Nora.

"Come on," she says. "Let's check upstairs."

The top floor is just two children's bedrooms, a bathroom, and the balcony. Empty, dusty, silent.

"All clear?" Nora asks, but Addis doesn't confirm.

"Can we stay up here?" he says quietly. "We don't have to go downstairs again, do we?"

"Not if we're all clear. Are we all clear?"

"All clear."

"Okay. Then we can stay up here."

"Until it's light out?"

"Yep."

"Okay."

"Are you tired?"

"Not really."

Nora looks at his face. He is shaken. Walking over a hundred bodies rotting in the street didn't faze him, but those three skeletons seem to have reached him in a deeper place. She doubts he will sleep tonight.

"Addy," she says. "Come out on the balcony with me."

They step out into the night air and lean against the railing, looking down at the street, watching the faint moonlight shimmer on the treetops as a gentle breeze teases the leaves. Nora drops her pack at her feet—the Carbtein cubes are surprisingly heavy—and digs out her lighter, along with some shredded phone book pages she's been using for tinder. She pulls the cop's weed out of her pocket and rolls a joint. Addis watches her intently as she lights it.

"What's that stuff feel like?"

She looks at him, holding in her lungful, then breathes it out and hands him the joint.

His eyes widen. "Really?"

"Sure. It'll help you sleep."

"Mom said it's bad for kids."

"No worse than for grown-ups. Same as coffee and alcohol."

"But Mom said those are all worse for kids."

"It's not that different. Grown-ups just don't like seeing kids in altered states. It reminds them you're a person, not some little toy they sewed their faces onto."

Addis looks at her for a moment. "Are you high already?"

Nora giggles. "Maybe. I haven't smoked in a long time."

"Dad said it stunts kids' brains."

Fuck Dad, she wants to say. *Fuck them both and any advice they ever gave us. When a corpse tells you how to live, do the opposite.* Instead, she clings to her herbal calm and says, "Oh well. None of us are gonna grow up to be doctors anyway."

Addis studies the joint. He puts it to his lips and takes a dainty puff. He coughs and hands it back to her, then stares at the trees for a minute.

A slow smile creeps across his face. "Whoa . . ."

Nora sucks in another hit and they both regard the moonlit sea of trees, rooftops poking through like distant islands. She is in love with this moment. She glances at her brother, hoping to see that dopey grin again and maybe find out what stoned-child philosophy sounds like, but the grin is gone. His face has turned abruptly blank, and Nora feels a spike of dread piercing her cloud of well-being.

"Mom and Dad left us alone," he says.

Nora releases the smoke in her lungs in a long sigh.

"They were supposed to take care of us. Why did they leave?"

So soon. She thought she'd have another year to prepare for this. She looks out at the trees and auditions lies in her head.

Maybe they went to find food and got lost.

Maybe they got bitten and didn't want to infect us.

I don't know why they left.

But she rejects these. Addis deserves truth. He is a child, but why does that make him any less deserving? Nora herself is a child; so are her parents—everyone is equally young and foolish in the wide lens of history, and the arrogant denial of this is what unraveled the world. So much easier to think of people as children when you want to lie to them. Especially if you're a businessman, a congressman, a journalist, a doctor, a preacher, a teacher, or the head of a global superpower. Enough white lies can scorch the earth black.

"Addis," she says, looking her brother in the eyes. "Mom and Dad left because they couldn't take care of us. It was hard to find enough food and they wanted drugs and we were slowing them down, so they left."

Addis stares at her. "Didn't they care what happened to us?"

"Maybe they cared a lot. Maybe they were really sad about it."

"But they still did it."

"Yeah."

"They left 'cause they cared more about food and drugs than us. 'Cause staying with us was hard."

Nora winces a little but doesn't back down. "Well . . . yeah. Pretty much."

Addis looks at the ground, his face slowly tensing into a scowl. "Mom and Dad are bad people."

She begins to worry. Is this right? Should a seven-year-old be swallowing a truth this jagged?

"Good people care more about people than food," he mutters. "They try to help people and don't give up even when they get hungry." There's a strange intensity in his voice. His child falsetto sounds lower, rougher. "Only bad people give up."

"Addis . . . ," she says uneasily. "Mom and Dad are fucked-up and selfish but they're not 'bad people.' There's kinda no such thing as 'good' or 'bad' people, there's just like . . . humanity. And it gets broken sometimes."

"But good people fix things. Good people stay good even when it's hard to." He is gripping the railing so tightly his knuckles have turned white. His face is filling with a rage Nora has never seen before. "Even if they're sick or sad or they have to lose their favorite stuff. Even if they have to die."

"Addis—"

"Good people see past their own fucking lives."

Nora freezes and her eyes go wide. The air around her feels strange.

"They aren't just hunger and math. They aren't just animals."

She grabs her brother's shoulder and tries to pull him away from the railing but his muscles are stiff as wood.

"Good people are part of the Higher," he says in that deep growl, and for a brief moment, Nora swears the color of his eyes is changing. "Good people are fuel for the sun."

"*Addis!*" she shrieks and shakes him hard.

He turns and frowns at her. "What?"

His eyes are brown. His voice is mousy. The faint rustle of wind in the trees reclaims the night, muffled by the blood throbbing in her ears.

"What . . . what were you just saying?"

He turns his sullen gaze back to the moon. "Mom and Dad are mean."

Nora stares at the joint in her fingers. Addis reaches for it and she reflexively flicks it off the balcony.

"Why'd you *do* that?" he whines, frowning at her. "It made me feel really good."

"I don't think it's . . ." She's too rattled to finish. She shakes her head. "No more."

"Fine."

They both study the moon, Addis pouting, Nora wondering where the cop got this baggie and if perhaps there were a few other spices mixed into those herbs. That sensation of charged air is gone now, leaving only the familiar fog of a standard high. She settles into it, trying to erase the image of her brother's eyes flashing like two gold rings in the moonlight.

She aims her flashlight at the moon. She imagines her beam touching its powdery deserts and takes some whimsical comfort from the thought. A small taste of escape from this awful place. Then she swings the light back to Earth, and it glints off the silver eyes of a rotting bald giant.

She manages not to drop the flashlight and stifles most of her scream. The man is standing in the middle of the yard looking dumbly up at her, his eyes unsquinting in the flashlight's beam.

"I told you to leave us alone," she says in a shaky whisper.

The man makes no response. Just stares. He has barely rotted at all since his death. He is gray all over, but the only other sign of decay is his lips, which have gone from full and sensuous to blue and slightly shriveled. It's a shame. They were his best feature.

"Nora?" Addis says, his eyes wide with fear.

"It's okay," she says, scanning the yard with her flashlight and running mental checks on all the doors. "We're safe up here." She shines the light back into the big man's eyes like a cop interrogating a suspect. "Where's the new guy?" she yells at him in her best cop-voice, trying to force some steel into her nerves.

The man looks over his shoulder; Nora follows his gaze with her light and notices the top of a head peeking over the wall of shrubbery that surrounds the fence. She can't help a little chuckle.

"What's with him? Shy?"

"Nora . . . ," Addis whimpers, tugging on her shirt.

"I told you it's okay, Addy, they can't get up here. Hey," she calls to the big man. "Where's your girlfriend?"

He raises his arm and points at the sky.

Nora looks up, frowns, looks back at him. "What's that mean?"

He continues to point.

"She's flying?"

He lowers his arm, raises it again.

"Maybe he means she went to Heaven," Addis offers.

"Do you mean she died?" Nora asks the man.

He lowers his arm and makes no further comment.

"Well hey, I'm real sorry for your loss, but go the fuck away. We're not letting you eat us."

He doesn't respond for a moment, then a low moan rises in his throat. The tone is unmistakably mournful, so resonant with despair it makes Nora shiver. When she shines her light into his eyes she sees pain, and it disturbs her in a way she can't explain. She feels an urge to *comfort* him. She remembers all the pamphlets she's read, the stories on the news and the warnings from her parents telling her what these creatures are. The tests done on them, declaring them nothing more than corpses experiencing bizarrely prolonged death spasms. But looking into this corpse's eyes, she can see that there's a man in there. And he's suffering.

She sighs and folds her arms, turning to her brother. "What are we gonna do with these guys?"

"Shouldn't we kill them? What if they get in?"

"This place is a fortress, Addy. They can't get in."

"What if they climb up here?"

"Zombies can't climb. They have a hard enough time walking."

"Okay."

"We've got to figure something out, though. They'll still be there in the morning."

The big man waits patiently. Nora can hear the new guy pacing anxiously behind the hedge.

"They're probably just hungry, right?" Addis says. "That one was trying to eat that wolf."

"They're always hungry. But they have to eat people; animal energy doesn't work. Maybe he hasn't figured that out yet."

"What about Carbtein?"

"What about it?"

"You said it was like life powder."

Nora's eyes drift. "Right . . ."

"So maybe we could feed some to them? And they'd get full and leave us alone?"

"Addis Horace Greene," she says in a tone of pleasant surprise. "You *are* super smart."

He grins.

"Let's try it. Toss him one."

Addis pulls a cube out of the backpack and unwraps it. "Hey!" he calls down to the man. "Eat this and leave us alone!" He throws the cube. It hits the man directly in the face. The man backs away, looking up at them in surprise.

Nora giggles. "That's *food*, dumb-ass!" she says, pointing down to where the cube fell. "It's human energy! You can eat it."

He looks down at the cube. He looks up at Nora. He picks up the cube, sniffs it, and stuffs the entire thing in his mouth.

Addis laughs. "He likes it!"

Nora watches him chew. "This could be a big deal, Addy. They could put piles of it all over the city and keep the zombies fed. Then maybe they wouldn't—"

The man spits out his mouthful in a gooey pile of white shards, then stares up at Nora as if waiting for more.

"What the fuck, man?" She pulls another cube out of her backpack and rubs it hard against her wrist, leaving red abrasions caked with white powder. "*Swallow* it!" She raises it over her head to throw. "It's human life, it's what you—"

Something clamps onto her wrist. A withered vise of leather and bone—a hand, but barely. She looks up into a face but finds no eyes, just gluey blobs stuck to the sides of empty sockets. A skeleton shrink-wrapped in flesh is crouching at the edge of the roof like a spider, bracing against the gutter with one hand and gripping Nora's with the other. Only the tendrils of blond hair dangling from its scalp tell her this was once a human woman. A warbling hum emanates from its bones.

Nora buckles her knees and yanks against the thing's grip but it's shockingly strong—her knees dangle above the balcony floor with her full weight grinding against her wrist. The creature bites the Carbtein cube out of her hand and chews briefly, then tilts its head and lets the chunks drop out in strings of brown saliva. It looks at the man far below on the ground. It looks at Nora. It shoves her hand in its mouth and bites off her ring finger.

What happens then happens so fast it barely reaches Nora's brain: blurry, disjointed images in flickery black and white. Before the pain in her finger even registers, her brother is standing in front of her and jumping up and swinging his hatchet; the creature's arm snaps off above the wrist. He is yanking her back into the house and slamming the balcony door and slapping her hand down on the floor and then he is spreading her fingers away from her ring finger and swinging his hatchet down hard. The remainder of her finger jumps away from her hand and rolls into one of the children's rooms. She stares at it, and when the hoarse scream rises in her throat, she's not sure if it's from the pain—a deep, aching agony that radiates through her hand and up into her arm—or from watching her severed finger turn gray, black, then shrivel up and slough away to bone right there in front of her.

"I'm sorry I'm sorry!" Addis is sobbing as he inches away from the blood pooling under Nora's hand. She wants to tell him it's okay; she wants to thank him and tell him she loves him so much, but she can see the creature through the balcony door's windows, crouched on all fours and tearing apart her backpack, crunching greedy mouthfuls of Carbtein and drooling it back out in slimy piles. "Why?" she screams hysterically at the door, watching her and her brother's future disappear into the thing's gnarled jaws. The thing just glances at her briefly and keeps chewing, and Nora feels her mind sinking into a dark well.

She wobbles to her feet, squeezing her left wrist tight with her right hand. "Come on," she hisses and staggers down the staircase. When she hits the bottom she pauses to listen. No breaking glass. No crunching wood. Even the sound of the thing's frenzied chewing has stopped, and the house is silent. Where did it go? Surely one knuckle wasn't enough to satisfy its hunger. That little nibble of finger food?

An unhinged giggle escapes her throat. Her head is swimming.

Addis dashes down hallways and sweeps his flashlight over doors and windows, checking the perimeter, but the house is still empty except for the family of skeletons reclining in the living room. Their yellowed faces sneer at Nora as Addis passes his light over them, casting all their awful edges in sharp relief.

She smells that burnt odor again. Plastic? Hair?

"Nora?" Addis whispers.

She sees a wisp of smoke pass through his beam and glances around in the dark.

"These skeletons . . . how come their skulls aren't open like the ones in the street?"

Nora freezes. She follows her brother's flashlight beam to where it rests on the father's cranium. And she notices—no cracks. No bullet holes. No gaping lobotomy. Inside that skull is an intact brain.

This is when she hears a noise, but not from upstairs. From the kitchen. A dry scraping, then the metallic squeak of an oven door opening.

Nora turns around. A skeleton is straightening up from behind the oven, holding a smoking baking pan in its bare bone hands. The pan's Teflon peels off the sides in smoldering flakes. The skeleton carries the pan into the dining room and sets it on the table, where it sizzles on the cherrywood, adding more bitter smoke to the already acrid air. The skeleton is wearing an apron. Bits of long hair cling to its thin film of a scalp. The baking pan is empty.

The father rises from its easy chair in a noisy clatter of bones. The two children follow. They all sit at the dining table and begin dipping forks into the empty pan, serving nothing onto their white china plates, shoveling nothing into their mouths, teeth scraping and grinding on the steel tines. Then in mid-bite, as if surprised by a dinnertime doorbell, they all pause in unison and turn their heads to look at Nora.

Addis is the first to scream. Nora grabs his hand, ignoring the pain in her finger stump, and rushes to the front door. She is reaching for the latch when she sees two decomposing faces peering through the door's window. She whirls around to head for the back door but the skeletal family is lined up at the end of the hall, staring with those grotesquely cheerful grins. The front door rattles violently. The big man is trying to force his way in. Nora has a flash of irrational hope, imagining for a moment that he is coming to save her, but then his fist smashes through the door's window and she sees the look on his face, no longer pain but pure, mindless hunger. Whatever she saw in him before is rapidly departing.

The man and his partner are at the front door and the family is planted at the end of the hall, clawlike fingers twitching and pinching the air. There is no exit.

Nora pulls Addis into the hallway half-bathroom, a tiny box containing only a sink, a toilet, and a narrow window looking into the side yard. The room is barely wide enough for two people abreast. A good enough place for a last stand.

"Stay behind me," she whispers. "If they get me . . ." She doesn't finish. There is nothing else to say.

She holds her breath and listens. Louder than anything she hears her heart pummeling her breastbone. Throbbing in her temples and roaring in her ears. The tiny howls of her finger nerves, reaching out into open space and grasping around for their cut endings.

The big man has stopped pounding the door. There is silence in the hall. Then footsteps. Slow, one at a time, bone feet tapping the hardwood like dog claws or stiletto heels. The click of a latch. Squeak of a door. More footsteps, much heavier, but softened by shoes. Then silence.

Nora tenses. She grips the hatchet in both hands despite the growing numbness in her right. Addis is huddled behind her on the toilet seat, breathing hard but too terrified to cry. Her wide stance fills the room's width, shielding him. She indulges in one selfish thought: if he dies, at least she won't be here to see it. She is his big sister. She gets to go first.

She glances back to tell him she loves him. The woman's shriveled face is grinning in the window. A spear of bone punches through the glass and through Addis. The spear lifts him, a hand grabs him, and he disappears through the window hole.

Nora is alone in the bathroom, staring into a dark yard of neat grass and trimmed shrubberies, just her and the soft chirp of crickets.

Her face contorts and trembles in a soundless shriek. She kicks open the bathroom door. The hall is empty. She runs through the wide-open front door and dashes around the house, waving her flashlight in wild arcs. She sees the back door swinging open and staggers back inside.

Everyone has gathered in the living room. The big man and the woman are kneeling on the floor in front of the coffee table. Addis lies on its ornate oak slab, his blood pooling in the engraved flowers and paisleys. The man and the woman gaze down on him and the skeletons lean in eagerly, angels in a satanic nativity.

Addis looks at Nora. He says something but it's too faint. The big man scoops him up in his powerful arms and rises to his feet. The man looks at Nora. The spark of awareness is still there, weakened and faded, but there, and so is the pain. Then the woman thing stands up and touches his arm. Its sharp fingers press until they break his skin. Nora hears that warbling hum rising in the room, vibrating from within the creature and all the skeletons too, a thick and dissonant chord like a hundred cracked wineglasses singing in unison.

Over the top of this noise, the creature speaks. Its jaw opens and a dry, rasping caw emerges, shrill and cruel, full of wordless rage bubbling up and blaring like a dictator's megaphone into the man's ear.

The man's eyes change. His brows and lips go slack. His pain and longing and uncertainty go away.

"No," Nora croaks. *"No!"*

The man bites into Addis's shoulder. Addis begins to shake.

Nora clamps her eyes shut so hard it hurts. She runs backward, she bumps into a chair then a wall then stumbles out onto the lawn. All she sees is blackness and sparks but in her mind the house is crumbling, brick disintegrating, walls toppling in on themselves and then a black cloud of dust that chokes the air and hides everything, erases everything, makes everything gone.

She grips her face in her hands, squeezing out all thought.

No.

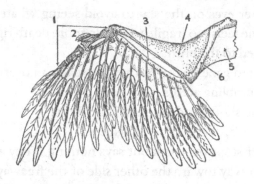

JULIE'S EYES OPEN HALFWAY. Morning sun refracts through the water in them, making abstract art in her lashes and salts. She has just woken from a long night of dreams, bad like they always are now. She dreamt she was a monster. She dreamt she was alone in an empty school. She dreamt a skeleton had stolen her mother's white dress and was dancing on a roof with her father.

She feels a rumbling under her and realizes the truck is moving. She sits up and wipes the crust out of her eyes. The sun has the shy, tentative angle of early dawn.

"Mom?" she says, and her mother's eyes appear in the mirror, blue like hers but paler.

"Hi, honey," she says.

Julie stretches her limbs. "Where are we?"

"Just coming up on Seattle. See?"

They crest a hill and the city skyline sweeps into view. She sees the Space Needle, still pointing straight and true, lights blinking calmly like nothing is wrong. The freeway begins to congest as they get closer to downtown. A permanent traffic jam of derelict cars crashed or abandoned in the street. Julie's father slows to weave through the mess, carefully bulldozing cars aside when necessary. Julie keeps her eyes on the sky to avoid seeing whatever is inside those cars. She feels too fragile to take in more death right now. She is already filled to the brim.

This upward gaze is why, as they approach an overpass, she notices a girl stumbling across it.

"Dad!" she shouts and points wildly. "Look!"

"Oh God . . . ," her mother whispers.

Her father stops the truck but says nothing. They all watch the girl make her way toward the other side of the freeway. Slow, shuffling steps. Empty, dull-eyed stare. A blood-smeared hand with a missing finger swinging against her hip.

Julie's father looks back at the road and drives forward.

"Dad!"

"She's Dead."

"We don't know that," Audrey says.

"You saw how she's walking. You saw her hand. Alone in an exed city without even a backpack? She's Dead."

"What if she's just hurt?" Julie demands.

"It's clearly a bite. If she hasn't converted yet, she will in a few minutes."

Julie cranes her neck to look back at the overpass. "Dad, we have to at least check!"

"What's the point, Julie?" For the first time this morning his eyes appear in the mirror, and Julie glimpses pain in them. "Do you want to make another new friend just to watch her become a corpse? Are you going to shoot her or will I have to?"

Julie's eyes sting and her mouth trembles. She looks at the girl, older than her, older than the boy she killed yesterday, maybe closer to Nikki's age, walking alone on a bridge.

She opens the truck's door and jumps out.

The truck is not moving fast but the pavement sweeps her feet out from under her and she falls, lands on her elbows and then her mouth; she feels a few teeth loosen. Heedless of the salty flood pouring down her throat, she scrambles to her feet and runs toward the overpass, screaming, "Hey! Hey!"

The girl on the overpass doesn't seem to hear her. She continues stumbling forward.

"You're not Dead!" Julie chokes through her tears. "You're *not* Dead! You can come with us!"

Steely arms wrap around her from behind and pull her off her feet. *"Julie,"* her father hisses. "Jesus Christ, Julie."

She collapses into her father's grip, sobbing uncontrollably as blood streams down her chin and onto her T-shirt. She feels the cracks in the world widening. She feels it breaking.

Her father looks up at the girl on the overpass. "Ma'am?" he shouts like a weary cop reciting procedure. "Have you been bitten?"

The girl stares at him.

"Are you infected?"

She wobbles on her feet and says nothing.

Julie's father scans the streets leading to the overpass, sizing up the risk and difficulty of reaching the girl, and shakes his head. He pulls Julie back toward the truck.

Julie tries to fight him but her body has gone limp. She feels his logic tugging at her brain but she fights that, too. His logic is sound. He's not incorrect. But he's wrong.

"Follow us!" Julie shouts hoarsely.

The girl on the overpass finally looks at her. Her gaze is unsteady, but so is Julie's, blurred by hot streams of tears.

"We're going to South Cascadia! There's a stadium with people in it!"

Her father shoves her into the truck and slams the door. She rolls down the window and sticks her head out. "If you're not Dead, come south! Meet us there!"

Without a word or a pause her father starts driving, resuming their slow crawl through traffic as if nothing has happened, but his face is harder than she has ever seen it. Her mother reaches back and dabs at her chin with a rag, soaking up the pink mixture of blood and tears. Julie's eyes lock with hers, pleading for something she can't articulate. Her mother's lips tremble briefly, then they stiffen. She breaks away from Julie's gaze.

"Your teeth might end up a little crooked," she says, staring straight ahead. "But you'll be okay. We'll bandage your elbows at the next safe stop." The Tahoe grinds against a rusted convertible and pushes it out of the way. A man-sized pile of rags crunches under the tires. "John, stop at the next department store, please."

"Why?"

Julie leans forward to find her mother's face in the mirror, but all she can see is the white dress, her mother's fingers tugging at the holes.

"I need some real clothes."

The sky is a pale, dry blue like it always is now, even on perfect, cloudless afternoons. Smog, dust, airborne radiation; Julie doesn't know what it is. But from old photos she knows the blue was deeper, once. Her father tells her it's just a trick of photography, but she doesn't believe him. She sees it in her dreams. Even when they're nightmares.

Julie has had many nightmares in her short life. She is twelve, but she has seen death from more angles than her grandfather did in forty years of military service. She will grow up quickly. She will harden in places she shouldn't and break apart in others, and she will bury both her parents before she's old enough to buy beer. But even now she knows: this is living. She won't object to it or call it unfair, even though it is very, very unfair. Life is only fair for the Dead, who get what they want because they want nothing. Julie wants everything, no matter how much it costs, and this is why she will change the world.

She watches the girl on the overpass shrinking into the distance. Their eyes meet across a river of cars. Just before the girl disappears, Julie drops something out the window.

• • •

"You're not dead!"

The tall man watches the short girl stumble toward him on the street below, blood trickling down her chin and arms, bright red instead of black because she is alive. The brute is screaming again because there is another Living girl even closer to him, this one tall with black hair and brown skin and life that smells like liquor. The brute wants to take it and drink it, but the tall man is not moving. He hides behind a rusty truck, peering through its windows at the mystery unfolding in front of him. The tall girl is only a few yards away, but he ignores the commands throbbing in his hands and teeth and just watches the tiny blond creature below.

She spits a mouthful of blood onto the asphalt and sucks in a lungful of air. "You're not dead!" she shouts in a voice so very different from the melodic tones he heard in the forest yet in its own way beautiful, a broken sound of grief and desperate hope. Somehow these emotions ring clear to him despite his growing inability to feel them, and he wonders with some amazement why the girl is talking to him.

"Dead . . . ," he croaks, slowly molding his tongue into the necessary shapes.

"You're *not* dead!"

His eyes widen. He is more confused now than when he woke up near a river with a mind as dark as deep space. What does she mean? What is she trying to tell him? He knows he is not alive. If he were alive, everything would be different. If he were alive he would be sitting on a park bench with a mug of hot coffee reading his favorite book for the fifth or tenth time, glancing up now and then to watch the people stroll by, and the city would smile and lean in and whisper: *That bench was shaped for your body. That book was written for your mind. This city was built for your life, and all these people were born to share it with you. You are part of this, living man. Go live.*

If he were alive, he would not be walking through a concrete graveyard with a crowd of corpses, looking for lives to erase.

So why does this girl insist he's not dead? He knows she is wiser than him. He heard it in her singing. Can he somehow believe her? He is not alive, that much is clear, but he *is* walking. He *does* have eyes, unlike the big man's shriveled girlfriend, who is barely distinguishable from all the person-shaped piles littering the streets. He hasn't fully surrendered to rot.

"Not . . . dead?" he murmurs, pressing his face against the truck's grimy glass.

"You can come with us!"

The girl's father has her now, dragging her away, and the tall man feels a sting in his eyes. After all this time and all the things he's given up, it seems there are still things he wants. The brute tries relentlessly to shove them aside, hammering down every desire that isn't hunger, but they remain. And he finds, to his surprise, that he wants them to.

Behind him, he hears the scraping of dry bone on pavement. He leaves the tall girl on the bridge and intercepts the others as they emerge from an alleyway. The big man, the small boy, and five creaking skeletons, their withered bones humming with the strange darkness that drives them. They would have killed the boy. They would have gleefully devoured his brain, a tiny sun hot and dense with life. But they restrained themselves for one simple reason: they need him to help kill others. They need to grow their terrible family, to add more teeth to their mouth so that it can eat the world.

As they sniff the air in the direction of the overpass, the tall man feels something move inside him.

It is not the brute.

"Guns," he wheezes.

They regard him blankly.

"Too . . . many guns."

He starts walking away from the overpass and after a brief hesitation, dazzled by the decisiveness of his movements, the others follow him.

The big man walks alongside him, giving him a curious look. The tall man returns it, unblinking.

"Name?" he wheezes at the big man.

The big man considers this with a troubled expression, as if he's been asked to do something unnatural. Finally, a hum builds between his lips. "Mmmm."

The tall man nods. "Rrrrr."

The big man nods. They keep walking.

They walk away from the tall girl on the bridge, away from the short girl and her family disappearing into the distance, away from this beautiful city and its silent condemnation. The tall man doesn't know where they're going and doesn't care. He is spent. His mind is mercury again, its brief surge of humanity melting into an oily residue on its surface, and he no longer understands the feelings he felt in that strange moment on the overpass.

But he did feel them. They did happen. They rest on the murky seabed of his mind, buried under sand and silt and miles of gray waves, patient seeds waiting for light.

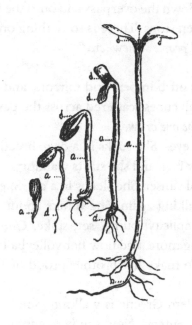

"YOU'RE NOT DEAD!"

Nora watches the apparition move toward her on the street below. Golden hair, azure eyes, fair skin like the saints on her mother's candles, except those saints never had blood running down their chins.

"We're going to South Cascadia!"

The apparition is moving away now, getting smaller.

"You're not Dead! You can come with us!"

Nora blinks, and the apparition is gone. She is alone on a bridge, overlooking miles of desolation. She stands there for a while, watching the apparition's truck disappear into the distance. The wind blows a beer can against her feet, bits of ash into her hair.

"What are we looking for?" Addis demands.

"Good people."

She stumbles down the overpass and onto the freeway, walks for a few minutes, then stops. There is something on the road.

"There are good people somewhere."

"Are you sure?"

The sun glints off bumpers and mirrors, and off the foil wrappers of thirty small cubes scattered across the pavement.

"There's got to be one or two."

She closes her eyes. She sucks in a deep breath. She gathers the cubes in a grocery bag, and she starts walking.

She walks until sunset. She sleeps in a car. She wakes up at sunrise and starts walking again. She thinks about the volleyball. Its smooth white simplicity; bump, set, spike. One clear thought to keep aloft, nothing more, and now her volleyball is this: to become a good person. To make her brother proud of her. And to find a way to save him.

So Nora Aynalem Greene is walking. She is sixteen years old, but now she is seventeen. Now she is twenty-four. She is seeking a cure for the plague, the curse, the judgment—people may never agree on what to call it. She will search for years until she forgets this city and its horrors, until she forgets she ever had a family and begins to think of herself as something that sprouted unbidden and unwanted through the concrete of an empty parking lot. But even then, alone in the driest desert, she knows that a rain will fall. It may be a long time, but not forever. Nora knows better than most that nothing lasts forever. Life doesn't, love doesn't, hope doesn't, so why would death or hate or despair?

Nothing is permanent. Not even the end of the world.

end

THIS IS NOT the end.

The end is darkness and fire. Madness and war. A quiet retreat into extinction on a drained and barren Earth. The end is the dissolution of all bonds and the dissipation of all warmth, the scattering of all hearts across the desert of the world.

This is not the end. We are not standing on that howling ledge. As dim as our skies are, as far off as we've wandered, we have not yet reached that hopeless place, and sometimes we dream that we won't.

What if entropy is a puzzle that life can solve? What if the Library has no ceiling and the ladder goes up and up?

We don't often indulge in such wild fantasies. Eons of disappointment have taught us restraint. But we are reading these strange lives and they are giving us strange hopes, because these people shouldn't be here. All three should be dead or Dead or at the very least broken—fearful, distrustful, alone in their despair.

But they are none of these things. They are alive and together on the roof of a stadium, waiting patiently for the sun.

Our thoughts bleed into theirs as we flip through their books, and they shiver. They chalk it up to the morning wind whipping over the roof. They write it off as nostalgia, but we are nothing so cheap. They feel a swell of sweet grief, outlines of memories they've forgotten or buried. They find tears in their eyes without knowing why.

We know their names now. Who they were and who they are, and who they hope to be. They huddle together on the blanket, three human beings out of the half-starved hundred million remaining on the earth, and though they have only faint suspicions that we exist, we sit close to them like friends—like family—willing them to feel our warmth.

We are almost full. We are near the brim. Soon we'll spill over and everything will change, but not this morning. Earth has a few more revolutions to make.

Acknowledgments

I thanked these people in *Warm Bodies* and I thanked them again in *The New Hunger*. With both books in one volume, I guess I have to thank them twice as hard. So, *superthanks* to everyone who's gone with me on this five-year mission: my editor, Emily Bestler, and everyone at Atria/Emily Bestler Books; my agents and also-editors, Joe Regal and Markus Hoffmann; Cori Stern for pulling me out of internet obscurity; Laurie Webb for holding the door open for me; and Bruna Papandrea, Steve Hutensky, and Gillian Bohrer for that crazy ride through Hollywood. And most of all, thanks to my family for always cheering me on. I love all of you.

Oh and my cat, Watson, for . . . being a cat.

For book updates,
follow Isaac on Facebook:
facebook.com/isaacmarionauthor

For dumb jokes and strange thoughts,
follow Isaac on Twitter:
@isaacinspace

For longer and stranger thoughts,
follow Isaac on Tumblr:
isaacmarionsbigwords.tumblr.com

For Isaac's music, visit:
isaacmarion.bandcamp.com

For photos of Isaac's adventures (but mostly of his cat),
follow him on Instagram:
@isaacmarion

And Snapchat:
isaacmarion

And for everything else:
isaacmarion.com

A hard climb toward humanity. A past that won't stay buried.
And an old plague with a new host far more dangerous than the Dead.

R steps out from the safety of the grave and into . . .

THE BURNING WORLD

Turn the page for an excerpt.

I AM CONCENTRATING FIERCELY on the art of driving—the contour and condition of the road, the speed and inertia of the car, the intricate interplay of throttle and clutch—so Julie hears them first.

"What is that?" she says, glancing around.

"What?"

"That noise."

It takes me a few seconds to hear it. A distant hum, three slightly offset pitches forming a dissonant chord. For a moment I think I recognize this sound, and fear stiffens my spine. Then Julie twists around in her seat and says:

"Helicopters?"

I check the rearview mirror. Three black shapes approaching from the east.

"Who is it?" I wonder.

"Nobody we know."

"Goldman Dome?"

"Working aircraft are practically mythical these days. If Goldman had helicopters, they would've told us."

The choppers roar over our heads and into the city. I am still new to Julie's world and not well-informed on the current political landscape, but I know the Dead are not the only threat, and unexpected visitors are rarely a welcome sight.

Julie pulls out her walkie and dials in Nora's channel. "Nora, it's Julie. Come in?"

Instead of traditional radio static, soft and organic, the walkie emits a distorted shriek. I don't need to ask Julie for a refresher to recall this piece of history: the BABL signal. The old government's last desperate attempt to preserve the nation's unity by smothering every argument. I can just barely hear Nora through the jammer's wall of noise, the ghost of a bygone era refusing to release its grip.

"—you hear me?"

"Barely," Julie says, and I wince as she raises the volume. "Did you see those choppers?"

"I'm at work but I—eard them."

"What's going on?"

"No idea. Rosso—alled a meet—ill you—there?"

"We're on our way."

"I'm at—ork, come—me before—eeting—want to show—omething—"

The sound of nails on a chalkboard enters the mix, and Julie cringes away from the walkie. "Nora, the jamming's too bad. I think there's a surge."

"—amn—ucking surges—"

"I'll see you soon. Cabernet out."

She drops the walkie and watches the helicopters descend into the streets around the dome. "Maybe Goldman's scouts salvaged them from an old base?" she offers feebly.

We plunge into the city, the corpse of a forgotten metropolis that most people call Post and a few thousand call home. The choppers disappear behind crumbling high-rises.

•   •   •

The cleanup crew has done a good job erasing the mess my old friends made of the city. All the bones and bodies have been cleared, the craters have been filled, and the walls of Corridor 1 are almost finished, leaving a clear and relatively safe highway to the stadium. But far more significant is the construction on Corridor 2, which has resumed from both ends after years of stagnation. The two largest enclaves in Cascadia are reaching across the miles that separate them. In practice, the merger is about nothing more meaningful than the safe exchange of resources, but I allow myself to imagine neurons in the brain of humanity attempting to forge a synapse.

One connection after the other. This is how we learn.

I pull into the stadium parking lot and find a spot between two Hummers, sliding in with only a few scrapes. As we head toward the gate, I glance back at our flamboyant red roadster and my brows knit with sympathy. It looks distinctly uncomfortable huddled between those two olive drab hulks. But despite Julie's tendency to humanize the inanimate, despite assigning it a name and a personality—the strong, silent type—Mercey is just a car, and its "discomfort" is just a projection of mine. Like that shiny red classic surrounded by armored trucks, I have struggled to find my place in this sensible society. The incongruity runs through every layer of who and what I am, but it starts on the outermost surface: my clothes.

Fashion has been a problem for me.

At first, Julie tried to convince me to keep dressing sharp. My original graveclothes clearly had to go—no amount of laundering could remove their grisly history—but she begged me to keep the red tie, which was still in surprisingly good condition.

"It's a statement," she said. "It says there's more to you than work and war."

"I'm not ready to make a statement," I said, shrinking under the incredulous stares of the soldiers, and eventually she relented. She took me shopping. We sifted through the rubble of a bomb-blasted Target and I emerged from a dressing room in brown canvas pants, a gray henley, and the same black boots I died in—always an odd pairing with my old businesswear but perfect for this grim ensemble.

"Fine," Julie sighed. "You look fine."

Despite the resignation it indicates, my neutral appearance is a comfort as we approach the stadium gate. Dressing vibrantly takes a courage I don't yet have. After all those years prowling the outskirts of humanity, all I want now is to blend in.

"Hi, Ted," Julie says, nodding to the immigration officer.

"Hi, Ted," I say, trying to make my tone deliver all the signals required for my presence here. Remorse. Harmlessness. Tentative camaraderie.

Ted says nothing, which is probably the best I can hope for. He opens the gate, and we enter the stadium.

• • •

Dog shit on lumpy asphalt. Makeshift pens of bony goats and cattle. The filthy faces of children peering from overgrown shanties that wobble like houses of cards, held barely upright by a web of cables anchored to the stadium walls. Julie and I broke no evil spell when we kissed. No purifying wave of magic washed the stadium white and transformed its gargoyles into angels. One might even say we had the opposite effect, because the streets are now crawling with corpses. The "Nearly Living," as I've heard some optimists calling them. Not the classically murderous All Dead, not the lost and searching Mostly Dead like our friend B, but not yet fully alive like I allegedly am. Our purgatory is an endless wall of gray paint swatches, and it takes a sharp eye to spot the difference between "Stone" and "Slate," "Fog" and "Smoke."

The Nearlies roam the stadium freely now, having proven themselves through a probationary month of close observation, but of course that doesn't mean they blend in. They float through the population in bubbles of fearful avoidance. People read the cues—stiff gait, bad teeth, pale skin tinted purple by half-oxygenated blood—and the flow of foot traffic opens wide around them.

They nod to us as we pass. Julie nods back with an earnest smile, but the look in their eyes makes me shrink inward. Respect. Even reverence. Somehow, they've gotten it into their rotten heads that Julie and I are special. That we ended the plague and are here to usher in a new age. They can't seem to understand that we did nothing they didn't do, we just did it first. And we have no idea what to do next.

• • •

Despite my distaste for stadium life, I have to admit the place feels a little less grim under its new management. Rosso has scaled Security back to pre-Grigio levels, reassigning some personnel to largely forgotten community services like education. Former teachers are dusting off their books and teaching arcane knowledge like history, science, and basic literacy. With fewer infection patrols and fewer guns aimed at the old and sick, the city feels a little less like a quarantine camp. Some areas have an atmosphere that could almost be called idyllic. I smile at a young boy playing with a puppy on the green grass of his front lawn, trying to ignore the scars on his face and the pistol in his pocket and the fact that the grass is Astroturf.

Anytown, USA.

"Hey, Julie," the boy says when he notices us.

"Hey, Wally. How's that beast of yours?"

He ignores the question and regards me nervously. "Is he . . . still alive?"

Julie's smile cools. "Yes, Wally, he's still alive."

"My mom said . . ."

"Your mom said what?"

The boy pulls his eyes away from me and resumes playing with his dog. "Nothing."

"Tell your mom R is a warm and wonderful human being and he's not going to stop being one. And neither are the others."

"Okay," Wally mumbles, not looking up.

"What's your dog's name?" I ask, and he looks startled.

"Um . . . Buddy."

I crouch down and slap my knees. "Hey, Buddy." The pup runs over to me with his tongue lolling. I ruffle his face, hoping he doesn't see me as a carcass to be gnawed. He sniffs my hand, looks up at me, sniffs my hand again, then rolls onto his back and offers his belly, apparently deciding I'm Living enough.

"We've got to go," Julie says, touching my shoulder.

"To the meeting?" Wally says, and it's our turn to look startled.

"You know about that?" Julie says.

"Everyone knows. They announced it on the speakers and told us all to listen. Is it about those helicopters?"

"Um . . . yeah . . ."

"Are we going to war again?"

Julie looks at me, then back at Wally, who can't be older than twelve. "Slow down, kid," she says. "And quit playing with your pistol."

He glances down at the gun in his jeans, realizes his fingers have been caressing it, and clasps his hands behind his back, blushing.

"We don't have any idea what's going on," Julie says. "For all we know, those choppers are an aid convoy from Iceland with crates full of candy bars. So don't be such a hawk." She grabs my hand. "Let's go, R."

I release Buddy back to his owner and we continue into the city, a little more apprehensive than before. Leave it to a child to shout what we've been whispering.

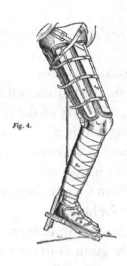

Fig. 4.

"WELL IF IT ISN'T Post's biggest celebrity couple!" Nora calls to us from across the warehouse. "Rulie? Jar? Have you picked a name yet?"

She's in full nurse regalia: baggy blue scrubs, latex gloves, a mask and a stethoscope hanging around her neck. She has attempted to make the scrubs more flattering by tying a thin belt around her waist, but the effect is lost among all the black gore smeared down her front. Her thicket of curls is tied back in a tight bun, but a few locks have come loose and fallen into her work, hardening into scabby dreadlocks. And yet somehow, she pulls off the look.

"Will you stop it?" Julie says, but she's smiling. "Things are weird enough."

"I bet they are." Nora stops in front of us and glances me over. "You're looking good, R."

"Thanks."

"How's life in the suburbs? How's life? How's being alive?"

"Um . . . good?"

"How's your kids?"

I squirm a little. "They're . . . staying with their mom."

"No progress?"

I shake my head, growing somber.

"When are you going to tell me what happened, anyway? I thought the airport was the base of the revolution. I thought you were out there spreading the cure."

"It didn't go . . . as well as we hoped," I mumble.

"I know you had a few incidents—"

"Nora," Julie says. "Can we talk about something else? The airport's not a fun subject for him."

Nora holds up her hands. "Sure. Sorry. Just excited to see you. I'd hug you, but . . ." She gestures to the mess on her scrubs.

"What is all that?" Julie says. "Do these ones still get violent?"

Nora cocks her head. "Have you not seen this place yet? Is this the first time you've visited me at work?"

Julie glances away. "It might be."

"Well, I'm sure being a suburban housewife doesn't give you much free time." Before Julie can respond to this, Nora turns and starts walking. "So anyway, come check this out. Patching R up was fun but that was just a few broken bones and knife holes—excuse me, superficial puncture wounds. We've gotten some much more interesting cases since then."

We follow her deeper into her workplace: a huge open warehouse converted into something resembling a hospital. The walls are corrugated sheet metal painted clean white, cords snaking around support beams to power EKGs, X-ray machines, artificial lungs, and small electric chainsaws. The place has been substantially reconfigured since I saw it last, organized and sterilized, but I know where I am.

"This place," I say, and then run out of words. "You used to . . ."

"Yeah," Nora says as she walks. "We used to dissect zombies here. Mostly we were trying to figure out new ways to kill you, but we also did a lot of our medical training here. You guys make excellent cadavers."

Julie frowns but doesn't say anything.

"We had to clean it up a bit, but all the equipment is basically the same, so it made sense to make this the zombie hospital. Before things changed we called it the Morgue, but now . . . well, we still call it the Morgue, but now it's ironic."

She leads us toward the far end of the building, where most of the action seems to be. Men and women and children lie on operating tables in varying states of decay. The scene is nearly identical to the one I saw before, but with a crucial difference: the young physicians here are not cutting corpses apart. They're putting people back together.

A young girl who is gray but otherwise whole requires little attention; one of the nurses stops by to check her pulse and other vitals but mostly leaves her to lie there, gazing around the room with an expression of confused wonder.

"How're you doing, Amber?" Nora asks her.

The girl slowly stretches her lips into a smile. "Better," she whispers.

"Glad to hear it."

Next to Amber is a man whose flesh is only slightly rotted, but he has suffered multiple gunshot wounds and they're beginning to bleed. His face is a mixture of excitement and fear as two nurses hover over him, working to remove bullets from long-congealed wounds. I give him a look of commiseration.

"Mr. T here's in about the same shape you were," Nora says to me. "So you probably know what he's going through."

I do. I remember the slow creep of awareness as I woke up like a drunk from a blackout, wondering what the hell happened last night. When did I get stabbed in the shoulder? When did I get shot four times? When did I fall off a roof and fracture most of my bones? I remember being grateful for my numbness then, the unexpected gift of natural anesthesia. But I somehow assumed it would end when my wounds healed.

"How do you heal the rotten parts?" Julie asks. "Skin grafts?"

"Well, that's where it gets weird. Let me introduce you to Mrs. A."

Nora moves to a bed in the corner, set apart from the other patients. A woman lies naked on a plastic tarp, and another tarp on the floor catches the various fluids oozing from her ruined body. This woman has been Dead a long time. Her flesh is dark gray and withered into grandmotherly wattles, though I suspect she's middle-aged. It has dried up and sloughed away completely in a dozen places, revealing the bones underneath. If I ran into this woman in my days of wandering the airport, I would have kept my distance, waiting for her to start grunting and hissing and clawing at her eyes. For that sour hum to rise from her bones.

"It's rare that they come to us when they're this far gone," Nora says. "I can't imagine what it took to break this lady loose, but look at her. Look how hard she's fighting."

The strangest thing about her is her eyes. Though the rest of her body is putrid, her eyes are incongruously whole. They stare at the ceiling with a fierce intensity, as if somewhere inside her she is lifting impossible weights. People and places and a lifetime of memories. A thousand tons of raw human soul hauled up from the depths.

Her irises are the usual metallic gray, but as I stare into them, they flicker. A brief glint, like a flake of gold in the sand of a deep river.

"What was that?" Julie says, but she's not looking at Mrs. A's eyes. She's leaning in toward her chest, pointing to a gaping hole that has rotted out of her ribcage. "Did you see that?"

"A flash?" Nora says. "Like there's a little mirror in there catching the sun?"

"Yeah . . . for like half a second. I thought I imagined it."

Nora nods. "That's the 'weird' I was talking about. And to answer your question about healing the rot . . . look closer."

Julie and I both lean in. The hole in the woman's side is . . . smaller. The edges are a little lighter. There are patches of pink in the tissues around it.

"What is it?" Julie asks in an awed whisper.

"I have no idea. I've never had less idea about anything. We've been calling it 'the Gleam.' Every once in a while it just . . . happens, and the Dead get a little less dead."

A strange sensation trickles through my core. A chill of uncanny familiarity, like recognizing an ancestor in a crowd on the street. I have felt this Gleam. In my eyes, in my brain, in my brittle, broken bones. I have felt it surround me and lift me to my feet, urging me onward. I catch the woman's eyes, wide and feverish with strain. "You're not dead," I murmur to her, too soft for Julie and Nora to hear.

"So it's healing them?" Julie says.

"I guess you could say that."

"Then why do they need medical attention? Why don't you just wait for 'the Gleam' to fix them?"

"Well, that's where it gets weirder. It doesn't heal the wounds. Only the rot."

"What do you mean?"

"It can revive necrotic cells and stitch together a huge disgusting hole"—she points at Mrs. A's chest—"but it skips the wounds."

"Skips? Like . . . intentionally?"

Nora shrugs. "Sometimes it seems that way. Sometimes you're looking at a slimy mess of rotten flesh and you don't even know there's a wound in there until the Gleam revives the area, and then suddenly there's a bullet hole, all bloody and fresh, like the Gleam remembered it was there and left it for us to fix."

Julie frowns at the hole, which seems to have shrunk a little further while we weren't looking. "That doesn't make sense."

"Wounds aren't the plague." Both women jump a little, as if they'd forgotten I was here. "The damage we do to ourselves is our responsibility."

Nora raises her eyebrows and juts her lower lip. "Wow, R. Your English has really improved."

Mrs. A shudders on her table. I catch a flurry of golden flashes in the corners of my vision that are gone before I can focus on them. Her skin begins to firm. The wrinkles fade and the color returns. Her real face is emerging from the rot, and I was right. She's young. Mid-thirties. The liquid lead is draining from her eyes, leaving a deep blue.

"She's coming back," Julie whispers, leaning in close, and there's a sudden tremor in her voice. "After all this time."

Nora is stone-faced. She slips on her surgical mask and goggles, and when I follow her gaze, I understand why. Red blood is pouring from gaping holes all over the woman's body. Areas that were black and desiccated when we arrived have blushed into raw, red wounds, and her newly Living lifeblood is leaving.

"That leg's gonna have to go," Nora mutters, examining what's left of her mauled thigh, which is now gushing semi-clotted blood. She reaches for the chainsaw.

"What do you—" Julie starts to ask, but Nora cuts her off.

"You'll want to stand back."

She doesn't wait for us to comply. She pulls the trigger on the saw and we duck for cover as a spray of blood draws a line on the wall.

By the time I straighten up, Nora is already stitching the stump. I see the flush of giddy hope draining from Julie's face.

"So it's a tease?" she says. "They come back to life just long enough to finish dying?"

Nora's eyes are unreadable behind the mist of blood on her goggles. When she's done with the leg she resumes patching the sieve that is Mrs. A's body, but it's quickly becoming apparent that the woman isn't salvageable.

"What's the point?" Julie's voice is faint. "If we can't save them, what's the point?"

"We can save some." Nora's needle is a blur as she sutures a bite in the woman's bicep. "You come back in the same state you died in, so if it was just a bite, you're fine. If it was a fixable injury, we can fix it. But if you died of a bullet through the heart or, say, getting mostly eaten . . ." She pauses, running her eyes over the hopeless mess of Mrs. A's body. ". . . then this is just an epilogue." She resumes her stitching with a stubborn intensity. "If you can fight your way out of Purgatory like our friend here, wonderful. I'm sure you'll get bonus points in Heaven. But you're still dead."

"The plague's not immortality," I murmur to no one. "Doesn't sustain life. Just protracts death."

"Fucking eloquent, R. Who knew you'd be our resident poet?" There's an edge to this that tells me to stop. She finishes one wound and jumps to the next. "Going zombie isn't a loophole in the rules." Her voice is hard, but the speed of her movements reveals her desire to be wrong. "The Gleam's not some great resurrection." She snips a thread and stands back to inspect her work. "Gone is gone."

Mrs. A is an island in a red sea. Her breathing, which had for a moment quickened to sharp gasps, is slowing again. After just a few minutes of new life, earned through perhaps years of titanic efforts, she is going to die again.

"Welcome back, Mrs. A," Nora says, doing her best to offer a comforting smile. "Sorry I couldn't . . ." She can't hold the smile; it quivers and falls. "Sorry I couldn't save you."

I catch Mrs. A's eyes. There is no blame in them, no fear or even grief. Her body is a horrific crime scene, but her face is serene. She turns her head slightly and opens her mouth, as if about to say something to me, but nothing comes out. She lets it go. Her trembling lips form a smile, and she closes her eyes. Her wounds stop pulsing.

Julie and Nora are silent, standing over the dead body like mourners at a funeral. I'm surprised to see a glint of moisture in Julie's eyes. It took her days to shed a tear for her father's horrific death; why should a stranger's bittersweet passing affect her like this?

"Julie?" I say softly. She doesn't respond. "You okay?"

She pulls her eyes away from the corpse and furtively rubs them dry, but the redness remains. "I'm fine. It's just sad."

Nora pulls the mask and goggles off her face and drops them on the floor, and just before she turns away to wash her hands, I glimpse a similar redness in her eyes. Have I missed something? What I just saw was gruesome and tragic, yes, but also beautiful. I saw a woman pull herself out of her grave and climb up to whatever's next. I saw a woman save her own soul. What did they see?